Sharon Kendrick once wo[...]
competition by describing h[...]
flown to an exotic island by[...]
powerful man. Little did she realise that she'd
just wandered into her dream job! Today she
writes for Mills & Boon, and her books feature
often stubborn but always to-die-for heroes and
the women who bring them to their knees. She
believes that the best books are those you never
want to end. Just like life…

When **Kali Anthony** read her first romance novel
at fourteen she realised two truths: that there can
never be too many happy endings, and that one
day she would write them herself. After marrying
her own tall, dark and handsome hero, in a perfect
friends-to-lovers romance, Kali took the plunge
and penned her first story. Writing has been a
love affair ever since. If she isn't battling her
cat for access to the keyboard, you can find Kali
playing dress-up in vintage clothes, gardening, or
bushwalking with her husband and three children
in the rainforests of South-East Queensland.

SEDUCE ME

SHARON KENDRICK

KALI ANTHONY

MILLS & BOON

First published in Great Britain 2025
by Mills & Boon, an imprint of HarperCollins*Publishers* Ltd,
1 London Bridge Street, London, SE1 9GF

www.harpercollins.co.uk

HarperCollins*Publishers*, Macken House, 39/40 Mayor Street Upper, Dublin 1, D01 C9W8, Ireland

Seduce Me © 2025 Harlequin Enterprises ULC

His Enemy's Italian Surrender © 2025 Sharon Kendrick

Royal Fiancée Required © 2025 Kali Anthony

ISBN: 978-0-263-34452-3

02/25

MIX
Paper | Supporting
responsible forestry
FSC™ C007454

This book contains FSC™ certified paper and other controlled sources to ensure responsible forest management.

For more information visit www.harpercollins.co.uk/green.

Printed and Bound in the UK using 100% Renewable Electricity at CPI Group (UK) Ltd, Croydon, CR0 4YY

HIS ENEMY'S ITALIAN SURRENDER

SHARON KENDRICK

MILLS & BOON

With thanks to Hilary 'Hils' Birch, violin virtuoso
and woman of encyclopaedic knowledge.

Also to the masterly clarinetist
Colin 'Colinas' Lawson.

You have introduced me to so much beautiful music,
for which I am forever grateful. xx

CHAPTER ONE

THE STORM ROARED, the rain lashed, and the inky-dark sky seemed to reflect the current state of Romano Castelliari's mood.

Which was angry, to say the least.

He had just returned from Turin where he had been poised to sign the deal of a lifetime. The purchase of one of Italy's most iconic car factories to add to his already impressive portfolio had been a long-held dream and for once he had allowed his stony heart to feel a flicker of anticipatory joy. And then, right at the last minute, the elderly owner had pulled out, citing a deep aversion to Romano's lifestyle as his reason. *'I want to sell my company to a family man,'* he had rasped. *'Not an international playboy.'*

The old man had been adamant, stubbornly rejecting every inducement Romano had offered, leaving the Italian billionaire—simmering with a quiet rage—to make his way to where his private jet waited. He was still simmering now.

'Porca miseria!' he raged, although there was nobody around to hear him. What right did Silvano di Saccucci have to refuse a deal on such flimsy grounds?

What right did anyone have to stand in the way of his wishes? Or to judge him like that?

Irritably, he continued to pace the corridors of his Tuscan retreat, glaring as the rain lashed against the windows of the ancient *castello*, obscuring the mountains in the distance with a heavy grey curtain.

He had never been a man who allowed himself to be governed by the elements and would walk, or ride, or hunt boar in almost any weathers. But this! This never-ending rain was yet one more intolerable fact to add to his growing list of inconveniences and if the coming weekend had not been fixed in stone, he might have taken himself off to somewhere warm, maybe Brazil, to watch one his cars competing in the Premio Mondo.

He scowled. Certain social events were inevitable when you were custodian of a vast Italian estate like this and, since he was rarely here, he always limited them to a few per year. This weekend was the baptism of his little half-sister's baby. Actually, Floriana was not so little any more, he reminded himself, for she was a wife now and a mother. But he was not looking forward to it, because such occasions always prompted intrusive questions— the most intrusive being the supposedly innocent query about when he intended having children of his own.

Innocent they most certainly were not, though he should have been used to fielding them by now. How many times had lovers looked deep into his eyes, with what he always considered a rather bovine expression? It usually happened after a particularly satisfying bout of sex, when they suspected he might have let his guard down, because they were foolish enough not to realise that he *never* let his guard down. When would they ever learn? 'You'd make such a good father, Romano,' they would coo, as if the idea had only just occurred to them.

This was a lie. He knew his limitations—the very same ones which had made Silvano withdraw his offer at the last minute. He had neither the desire nor the tolerance to settle down, despite the growing pressure to do so with every year which passed. A shudder of distaste whispered its way over his skin. Why create a situation which would inevitably draw his memory back to his own, wretched childhood?

And now he had opened a floodgate to the rogue thoughts which came tumbling in. Because it had been a night like this, hadn't it?

His body tensed.

The night his mother had taken him away. He remembered rain lashing down on him as he had been carried outside in her arms. The howl of the wind as he had been bundled into the back of a waiting limousine. He recalled the pungent smell of some sickly sweet and cloying smoke and then...nothing—until he had awoken in an unfamiliar house with his mother kissing an unfamiliar man who was not his father.

Romano felt a pulse begin to hammer at his temple. The ordeal had lasted a full three years before he was free again. But you could never really be free of your past, could you? Good or bad, those experiences made you the person you were. Every criticism laid at his door, he could trace back to that interlude. He accepted that it accounted for his lack of feelings. His chosen remoteness from other people. His sense of always being on the outside, looking in. The man who never really fitted in anywhere.

And that was the way he liked it.

Because he didn't want emotional mess. He had no intention of going through that again. He didn't want pain, or insecurity. He lived his life in a carefully controlled way and if anybody ever dared challenge him, then he cut them out with a ruthlessness which came as easily as breathing to him.

He threw another log onto the massive fire which burned so brightly in the castle's entrance hall, splashing the dark panelled walls with red and gold and providing some much-needed warmth, because it had been freezing when he had arrived at the empty *castello*. At least he had been granted an unexpected day's grace before everyone else got here. His half-sister and her family, along with his stepmother, had all been delayed, which meant he would be able to spend the rest of the evening alone. He swallowed. Trying very hard not to think about the other guest…

The unwanted one.

The spectre at the feast.

The green-eyed witch with the cascade of copper curls.

The woman who…

Romano caught a glimpse of his glowering features reflected back from one of the antique mirrors and his scowl grew deeper.

Why the hell had his half-sister chosen to bring that infernal woman here, when she knew how much he disliked her? He could feel his muscles bunch, his body becoming iron-hard and tense. Why make someone like Kelly Butler godmother to a Castelliari child when she had always been the most unsuitable of Floriana's friends? Hadn't the stubborn redhead already caused enough trouble with her interference? With her stubbornness and her insolence?

And hadn't that trouble been compounded by the way she had made him feel? By the shameless sexuality she had exuded, which had licked at his body and soul with a taunting heat, made worse by the fact that she had been forbidden to him...

His turbulent thoughts were interrupted by a distant sound. A muffled banging, which was barely audible above the banshee scream of the storm. At first he thought it might be a stray branch, dislodged from a tree, which had hurled itself against the door, and better left until morning to investigate, when the wind suddenly dropped and he heard it again, more clearly this time.

A voice.

His forehead creased.

A woman's voice.

Turning away from the blaze of the fire, he pulled open the heavy door to the howling gale, unprepared for the vision who stood in front of him. At first he barely recognised her as the light from the castle spilled out onto the courtyard, bathing her in a golden halo. Her hair was plastered to her head and her shoulders were hunched in a useless attempt to resist the onslaught of the driving rain. But then she looked up and said his name—said it in that soft, witchy voice of hers—and he could do nothing about the sudden thickness which gathered in his throat, nor the unwanted stab to his groin. His gaze raked over her with unwilling hunger and he swallowed. He had forgotten how tiny she was.

'Get inside,' he bit out.

Obediently she nodded, stumbling over the threshold into the hall. As he shut the door on the forbidding night, he found himself thinking he'd never known her quite so compliant. Or so vulnerable. There was no rebellious challenge on her heart-shaped face tonight. Her rain-streaked cheeks were pinched as she stared up at him, but in the firelight her eyes were as bright as he remembered them. Green eyes, he thought. Green with promise. Even when wet with rain, they were the eyes of a sorceress.

He wanted to ask her why the hell she'd turned up so early but she was shivering so violently that instead he jerked his head in the direction of the fire. 'Stand over there and take off your damned coat,' he ordered roughly.

Her teeth were chattering so much that she could barely get the words out, but she tilted her chin to stare at him defiantly and *this* was more like the Kelly he knew.

'Y-you haven't lost any of your bossy instincts, I s-see!' she declared.

'Quit the analysis and concentrate on what you're supposed to be doing—or rather *un*doing,' he snapped back. 'Which are the buttons of your coat.'

But her ungloved and presumably frozen hands seemed incapable of accomplishing even that simple task and Romano gave an impatient click of his tongue as he moved towards her.

'Shall I?' he growled.

Her nod was grudging, the recalcitrant set of her lips achingly familiar. 'If you want.'

If he wanted? Romano gave a short laugh. What he wanted was something quite different.

For her to be as far away from him as possible. Out of sight and out of mind.

Oh, yeah?

Wasn't the truth something much more fundamental? Something carnal and urgent, which flared up inside him like a sudden fever, despite the pathetic and sodden image she presented? Wouldn't he have liked her lying beneath him, that soft and petite body opening up to welcome him?

And hadn't she always had that effect on him?

He remembered the clumsy pass she had made when she was barely eighteen years old. His obvious shock that his sister's friend could have been so glaringly obvious how much she desired him had fuelled his worst prejudices about women and made him worry about her influence on Floriana. He had rejected her swiftly— some might even have said cruelly—but he'd needed to do that. Because hadn't he been appalled at just how much he had wanted her, despite her unsuitability and the fact that she had been out of bounds? Because no way would he have contemplated having sex with the eighteen year old best friend of his little sister, no matter how great the temptation.

His breathing shallow, he slid open the buttons of her sodden jacket and slipped it from her shoulders, taking great care to keep all contact with her body to a minimum. But even the featherlight brush of his fingertips against her shoulders felt like wildfire rippling over his skin. 'Didn't it occur to you to wear something waterproof and warm?' he demanded huskily as he hung the dripping garment on a nearby coat-stand. 'Or did you think the fashion police would be watching your every move?'

'I wasn't expecting the weather to be quite so foul, if you must know!'

'You think the sun always shines in Tuscany, do you, Kelly?' he questioned sarcastically.

'Not when you're around, that's for sure! It probably wouldn't dare to show its face. Anyway…' She glanced around, her hair resembling a rapidly forming halo of fire as the heat began to warm her curls. 'Where's Floriana?'

'Let's get you dry first, shall we?' he clipped out impatiently.

'You're making me sound like a dog who's just jumped in a puddle.'

'A dog would show more gratitude.'

'Ah. So that's why you've got a face even more like thunder than usual. Aren't I showing the correct degree of appreciation, Romano? Do you want me to bow and scrape to you and simper my thanks?'

'I want you to shut up for a while, if such a thing were humanly possible.'

'I'm surprised you're talking about being human, when everybody knows you're the devil incarnate,' she mumbled.

But Romano's retort died on his lips, his gaze reluctantly drinking in her appearance despite the fact that she was wearing little he found commendable. Her striped sweater made her look like a cartoon character and her jeans were surprisingly practical and sturdy. And yet… How could she manage to make such a commonplace outfit look *sexy*? 'You're soaking,' he observed unevenly.

'Tell me about it.'

'Where are the rest of your clothes?'

'In the car.'

'I didn't see a car.' He frowned. 'In fact, I didn't hear a car.'

'No. It conked out, halfway up the drive.'

'Conked out?' Despite his fluency in four languages, the English colloquialism was unfamiliar to him.

'Broken down. It won't budge. I ran over something in the road and I think I've done something to the wheel.'

'You think?'

'Okay, I have!' she shot back. 'We don't all have limos on tap, you know! The satnav stopped working and I got hopelessly lost. Even if the roads weren't currently looking like rivers—this is a godforsaken place to find.'

'It's a castle on top of a hill—how hard can it be?'

'A few signposts along the way might have been helpful!'

Softly, in Italian, he cursed. 'Give me the car key and wait here,' he ground out, grabbing a jacket.

Kelly told herself she was glad to see the back of him as he took the key and slammed the centuries-old door behind him, even though the back of him was almost as tempting as the delicious front of him. The journey here had been an absolute nightmare—like an animated version of the worst kind of fairy tale. Tall, creaking trees. Perilous drops into unseeable forests. A castle she had never liked, which had risen up before her, vast and daunting. And then, waiting inside was the ogre. The beast.

Except that he was neither of those things.

She fanned her face and tried to get her breathing back to normal, but it was a big ask, because how could anyone ever act normally when Romano Castelliari was around? That had always been her problem when he had been in the vicinity. There was something almost *dangerous* about his beauty which set him apart from other mortals. His muscle-packed frame—all six feet plus of it. His eyes as dark as a starless night. Eyes which seemed capable of looking into your very soul—which was total fantasy on her part, because he'd never looked at her with anything but contempt.

She remembered the first time she'd ever seen him. She'd been peeping from an upstairs window at school when he'd arrived to take his sister out for lunch, in a shiny black car, with a chauffeur at the wheel. Had he known she was watching? Was that why he glanced up, dark eyes narrowed, his black hair ruffled in the light breeze? But that first sight of his face had come as something of a shock, for he had none of his half-sister's sunny expression. She remembered thinking how cold his features looked. How hard and forbidding. But there was something about the sensual curve of his lips which badly made her want to kiss him. And just like that, she had lost her heart to him even though a man like that was never going to look twice at a schoolgirl, despite the fact that she'd been nearly eighteen and just about to go away to college.

Was that why she had taken to dressing up like an amateur seductress every time she saw him and making out as if she were always on her way to a party, much to his sister's amusement? Because Flo had known the truth. That Kelly was the person least likely to have a wild social life. Not that Romano had appeared to notice her, no matter what she wore, or how she behaved. Which was why she had mistakenly brought things to a head and asked him if he fancied going to the pub for a drink on the last day of term, wearing a tarty outfit she'd borrowed from one of the other pupils. Hadn't she *deserved* the derisive curve of his lips which had followed?

'Go away, little girl,' he had drawled contemptuously and she had done just that, hurt and humiliated.

Stop it, she thought distractedly. Just *stop it*. Romano Castelliari's gorgeousness had never been in any doubt and she'd left behind her hero worship a long time ago. Good job too, because, judging by his behaviour since she'd arrived at his castle, he was still a judgemental snob and control freak. Nothing has changed, she recognised. He still doesn't like you. And you don't like him. End of story.

And hadn't she got other stuff to think about? Scary, urgent stuff. Like, how was she was going to scramble together enough money to pay her rent now that the restaurant she worked in had finally gone bust? The part-time job didn't pay much but it just about supplemented her meagre takings from the market stall.

But it was still a constant juggle, keeping all the balls in the air, and now one had come crashing down, she wasn't sure how she was going to manage in the short term.

In an attempt to distract herself from the teeming of her worried thoughts, Kelly wondered where everyone was. Cocking her head, she listened for sounds of life but she could hear nothing other than the crackle of flames and the howl of the wind. Come to think of it, she hadn't noticed any other cars when she'd been banging on that ancient door for what had seemed like hours, had she? A flicker of apprehension whispered over her skin at the thought of being alone in this vast *castello* with the Italian billionaire, but her musings evaporated when Romano reappeared a few minutes later, removing his dripping jacket and depositing her battered suitcase on the flagstoned floor.

'Did you get manage to get it to start?' she questioned.

'No,' he snapped.

'But it's a hire car,' she wailed, thinking about the damage clause in the contract she'd signed.

'I'll make sure it's moved off the road tonight,' he said, from between gritted teeth. 'And get someone to look at it properly in the morning.'

'Okay,' she said, her gaze reluctantly straying back to his body. She'd never seen him dressed so casually before, in jeans and a black cashmere sweater. Did he realise that the taut denim stretching over his thighs was positively indecent—causing her heart pound in a way which made her feel almost dizzy? Did he *enjoy* making women desire him? She cleared her throat, wondering why she had suddenly morphed back into that same star-struck teenager. Focus, she thought. Just *focus*. 'You still haven't told me where Flo is.'

'She's stranded. In France. In the snow. In that godforsaken place they choose to call home. They won't be here until tomorrow.'

'*Tomorrow?*'

'Didn't she call you to tell you?'

Kelly bit her lip. 'She might have tried, but there was hardly any signal when I was driving through the mountains and now my phone's completely dead.'

'I see.' There was a pause. 'Plus your car has "conked out".' He surveyed her with a steady look, his dark eyes laced with undeniable mockery. 'Anyone would think you *wanted* to get yourself stranded in the middle of nowhere with me, Kelly.'

'Why? Do women often engineer situations to find themselves alone with you, Romano?'

'You'd be surprised,' he drawled.

'I'd be *very* surprised if anyone should actively seek out your company, yes!'

He smiled at this—just a flicker of a smile but powerful enough to break through the outer layer of her bravado, like the warm lick of the sun beginning to dissolve the edges of an ice lolly.

'Would you really?' he questioned silkily, and Kelly felt the beginning of a blush begin to heat her skin as she recalled the tarty dress she'd worn to ask him out and the cringe-making way she had fluttered her eyelashes.

'Anyway, where's your army of servants?' she put in quickly, in a not very subtle attempt to change the subject.

'There are no longer any resident servants and, believe it or not, I do allow them to have time off. This isn't medieval England. I'm a very considerate employer.'

'What about your mother—isn't she here?'

There was a pause. 'My stepmother, you mean,' he corrected.

Kelly screwed up her nose. 'I thought she'd always treated you like a son.'

'Rosa has never treated me with anything but kindness,' he agreed, his mouth flattening into a hard and unremitting line. 'But I am not her son,' he asserted.

Kelly could hear the frost edging his voice, which made it sound as brittle as ice. Hadn't his mother died when he was very young? She couldn't remember. Despite her sunny nature, Flo was always reluctant to dwell on the past.

'Every time it is ever mentioned, there are always tears. Always some sort of scene, or row. So I block it out,' her schoolfriend had once told her.

'Rosa will be arriving with Floriana tomorrow,' he informed her.

'And what about your brother? Sorry, half-brother,' corrected Kelly hastily as she remembered Flo's fierce and dogmatic brother, Riccardo, who had apparently been tamed by his love for the sweet Angie, his former secretary. 'Is he coming?'

'No. They're in New York and Angie is heavily pregnant so they can't fly,' he said, his cold gaze sweeping over her, before he gave a heavy sigh of resignation. 'And in the meantime, it looks as if you're here to stay.'

'There's no need to look so pleased about it.'

'I'm not going to pretend something I don't feel, Kelly.'

'You'd obviously rather I wasn't here.'

'Yes, I would. I never wanted you here in the first place.' He shrugged. 'I would have been quite happy never to have set eyes on you again. Actually, scrub that. Deliriously happy might be a more accurate description.'

'Believe me, the feeling is entirely mutual.'

They glared at each other across the fire-splashed entrance hall.

'But while we could easily spend the rest of the evening trading insults,' he continued silkily, 'it might be more sensible if you went upstairs and got changed out of those damp things. I don't want to have to ring the local doctor and tell him that one of the guests has come down with pneumonia. Apart from anything else, he would hate to be disturbed in the middle of dinner.'

Kelly opened her mouth to respond with something smart but her brain was being scrambled by mixed messages, because Romano Castelliari was suggesting she take her clothes off and her nipples were growing hard beneath her chunky sweater as a result. How crazy was that—that a few careless words could provoke such a reaction? Why was her body betraying her in such a way when she didn't even *like* him? Please don't let him notice, she prayed, crossing her arms tightly across her chest the way she did when she was working on the market stall.

'I have no idea where Floriana was intending to put you, but there are a number of guest rooms on the second floor available,' he continued. 'Any preferences as to which one you'd like?'

Indignation rode to her rescue, dragging her attention away from her aching breasts. 'How would I know?' she demanded. 'Last time I was here I was made to sleep in a local hotel—presumably because I wasn't considered good enough to stay in your precious castle!'

There was a pause as their gazes clashed. 'I think we both know I was trying to keep you away from my sister as much as possible.'

'Even though, as her bridesmaid, I was supposed to be on hand at all times?'

'I didn't like your influence over her.' His black eyes glittered. 'And it seems my judgement was entirely correct, since you encouraged her to run away the night before her wedding, jilting the man she was supposed to marry and bringing shame and dishonour on the entire Castelliari family.'

'Surely her happiness was more important than the reputation of the family?' she protested. 'And I didn't influence her at all. The whole thing was her idea.'

'You could have stopped her,' he ground out. 'You could have come to me.'

Kelly stilled. 'Why would I do that? Not only were you the last person I would ever turn to for advice— she was being offered up like some ancient sacrifice to an older, richer man!'

'Stop being so melodramatic,' he snapped. 'Count Alphonso de Camino would have made an excellent husband. He would have provided for her. Unlike her current one.'

Kelly heard the criticism implicit in his tone. 'But Floriana is happy with Max,' she defended.

'And for how long?' he retorted. 'She won't stay happy unless she has some money.'

'So give them some!'

'You think I haven't tried?' he demanded. 'But not only is he poor—he is proud. It is the worst possible combination.'

She stared into his dark and brooding features. 'Did you really want her to marry a man she didn't love?' she whispered.

At this he tensed, his powerful body growing still. 'Please. Do not speak to me of *love*,' he said, his voice filled with venom. 'It's nothing but a lazy word for lust—which screws up people's lives if they're stupid enough to believe in it.'

'And you don't.'

'Of course I don't,' he answered scornfully.

'What a *cynic* you are, Romano,' she breathed and was about to turn away when his expression stopped her. Startled her. And suddenly she couldn't tear her gaze away. Because he looked…

Kelly swallowed. Everything about Romano Castelliari seemed like a contradiction in that moment. Like ice and fire. Like need and contempt. His features were stamped with bitterness. Impatience, too—probably because a little nobody like her had the temerity to speak to a powerful billionaire in such a way. But she saw something else as he followed the movement of her hair falling back down to her shoulders, like a man who had just been hypnotised against his will. Something in his eyes, which echoed the molten rush of longing which was gathering low in her belly. Heat began to flood through her pelvis, filling her with unfamiliar hunger and frustration, making her want to grind her hips against his and ask him to…beg him to…

Her throat dried. How was it possible to want someone you hated so much?

To want him to touch you so badly that your life felt as if it would be incomplete if he didn't?

She knew he still blamed her for her part in what had happened. Floriana's carefully choreographed wedding to the middle-aged count had never happened—mainly because the bride-to-be had run away in the middle of the night, aided and abetted by Kelly. And Kelly had been at her side when Floriana had married Max, the man she'd loved for so long. Emotions had been understandably raw for a long time afterwards, which probably explained why Floriana and Max's first baby had been baptised in a low-key family ceremony, to which Kelly had most definitely *not* been invited.

But that was all in the past. Now they had an adorable baby girl and the couple were determined that Kelly should be Allegra's godmother. Things had moved on, tempers had cooled and they were all grown-ups, weren't they?

Surely she could manage to be civil to the brooding billionaire for one short weekend of her life.

But it wasn't easy when he was looking at her like that. Making her skin feel too tight for her body. Making her want things she had no right to want. Not from him.

She licked her dry lips. 'Weren't you about to show me my room?'

Imperiously, he inclined his dark head and somehow the sensual spell he had woven was broken.

'Come with me.'

She followed him up the sweeping staircase, remembering how unwelcoming she'd always found this huge castle. How she had never really fitted in. Because she was different, she'd always known that. She wasn't like them. Floriana had money and class and connections going back centuries, while she, Kelly, had nothing.

Trying to keep up with his long-legged stride, they reached the second floor where, at the end of a long corridor adorned with faded silk rugs, he halted in front of a door and pushed it open.

'You can stay in here,' he growled abruptly, putting

down her suitcase but making no attempt to enter the room, as if the interior was in some way contaminated. 'You should find everything you need. The bathroom's just along the corridor.'

'Oh, dear. No en suite?' she joked weakly, trying to distract herself from the fact that very nearby was the most enormous bed.

'It's a castle, Kelly.' The granite line of his jaw tightened. 'Not a hotel.'

No. A hotel would never have employed such a grim-faced guide as him.

'Come down when you're ready,' he continued. 'And I'll fix us something to eat.'

And with that, he turned on his heel and was gone and Kelly was left feeling as if somebody had sucked all the oxygen out of the atmosphere. She blinked, wondering if she'd misheard him. Was he actually offering to make her dinner? The rugged car tycoon rolling his sleeves up and cooking? He probably meant pulling the cling film off the top of a ready meal and shoving it into the microwave. She couldn't imagine that Romano Castelliari had ever had to lift a finger in the kitchen—not with his countless servants and myriad lovers.

Peeling off her damp clothes, she hung them over one of the radiators and sighed. That was one outfit out of action until it was dry enough to wear again. She stared bleakly into her small suitcase. Her cheap airline ticket meant her luggage was weight-restricted with not a lot of wriggle room, but even so… She glanced up at a lavish tapestry hanging on the wall and swallowed. She didn't really have any clothes which were suitable for a christening in a billionaire's castle. She used her imagination and what little money she had to make her own clothes, but no way was she going to be able to hold her own among the A-listers, who would doubtless be wearing designer.

She pulled out a dress and studied it—she'd made it herself from a bolt of claret-coloured velvet she'd bought cheap at the market. But a dress meant legs and somehow that made her feel…vulnerable.

No. He makes you feel vulnerable. He only has to look at you and you start to melt.

She found the enormous bathroom—as modern as the castle was old. The water was pleasingly hot and the soap high-end, scented with bergamot and lavender, and for the first time since she'd arrived, she felt vaguely human. Back in her room, she tamed her wayward curls and put on a pair of handmade silver earrings which caught the light as she peered in the mirror, but the eyes which stared back at her were uncertain. He made her feel twisty and strange but she mustn't let Romano Castellani intimidate her or realise how much she still wanted him. Because all that was history now.

But her fingers wouldn't stop trembling as she slipped from the bedroom.

CHAPTER TWO

HE SENSED HER before he saw her. Before she'd even made a sound, he knew she was there—as if she had activated some sixth sense to alert him to her presence. How the hell did she make that happen? Romano wondered frustratedly. And why her, of all people?

Abruptly, he turned to find Kelly Butler hovering in the doorway of the castle kitchen, looking as if this was the last place she wanted to be. Or as if he was the last person she wanted to be with. Well, that makes two of us, *cara*, he thought grimly, though the wild thunder of his heart as he shot her a censorious look made a mockery of his sentiments. Her velvet dress clung to her generous curves and the worn fabric seemed curiously appropriate in this ancient setting, as did the richness of its claret hue. He could see the glint of silver at her ears and the swing of her lustrous hair and thought how big her green eyes looked in her heart-shaped face. She looked like a painting come to life and silently, he cursed the rapid trajectory of his thoughts and the corresponding hardening of his groin.

'Sit over there,' he said, gesturing towards the table with the abrupt slice of his hand. 'Dinner won't be long.'

'If you don't mind, I'd rather just walk around for a

bit,' she said, stepping into the warm room and looking around. 'I've been sat in that wretched car for hours.'

'Suit yourself.' But Romano's careless shrug as he met her witchy gaze wasn't really representative of his feelings because he *did* mind. He didn't want her close enough to be able to detect her body heat, or smell the subtle drift of her perfume. Or to watch her petite form as she moved around the vast castle kitchen, peering this way and that with a guileless curiosity, her thick curls swinging around her shoulders. He wanted her seated at the table, half hidden from view. Because if she continued to walk around the place looking like...

His throat grew dry as he adjusted to this new-look Kelly Butler. The *femme fatale* schoolgirl who had morphed into the wild-looking art student had matured, it seemed. There was no tiny dress barely covering her bottom, her breasts straining against tight satin. Nor those horrible all-black clothes and clumpy boots which had followed—the front of her hair dyed a startling shade of purple and a small silver ring laced through her nose. Every time he'd seen her he had been nothing but critical of her appearance, but on a visceral level he had been unable to deny his attraction towards her. Yet he had always kept her at a chilly distance. He knew that women fell for him—hard—and he never encouraged unrequited love in order to feed his ego. More than anyone else, his half-sister's wild-child friend had been strictly out of bounds and he had found it curiously easy to transmute his undeniable attraction towards her into disapproval. He found it easier to dislike her than to desire her.

He hadn't seen her for years until the night before

the wedding which had never happened, when she had been properly grown up and the chemistry between them had been almost off the scale. He remembered the way she had looked at him—with hunger and promise glinting from those magnificent emerald eyes. The way her curls had coated the luscious curve of her breasts with fiery corkscrews. And he could recall quite vividly how urgently he had wanted to lick her nipples. If she hadn't run off with Floriana into the night, who knew what might have happened? Would they have ended up in bed together? He gave a short laugh. Maybe. At the end of the day, he wasn't made of stone and at least he might have been able to get her out of his system. He'd had a lucky escape, he concluded grimly.

Only right now, it didn't feel so lucky. If he had bedded her, at least he would be immune to her charms, because once you'd been intimate with a woman, inevitably she began to bore you. He certainly wouldn't have been left wanting nothing more than to run his fingers through those magnificent curls and kiss the crumpled petals of her lips. Silently, he registered the deep shadows beneath her eyes, as if sleep had been at a premium of late. Was she still a party animal? he wondered acidly. Was that why she was looking so worn out?

'What do you want to drink?' he questioned roughly.

'Just water, please. Don't look so surprised, Romano. Did you imagine I'd grab the bottle and start drinking it by the neck?'

'Why not? I imagine that old habits die hard,' he drawled. 'Isn't that what you used to do at your sixth-form parties?'

'Oh, *that*,' she responded airily. 'It's so long ago I can

hardly remember. And you don't have to wait on me, you know. If you tell me where the glasses are, I can easily help myself. I'm very self-sufficient and house-trained.'

'No.' His voice was terse as he reached into the refrigerator, pulling out a bottle and tipping water into a tumbler and handing it to her. 'I don't want you getting in my way.'

'Of course you don't,' she said, sipping at the water and then putting the glass down on the table with a sigh. 'Flo was right, you are a total control freak.'

'I don't deny it.'

'I should have realised that a man like you would regard that kind of remark as a compliment.'

'What's bothering you, Kelly?' he taunted softly. 'Do you prefer the kind of man you can just push around? Who obediently does everything you want him to? A *yes* man?'

She was chewing on her bottom lip as if his comment had made her feel uncomfortable. Was that because he'd touched a raw nerve and she really *did* like her men submissive? As their gazes clashed in hostile duel, he tried to quash the first evocative shimmering of sexual fantasy.

'Look, this isn't going to work, is it?' she said, her question shattering his erotic thoughts. 'Maybe it's better if I just go back up to my room and leave you in peace.'

'You've been travelling all day.'

'And?'

'And you need to eat something.'

'I can always take a sandwich up to my room.'

He shuddered. 'You are *not* picnicking in one of the castle rooms. That's not how we do things here.'

'The working-class girl who doesn't know how to behave, you mean? Or are you afraid it might attract rats?'

'Are you trying to shock me, Kelly?'

'I wouldn't have to try very hard, would I, Romano? You're so incredibly easy to shock!'

A faint smile touched the edges of his lips. 'I'm sure we can just about manage to endure each other's company for the duration of a meal, without killing one another, if we put our minds to it.' He slanted her a steady look. 'Don't you think that might be possible?'

'It might,' she agreed grudgingly.

But as he turned away to tend to something on the giant range, Kelly realised she didn't actually want a sandwich—nor anything else for that matter. How could she possibly think about anything as mundane as food when Romano was waltzing around the kitchen in front of her like that, dextrously wielding pans like a sexy conjuror? The powerful magnate looked completely at home in this setting and it wasn't a bit what she had imagined. And, disturbingly, it felt uncomfortably *intimate* to be alone together like this, with tall cream candles burning on the table. Like the kind of thing a *couple* might do together.

Though what would she know? She'd never been part of a couple. Never even witnessed at close quarters what it might be like to be in a relationship. Was her mother's attitude towards men responsible? Had she gradually absorbed all that mistrust and negativity she'd been spoon-fed over the years? Or maybe the real reason was more troubling…that she was one of those people who simply wasn't cut out for romantic partnership.

She watched him tossing salad and grating Parmesan before placing everything on the table, along with two steaming bowls of pasta.

'Sit down,' he said curtly.

She slid into the seat opposite him. Say something, she thought—but the only thing she could think of was how his hard features gave nothing away. She cleared her throat. 'I didn't know you could cook.'

He raised his brows. 'Surely you're not implying that, because I'm a man, I can't fend for myself? Isn't that a very sexist assumption to make?'

'I was just going on what I know.'

'Which is?'

She wound some pasta around her fork and ate some more before answering, realising just how hungry she was. 'That you're a man who has been waited on all his life.'

Had she thought his features gave nothing away? Then she had been wrong. Because suddenly his expression became shadowed, his ebony eyes growing hooded, but not in time to hide the unmistakable glint of irritation. 'Is that how you see me, Kelly?' he questioned silkily. 'As a spoiled little rich boy who's always had everything handed to him on a plate?'

'Well? Aren't you?'

'I might have been born rich, but I taught myself the art of self-sufficiency a long time ago because I never wanted to rely on anything or anyone, and that's the reason I can cook. Now eat,' he added roughly. 'You look as if you could do with feeding up and the shadows be-

neath your eyes suggest you're crying out for a decent
night's sleep. I suppose you've been burning the candle
at both ends as usual?'

Well, yes, she had—but not in the way he was probably imagining. 'Surely you know all about my crazy
life?' she questioned carelessly. 'Floriana must have
filled you in.'

'We don't speak that often,' he answered repressively.
'And when we do, it's never about you.'

No. That didn't surprise her. She imagined she'd be
the last topic of conversation Romano would be interested in discussing. If anyone else had asked the question, she might have given the true and somewhat
uninspiring version of how she lived—that her social
life was practically non-existent. That she worked as a
waitress most evenings and spent the rest of the time
making silver jewellery to sell on a market stall not far
from where she lived. That life was mostly hard work
juggling all the components and trying to earn enough
money to pay the rent. Her heart pounded as her brand-
new reality slid into her thoughts. Because now the restaurant had shut, she didn't even have her waitressing
job to fall back on and she wasn't sure how she was
going to be able to make ends meet...

But she wasn't going to justify herself to him, or hope
to tug at his heartstrings by telling him a sob story,
because what good would it do? She didn't want his
sympathy. And in some ways, wasn't it easier when
he looked down his proud and patrician nose at her?
Imagine if a modicum of respect started creeping into
in that mocking black gaze. If he regarded her with anything other than hostility, wouldn't that only increase

her vulnerability around him? So feed his prejudices, she thought defiantly. Let his disdain wash over her!

'I just try to live life to the full,' she told him carelessly, shrugging her shoulders so that her waterfall earrings shook, and noticing that his attention had been momentarily captured by the jangly noise they made. 'One long non-stop party express. You know?'

'Yes, I know.' He glowered. 'I remember how you constantly led Floriana astray when you were at school.'

Kelly sucked in her cheeks, because at least now she was on familiar territory. Didn't he realise that it had been simpler for everyone to blame *her* for their youthful misdemeanours and make her into the convenient scapegoat? The daughter of the school matron was always going to be a more suitable target than the daughter of one of the richest men in Italy, who regularly donated to the school fund. If there had been any leading astray it had been done by Floriana, not her. But friends didn't grass each other up, did they? Especially not after all this time. And really, their supposed crimes had been nothing greater than missing the last train home and having to spend a fortune on a taxi to get back—or trying out a cigarette and then being sick in a hedge.

'We were a little wild,' she conceded.

'Maybe you still are?'

'Maybe I am,' she agreed, really warming to the theme as she acknowledged the hostile judgement in his voice. Because this felt familiar... Romano looking at her with nothing but censure gleaming from his black eyes. 'Still the wild-child art student at heart.'

She saw a pulse begin to flicker at his temple.

'And what about men?' he continued softly.

'I'm not sure I understand, Romano.' She batted her eyelashes at him with exaggerated innocence. 'What about them?'

'There are…many?'

Kelly froze. It was probably the most insulting question he could have asked and she might have forgiven him, thinking that something had been lost in translation, were it not for the fact that his English was as good as hers. She wondered how he would react to the truth, which was that she barely had the time to actually date anyone, even if she ever met anyone she remotely fancied, which she never did. But she wasn't going to come across as some sad loner, let alone an inexperienced virgin. Far better he continued to think of her as a brazen party girl—because wouldn't that afford her some sort of immunity? Brushing her hair away from her face, she fixed him with a look of challenge. 'What do you think?'

His mouth pleated. 'I don't think you'd care to hear my thoughts on the subject.'

'Oh, do tell me. Please. I'm fascinated.'

'If you must know, it wouldn't surprise me to discover that you have acquired a multitude of men with whom to amuse yourself.'

'An actual multitude,' she repeated faintly.

'Why not?' His mouth hardened. 'You are a very beautiful woman.'

It was the last thing she had expected to hear and Kelly's hand shot to her neck, trying to conceal the sudden blooming of her skin. He'd said… She swallowed. He had actually said she was beautiful. And wasn't it insane that the compliment somehow managed to cancel out the hateful remarks he'd made earlier? She could feel her nipples tightening beneath her velvet dress and suddenly she didn't have a clue how to respond. Should she thank him and purr with pleasure, which was what she felt like doing? How did you respond to a compliment from your arch-enemy without losing face?

Until his next words drew her up short.

'But I think you should be careful about your lifestyle choices,' he continued remorselessly. 'Because sooner or later, age will catch up with you.'

'Age will catch up with me,' she repeated.

'Of course it will. And it's not a good look, Kelly. Believe me. I've seen what happens to party girls. It takes its toll.' He leaned back in his chair and studied her, his gaze cool and assessing. 'The desperate moth who is drawn to the flame is bound to get its wings burned.'

'Wow. And for a minute there I thought you were actually being nice to me.' Kelly slammed down her fork. 'Well, since you've rubbished me and my life, why don't we shine the spotlight on yours?'

He shrugged. 'Be my guest.'

She pushed her plate away. 'Flo says you're hardly ever here these days.'

'So what? I have an estate manager who is perfectly capable of dealing with everything. I don't personally have to pick the grapes or the olives, or go down to the meadows to milk the cows, or supervise the labelling of the wine, in order for the agricultural side of the Castelliari empire to thrive.' His voice was low and mocking. 'Logistically that might prove a little difficult since I also have a car factory in Turin as well as an international racing team to run.'

'Which you were lucky enough to inherit—'

'And which were both on the point of collapse when I took over,' he interjected icily.

'Yes, you turned them around.' She held her palms up in mock appeal. 'I concede. Not just a privileged rich boy, then.'

His eyes narrowed. 'Your point being what, exactly?'

'That you're a jet-setter, Romano—certainly not a gentleman farmer. You live life in the fast lane. What right do you have to warn me about burning the candle at both ends when you do exactly the same? You're always being pictured coming out of nightclubs all over the world. So it's a bit rich you making snide comments about the number of men I'm supposedly dating, particularly when you're never pictured with the same woman twice.'

The dark gleam of his gaze became thoughtful. 'You seem to know a lot about my life, Kelly.'

'It's not rocket science. There are pictures of you splashed all over the Internet.'

'Which you naturally spend a lot of time studying?'

'Oh, get over yourself! I get the occasional alert— probably because you have the same surname as my best friend. But anyway, that's beside the point,' she gabbled, terrified she was going to come over as some kind of stalker. 'What I'm trying to say is that it's one rule for men and another for women. Even now. If a woman goes out and has a good time, then society attaches labels to her which are deeply unflattering. But if a *man* does it—well, that's a whole different story.

Anyway, I think this conversation has run its course, don't you?' She pushed back her chair. 'Thanks for dinner,' she added stiffly. 'I think it's time I went to bed.'

But as she got to her feet, he mirrored her movements, rising to his feet so that his tall frame towered over her, bathing her in its dark and formidable shadow and making her feel curiously *fragile*. His powerful body seemed to ripple with energy and as Kelly felt the sweet liquid rush of reaction, another inconsequential thought skittered into her head. Why weren't other men more like Romano? she wondered desperately. Why did it have to be *him* who made her feel like this?

'I'll see you upstairs,' he said.

'I'm perfectly capable of getting back to my room without your help.'

'Given how long it took you to find your way here by road, I think it's inadvisable to take any more chances, don't you? I don't want you wandering around the castle at night and disturbing me.'

'You're so sarcastic,' she snapped.

But she was secretly glad of his company as they navigated the twisting subterranean corridors leading from the vast basement of the castle. She could hear the sound of creaking as the ancient building began to settle down for the night and, as they mounted the sweeping staircase, she found herself wondering how many different pairs of feet had walked this way over the years. Had Romano brought any of his lovers here? And why was it so easy to imagine that muscular body of his naked on a bed, with the pale light of the moon bathing his rippling flesh with silver?

Deliberately, she blocked the fantasy. Concentrate

on his flaws instead. Heaven only knew but there were enough of them. His cold and judgemental nature, for starters. His cynical attitude towards love. The way he tried to control his sister's life.

She tilted her chin to look up at him. 'I suppose I'd better try to get rid of these unsightly black shadows beneath my eyes,' she said, pointedly referencing his remarks of earlier. 'Before everyone else gets here.'

There was a long pause as he met her gaze and for a moment the condemnation in his eyes became something else. A flash of ebony fire, which seemed to burn right through her skin and make her dissolve from the inside out. Suddenly Kelly was finding it difficult to breathe and her knees were feeling decidedly unsupportive.

'I didn't say they were unsightly,' he said abruptly. 'It was a criticism of your lifestyle, not your appearance.'

He turned away and quickly she pushed open her bedroom door, resisting the urge to stand watching him, terrified he would turn round and see the pinprick thrust of her aching breasts. That he might then understand that, although she had never really liked him, she had never stopped wanting him.

CHAPTER THREE

'KELLY. KELLY! Wake *up*!'

Reluctantly surfacing from the landscape of her fractured dreams, Kelly kept her eyes tightly shut, aware of bright light flooding onto her closed eyelids and the aroma of fresh coffee filtering towards her. She didn't want to wake up. It had taken her long enough to get to sleep because her body had been so, so…restless. She wanted to stay in this heavenly half-world which her unconscious had created, one where Romano Castelliari was licking very slowly down her neck, his fingers whispering beneath the hem of her dress towards her knickers.

Her throat dried.

Since when had she started having erotic dreams about her arch-enemy?

Her eyes snapped open to see Floriana opening the shutters of her bedroom windows and she was glad of the momentary reprieve to compose her flushed face and steady her thudding heart. Hastily adjusting the cosy jacket of her winceyette pyjamas, she sat up in bed, noticing the creamy cup of cappuccino which was sitting on the bedside table and which Floriana must have placed there. And in spite of her mixed-up feelings, Kelly smiled—but then, her schoolfriend always had that effect on her, even though they didn't get to see each other as often as they'd like. They had known each other since they were thirteen, when Floriana had arrived at the highly competitive school where Kelly's mum had been matron, which meant she'd got her fees paid and had supposedly had exactly the same opportunities as all the other pupils in the posh establishment.

But that hadn't been the case. Kelly had never been allowed to forget for a single moment—not by her peers, her teachers and sometimes, by her mother herself—that she was a 'charity case'. And that her existence was powered by other people's generosity. Her uniform was second-hand and so were her books. She never went on school trips. She was never invited to anyone else's house during the holidays—but there again, she never had anywhere to call home to invite people back to. The minuscule apartment above the sanitorium which came with her mother's job looked more like a waiting room.

Only Floriana Castelliari had been different. Floriana had actually *liked* her. Apparently she had begged her parents to let her attend the prestigious English boarding school, mainly, it transpired, to escape from her domineering older brothers, Riccardo and her half-brother, Romano. Romano in particular had brokered his sister's marriage to a wealthy count more than two decades her senior and, for a while, Floriana had gone along with his plans and pictured herself as his bride. But people changed their minds, didn't they—often at the last minute? Better to discover that something was wrong before you entered into it, sooner rather than later—especially when it involved something as important as marriage.

Shuffling further up on the feathery bank of pillows, Kelly focussed her attention on her friend. 'Morning, Flo.'

'Ah! You're awake—at last!' Floriana turned around and gave a huge smile, tucking a strand of hair behind her ear. 'I thought you were supposed to be a lark! I've brought you some coffee.'

'So I see. *Grazie.*' Kelly yawned. 'What time is it?'

'Nearly eleven.'

'Are you serious?'

With perfect yet slightly inharmonious timing, several clocks began to boom out from different parts of the castle.

'Listen for yourself,' said Floriana, bouncing across the room like a sunbeam, her dark hair shining in the pale sunshine which flooded in through the tall castle windows. 'Thank heavens we're here,' she announced, bending down to give Kelly a big hug. 'I tried to ring you to say we were going to be delayed but I think your phone must have been dead. I heard you got lost and pranged your car and then turned up on the doorstep looking like a drowned rat.'

'Did Romano say that?' asked Kelly carefully.

'Well, he growled it out in his habitual bear-like way, but that was the gist of it, yes. I gather it was just you and him here for the evening. No staff here.' Floriana studied her mischievously. 'Given the history of your mutual loathing, how did that work out? *Madonna mia*, but I'd love to have been a fly on the wall.'

'We managed to pass a few hours without coming to blows.'

'*Brava!* And what did you do?'

'He cooked me supper,' she informed her friend evenly.

'Did he? That was surprisingly well behaved of him. I've been told he's good, though I've never actually sampled his cooking.' Floriana frowned. 'And you look as if you could do with some feeding up.'

A pulse fluttered at her throat. 'That's exactly what—'

'What?'

She shook her head. 'It doesn't matter.'

'It does matter.' Floriana's eyes narrowed perceptively. 'Something's wrong, isn't it, Kell? I can tell.'

Kelly chewed her lip. She hadn't been planning on saying anything, not on the weekend of her goddaughter's christening. Why impart all her personal doom and gloom and risk bringing the atmosphere down? But the tension had been building up inside her ever since she'd been given the news and it had to go somewhere, and Floriana was looking at her in a way which was making stupid tears start stinging at the backs of her eyes. She was trying to remember the last time someone had looked at her so sympathetically and came up with a great big blank. And if she couldn't confide in her oldest friend then who *could* she confide in?

'Just money,' she said, attempting a careless shrug.

'*Just* money?'

'The restaurant where I've been a part-time waitress for the past four years has gone bust,' she elaborated, the words tumbling out in a rush. 'And so I'm out of a job. Hopefully I'll get another one as soon as I'm back from Italy.' She pulled a face. 'But in the meantime there's a slight cash-flow problem and the small matter of paying my rent.'

'I will lend it to you,' said Floriana impulsively. 'How much do you need?

'No, you won't. I would never borrow from a friend,' answered Kelly fiercely. 'And anyway, from what I gather, you haven't got a whole load to spare.'

Floriana frowned. 'That's what Romano told you?'

'In his usual bear-like way, yes!' Kelly shrugged. 'He implied that your lifestyle was hand to mouth. Is that true?'

'I guess to someone with my brother's extravagant life-style, it is. Not many people have planes and properties and car factories.' Floriana stared down at her plain gold wedding band before looking up again. 'You know Romano wants Max to take over the running of this estate?'

Kelly shook her head. 'No, I didn't. Wow. Is that what you want, Flo?'

Floriana sat down on the edge of the bed and began pleating the heavy brocade cover between her fingers. 'I don't know. In some ways, it would be great. I love Tuscany and I've still got friends here, and our place in France is lovely but…well, it's hard. I'm not going to deny that. We've got a tiny smallholding and the land isn't that fertile and it's miles from anywhere—hence getting stuck overnight in the snow.'

'So what's the problem? Surely the answer is right here for the taking?'

Floriana gave a brittle laugh. 'I'll give you three guesses, and it's all to do with the stubbornness of men. Max doesn't want to be beholden to Romano and although Romano isn't the least bit interested in being a farmer, he just won't let go. You know what a control freak he is. He still wants to make all the decisions. And Max says that would drive him crazy. He says it took long enough for him to demonstrate he was worthy of being my husband after we'd eloped, but he doesn't want to have to keep proving himself for the rest of his life. He says he'd rather be poor than have to keep kowtowing to Romano.'

'And what about you? What do *you* want?' questioned Kelly quietly.

Floriana shrugged. 'I love my husband,' she said simply. 'And you know what they say. If he's not happy, then none of us are.' She stood up and smoothed down her dress. 'Now, are you going to laze there in bed all morning, or are you going to get up and come and see your gorgeous goddaughter?'

Kelly laughed. 'I'm on my way.'

'Well, you'd better get a move on, or it'll be lunch time—and you know what a stickler Romano is for punctuality. Particularly as a load of extra staff have just arrived. He's ordered caterers and florists and nannies, as if we're expecting hundreds of guests, and now he wants everything run like clockwork.' Floriana gave a heavy sigh. 'I thought the years might have softened him, but they seem to have done the opposite.'

Kelly blinked. It wasn't a word she'd ever associated with the Italian billionaire—in fact, soft was the very antithesis of his steely character and iron-hard body.

She gave a bitter smile.

Soften him?

Not in this lifetime.

Romano sat at the head of the table and made no attempt to hide his irritation. 'Where is she?' he demanded, with a pointed glance at his watch.

'Not *she*, Romano,' observed his stepmother mildly. 'Her name is Kelly.'

'I know what her name is, Rosa,' he said impatiently. As he tapped his finger like a metronome against the linen napery, his gaze swept around the table, encompassing Rosa, his brother-in-law, Max, who was tearing off a piece of bread to give to his four-year-old son, Rocco, before finally coming to rest on his sister. 'I was just wondering whether *Kelly* was intending to grace us with her presence any time soon.'

'She just wanted to see Allegra before lunch and give her a cuddle,' said Floriana quickly. 'Oh! Speak of the devil! Kelly. Here you are. Come and sit over here, next to me.'

Romano felt himself grow tense as Kelly walked into the castle dining room, though he doubted it was noticeable to anyone else. His heart might be pounding uncomfortably beneath his silk shirt and his muscles bunching low in his gut, but his face didn't betray a smidgeon of reaction. When he put his mind to it, he was easily able to conceal the few emotions he had been unable to eradicate completely. The lessons learned during his early childhood hadn't *all* been in vain, he thought caustically. He had learnt very early to construct an icy barrier around himself, designed to protect himself from the squalid world in which he had existed. His very survival had depended on it. And old habits died hard, he concluded grimly. Perhaps he should be grateful for the stony countenance he was able to present as he watched the redhead sit down opposite him, even if inwardly he was cursing her for the uncomfortable night he had endured.

He had barely slept a wink and he knew exactly why. Despite his recent punishing schedule and the bitter disappointment of his failed takeover bid, he had lain wide awake for hours. The quietness and solitude of the Tuscan estate might have provided balm to his troubled spirit if he had been alone, but he had not been alone. Because *she* had been here. Admittedly, tucked up in a far-flung corner of the castle, but here nonetheless. And she might as well have been in the adjoining room, he had been so achingly aware of her presence. No matter how hard he had tried to sleep, he had found himself unable to stifle the urgent throb of his body, as he had pictured her compact curves and fiery curls.

'Zia Kelly! Zia Kelly!' yelled young Rocco with excitement, scrambling down from his seat beside his father and hurling himself into Kelly's arms.

'Woo! Rocco!' she responded, as she scooped the child up into her arms and whirled him round. 'Haven't you grown?'

'I'm the tallest boy in the class!'

'I bet you are.'

'Perhaps we could get on with lunch now?' interjected Romano coolly.

'Of course.' Slowly putting Rocco down, she led him back to where he'd been sitting. 'We'll play after lunch,' she promised the little boy quietly, before sliding into her own seat.

Romano stared across the table at her and despite the irritation she always provoked in him, he could do nothing to quash his instant stab of desire. To his astonishment, he noted that she was wearing exactly the same dress as she'd had on at dinner last night, although in the daylight the claret velvet looked garish and wrong. Who wore the same item of clothing two days running? he wondered in disbelief. Certainly, every woman of his acquaintance would have been horrified at the very idea. But that didn't change a thing, did it? He still wanted her. He had always wanted her, from the moment he'd met her in that first, sweet flush of womanhood. Little Kelly Butler with her unkempt appearance and her wilfulness and her wild ways. The woman who always got underneath his skin—but never in the right way.

'I'm not late, am I?' she questioned sarcastically, shooting him a challenging look as she shook out her napkin.

'Very nearly,' he answered repressively.

'Oh, Romano, don't be such a grouch,' chided Floriana. 'Here, have a little wine, Kelly. I'll lend you my sunglasses in a minute and then you'll be able to blot out the glare of Romano's stare.'

Kelly bit back a smile, glad that her friend seemed to have learned to stand up to her domineering older brother at last. She took a sip from the small glass of red wine she'd been offered, grateful for the warmth which flooded through her, something she was going to need quite badly if she continued to be subjected to Romano's frosty gaze. What torture it was, sitting across the table from him like this, when his dark eyes were icing out a barrage of conflicting messages. Unlike last night, today they had an audience and, for the sake of harmony, she needed to temper her response to him.

'This is lovely,' she said politely, gesturing towards the beautifully laid table, with its heirloom china and low bowls of white roses, although she couldn't actu-

ally detect any of the flowers' perfume. She turned to
Floriana's mother and smiled. 'It's so nice to be at the
castle again, and for such a joyful occasion.'

'Indeed,' said Rosa, as two servants entered the room
and began placing dishes on the long table. 'It's been
a long time since we've seen you, Kelly. How are you,
my dear?'

Kelly was wondering how best to bat off the question
in a way which would shut the subject down before it
had even started, when Floriana leapt in on her behalf.

'Not great, actually. Kelly's in a fix. She's out of
work, Mamma!' she declared dramatically. 'She lost
her job this week.'

Kelly saw Romano's lips harden into a forbidding
line. Bring on the negative judgment, she thought fa-
talistically, and wasn't disappointed.

'One hesitates to ask why,' he intoned coolly, slanting her an arrogant elevation of his dark brows. 'Did it
have anything to do with your timekeeping?'

She was so tempted to say something shocking just
for the sake of it.

They accused me of flirting with the customers. Or,
They caught me with my hand in the till.

But Rosa was there and she needed to behave herself,
and so Kelly sought to make her explanation as succinct
as possible. 'I've been working as a waitress, to supple-
ment the money I make on my market stall.'

'Market stall?' Romano choked out.

'That's right. I sell earrings, made by me.' She saw
Romano's lips harden even more as she moved her finger to her left ear and brushed the tip against a swaying cascade of miniature silver stars. 'It's a very lively

little market. Every day except Mondays and Tuesdays. People come to Granchester just to visit it. Maybe *you* should, Romano, next time you're in England. You could pick up a five-pack of socks for under a tenner.'

Floriana was looking at Romano, seemingly oblivious to the private battle which Kelly was conducting with her half-brother, or the look of utter horror on his face.

'She can't pay the rent,' Floriana told him baldly. 'And she needs a job. Just a temporary one to tide her over until she can get something else. You must have a job she can do, Romano. You have a massive workforce.'

For all her determination to be flippant, Kelly couldn't deny her heartsink moment when she saw Romano's reaction, for he made absolutely no attempt to hide the disdain on his face.

'I don't think so,' he said.

'Why not?' persisted Floriana.

'Unless your friend has recently qualified in mechanical engineering, I fail to see how she could possibly be of use to me,' he clipped out coldly.

'I don't mean an expert's job,' protested Floriana. 'I mean something a bit more casual. What about cleaning? Please, Romano. Kelly's a dab hand with a duster and the castle could do with a bit of a spruce. Nobody's been living here for ages—and it shows.'

'I agree with Floriana,' said Rosa unexpectedly. 'I discovered a cobweb on one of the upper floors earlier and it was distinctly dusty up there. Obviously none of the christening guests will be venturing up that far, but it does imply a certain sense of *decay*, which has never been present before. What harm could it do?'

'Honestly, it doesn't matter. It's a mad idea,' put in Kelly quickly.

'A completely mad idea,' Romano agreed, and this time made no attempt to hide the exasperation which tempered his words. But annoyingly, nobody was saying anything. They were all looking at him instead. His stepmother enquiringly. His sister pleadingly, and his brother-in-law, he suspected, with a hint of amusement lurking in his eyes. As though he were witnessing Romano being backed into a corner and was wholly enjoying this unusual spectacle. In fact, only Kelly looked as horrified as he felt and that rankled with him, too. Did she think herself too good to clean his castle? And it was that, more than anything, which made him slowly incline his head before lifting it again to clash with the green gaze of the redhead on the other side of the table.

'Very well,' he agreed, giving a heavy sigh. 'If that is what you wish, I will allow you to clean my castle.'

'Allow me,' repeated Kelly so quietly that only he might have heard—or was he simply reading her lips?

'For which, naturally, you will be adequately compensated.' He frowned. 'I imagine there is enough work to keep you employed for ten days—will that be sufficient?'

'Oh, that's fantastic. Thanks, Romano,' said Floriana brightly. 'What do you say, Kelly? Isn't that the answer to all your prayers?'

What could she say? Kelly tried not to squirm in her seat, though it wasn't easy because they had all turned to look at *her* now. And yet the only thing she could see was the hostile expression on Romano's face, which annoyingly managed to be as sexy as hell. There were a million things she wanted to say, the chief one being a suggestion that he could take his offer and stick it where the sun didn't shine.

But that would be like shooting herself in the foot, especially when an unexpected injection of much-needed cash would be a temporary lifesaver. Her problems were real and she couldn't let pride stand in the way of what sounded like a genuine offer. And while there were many criticisms she could level at the controlling tycoon, instinct told her he would pay her fairly. Romano Castelliari wasn't an exploitative man, she recognised— just a cold and occasionally cruel one.

'It's very generous you, Romano. Thank you. When would you like me to start?' she added sweetly. 'Shall I wash up after lunch? Polish some of the furniture before the service starts?'

The brief gleam in his jet-dark eyes was the only indication that he had acknowledged the barb. 'That won't be necessary. After the christening party have left for Rome,' he said icily. 'Will be when your employment officially begins.'

I guess that's when my clothes turn into rags, Kelly thought irreverently, but she didn't say another word.

CHAPTER FOUR

ROMANO STOOD BY the font at the altar, his back ram-rod straight as he waited for the christening party to arrive. The church was cool, with the light muted by the approaching dusk, and the powerful scent of lilies pervaded his nostrils with a cloying intensity. He didn't like churches at the best of times but this one pressed all the wrong buttons. It had hosted Castelliari weddings, and baptisms—including his own—but for him it symbolised only one thing. He felt the ice of his skin and the cold clench of his gut. He had worked hard not to think about those earlier times and for the most part had been successful, but the rainbow light bleeding through these particular stained-glass windows onto the faded flagstones was enough to drag them up from the recesses of his mind.

He swallowed.

The funeral.

He remembered how obscenely small his mother's coffin had looked as he had walked into the church behind it.

The memories shot back with painful clarity.

The congregation turning to regard the solemn five-year-old with pity pouring from their eyes. Had they been expecting tears? Hysterics? Had they been surprised—maybe even disappointed—by his total lack of reaction? By an expression he had overheard someone whispering: *'Freddo come il marmo.'*

As cold as marble.

He hadn't felt a flicker of sorrow. Why would he?

Even now he could recall how empowering it had felt to defy the expectations of those adults around him. To show them that he could be strong. That he didn't need their damned pity.

His gaze flickered around the waiting congregation. There was nobody here who would remember that day. Most of them were dead—certainly the ones of his father's generation, or older—and the others he had deliberately lost touch with. His stepmother hadn't even met his father at that point and, though she must have known the story, she'd been wise enough never to broach the subject with him, and he knew for a fact that Floriana had never been told the story about what his mother had done to him. They had shielded her from the sordid tales of drugs and sex. They had wanted to protect his young half-sister, in a way they had never been able to protect him...

The opening of the church doors was welcome distraction from the ugly stream of his thoughts but, instead of a moment's respite, he was awarded with the loud hammer of his heart as he saw the woman following his half-sister into the church. Floriana was carrying the baby, with Max beside her, holding onto young Rocco's hand. But the only person Romano could see was the redhead who accompanied them, her frame so tiny and petite—her hair the brightest thing in the entire place.

He expelled an unsteady breath as she sashayed into view, her nubile grace as electrifying as ever. He had managed to avoid her since that excruciating lunch earlier, when... He shook his head very slightly for he still couldn't believe what had happened. .

When he had been railroaded into giving her a spurious kind of employment.

As his cleaner.

Did that mean he was about to subject himself to the wild fantasy which had been hovering on the edges of his mind ever since? Of Kelly Butler with her hands all wet and gleaming, bending over a bucket of soapy water, those pert buttocks tight and clenched as she moved to and fro with her scrubbing brush.

His throat dried.

Had he been insane?

Very probably.

But the fact remained that he now had a problem and he needed to work out how best to deal with it.

As she walked towards the font behind his sister, he attempted to judge her negatively—not a big ask since she stood out from every other woman in the small church. The handful of Floriana's friends who had been invited were wearing quietly expensive designer outfits, as befitted a small christening for a member of one of Italy's premier families. But not Kelly Butler. Her diaphanous dress was splashed with a meadow of flowers—the delicate fabric falling almost to the ground, just above narrow ankles, which were clad in soft-buttoned leather boots. Her jacket was leather, too—nipped in at the waist as if to emphasise the gentle curve of her hips. Her hair was a blaze of fire, tumbling in fiery curls all the way down her back, two waterfalls of silver streaming from her tiny ears. What she wore was completely inappropriate for the occasion and yet...

'Hello, Romano,' she said sweetly as she reached him.

'Kelly,' he responded curtly, with a brief nod of his head.

'My last few moments of freedom before I have to start calling you boss,' she whispered.

Romano's gaze remained fixed ahead as he deliberately declined to answer and waited for the priest to begin the service. He felt a tug on his jacket and looked down as his nephew, Rocco, held up a tiny toy car—a replica of the one made in Romano's own factory. The boy fixed him with a gap-toothed grin as he mimed the vehicle travelling at speed along the top of the pew but Romano gave a brief shake of his head, noting the boy's look of disappointment as he let his hand fall. Had Floriana taught her son nothing? he wondered censoriously. He might wish he were anywhere else but here, but he was a stickler for tradition. Hadn't the child been instructed never to play inside a church?

And why was Kelly glaring at him like that as she smoothed the ruffled hair of the little boy?

His sister turned to him, cradling the infant in her arms. 'Would you like to hold Allegra?' she whispered, but he shook his head, ignoring the faint look of hurt which crossed her dark eyes.

Would it shock her to know that he had never held a baby?

That he had never *wanted* to hold a baby.

'I will,' said Kelly, with another wordless look in his direction.

Unwillingly Romano's gaze was captured as she carefully took the infant, who promptly began to whimper. But instead of handing her straight back to her mother, Kelly held out her little finger for Allegra to suck and the baby latched onto it immediately. It was an instinctive gesture—though what did he know?—which somehow didn't seem to fit well with his racy image of her. At that moment she more resembled a famous painting he had once seen of the Madonna—serene and oh-so-soft rather than an all-night party queen. As the child quietened with an ecstatic little bleat, Romano felt the inexplicable clench of something unfamiliar inside his chest. Suddenly he was finding it difficult to concentrate. To breathe.

And he didn't know why.

The swell of music momentarily distracted him and he forced himself to join in with the responses, but he was glad when the service ended and he could escape, emerging into the spring dusk and sucking in a lungful of mountain air in an attempt to clear his head. A line of cars was waiting to take them back to the *castello*, but he stood back until everyone else had departed, ensuring that he travelled without company. Alone at last in the limousine, he stared out of the window at the pale indigo of the darkening sky—perplexed and irritated to find himself still thinking about Kelly Butler.

Back at the castle, where servants were carrying trays of champagne and canapés to the gathered groups of guests, he saw a temporary escape route. Quickly excusing himself, he went upstairs to his office, citing the need to telephone a colleague in Sydney and ignoring the look of frustration on his half-sister's face. But the call went on longer than he'd intended. Or maybe he had deliberately prolonged it. Because when he came back downstairs, it was to find everyone standing in small groups, chatting amicably and—much too late now, of course—he wondered if he could have got away with a total no-show.

But he knew what was expected of him and how best to deliver it and the eager expressions which greeted his arrival made it obvious that, in a sense, they had all been waiting for him. He gave a mirthless smile. No surprise there. It happened all the time. It was one of the drawbacks of being a billionaire. Of being a 'money magnet', as his good friend Javier Estrada always put it. It was why some of his peers used permanent body-guards, though he could never have tolerated such an incursion into his privacy. With a skill born of endless practice he was able to adapt, chameleon-like, to any given situation—and at a rare family gathering like this, it was always best to adopt a low-key demeanour and attempt to blend in.

So he moved from group to group, exchanging pleas-antries as he sipped from a glass of vintage champagne, graciously receiving compliments about the castle, the garden and the quality of the wine as he batted away the intrusive questions he had already anticipated.

Yet all the time he was aware of one person who dominated the periphery of his vision. Infuriatingly, his sole focus. Kelly Butler was at the far end of the room in her inappropriate dress and bright earrings, yet he was having to work very hard not to turn his head to stare and drink in her beauty. Suddenly he wondered how the hell he was going to get through the next few days, when the thought of being alone with her for an entire week was stretching before him with unendurable provocation.

But he couldn't keep avoiding her.

There was surely only one way to get her out of his system—and if he couldn't have sex with her, then the solution was to talk to her as much as possible, because didn't all women have limitations when it came to conversation? A wry smile curved his lips. In his experience, even highly educated career women were notoriously predictable when they chatted. A few seconds in his company and all they could do was flirt and portray themselves as ideal wife material, which bored the pants off him. There was, of course, one exception to the rule. She may have consistently annoyed the hell out of him but nobody could ever have accused Kelly Butler of being boring.

He walked across the room to where she stood in her floaty dress, nursing a glass of orange juice.

'Having a good time?' he enquired conventionally.

The look she directed at him was unfathomable. 'I was.'

'Try not to be too combative, Kelly,' he murmured. 'It will make lines appear on your forehead.'

'I suppose all your girlfriends have them Botoxed out?'

He shrugged. 'I really wouldn't know.'

Kelly clutched her glass a little tighter. No, she bet he had no idea about what his girlfriends did with their lives, unless it involved fawning over him. No wonder his ego was so colossal. She'd observed the way all the other guests had practically prostrated themselves in front of him, and his admittedly gracious response had made her blood boil. Smug, or *what*?

And in the meantime she was stuck.

Stuck here, with him.

No, not just stuck with him.

Working for him.

She knew Floriana had been acting out of the goodness of her heart but how Kelly wished she'd kept her impetuous question to herself. She felt embarrassed colour rising in her cheeks. She knew Romano had always looked down his nose at her. That he saw her as the poor girl from the wrong side of the tracks. Was he quietly laughing to himself at this latest development? Maybe he thought that cleaning for him would make her accept her place and that this new, servile role might reinforce her real Cinderella status in the lives of the Castelliari family once and for all.

But it was a done deal and there was no point being ungracious and sulking about it. So embrace it, she told herself fiercely. Show him you're not too proud to earn an honest buck. Concentrate on the positives, not the negatives. And not the kind of positives which involved drooling over the charcoal suit he was wearing, which hugged his muscular frame to perfection.

She forced the words out. 'It's very kind of you to give me work.'

'A kindness I would have preferred to forgo,' he commented acidly.

'I kind of worked that out for myself from the look of horror on your face.'

'I had no idea I made my feelings so transparent,' he said, frowning a little as he loosened his silk tie.

And annoyingly, Kelly found herself transfixed by that simple movement, especially when he undid the top button of his shirt to reveal a tantalising glimpse of chest hair, dark against the olive gleam of his skin. 'Do you want me to give you a get-out clause, Romano?' she enquired hoarsely, desperately trying not to stare. 'Because it really won't be a problem if you do. I'm well aware that you were railroaded into it.'

'I do not renege on promises.' He raised his eyebrows. 'And besides, how else will you pay your rent?'

'Like *you* care!'

He gave a short laugh. 'Even I am not hard-hearted enough to see my sister's friend being kicked out onto the street.'

'Bad for your image, I suppose?'

'I don't spend my whole life trying to enhance my image, Kelly.'

'Perhaps you should.'

He raised his eyebrows. 'Or perhaps you're attempting to exasperate me so much that I'll just tell you to go to hell?'

She sucked in a deep breath, hating his shrewdness. Hating the fact that she was depending on his benevolence and that only a fool would flounce out of the room in a huff, which was what she felt like doing. And hating most of all the way he made her feel like no man had ever done before. Weak and strong and invincible yet vulnerable, all at the same time. 'No,' she said, wondering why her voice sounded so squeaky. 'I don't want that.'

'Then we'll just have to make it work, won't we?' He slanted her a steady look, which was underpinned with warning. 'You can easily keep out of my way. It's a big castle.'

'Our paths need never cross,' she agreed readily. 'I'll look on it as a personal challenge to stay as far away from you as possible, Romano—as well as eradicating every cobweb in the building, of course.'

But he didn't smile at her flimsy joke. His black eyes were narrowed with curiosity. 'You seem to know my nephew very well,' he observed.

'I make video calls as often as I can—and Rocco loves to chat.'

He didn't seem satisfied with her response.

'And do you often visit them in France?'

She opened her mouth to skate over the question, when something stopped her. Because the best thing about this weird situation—possibly the only good thing—was that she didn't have to pretend to be anything she wasn't. He might not like her or approve of her forming a close bond with his nephew, but she didn't have a single thing to lose. And surely that gave her the freedom to speak the truth to him.

'Hardly ever,' she said. 'I can't afford it. Unlike you, who can, but never does.'

'Excuse me?' His words were discharged in a disbelieving hiss.

'You know very well what I'm talking about,' she said, swallowing a little as she thought whether or not it was wise to proceed, because the expression on his stony features was more than a little forbidding. But so what? Nothing ventured, nothing gained. 'You never go and see them, do you? Floriana said you'd been once—that you zoomed in by helicopter and zoomed straight out again, without even staying for dinner.'

There was a pause.

'I have a busy lifestyle,' he answered repressively. 'I happen to run a giant organisation. You don't think that eats into my time?'

'I'm sure it does. But that's not the real reason why you don't go, is it, Romano?' she challenged. 'You manage to find time in your packed diary for all those fancy Premio Mondo car races, and the parties, and gallery openings and—'

'How dare you take me to task in this way?'

'I dare because there's a gorgeous little boy who would love to get to know his *zio*, but never gets the chance. And time is marching on, Romano. He'll be a sulky teenager before you know it and—'

'That is enough,' he snapped, before sucking in a deep breath, as if to temper his icy retort with something a little more reasonable. 'If only my sister would allow herself to see sense, she could base her family here, which is far more accessible than their current location—'

'I didn't find it that accessible,' she objected, remembering her journey.

He glared at the interruption. 'But she stubbornly refuses to accept my offer.'

Kelly opened her mouth to suggest why that might be, but hadn't she already said enough? What was the point of accusing him of being a total control freak? He was an intelligent man. He must know that and even if he didn't... Did she really think he was going to radically change his personality, on her say-so? What did she think might happen—that he would nod and smile and thank her for her insight? At the moment his face was so granite-grim, she couldn't imagine him ever smiling again. 'Oh, look,' she said, her words tempered with relief. 'Here comes Floriana. Let's try and act normally, shall we?'

'I don't think I know what normal is, around you,' he snapped.

'You and me both,' she shot back, yet as Floriana made her way towards them, Kelly was aware that, in some weird kind of way, it almost felt as if she was *colluding* with him.

CHAPTER FIVE

ROMANO LAY ON the giant bed, wide awake.

Again.

This was unconscionable, he thought, throwing the rumpled covers away from his sweat-sheened skin. He was a man who had taught himself to sleep with enviable deepness, once he had trained himself out of the nightmares which had once haunted him. But not tonight. He gave a bitter laugh. Nor last night either. He stared out of the window, where the bright silver of a crescent mood was etched starkly against the black sky as he tried desperately to concentrate on something—anything—other than the image of flashing emerald eyes and copper curls and a pair of rosy lips which had poured forth a stream of insolent criticism. But the memory of Kelly Butler was more persistent than any fever.

He let out a ragged sigh, knowing it wasn't simply her beauty which was making him feel like a man obsessed. He stared at the lacy flicker of moonlight which was dancing through the leaves outside his window. Because hadn't her insolence rankled? How dared she take him to task over his perceived failures as an uncle? She had no right to speak to him like that. Not even a member of his own family would dare to do so. Come to think of it, he couldn't think of a single other person who would have had the temerity or the courage to address him with such brutal frankness.

Yet somehow her words had bothered him—or, rather, the sentiments behind them had. *Was* he a bad uncle to little Rocco? He frowned. He put money into the child's account every month and had written his will so that Rocco and his sister and any future siblings would inherit every euro of Romano's estate. *Sì*, it was true he didn't interact much with him, because he was stricken with a strange kind of paralysis around children. Up until the age of five he had existed without the company of other children. His heart had become stony, his spirit deadened. What kind of example would he be for the little boy—what could he offer him, other than cynicism?

He lifted up the glass of water at his bedside and put it down again. He needed something stronger than water. A slug of grappa perhaps, which might blot out his restlessness and help him get the rest he craved.

Pulling on a pair of jeans, he failed to grab a T-shirt or sweater, even though the night was cold. Because the chill on his bare torso might benefit him. It might even serve as the non-wet equivalent of a cold shower, he reasoned with a savage trace of humour.

The night-time creaks of the *castello* were familiar but, as he descended the curving staircase, he could hear unusual clinking and thudding noises which definitely weren't. He frowned. Had he left a window open, so that a bird could fly in? Was an owl or a bat currently incarcerated in the bowels of the *castello* and wreaking havoc? Following the distant sounds which eventually led him to the scullery, he pushed open the door, totally unprepared for the sight that greeted him—which managed to be both domestic and erotic—of Kelly Butler with her back to him, bent over one of the sinks, seemingly lost in thought. For a moment he stood in silence, allowing his gaze to absorb the unexpected vision she presented to his cynical gaze.

Her thick red curls were tied back in a black velvet band and her hands were deep in soapy water, with a row of crystal glasses draining neatly on the side. She was wearing a pair of pyjamas of a type he had never seen before—certainly none of his lovers would have dreamed of sporting such robust-looking nightwear. Because these weren't made of gossamer-fine silk which whispered against the flesh—intended to reveal almost as much as they concealed. These, he noted sourly, were made of a thickly unattractive material he had once heard described as… He frowned. What was it? Winceyette? *Sì*. The word had been so extraordinary that he'd never forgotten it. Disbelievingly, he registered a pattern of bright sprigs of cherries splashed against a dark background. She couldn't look more different from the occasional forbidden fantasy he had entertained about her, yet still he had difficulty tearing his gaze away.

'Kelly,' he said quietly, for he had no wish to startle her.

But she spun round anyway, her plump lips forming a cushioned circle of surprise, her eyes widening as she clutched a dripping brush she was brandishing before her like some sort of a weapon.

'Romano!' she cried.

'Why, who else were you expecting?' he demanded sarcastically—mostly to divert his attention from the fact that she could look so ravishing, despite the roomy swamp of her practical pyjamas. 'The resident castle ghost?'

Her eyes grew even wider. '*Is* there a castle ghost?'

'I have no idea. I don't believe in ghosts,' he snapped, shaking his head with an impatience he didn't bother to hide. 'What on earth are you doing down here at this time of night?' He glanced up at the ancient clock on the wall. 'Or should I say morning?'

'Sorry. I didn't realise there was a curfew.' She put the dripping brush down. 'Isn't it obvious what I'm doing? It suddenly occurred to me that there were probably a load of dirty glasses left in the dining room after the servants had all gone home for the night, since none of them are resident any more.' She shrugged. 'And I... I couldn't sleep. So I thought: why not do something useful?'

'I thought I told you not to do anything until the others have left for Rome?' he husked, unable to stop his brain from registering the quivering movement of her breasts beneath the voluminous nightwear. 'Until then, you are here as a guest. The housekeeper will be here in the morning. She can finish off.'

'Suit yourself. Anyway, what are you doing up at this time of the—' irreverently, she wrinkled her snub nose at him as she dried her hands on a nearby cloth '—*morning*?'

'I couldn't sleep. I came down to get myself a drink.'

'You haven't got a drink problem, have you, Romano?' she questioned delicately.

'No, I damned well—' he retorted, when he saw from the unmistakable twitch of her lips that she was teasing him and, for some reason, this also infuriated him. Turning away from her witchy-eyed distraction, he surveyed the glasses draining on the side, his desire for grappa gone. 'You don't need to do any more tonight,' he growled reluctantly. 'But thanks.'

Kelly nodded, even though he had his back to her and couldn't see, unable to formulate a coherent response to that grudging praise. Not when he was standing there like that—driving every sane thought out of her head. With hungry greed, she stared at him, even though she knew it was a mistake. Because this was Romano as she'd never seen him before—not even in her wildest teenage dreams. She'd certainly never seen his bare torso before. She associated him with pristine suits, silk shirts and handmade shoes—as befitted his status as one of the wealthiest men in Italy.

She couldn't help but marvel at the silken flesh which covered the rippling muscle, visually devouring his powerful frame inch by inch, as if trying to permanently commit it to memory. Broad shoulders tapered down to narrow hips and his jeans were low-slung and snug against his bottom. His feet were bare too and…they were really quite *big*. Her heart raced. She wasn't used to being in such an intimate setting with a man, though obviously she'd seen people half naked before—but being surrounded by random strangers strutting around in too-tight trunks down at the local swimming baths was nothing like *this*.

'You should go back to bed,' he said, still with his back to her, his voice oddly tight.

'I guess I should.' But still she didn't move. Actually, she couldn't. Her feet seemed to be rooted to the spot—as if her body were refusing to take her away from where she most wanted to be. And something strange was happening. A cocktail of emotions was building inside her—filling her with an intoxicating sense of need. She wanted to explore him. To touch him and kiss him and run her fingertips all over that satin flesh. Deep down she had always wanted that.

And he had rejected her. Made her feel crass and foolish and out of her depth.

So get out of here before you do something you'll regret. Learn from the lesson he took a cruel pleasure in teaching you.

'Romano,' she said, meaning to say a calm goodnight to him. At least, that was what she told herself. Only suddenly her voice didn't sound like her voice any more. It was coming out all wrong and there was a husky quality to it. A tiny, questioning lilt as she uttered the last, breathy syllable of his name.

He turned round and Kelly couldn't hide her surprise as she stared up into his face, because this was a Romano she didn't recognise. He looked conflicted. Almost...*savage*. Suddenly, she caught a glimpse of the primitive man who existed beneath the veneer of sophistication she had always associated with him. It was as if a silent and anguished battle was taking place behind the symmetry of his hard features. His lips were flattened into an accusatory line but his eyes were smouldering—they reminded her of the glowing coals you found at the bottom of a fire, their intense heat often taking you by surprise.

'Don't,' he commanded softly.

'Don't what?'

'Don't say my name like that.'

She blinked. 'Like what?'

'Like what?' he mimicked, before giving a short and bitter laugh. 'Do you really want me to spell it out for you, Kelly?'

'I was rather hoping you might.'

His voice dipped. It was gravel. It was honey. And it whispered over her skin like the brush of a feather. 'Like you're running your tongue up an ice-cream cone and trying to catch the drips.'

Kelly may have been innocent in many ways but she wasn't completely naïve. She'd read enough books and seen plenty of films and Romano's words were graphic enough for her to realise exactly what he meant. Heat flooded her cheeks and she could feel the push of her tightening nipples rubbing against the pyjama top. Because the craziest thing of all was that she *wanted* to do exactly what he was hinting at. She *wanted* to lick him.

'Have I shocked you, Kelly?' he taunted softly.

Somehow she kept her voice steady. 'Why, is that what you're trying to do?'

'No. There's only one thing I want to do right now,' he said, his voice as taut as a piece of elastic which had been stretched to breaking point. 'And that is to kiss you.'

Their gazes locked. His ebony gaze was splintered with fire and Kelly realised what a massive admission this was for a man like Romano to make—a man who had once taken great pleasure in rejecting her. And if it didn't sound in the least bit romantic, that was because it wasn't. In fact, that was the last way you would describe it. His desire for her was obviously an irritant. Like an annoying itch which needed to be scratched.

But wasn't it the same for her? She didn't want to feel this way about him. The odds were stacked against any kind of relationship between them, she knew that. He didn't like her, or approve of her—he never had. He was much too rich and she was much too poor. She came from the opposite side of the tracks. She was wrong for him in so many ways. And he was wrong for her. She didn't need a heartless control freak as her first lover and if she walked away now, she would occupy the moral high ground. She would be seen as the victor in this futile sexual battle and it was a very tempting prospect.

But not nearly as tempting as the alternative...

Because mightn't this help her break the deep spell he had cast on her? Wouldn't kissing him free her from the crazy fantasies she'd nurtured all these years, no matter how many times she'd tried to wean herself off him? Because everyone knew that reality could never match up to fantasy.

She met the hard glitter of his eyes and suddenly all her reasons for refusing melted away. 'So kiss me,' she urged him recklessly. 'I'm not stopping you.'

She saw a pulse working at his temple as he nodded, as if her husky suggestion were only confirming something he already knew. Had she capitulated too easily? Even if she had, she didn't care because he was walking across the castle kitchen towards her and she couldn't think of anything other than the incredible fact that he was pulling her into his arms. The breath caught in her throat as his long fingers spanned her waist, his touch making her sizzle beneath her thick pyjamas.

'This is your last chance, Kelly,' he warned softly, his black eyes glinting. 'But I'm telling you now that things will never be the same if I do this.'

Kelly bit her lip. Did he imagine she would never recover from his lovemaking and she would be weeping into her pillow for the rest of her days? Oh, the predictable arrogance of the man! She wondered what he'd say if he knew she was only doing this to get him out of her system. To rid herself of his lingering presence once and for all, because nothing else had worked. 'Oh, I think I'll just about manage to survive,' she declared, through lips which already felt thick with anticipation.

Tilting her chin with his thumb, he stared down at her for a long moment, before slowly bending his mouth to hers. And although Kelly thought she was prepared for his kiss she was mistaken, because it wasn't what she was expecting. She swayed. Just what *had* she been expecting? A brutal crushing of his lips? A blatant demonstration of sexual mastery? Yeah. All that. But...

Not this.

She gasped as his lips whispered provocatively over hers. Why, their flesh was barely touching, so how could it possibly feel this good? It was as if he was tantalising her in slow motion, making all the unfulfilled desire inside her burst into sudden and vital life. Heat flooded her as his lips coaxed hers apart, allowing him to slide his tongue inside her mouth, and it felt so intimate, she thought dreamily, as she slid her arms around his neck. And so easy. As if she'd been waiting all her life for a man to kiss her like that. It made every other kiss she'd ever had—and there hadn't been many—seem like a travesty.

He made a small growling sound as he deepened the kiss, his fingers weaving themselves through her curls, and she felt her hairband loosen. And now his hands were roving over her pyjama jacket and he was uttering something urgent in Italian, cupping her breasts through the thick material, as if he were silently weighing the engorged flesh—as people sometimes did when they were buying melons in the market. She gasped as he turned his attention to her nipples, and the tips were so hard that they felt like bullets.

'Please,' she moaned, with a restless writhe of her hips.

'Please, what, Kelly?'

But he didn't seem to be expecting an answer and Kelly choked out a sigh of relief as at last he began to undo the jacket buttons with shaking fingers—briefly marvelling that she could make such a man tremble like this. The cool air hit her heated skin and she heard his silky murmur of approval as he bent his head to one thrusting mound, drawing a tight bud into his mouth and beginning to lick it with sensual precision.

'Is this what you wanted?' he queried, his voice muffled against her flesh.

'Yes,' she whispered.

'I can't hear you, Kelly.'

'Yes!' she burst out. 'You know it is!'

'*Sì,*' he answered, almost grimly. '*Lo so.*'

Almost giddy with pleasure, she closed her eyes as he began to tease her puckered flesh with his tongue. Her body felt boneless, her blood thick and sweet. She was dissolving beneath his touch. She moaned as he slid his hand beneath the waistband of her pyjama bottoms, seeking access to where the aching was fast becoming unbearable. She heard his low laugh of pleasure as she opened her thighs for him, as if this were something she'd done a million times before. Again she moaned as his finger glided over her slick flesh, making contact with that most intimate part of her, and instinct made her angle her hips towards him as she sensed his sudden hesitation.

Was she doing everything she was supposed to do? Was he expecting her to touch him back—and if so, where did she even begin? Through the denim, perhaps—or did she carefully unzip him, where the fabric was straining over that formidable mound? She was a bit daunted by that, because she had never undressed a man before. Her throat dried. And there were other considerations, too. Should she tell him she was a virgin, or might that put him off?

'Romano,' she whispered, when suddenly he drew back from her, shaking his dark head.

'Not here,' he groaned as he straightened up. 'And not like this.'

She gazed at him in confusion. 'What's wrong?'

'We're going upstairs,' he growled.

'Wh-why?'

'Why do you think? Do just want me to take you over there on that table where the servants will have their morning coffee?' he demanded, his breathing unsteady. 'Or would you prefer it up against the wall?' He tilted her chin with his finger, so that their eyes were on a collision course. 'Is rough and ready how you like it best, Kelly?'

Now didn't seem the right time to tell him that she didn't have a clue how she liked it—and besides, wasn't conversation redundant when he was lacing his fingers through hers and leading her out of the kitchen? But when they reached the doorway, he stopped, his whole demeanour altering as he let go of her hand. And suddenly, his features were shuttered and his black eyes were empty. All that blazing hunger had gone—just as if it had never been.

'I want you to go upstairs. Alone. I'm giving us both the opportunity to change our minds. A breathing space, if you like,' he elaborated unsteadily. He gave a short laugh. 'It might be better for both of us if we did.'

It was then that Kelly realised that this could all come to nothing. That passion could wither just as quickly as it had bloomed. And then what? Didn't this near-encounter have the power to torture her with unfulfilled promise—the ripples of it persistently lingering, leaving her hollow and aching and unable to move on? She wanted to hurl herself into his arms and plead with him to just have done with it—to ease her longing and frustration right now, and set her free. But she realised Romano Castelliari had probably spent a lifetime being begged to do things by women and that his ego and famous double standards would despise any kind of neediness on her part.

Which was why she managed to shrug in a nonchalant way, feeling a tug of triumph as she watched his gaze flicker reluctantly to the sway of her breasts. 'Suit yourself,' she said insouciantly, but he caught hold of her wrist.

'Leave your light on if you want me,' he told her roughly. 'If the room is in darkness, we will forget this has ever happened. Now go. Quickly. Just go.'

CHAPTER SIX

HE WAITED.

For fifteen long minutes, which ticked by with unbearable slowness, Romano waited, convincing himself that Kelly must have had second thoughts by now. Of course she would. They were sworn enemies, weren't they? They had history. And why the hell was he giving *her* the power of making a decision? There was nothing stopping him from turning off his light and going to sleep and putting it out of his mind completely. He'd spent a whole lifetime asserting his self-will and sense of control and it had never let him down before.

But tonight he seemed powerless to resist the urgent demands of his body. He couldn't seem to shake off the memory of how good she had felt in his arms, just as he couldn't seem to eradicate the scent of her sex, which lingered on his fingers. Actually, he didn't even try. Just lay there drifting them beneath his nostrils and imagined putting his mouth to that sweet, moist spot. Until, like a man enchanted, he slipped from his room, silently making his way to the second floor where his nemesis lay, his heart pounding erratically when he saw the thin shaft of golden light spilling out from beneath the wooden door.

His groin hardened as he acknowledged the silent

invitation, but still he made an effort to fight it. Go, he urged himself, with a sudden swift stab of desperation. Go now, while you still can. But despite the reservations which were stabbing into his mind, he found himself pushing open the wooden door and closing it quietly behind him.

She was in bed, waiting.

A siren.

He swallowed.

No, certainly not that. A siren would have removed those pyjamas and been lying there, artfully posed, with all her delightfully naked flesh on display, while all he could see of Kelly was the spill of red hair over those cherry-covered shoulders. Yet that didn't seem to matter. His stomach curled as he acknowledged the blatant temptation she exuded, propped up against a bank of white pillows, looking impossibly tiny in the four-poster bed.

'You left your light on,' he observed softly.

'That's right,' she said, but he noticed that her voice sounded a little shaky.

'You've still got time to change your mind.'

'Will you only be convinced if I hold up a placard saying, *yes, please*?'

With a powerful beat of anticipation, he walked over to the bed and sat down on the edge, idly lifting a handful of bright curls and letting them fall again so that they caught the light from the lamp like a flame. Slowly, he traced his finger along the line of her jaw and the quivering curve of her lips and felt her breathing quicken. He took his time before he bent his head to kiss her, for as long as it took her to dissolve all over again, which wasn't long. Within seconds she was moving restlessly in his arms, running her fingers frantically through his hair, and he felt his groin grow even harder. Disbelievingly, he shook his head. Had he ever been this hard before?

With a groan he disentangled her arms and stood up so that he could begin to undress and this, too, was different. He had undressed before countless women in the past, usually to murmurs of approval or very graphic descriptions about the generous dimensions of his manhood. But never had he been so painfully aware of his audience. He wanted to tell her to stop looking at him like that, with that curious mixture of hunger and shyness, as he carefully slid the zip down over his aching hardness. Was that how she operated in the bedroom? he wondered with a grim kind of resentment. Providing her lovers with the ultimate fantasy of innocence and experience in order to turn them on? If that were the case, it was certainly working.

Climbing into bed, he pulled her against him and her lips sought his almost clumsily as he began to remove her pyjamas. Yet for once he was clumsy, too. There was none of his usual finesse as he roughly dealt with the offending garments and threw them to the floor. Not that she seemed to mind. Or even to notice. Her attention was focussed totally on him. She was all soft and responsive flesh, moaning a little as his thumb circled each nipple and moaning some more as he slid his hand between her legs.

'You're going to need to keep the noise down,' he warned her softly as he stroked the firm silk of her thigh.

'I will,' she whispered.

He found the liquid heart of her. Began to beat a steady rhythm against her molten skin. Saw her bite down on her lip as he felt a rush of honeyed heat against his fingertips. Suddenly she was writhing her hips with urgent and purposeful frustration and when he glanced down at her face and saw what was about to happen, he had to claim her lips in a crushing kiss to quieten her. He felt her spasm around his finger, over and over again, her little bleats of fulfilment absorbed by the pressure of his mouth, until finally she grew still.

In the apricot lamplight he could see two flares of colour arrowing her high cheekbones as she slumped back against the pillows. 'Oh,' she whispered, her eyes wide and dazed as she stared up at him. 'That was...'

'Quick?' he murmured.

She nodded. 'Did you...mind?'

'Your enthusiasm is...refreshing,' he observed cryptically.

It was a remark he had never made within the bedroom before and it appeared to have given her the green light because suddenly she came at him like a little dynamo, kissing his nose, his eyelids and jaw and softly nipping his earlobes in a display of what felt almost like *gratitude*. Her unconstrained zeal was wildly arousing but Romano knew he needed to take command. If she didn't slow down and continued to move against him like that, there would be consequences and he was a man who always prided himself on his pace and performance.

He reached for a condom, but after he'd stroked on the protection, she climbed on top of him and suddenly his control was slipping away. The warm, sweet weight of her was irresistible. Her breasts were swaying against his skin as he curved his fingers possessively over the pert silken globes of her buttocks and suddenly he was rocked by the urgent need to possess her.

'Kelly,' he groaned.

'What?'

'You're so...' But for once he was lost for words.

'So are you,' she whispered back, using that same erotic verbal shorthand as she stroked her fingertips over his back.

He had intended to flip her over so that he could drive deep inside her—demonstrating his preferred position of dominance—but his swollen tip was so tantalisingly close to her wet folds that he found himself edging inside her. He swallowed, compelled by an urgent need to possess her. He just couldn't stop himself.

But something else could.

Romano wasn't sure exactly when he realised.

When he met that first resistance, or when she gave a tiny ȳelp of pain?

It was heaven to be inside her, but hell to realise the significance of that small cry. He tried to withdraw but by then he was too far gone. He lifted his head to kiss her and slowed his movements down, so that her body could learn to accommodate his, and once she had relaxed, he filled her completely. With a fierce and primeval need he moved inside her molten heat, aware of the encroaching sensation of something he couldn't define. Something he'd never experienced before.

Was it because she felt so tight that this felt so overwhelming, or because for so long it had formed the basis of his most forbidden fantasy? Suddenly he realised that for the first time in his life he wasn't going to be able to wait for her. That he was powerless to stop himself coming and it was happening now. He was falling from a great height. He was *out of control*. His seed was being torn from a body which felt as if it were being splintered into a million pieces, and Romano choked out his shattered disbelief as he orgasmed.

He didn't know how long he lay there, gathering together his breath, stunned and disbelieving that he had allowed himself to walk straight into a honeytrap, as old as time itself. But he didn't focus on it until after he'd made love to her again, this time ensuring that he brought her to another rapid orgasm, which had her blissfully choking out his name.

And then came the anger.

Kelly lay very still, scarcely daring to breathe, let alone speak. She thought he must be asleep. In a way, she hoped he was because she needed to get her thoughts together and work out what she was going to do when he opened his eyes. First up, she needed to dial down her instinctive reaction, which was to spill out her gratitude and delight and tell him that he was the most incredible lover. She didn't need to. He must know that. He had been everything she could have hoped for—and more.

The way he had stilled when he had first entered her and tangled his fingers into her hair until the pain had passed. And after that he'd been so...so...*wild*. He had choked out his own delicious pleasure and then explored her with breathtaking thoroughness, bringing her to another shuddering orgasm, which had made her want to weep with pleasure. A lump rose in her throat. Never in a million years would she have guessed it would be the grouchy and authoritative Romano Castelliari who could make her feel as if she could soar like a bird through the starlit heavens. Who knew?

For a long time she'd worried she wasn't like other women. Mostly because there weren't many virgins as old as her. Over time her innocence had become a silent, nagging burden, rather than the badge of pride she'd been brought up to believe in. She'd wondered if her mother's jaundiced proclamations about how men could never be trusted had scared her off so much that she would never be able to respond to one sexually. That she was...

She remembered the word flung at her by her first and only real boyfriend, when she'd refused to go to 'first base'—which she had thought was a pretty horrible way to describe touching her breasts. He'd said afterwards that he'd read it in an old book and it was supposed to be 'ironic', but at the time...

'You know there's a word they use for women like you, don't you?'

No, she hadn't known and so, rather stupidly, she had asked him.

'Frigid. I'm afraid you're frigid, Kelly.'

Well, she certainly hadn't been feeling frigid a few minutes ago!

She had been feeling...

She swallowed.

Wanton, yes. But something else, too. As if she'd just discovered a side of herself she hadn't known existed, which went far deeper than the giving and receiving of pleasure. When Romano had been inside her, she had wanted to weep and marvel at the way she could feel powerful and yet vulnerable all at once. She'd felt *emotional* and that was dangerous, because that made you susceptible to being hurt. Hadn't her mother spent her entire life telling her that?

But she mustn't jump ahead of herself.

She wasn't sure how to behave but instinct urged her to play it cool, even though she wanted Romano to make love to her again as soon as possible. She wanted that more than she could remember wanting anything. But it was weird having made the transition from enemies to lovers and she wasn't quite sure how to handle it.

Tentatively, she laid her hand over his heart and felt the powerful beat beneath her palm.

'Are you awake?' she whispered.

Romano took a moment before he answered, too preoccupied to trust himself to answer. *Oh, stupido sciocco*, he raged silently! What a fool he was. His jaw tightened. Not just for making love to a woman who had always been forbidden to him, but compounding it a million times over with his subsequent behaviour. Why her? he wondered resentfully. Why did it have to be Kelly Butler, of all people, who had made him behave like some sort of caveman? Who had felt almost *helpless* in her embrace, yet at the same time had revelled in it. Who had come almost as soon as he had entered her. What the hell was the matter with him?

He turned his head just in time to catch the wary look she was slanting in his direction, before her long lashes fluttered down to conceal it, and that was when reality kicked in. Because she was good at concealment, he realised bitterly. Good at lots of things. Lying and deceit to name just two. But why should that come as any surprise? She was a woman, after all.

'You didn't warn me,' he observed, his voice deliberately neutral.

She nodded, her hair rippling against the snowy white of the pillows like the burst of a flame. 'That I was a virgin, you mean?'

'Now is probably not a good time to try and play the innocent, Kelly. Because you aren't. At least, not any more.' He gave a cynical laugh. 'Why didn't you tell me?'

'Because...it didn't seem appropriate. It was difficult to find the right moment. Surely you can understand that.' Her green eyes were filled with appeal. 'It might have spoiled the mood.'

'Damned right it would.'

'I'm just not sure how these things work.' She tiptoed her fingers over his chest. 'Should I have asked how many lovers *you'd* had—and if I had, wouldn't you have accused me of prying?'

'Don't try to change the subject,' he snapped, batting away her hand. 'It would have been a courtesy to have told me, that's all.'

'A *courtesy*?' Her voice threatened to rise, but he heard her suck in a deep breath before she lowered it again, as if she was afraid of being overheard. 'You mean like letting your neighbour know if you're intending to park in their spot?'

He resisted the desire to smile. 'Please don't wilfully misunderstand me, Kelly.'

'There's nothing wilful about it, I can assure you. I'm just wondering why you seem determined to catastrophise what just happened.' She hesitated. 'I enjoyed it and presumably you did too. Well, you appeared to,' she added, almost shyly.

'Of course I enjoyed it. You know damned well I did. But that's not the point. You misled me,' he accused, steeling himself against that doe-eyed look as he remembered the way she had behaved at school. 'You've always made out you were some kind of good-time girl. You were even doing it the other night when you arrived, with all your talk about a *"non-stop party express"*.' He glared. 'Remember?'

'I was only confirming your prejudices, Romano. You always did seem determined to think the worst of me—especially when I dropped out of art school, or so Flo told me.' She shrugged. 'Why should I be the one to spoil your fun?'

Romano tightened his lips, because that shrug didn't help. It reminded him that she was naked and it made those glorious breasts move with unfettered provocation, the nipples dancing as if to invite the lick of his tongue. With an effort he tore his gaze away and met the question in her eyes. 'If I'm such an abhorrent and prejudiced person,' he continued coolly, 'then why have sex with me—particularly when it was your first time?'

There was a pause.

'Is your ego in such need of a boost that you want me to tell you you're irresistible?'

'My ego needs no such reassurance. And I guess you've got what you've always wanted. You've realised your schoolgirl ambition to have your wicked way with me,' he added with soft mockery.

'That's right. I have,' she agreed, and he wondered if

he'd imagined the brief disappointment which clouded her eyes before it was replaced by the defiance he had always associated with her and, once again, he felt the unwilling twist of desire.

'You were a hunger I had to feed, that's all,' she continued insouciantly. 'A hunger which never really went away. There you go again, looking so shocked. You're terribly old-fashioned at heart, aren't you, Romano?'

'My principles remain constant.'

'How very admirable.'

'So, it was simply sexual desire?' he elucidated deliberately, in an attempt to distract himself from the fact that they seemed to be flirting again. 'Nothing else?'

'Why, should it have been?' She wriggled a little on the bed, as if the direct fire of his eyes was making her self-conscious. 'Is it a prerequisite for taking a woman to bed that they need to be in love with you?'

'On the contrary,' he bit out, the words leaving his mouth as if they were poison. 'I thought I'd made my views on *love* abundantly clear.'

She looked puzzled and he braced himself for what he knew was coming.

'I don't understand why you're so…vehement about it.'

'You aren't intended to understand. And the why is irrelevant. If a woman believes she's "in love" with me—with absolutely no encouragement on my part—then I'm afraid she's history.'

She expelled a sigh and shook her head a little. 'Wow,' she said at last. 'That's probably the most cold-hearted thing I've ever heard you say—and it's a pretty crowded field to choose from.'

But Romano refused to rise to the barb. He wasn't particularly offended by her accusation, because it was true. The subterfuge and deceit of his early years had always made obfuscation particularly abhorrent to him. In business as well as in personal matters, he was known for plain speaking, even if it gathered a few enemies along the way. 'I'm just telling you the truth, Kelly, in case—'

'What? In case I join that vast number of women you've left weeping into their pillow? Rest assured, Romano—look! My eyes are completely dry.'

In an attempt to deflect another unwanted smile, which was hovering at the edges of his lips, he scowled. What *did* he want from her? Especially now. More sex? Yes, that, of course. The hard pound of his heart was reinforcing just how much he would like to be inside her again, only, this time, to take it more slowly. He would like to prolong the pleasure until she was sobbing out his name, over and over again. For, despite her spiky words, he could see the tremble of her lips, just as he could almost taste the undercurrent of desire which was rippling through the air towards him. But he closed his thoughts to the possibility of a repeat performance, even though her fleshy curves were outlined so invitingly beneath the rumpled bedding.

Because Kelly was different from other lovers and not just because she had been a virgin. She'd been on the periphery of his life for a long time and her role as his sister's friend and his niece's godmother would guarantee she'd be rocking up to family events a long way into the future. This one episode could be safely contained, *sì*. They could write it off as a hot-blooded moment of impetuosity. But having sex with her again would complicate matters and no way should he be contemplating further intimacy just to demonstrate his sexual prowess.

Averting his eyes from the glow of her body, he rose from the bed, determined to put some distance between them and although he couldn't help notice the disappointment which briefly clouded her features, she didn't try to stop him. Reaching for his jeans, he forced his mind to race through a calendar of the days ahead. 'Floriana and her family will be flying to Rome with my stepmother tomorrow—'

'Which I suppose is when my employment as your cleaner officially begins.' She tucked her hair behind her ears and gave him an exaggerated smile. 'I can hardly wait!'

And oh, how he wished she would suddenly announce that she was no longer able to fulfil her obligations. Didn't he *want* her to flounce back to England and tell him she never wanted to see him again because of what had just happened? Of course he did. But if she was determined to see the deal through, he could hardly renege on it simply because her beauty and her defiance had called out to something deep within him and he had been weak enough to answer that siren call.

'Obviously, we are going to have to negotiate how to behave around each other when we are alone in the *castello*,' he said carefully.

'Is that code for wanting me to appear servile whenever I'm in your presence?'

'No, it is not,' he snapped, his conciliatory mood vanquished by her too-smart response. 'I'm talking about keeping expectations real.'

'Go on,' she said.

He nodded, observing her sudden stillness and knowing now was the perfect moment to dash any futile hopes she might be nurturing. 'I can't offer you anything permanent, Kelly.'

'I assume this isn't about the cleaning job?'

'You know damned well it isn't.' He gave an impatient click of his tongue. 'I don't want marriage, or children. I don't want a family. I'm not looking for someone to share my life.'

He waited for her to challenge him. Or pout. Or do that thing of pillowing her hands behind her head to accentuate her breasts so the pert thrust of her nipples would be outlined provocatively beneath the concealing sheet.

But she didn't. She didn't say another word. For how could she possibly be familiar with the post-sexual ploys women used when they were trying to get you to change your mind, when she had been such an innocent?

And he had been the one to take that innocence.

Turing his back on her, he pulled on his jeans, telling himself it was pointless to keep staring into those fathomless eyes, with all their soft green promise.

But wasn't the real reason for presenting his forbidding back view that he didn't want her to get any inkling of her sensual power over him? Or to witness the hard spring of his erection and realise just how much he wanted her.

CHAPTER SEVEN

DETERMINED NOT TO repeat yesterday's sin of oversleeping, Kelly was up with the lark, creeping along the corridor to the bathroom and submerging herself in a deep bath. But the hot water and scented bubbles did little to relieve the aching deep inside her, no matter how hard she scrubbed her skin with the fancy bergamot soap. She could still feel him. Smell him. Taste him.

What had she *done*?

She swallowed.

Lost her virginity...

No. That phrase implied carelessness and there had been nothing remotely careless in her reaction to the Italian billionaire who, up until last night, she had always considered her enemy. He'd given her plenty of opportunity to dismiss their passionate kiss in the kitchen, but she hadn't taken it, had she? On the contrary. She had left the light on in her room, burning like a bright flag of welcome—as she had lain in bed waiting for him. She'd thought that sort of thing only happened in films. Although she supposed that if it had been a film, she would have been wearing something a bit more flattering than a pair of winceyette pyjamas.

The sex had surpassed all her wildest expectations

and then some. But after it was all over and she had been lying there, trembling with the sweet aftermath of all that passion, he had unleashed his insulting conclusion.

'You've got what you've always wanted.'

In some ways he was right, but in other ways he was wrong. She *had* always wanted him—she wasn't hypocritical enough to deny that. A fumbling pass she'd made all those years ago had planted an unwanted seed inside her. Yes, she'd always fancied him, even if she didn't want to feel that way. But hadn't she thought that the fulfilment of all that reluctant longing would bring about some kind of satisfaction—maybe even a sense of peace? Of course she had. Ticking that particular box was supposed to have freed her from his sexy influence, leaving her able to move on with her life. Whereas this morning she felt restless and empty. As if she had left something unfinished.

No.

He had been the one to do that—and it had been deliberate. He'd made it plain he regarded the sex as a mistake. He had spelt out in the most coldly emphatic terms that he wasn't looking for a relationship and then had turned his back on her and walked out of the room, and she was going to have to live with that. In time she would learn to forget Romano Castelliari and all the pleasure he had given her, and time was a great healer. At least, that was what everyone said, and surely they couldn't all be wrong.

Pulling on the jeans and sweater which had dried on the radiator, she plaited her hair, reached for a pair of silver earrings, and went downstairs. Floriana and Max were just finishing breakfast but, thankfully, there was no sign of Romano. In a corner of the sunlit dining room, the baby was sleeping peacefully and, as Kelly wandered over, her heart gave an inexplicable wrench as she gazed down at her dozing goddaughter. Was this what first-time sex did to you? she wondered. Did it make you aware of all the possibilities which lay open to you as a woman and question whether you would ever have a baby of your own?

And why should it fill her with a terrible sadness to think that perhaps she wouldn't?

'Are you going to have a *cornetto*?' Floriana asked, breaking into her reverie as she proffered the basket of pastries. 'Max went down to the bakery for them first thing. I always forget how good they are here...stuffed full of *marmellata* and absolutely scrumptious.'

But Kelly shook her head as she walked over to the table. Her stomach was far too knotted to be able to contemplate eating and the thought that Romano might suddenly stroll into the dining room was making her jumpy. 'I'll get something in a while,' she prevaricated, pouring herself a glass of juice. 'Thought I'd go out for a walk round the estate. Anyone like to join me?'

'I'd love to, but Allegra's due a feed and there's a whole stack of christening presents to open. Let's have coffee when you get back.' Floriana smiled. 'And at least the nanny has taken Rocco off to play—that child has so much energy. Oh, and before I forget—' She reached into the back pocket of her jeans and withdrew a familiar piece of black velvet, which she dangled from her finger. 'This wouldn't happen to be yours, would it?'

Kelly's heart started pounding. 'Y-yes, it's mine,' she said, her fingers closing around the hairband as she remembered Romano's eager fingers loosening it. 'Wh-where did you find it?'

'The housekeeper said it was lying on the scullery floor when she arrived for work this morning. She wasn't quite sure how it got there. Kelly? Are you okay? You've gone really red in the face.'

'That's because it's very...hot in here,' croaked Kelly, fanning her face like an old-fashioned Victorian heroine.

'You think so? Must be your English blood.' Floriana laughed. 'Feels more like the North Pole to me, but of course that's what happens when it's uninhabited for most of the winter—doesn't matter how much you try to whack up the heating, it never really warms up. I'm going to tell Romano that if he isn't going to live here, then at least he could rent it out.'

'Or you could move in here yourself,' drawled a deliciously deep voice as Romano strolled into the dining room.

Kelly didn't want to stare but surely it would have looked odd—and rude—if she continued to study her glass of *succo* as if it were a crystal ball and ignored the man who had just walked in. Trying to behave naturally, she nodded him a polite greeting, doing her best not to react to the oxygen-draining power of his presence. But even a block of stone would be turned on by him, she thought grimly. Particularly when he looked like the very personification of sexual fantasy.

He was dressed in riding clothes—leather boots, old-fashioned breeches and a pale shirt, which clung damply to his torso. His ruffled hair was damp too and his face had the soft glow of exertion. He looked as if he'd stepped from another age, when the custodian of a *cas-*

tello like this would have total authority over everyone and everything.

And doesn't he? she asked herself frantically. *Doesn't he? Not much has really changed since his ancestors pitched up here and started constructing these ancient towers and thick walls.*

'It's a very kind offer, Romano,' Floriana was saying to her half-brother. 'But we told you we could never move in here, not with you acting like mission control from wherever you happen to be in the world. Ask Kelly what she thinks.'

'Why should we?' His black eyes glittered ominously. 'It's nothing to do with her.'

'Because she's my friend,' answered Floriana stubbornly. 'And she'll be able to give you an impartial opinion.'

'Is that so?' said Romano softly. 'Funny. I never really had impartiality down as one of Kelly's strengths but maybe it's time for her to prove me wrong. Go ahead, then, Kelly.' Dark brows were raised in question. 'The floor's all yours.'

They all looked at her and Kelly felt like someone who had wandered onto a darkened stage before suddenly being illuminated by a spotlight. Three pairs of eyes were fixed on her but the only person she was conscious of was Romano. Their gazes met and held. For how long? A second? A minute? Long enough for her to suspect that he had the ability to peer into her mind and know how much she ached for him.

And suddenly she could barely breathe. Or think. Because how were you supposed to behave in the cold light of day when you'd been naked with your host the night before, and he'd been sliding his fingers between your thighs? When he'd taken you to the stars and back, before turning round and berating you for deceiving him? Usually she would be glaring at him. Should she do that now? Or did he think that, by his having pleasured her, she would now give him her support in return?

But she couldn't ignore the undisguised appeal in Floriana's eyes and Kelly realised she couldn't let her friend down. He'd asked the question, so answer it. 'It's obviously a very kind offer, Romano,' she said, as diplomatically as she could. 'But I totally get why they're not biting your hand off to accept it.'

'Perhaps you would care to elaborate,' he suggested.

She ran the tip of her tongue along her bottom lip, trying to ignore the undertone of hostility in his voice. 'I think if you're always on the periphery, pulling the strings—then Max and Floriana won't feel as if they can put their own stamp on the place—'

'I have no objection to them making alterations,' he interrupted icily. 'Provided they are reasonable alterations, of course.'

His eyes had narrowed with calculation and Kelly suddenly got an inkling of the full extent of his power. He wasn't used to being challenged, she realised. Or refused. People rarely said no to him and when they did, he simply wouldn't accept it. And suddenly she felt infused with her own kind of power. She was poor, yes, and she didn't have a fancy status, but at least she wasn't answerable to anyone else—and didn't that confer a unique kind of independence upon her? Even if he sacked her for insubordination, she could always find something else, because jobs as cleaners, or barmaids, or waitresses were ten a penny.

'It's no fun if they have to ask your permission before they can do anything, Romano,' she ventured. 'How are Max and Floriana supposed to feel like it's their for-ever home, if they have to run everything past her fierce big brother before they can even slap some paint on a wall?'

'Fierce?' he echoed ominously.

'Oh, come on. You're not totally devoid of insight.' She met the ebony burn of his eyes without flinching. 'Surely even *you* aren't going to deny that!'

A disbelieving silence followed, broken only by Floriana's soft interjection.

'Wow.'

Kelly blinked, becoming dimly aware that the married couple had been following the heated exchange with total fascination, their heads turning from side to side, like spectators at a tennis match. And suddenly she realised that she and Romano were behaving very differently towards each other, and wouldn't Floriana and Max wonder why? Because having sex with someone changed everything, didn't it? It had to. They had crossed a line last night and they could never go back, no matter what happened in the future.

Once again she could feel herself blushing, the blood rushing to the roots of her hair, which she knew only too well was a deeply unflattering look for a freckly redhead. She needed to get out of there, before any more giveaway emotions spilled out. 'But this is family business, not mine,' she added hastily. 'And I need some fresh air. I'll see you later, Flo. I'll kick a ball around with Rocco and then we can have some coffee before you head off.'

Exiting at speed, she went outside into the pale February morning, only dimly aware that there was a slight nip to the air and she should have gone and found her jacket first. Rubbing her hands up and down her arms, she began to walk. How was it going to be possible to stay here, working for him—*cleaning* for him for ten days—when her feelings were so conflicted? Because when he'd walked into that dining room just now, she'd felt like the same starstruck schoolgirl who had peered down at him from the window of the sanitorium all those years ago. Why should that be? Yes, he had been an amazing lover—no surprise there—but surely exposure to his emotional coldness should have killed off her long-term crush. Just let me feel…*nothing*, she prayed silently. That wasn't too much to ask, was it?

She continued to wander around the sprawling estate, remembering much of the layout from the days leading up to Floriana's aborted marriage to the count. Back then, the place had been buzzing. She remembered lanterns strung from the trees, a string quartet flown in from Rome and a pre-wedding feast of unrivalled splendour—and in the end it had all been for nothing. Yet now she wondered if things could have been done differently. If the union could have been called off in a way which didn't involve a tear-stained Floriana's middle-of-the-night exile from Italy. *Should* she have gone to Romano? Kelly wondered. Risked his wrath and appealed to his better nature? Did he even have one?

Her footsteps took her along a path between two tall rows of cherry trees, their tips frothy and pink with early blossom. Tiny violet flowers were growing in profusion beneath them and nearby shrubs were fragrant with waxy white blooms. Despite the faintly neglected air of the *castello*'s interior, the terraced gardens were as stunning as ever and the jaw-dropping views over the valley were unchanged. Birds were singing their hearts out and, from the other side of the valley, Kelly could hear a church bell ringing. In that moment everything seemed so delightfully *Italian* and she found herself wondering why Romano was so averse to making such a glorious place his permanent home.

She was so lost in thought that at first she didn't properly register the crunch of gravel, but then she realised she was no longer alone and she despaired of the traitorous leap of her heart when she guessed who it must be.

Abruptly, she stopped and turned, wanting to surprise him, but he seemed to be expecting it, his cursory nod failing to disguise the faintly combative light which gleamed from his black eyes. She shivered as their gazes clashed and she hoped he hadn't noticed. So now what? Should she greet him in a cheery manner? That didn't seem appropriate somehow. The fact that she didn't officially start work until the others had left for Rome was a mere technicality. From here on in he is really your boss, she told herself, and might have bobbed a sarcastic curtsey if she hadn't been so taken aback by his appearance.

Because in the time it had taken her to traverse the vast estate, he must have showered and changed for his damp riding gear had been replaced by an immaculate charcoal suit and a dark shirt. Strength and power emanated from every hard sinew of his body and Kelly sucked in an unsteady breath, tortured by the sudden the memory of how magnificent he had looked when he was naked. With black hair glinting in the sunlight and his skin glowing with health, he looked vital and virile. But his eyes were like ice. Dangerous black ice.

Yet despite his emotional coldness, all Kelly could think of was how much she wanted to touch him. With some of the confidence she had acquired in his arms last night, she wanted to lean in and breathe in that potent masculine scent. She wanted to trace the shadowed curve of his jaw with her finger and burrow her hands underneath his shirt so she could feel the satin of his skin. And that was the very last thing she should be thinking, when he hadn't been able to get out of her bedroom quick enough last night.

'You seem to make a habit of jumping out and scaring people,' she exclaimed crossly.

'I was calling your name, but you seemed oblivious. Anyway, you don't look in the least bit scared to me.'

'I'm pretending.'

'*Sì,*' he drawled acidly. 'Pretence is one of your undoubted talents, isn't it, Kelly?'

How did he manage to make an insult sound so... *sexy*? Was it because it was accompanied by the mocking gleam of his eyes, which was making her think about kissing him? She was breathing a little too rapidly and her heart was slamming against her ribcage. 'What do you want?' she questioned weakly. 'To fight?'

'I suspect our fight would finish very differently from the way it started, *cara.*'

She swallowed. 'Please don't call me darling, when we both know you don't mean it.'

'Your command of the Italian language is coming along leaps and bounds.'

'Yes. Obviously I've been quick to learn the words for "tyrant" and "despot"!'

He laughed as he glanced up at the strawberry milk-shake blur of the blossom overhead, before lowering his head to survey her from between shuttered eyes. 'Did you tell Floriana?'

'Tell her what?'

He gave a click of irritation. 'About what happened last night.'

'That depends what you're referring to, Romano. A lot of things happened last night,' she declared. 'There was a party after the christening, during which you did your best to showcase how well you could glower and stomp around the room. Much later, I did the washing up, and—'

'Don't play games with me, Kelly,' he warned softly.

Kelly bit her lip. How would he respond if she told him she didn't know how else to behave? Flippancy seemed a safer bet than vulnerability and surely insolence would protect her against this dangerous and de-stabilising rush of emotion. Because, standing here in the pure light of the early spring morning, it was hard to get her head around what they had done. This hand-some and intimidating man had been her lover. He had explored her in a way which no other man had before. He had been *inside* her. He had choked out something helpless as he had come and this kind of thing happened to women all over the world, every single day. Did it make them feel different, too? As if a new person were inhabiting the same skin. As if she didn't really know herself any more. She cleared her throat. 'I take it you're referring to our ill-advised grapple in the bedroom?'

His brow creased. 'Our *what*?'

'Oh, come on, Romano. We both know your English is good enough not to require a dictionary definition of *grapple*.'

A hiss of air was expelled from his lips. 'You insult me, Kelly Butler,' he told her quietly. 'Was that your intention?'

'Well, maybe a bit, yes,' she admitted. 'You're so easy to wind up. But I'm also trying to be realistic. Because how else would you describe what we did? Surely you wouldn't want me to put a romantic spin on it? Because that would be completely false. And since it was nothing more than physical, then why would I embarrass Floriana by telling her? She probably wouldn't believe me anyway. She knows how much we dislike one another. It wasn't my finest hour.' She gave a short laugh. 'Nor yours, I imagine.'

'*Porca miseria*, but your tongue can wound,' he observed wryly.

'Maybe it's good for you to know how it feels, because yours can too.' She could hear the faint vibration of a phone sounding in his breast pocket but he didn't answer it. 'Look, somebody's trying to get hold of you. Take your call. I'm going back to the castle.'

'The call can wait. I will come with you.'

She shrugged, as if that might somehow cancel out the excited leap of her heart. 'Suit yourself,' she said carelessly, once again noting the superb cut of his clothing. 'And speaking of suits—why are you dressed like that?'

Romano fell into step beside her, wondering how she could manage to look so attractive in the striped sweater he'd seen before and an oversized pair of crumpled jeans. He had deliberately absented himself from the *castello* this morning, even though he was curious to see how she would react to him in the cold light of day, wondering if she would gush or pursue him, as women always did after sex. But not Kelly. She hadn't sought him out on his ride to gaze at him with admiring eyes, nor looked at him knowingly when he'd walked into the room as if to remind him of last night's intimacy. She had been nothing but her usual feisty and combative self and had given him a very honest piece of her mind, without any apparent heed of the consequences. Once again, she had confused him.

A reluctant sigh left his lungs. She was a puzzle, this unexpected virgin who had given herself to him with such sweetness. And Romano did not like puzzles.

He liked answers.

Facts.

Certainty.

Because all of those things guaranteed control and that was the only thing he trusted. Control meant you didn't panic, or scream. It had been the earliest lesson he'd ever learned. The only lesson which really mattered. A forbidden image flashed into his mind and he tensed as he recalled that lost little boy, alone with his mother's body.

No. A pulse flared at his temple. Some things you never forgot, no matter how hard you tried.

For a while last night, he had lost some of his habitual control and it had unsettled him. Back in his room, he had been determined to put the redhead out of his mind and, for a man who had always been able to compartmentalise his lovers, it should have been easy. But eyes as bright as emeralds had ambushed his dreams and those fleshy curves had taunted him with remembered rapture and he had woken this morning, aching and hard and out of sorts.

'What *did* make you drop out of art school?' he questioned suddenly.

Her footsteps momentarily faltered on the gravel path and he saw the hesitation on her face. The sudden unexpected flash of pain. And then her expression became blank again.

'My mother was sick.' She started walking again, increasing her speed as if she didn't want him to keep up, but he did, his long stride easily outstripping hers.

'Tell me about it, Kelly,' he urged, remembering that when he'd heard, he'd naturally assumed she was flighty—without the staying power to tackle a three-year degree course.

'There's not really that much to tell. I moved in with her to nurse her, though it was a bit cramped. She had a little flat she'd bought when she retired as matron, and when she died, I...'

'You what?' he questioned, more gently than usual, and he wondered if that explained her somewhat startled look as she came to a halt again and blinked up at him, almost as if she had forgotten he was there.

'By then it was three years down the line and I didn't feel like going back and being a student again. I'd seen too much that was...grim and...' She shrugged her shoulders, her throat working convulsively. 'I don't

know. Apart from the fact that we'd managed to ac-
crue quite a bit of debt while Mum was ill, it just seemed
sort of irrelevant to sit around discussing art and politics
while everyone around me was getting drunk.'

'And your father?'

Her eyes narrowed and he wondered if she would shut
the topic down, but she didn't and when she spoke her
voice was very quiet. 'I never knew my father.'

'At all?'

'No. He was a doctor, apparently—a very junior doctor at the hospital in London where my mother trained
as a nurse. She'd come from a very rural area of Ireland
and was pretty naïve about life in the big city.'

He flinched, but didn't say anything, just waited for
her to continue.

'My dad was a bit of a charmer, by all accounts, and
he and Mum hooked up. But getting pregnant had never
been part of his plan. In fact, he was horrified when she
told him and he dumped her.' She swallowed. 'She got
in contact with him when I was a few months old but
by then he was engaged to somebody else. Somebody
quite posh. Somebody like him, of course. Apparently,
he was quite rude to my mum. Told her to take him
to court if she wanted money and, of course, she just
crumbled at that. So she was on her own.'

'And what about her family?' he shot out. 'Didn't
they support her?'

She pursed her lips as if choosing her words carefully. 'They were very old-fashioned and concerned with
what they perceived to be right or wrong. They told her
they would never open their doors to a child born out
of wedlock, and they meant it.'

'So you've never met them either?'

'Nope.' She drew her shoulders back, the spill of her hair the colour of marmalade in the morning sunshine. 'Most people don't keep going back for more and more rejection, Romano,' she added proudly. 'It's a survival thing. I think she was trying to teach me to be resilient, which was why she always used to drum in how awful men were at heart and how they would always try to take advantage of you. Now I can see that her attitude was extreme—but it definitely brushed off on me. I guess that must have been one of the reasons why I was so inexperienced...'

He shook his head as her words tailed off, angry with himself. Angry he hadn't known about her sick mother and her purity and the fact that the 'brittle party girl' persona had been nothing but a mask. But he was angry with her too, for keeping this information to herself—because wouldn't he have behaved differently if he *had* known? Almost certainly. He would have kept her at arm's length. She would have remained a fantasy woman, not one who had the power to enter his dreams.

But he hadn't been interested in delving into her past, had he?

He hadn't been able to see past the lure of her lips and her tiny, shapely body.

'I'm going to Turin,' he announced abruptly, because hadn't that been the reason he'd come out here to find her, to tell her that?

'Oh?' Her eyes narrowed. 'Why?'

Romano furrowed his brow. He could explain that he had business to attend to, which would be true. He *always* had business to attend to—his punishing schedule ensured that. But evasion would serve neither of them well, and perhaps he was motivated by a need to make things clear to himself, as well as to her.

'Because I've decided it isn't going to work, us being here together,' he said flatly.

'Why not?'

'Are you really so naïve, Kelly?' And then he scowled, because yes, of course she was, and suddenly he knew he couldn't bear to take advantage of her, not when he had misjudged her so badly. Wouldn't leaving her alone be the best thing he could do for her? Because what was the alternative? 'What do you think is going to happen if we stay here after everyone else has gone?' he demanded. 'How is that going to work? Me going out of my way to avoid you. Both of us trying not to think about what we did last night, with both of us unable to forget?'

'It's a big enough place for our paths never to cross,' she pointed out practically.

'And what about mealtimes?' he continued, her reasonable tone only adding to his ire. 'You think we're going to sit chastely across the table from one another when there's only one thing on our minds?'

'Speak for yourself,' she protested. 'I'll be so hungry after cleaning this massive great pile of yours that I won't be able to look at anything other than my plate.'

He shot her a steady look. 'Are you saying you don't want me, Kelly? That you're not wishing I'd pull you into the shade of that cypress tree and make love to you even now? No,' he added grimly as he saw the molten dilation of her green eyes. 'I thought not.'

'So does this mean you're going to sack me, before I've even started?'

He shook his head. 'No, of course I'm not going to *sack* you. But I'm not staying here. You're too much of a temptation. I will arrange for some of my security people to stay on the estate to keep an eye on the place while you're here. Graziana is the housekeeper. You will report to her—she'll come in from the village every day. My assistant has arranged for your hire car to be returned and she will arrange your transport back to England once your employment is up. I think that's everything.' He glanced at his watch. 'You're not frightened of being here on your own, are you?'

'Huh! It would take a lot more than being stuck in a billionaire's fortified *castello* to scare me!' she retorted, with a touch of her customary fire.

'Good. Because let's be clear about one thing.' He glanced up and his voice dipped, as if the flock of flamingos flying overhead was capable of understanding his words. 'I'm not having sex with you again, Kelly. Do you understand?'

CHAPTER EIGHT

IN THE COSY warmth of the castle kitchen, Kelly had just finished munching her way through a delicious breakfast when the housekeeper put a brown paper parcel on the table in front of her.

Kelly looked up at her. 'What's this, Graziana?' she asked. 'It's not my birthday.'

The housekeeper smiled. 'Something you need,' she responded enigmatically.

More than a little intrigued, Kelly ripped open the paper to reveal several neatly folded pale red garments, which looked oddly familiar. Shaking one out, she found a roomy tunic with the word *Ragno* piped in ice-blue on the breast pocket, above a tiny logo of a sports car in exactly the same shade. She blinked. Of course they looked familiar. They were the uniform of the *castello* and worn by all members of staff—in fact, Graziana was wearing one right now. They had obviously been designed for all shapes and all ages because the matronly housekeeper from the village looked supremely comfortable in hers. But while the baggy trousers and tunic top might be practical for getting down on your hands and knees and scrubbing flagstones, they looked more like a pair of unflattering hospital scrubs. Accompanying them was a card bearing the company name, informing her that they were from the CEO and signed in Romano's absence by an assistant!

'Why such a weird colour combination?' she said, almost to herself.

'It is colour of Ragno racing cars,' answered Graziana slowly.

'Of course it is,' said Kelly, rising from the table, her rapidly cooling coffee now unwanted. Hadn't she seen all those photos of Romano on the Internet when the Ragno car had won yet another Premio Mondo race, pictured beside a gleaming ice-blue machine flashed with scarlet—usually with a similarly gleaming woman draped all over him?

She carried the package upstairs, her head buzzing and not just because Romano had provided her with a hideous uniform in a colour which didn't suit her and clashed like mad with her red hair. It hurt that he seemed determined to reinforce her servile status and drive home the fact that she was no longer his lover. Accept it, she told herself fiercely. Live with it. You are nothing but his humble...

Cleaner.

Glumly, she pulled the roomy tunic over her head and stared at herself in the mirror, thinking how much had happened in the last twenty-four hours in this beautiful corner of Tuscany. After Romano's departure, she'd spent the rest of the day with Floriana and her family, batting off curious questions from her friend about why her half-brother had left so abruptly. It had taken a huge effort to behave normally and in a way she'd been pleased when they had all departed for Rome, and her work could begin in earnest. Because the sooner it started, the sooner it would be over. She could collect her generous pay cheque, go back to England to lick her wounds and forget that her steamy encounter with the powerful billionaire had ever happened.

And that was another thing. She gave a heavy sigh. If she'd thought this might be a job in name only, she had been quickly disabused of that idea by a lengthy list of instructions sent by yet another of Romano's assistants and delivered by one of the security detail which was now stationed in various cottages dotted around the estate. As she pored over the endless dos and don'ts of cleaning such an historic building, she began to get a true idea of the reach of the Italian billionaire's network of power.

Just how many assistants did he have? And what must it be like if you had people to do your every bidding—if you could retreat behind the protective patina of money and influence any time the inconveniences of life intruded? Wouldn't that make you arrogant and unknowable? She pulled a face at her reflection. In Romano's case, yes and yes again. But he was paying her handsomely for the work and that was the most important thing. Had she forgotten the grim reality of her life back home? Because this was more than a job. It meant she would be able to pay her rent for the next few months until she got back on her feet.

No stranger to hard work, she soon got into a routine, toiling from dawn to dusk and deriving immense satisfaction every time she consigned yet another cobweb to the bin, or carefully polished one of the antique silvered mirrors. Bit by bit, the castle began to look less like a corporate venue and a bit more homely. She even picked some flowers and dotted them in a few strategically placed vases to make the vast space seem more welcoming and she thought they looked way better than the rather corporate selection of scentless hothouse roses which had been ordered in for the christening. Graziana arrived each morning with breakfast, leaving home-cooked food for the rest of her meals, and Kelly would often take her lunch outside, munching on a mozzarella salad while the birds sang and thinking that she'd never been anywhere quite so beautiful.

Night-times were different of course. They could be long and hard and painful. She'd spoken the truth when she'd told Romano that she wasn't scared of being alone in the castle, and she wasn't. Fear was being young and alone with your sick mum. Fear was the worry of being kicked out of your tiny bedsit and wondering if you'd be made homeless. But other things could certainly keep you awake. Bittersweet memories for a start, which flashed into her mind with disturbing clarity and made her shiver beneath the feathery duvet.

Romano undressing her.

Romano inside her, big and hard and warm.

Romano making that soft, wild sound which had made her wrap her arms tightly around him while he had lain there, shuddering almost helplessly.

He hadn't been so protected by his patina of power then, had he?

In that moment she had felt so unbelievably *close* to him. In every way. As if two people really had become one, just like it said in all the books you weren't supposed to believe. His gentleness and consideration had been almost as potent as her desire for him and a powerful emotion had welled up inside her, making her want to blink back tears, until she'd forced herself to realise that she was chasing after an illusion. Because Romano had left her bedroom as if the hounds of hell were snapping at his heels, hadn't he? He had only ever wanted sex from her—and he didn't even want that any more. He'd made that painfully clear the following morning, in the bright Tuscan sunshine, surrounded by birdsong and blossom, his brutal words making a mockery of the romantic setting. He'd made it sound as if he had done something he bitterly regretted and wished he could rewrite the past.

But nobody could do that. Kelly gave a mirthless smile. Imagine how different the world would be if you could.

At least today was her last day of work at the castle and tomorrow she was catching a flight back to England. She had stubbornly refused the offer of a lift in Romano's private jet, so a commercial ticket had been booked to take her to Luton airport and a car was picking her up in the morning. The countdown to never seeing him again was nearly at an end.

The daylight was fast disappearing and Kelly was upstairs attacking an ancient wardrobe in the attic when her phone started ringing. Picking it up with dusty fingers, she saw it was an unknown number and, grateful for a little respite, clicked onto the call.

'Hello?'

'Kelly?'

Her heart did something complicated as a delectably recognisable voice rippled down the line, making her feel as if he were brushing verbal velvet over her skin. Sucking in a deep breath, she tried to stay calm, but her the thumping of her traitorous pulse was off the scale. 'Romano?' she verified unnecessarily.

'Of course it is,' he shot back, and there was a pause. 'What are you doing?'

A bizarre thought flew into her mind as she remembered a film she'd once seen about phone sex and the X-rated responses the woman had given to that very same question. 'Dusting out a wardrobe,' came her own repressive reply. 'Don't worry, Romano, I know it's my last day but I'm not skiving.'

A few seconds ticked by. 'I wish to talk to you.'

Her fingers squeezed the phone. 'Isn't that what you're doing right now?'

He made an impatient sound. 'In person.'

'But you're in Turin.'

'No, I'm not,' he growled.

Her heart missed another beat. 'Where are you, then?'

There was another pause and when he spoke she could detect a different quality to his voice. There was resentment, definitely—but something else, too. Something which sounded like desire—although what would she know?

'At the bottom of the hill,' he bit out.

'This hill? You mean here, in Tuscany?'

'Of course I mean here *in Tuscany*!' he exploded. 'Where else would I mean?'

Ask him why. She should definitely ask him why. But part of her suspected she already knew the answer and if she challenged him, didn't that run the risk he might change his mind? Because from where she was standing it seemed as though Romano was backtracking on his grim intention not to have sex with her again, and her heart gave an excited leap. Because wasn't it kind of sexy and empowering that he was asking *her* permission to come here, rather than just rocking up to the house, as he was perfectly entitled to? 'Okay,' she said carelessly. 'I'll talk to you.'

Romano's heart was racing as he cut the connection and powered his car up the hillside, waving away the security guards who swarmed to the gates and seemed surprised to see him. You and me both, he thought grimly, trying not to scorch the tyres as the Ragno came to a screeching halt in front of the *castello*. But clearly his brain wasn't functioning properly and neither was his body, because something made him ring on the old-fashioned doorbell, as if *he* were the guest and she the proprietor. After a couple of minutes, she pulled the door open and when he saw she was wearing the uniform he had sent for her, he momentarily froze. *Porca miseria!* It swamped her tiny frame and didn't suit her and the fact that in no way did she resemble the erotic fantasies he'd been nurturing about her should have been enough to kill his sexual hunger stone-dead. The scraped-back hair and sneakers only added to her subservient image—the plain silver studs at her ears functional rather than decorative. Yet somehow her very ordinariness was making his blood thunder.

He stepped over the threshold and shut the door behind him, meeting the glittering question in her green eyes as she backed away and surveyed him warily from across the wood-panelled hall. Did she think he was going to leap on her, like the big bad wolf?

And didn't he want to?

'Who else is here?' he demanded.

'Nobody. Unless you count the men in black swarming around the place, whose binoculars keep flashing every time I set foot outside.' Now there was a tilt of her chin and a flicker of the defiance he knew of old. 'So, what do you want to talk about, Romano? I presume you're not here to check up on my work—although I'm quite happy to escort you around the *castello* so you can run your fingertip along the surfaces to check for dust. Speaking of which—I've still got that wardrobe to finish and it won't clean itself.' She raised her eyebrows. 'So if you wouldn't mind cutting to the chase?'

Romano stared at her with frustrated amusement as he thought how differently this scene would have played out if it had been any other lover. Women who would have correctly interpreted his desire and mood and played along with whichever fantasy he demanded. Or perhaps even prompted it with a little fantasy of their own. They certainly would have bothered to brush their hair and apply a little lip gloss!

A pulse began to beat at his temple. For days now, he had been waiting to hear from her—some irrelevant message contrived solely for the purpose of resuming contact between them. It was why he had deliberately instructed his assistant to include his personal phone number on all communication with her.

But there had been nothing.

When before had he stared at the blank screen of a phone, willing it to ring, frustrated as he had paced around his giant office on Turin's prized Via della Consolata? Never! Eventually, he had dialled the head of the security detail he'd assigned, demanding to know why there had been no report delivered to him, and whether or not the Englishwoman was safe. Totally safe, the ex-special services veteran had reassured him hastily, before launching into a detailed account of Kelly's comings and goings. The *signorina* had walked here, and the *signorina* had walked there. For her lunch on the terrace, the *signorina* had eaten a panino with…

'Have you been *stalking* her?' Romano had demanded, quite unreasonably, and the bodyguard had attempted to defend himself.

'*Mai, no, signor!* But the *signorina*'s hair is so bright,' the hapless man had continued dreamily. 'It is hard to miss.'

Abruptly severing the connection, Romano had taken matters into his own hands. If he wanted to see her, then why not just bite the bullet and get on with it? Which was how he now found himself staring at her across the wood-lined hallway, uncharacteristically unsure how to proceed as he stared into a pair of eyes as green as the tail feathers of a peacock.

'I don't want to waste time talking,' he admitted, on a growl.

'But you just said—'

'I want to take you to bed!' he declared.

Such heartfelt though undeniably clumsy words would never usually have passed his lips, but Kelly obviously failed to appreciate the honour he was affording her. It should have opened the floodgates, redirecting some of the unbearable tension which was building up inside him by causing the tiny redhead to hurl herself eagerly into his arms and to ask him what they were waiting for. But she didn't budge, just lifted her chin with a quiet dignity.

'You told me you didn't want to have sex with me again.'

'Okay.' The shrug of his shoulders was reluctant. 'I was wrong.'

'Sorry?' She tipped her head to one side. 'I didn't quite hear that.'

'I was wrong!' he exploded.

'All right! There's no need to shout!'

Romano's eyes narrowed. Had he thought she was a stranger to games? In that case, why was she playing him now, like a connoisseur? And why the hell was he letting her? 'But I meant it when I said I don't want a relationship,' he elaborated.

'Do you always lay down your terms quite so brutally, Romano?'

'No,' he said softly. 'Most women don't need to be told.'

'But I do?' Her green eyes burned into him. 'Because I'm so desperate, I suppose?'

He shook his head. 'Because you know nothing of how adults conduct their sexual affairs.'

Still she didn't move, just fixed him with that sensual, insolent look. 'Do you want me to beg you, Kelly?' he questioned mockingly. 'Are you holding out for dinner by candlelight?'

'We've already done that, remember?' she returned flippantly. 'And it didn't end well.'

'What, then?' he questioned silkily as their gazes clashed and held. 'Tell me what it is you want.'

He saw her defences crumble. Saw the way she

chewed on her lip. The momentary hesitation as she read the expression in his eyes and then her own dawning recognition that she had pushed him as far as he would go and he would capitulate no further.

'I want *you*,' she said, almost angrily, pacing towards him as if she were going to pummel his chest with her tiny fists. 'You know I do!'

He gave a softly triumphant laugh as she reached him and he pulled her into his arms, and that unexpected fusion of laughter and desire was as potent as anything he'd ever experienced. Fierce need consumed him but he knew he needed to rein this in. To demonstrate to them both that he was fully in command. He must not give her the power of knowing just how much in her thrall he was at that precise moment. He lowered his head in slow motion—watching the way her lips opened to meet his, like a baby bird wanting to be fed, but deliberately he kept his mouth hovering just out of reach. He could feel the warm rush of her breath before, at last, he touched her and his pulse thudded loudly in his ears. How could a kiss possibly be this good? he wondered helplessly. Her breasts were pushing against his chest, their tips as hard as diamonds. His groin was like a rock and he felt her shiver violently as he deliberately pressed the outline of his erection against her.

'Oh!' she exclaimed.

'Does that daunt you?' he taunted, dragging his mouth away.

Her eyelashes fluttered open as she met his gaze with what looked like genuine interest. 'Should it?'

'*Porca miseria,*' he groaned. 'You are so untutored.'

'Then teach me,' she whispered, and suddenly she

was all soft, sweet submission. 'Teach me everything you know.'

Her breathless demand almost felled him until desire consumed him once again, setting his body on fire and making him so hot for her he couldn't think straight. He thought about taking her upstairs but he didn't want to wait that long. He couldn't. Yet the practicalities of stripping off those clown trousers forced him to abandon his most basic of instincts, which was to take her now—here—where they both stood. Her back against the panelled wall. Her panties on the floor. Her gasps echoing his own as he pushed deep inside her.

He sucked in a ragged breath. Surely it was better to demonstrate the steely constraint which always seemed to desert him whenever she was around and which was now balanced on a knife-edge. Because wasn't that the whole point of this? Not just to feed his hunger, and hers—but to take his fill of her until both their appetites were sated and she could resume her rightful place in his life.

In the past.

Uttering a harsh expletive, he picked her up in his arms and began to carry her upstairs and she didn't cry out in surprise or ask him what the hell he was doing, even though he could barely believe he was behaving in such a Neanderthal way. She just whispered his name against his neck—which made the walk up the sweeping staircase seem unendurable.

Yet he couldn't seem to break out of this testosterone-fuelled zone as he kicked open his bedroom door and kicked it shut again, before carrying her across the vast space and setting her down beside the bed. 'Now,' he said, his fingertips roving over the bright red fabric of her uniform. 'I'm trying to work out the most provocative way of removing this…'

'What's *brutta*?' she questioned, fixing onto the harsh word he had uttered underneath his breath.

'Ugly,' he growled. 'No, not you—these,' he said, disparagingly twanging the elasticated waistband of the matching trousers.

'Well, you're the one who decided I should wear them, presumably.'

'Not me. One of my assistants,' he amended impatiently—for did she really imagine he would trouble himself with such a minor detail?

'Ah, yes. One of your trillions of assistants…' Her interruption trailed off as he slithered the trousers down over her hips and since he knew she was holding her breath as she waited for him to touch her groin, he deliberately avoided the area.

She expelled the breath, her words becoming tinged with frustration. 'Just how many assistants do you have, Romano—and is there some kind of pecking order?'

'Shut up,' he told her softly and, to his astonishment, she did.

'I like you much better like this,' he purred appreciatively.

'Like what?'

'Compliant.'

'Make the most of it, it may not last.'

He laughed softly as he pulled the tunic top over her head, causing the red curls to tumble down around her shoulders as she stood before him clad in nothing but her underwear. Suddenly it felt as if his throat were composed of nothing but dust, yet swallowing gave him no relief. Was it the way her lashes shuttered to shield her incredible eyes in an expression which was close to shy which made her look so unbelievably provocative? And yet, there wasn't a whisper of silk or lace in sight, so how come...?

'You look delectable,' he breathed raggedly.

'D-do I?'

'Utterly.' He whispered his fingertips over her bra, puzzled as to how she could transform such a functional garment into something so tantalising. Maybe because her breasts were spilling out over the black fabric like two generous scoops of ice cream and the curve of her hips was emphasised by the plain panties.

'Now you must...undress me,' he instructed unevenly.

'Must?'

'Please, Kelly.'

Kelly nodded because the raw need in his voice was stupidly flattering, as was her suspicion that the word *please* didn't often pass the lips of Romano Castelliari. Lips which were currently kissing the top of her neck in a way which felt...

Helpless?

No.

A man like this would never be helpless.

Her heart was racing as she pushed the black leather jacket from his shoulders and let it slide to the floor. Next came the dark shirt, which she tugged open to reveal the olive silk of his ripped torso. The shirt joined the jacket as her fingers moved tentatively towards his jeans because, in truth, she *was* rather daunted by the thought of taking them off. But wasn't there a bigger part of her which was eager to learn how to please him? She hesitated for no more than a moment before sliding the zip down over his formidable hardness.

'Your fingers are very nimble,' he groaned.

'Well, I do make jewellery for a living,' she replied pertly, as his erection nudged against her hand through the black silk of his boxers and, instinctively, she began to circle her palm over the rocky bulge.

'Don't do that,' he groaned.

'What?'

He shook his head as he removed her hand, swiftly disposing of her bra and panties before removing his own shorts with equal efficiency. And now they were both naked and some tiny vestige of wounded pride prompted Kelly to ask why he'd changed his mind about having sex with her again, but something stopped her. Because mightn't that make him reflect on the wisdom of this and mightn't he change it right back again? And she couldn't bear that. No, she couldn't.

His skin was warm as he tumbled them down on the bed and she lay back against the pillows like a willing sacrifice as his glittering gaze raked over her in a way which was making her tremble. Because she wanted this. No. *Needed* this. Her body felt as if it would crumble if he didn't make love to her again. Yet she was clinging to the hope—or was it fear?—that it couldn't possibly be as good as last time. And if it wasn't—if it had been a fluke—then surely that would put everything into perspective. Wouldn't it enable her to stop thinking about him and stop wanting him so much? She would put it down to experience and be able to walk away.

It wasn't a fluke.

Kelly realised that from the moment he started stroking her, and with luxuriously slow precision began to massage her nipples. The exquisitely sensitive flesh puckered on top of each engorged mound. She could hear her breathing quicken as he drifted his fingertips downwards, lingering a little on the swell of her belly before tangling themselves in the silken curls at the apex of her thighs. She held her breath as finally he located the place where all her nerve-endings seemed centred and began to beat a delicate tattoo on the tiny, sensitised bud. Pleasure and frustration merged into one potent shot and, writhing urgently, she gasped, her need for release growing stronger by the second. For a while it was enough, until suddenly it was no longer enough and her eyelashes fluttered open to find him watching her. Watching her reaction.

What did he see in her face as he slipped his finger inside her? A slow smile curved his lips as it came away slick and wet and she was shocked and thrilled when he actually *licked* it.

'You come very quickly when I do this,' he observed, almost clinically. 'But I want to be inside you.'

This too sounded like the antithesis of romance but Kelly didn't care. No point in chasing after something which didn't exist, and she was so pent-up with longing that she couldn't think of anything other than what he was going to do next.

'What are you waiting for, then?' she whispered, instinctively spreading her thighs for him, and he groaned as he reached for a condom.

And now she watched *him*—watched in rapt interest as he sheathed himself with hands which weren't quite steady, observing the incredible tension which was shadowing his chiselled features. 'Are you *trying* to unsettle me?' he demanded.

'How am I doing that?'

'By looking at me with those big eyes. Making me—'

'Making you what?' she whispered as he moved over her.

'It doesn't matter,' he growled.

He filled her to the hilt. Long and hard and deep, and Kelly moaned as he began to move inside her. And this time there was no pain or shock or accusation. This time it was all about pleasure and she happily gave herself up to it. Sensation swamped her as the heat began to build, the ripples growing stronger and stronger as he orchestrated her response. He was velvet and steel. Carnal yet experienced. Powerful and passionate, his delving kiss only adding to her sensual overload. Higher and higher he took her, the deft thrust of his hips making it so that she could barely think or move or breathe. And then it was happening all over again. Sweet spasms convulsed her, jack-knifing through her body, and she was aware of his own urgent cry as he bucked inside her. And somehow that simultaneous orgasm—because, of course, that was what it was—felt like the most amazing thing which had ever happened to her. Was that why she choked back a little sob, because in that moment she felt so overwhelmed by emotion?

He lifted his head to stare down at her and something like ice entered his black eyes. 'Please don't cry,' he said roughly and rolled away from her.

'I'm not crying!'

'Good. Because tears leave me cold.'

The spell was broken, his cruel candour shattering her illusion and momentarily taking her breath away. But she couldn't accuse him of raising her hopes, could she? He wasn't doing anything different from what he had projected he would do. This was all about pragmatism, not fantasy—so shouldn't she match his emotionless attitude, if only to keep her pride intact? 'So now what?' she questioned, her deliberate air of insouciance making her voice sound casual.

He turned to look at her, the relief in his gaze apparent before his lips curved with faint amusement. 'We fall asleep,' he said, stifling a yawn. 'And then I wake you. Or you wake me—traditionally by rolling those luscious curves against me to make me very, very hard—and we do it all over again. We repeat that as many times as it takes before we decide we're hungry or thirsty, or both, and one of us gets out of bed to go and find us something to eat and drink—which will probably be you.'

'That's a very sexist remark, Romano.'

'I don't deny it. Although, if you remember, I have actually cooked for you before.' His black eyes glittered as if he were being reluctantly forced to acknowledge the subtext of her question. 'Are you asking for a timetable, Kelly? Do you want to know how long this will last? Because I can't tell you that. I can't tell you anything other than at some point it will end. So…if you're seeking permanence or a ring on your finger…if you want to change your mind and walk out of here, then, please, be my guest.'

Kelly met the challenge which gleamed from his ebony gaze, recognising this as a make-or-break moment. They weren't the easiest words to hear, but he hadn't said anything she didn't already know. Yes, of course, she could coolly announce that she'd had second thoughts and know he would watch her walk away and not make the slightest effort to change her mind. He might even admire her more if she had the courage and the pride to do that. But why cut her nose off to spite her face when she wanted him so badly? She bit her lip. As long as she accepted that there was to be no fairy-tale ending, she would be okay. She *had* to be okay. 'I don't want to change my mind.'

'Good,' he purred and pulled her back into his arms.

She traced the shadowed line of his jaw. 'But I meant what I said, about you teaching me everything you know.'

'So that another man will one day benefit from my expertise?'

'I guess that's the logical conclusion.' She raised her eyebrows. 'Surely you don't expect me to live like a nun for the rest of my life, just because you don't want me? And there's no point scowling at me like that, Romano. I'm just trying to be honest with you.' She hesitated. 'Will you be the same with me?'

He gave a short laugh. 'I thought I had been.'

'Not honest enough. I feel like I hardly know you.'

There was a pause. 'That sounds very much like an ultimatum,' he offered silkily.

'Not really. I just…' She hesitated. 'I don't want to feel as if I'm in bed with a stranger.'

'But you know me better than a great many people, Kelly.'

'Maybe I do, but there's so much I don't know.'

'Like what?' he questioned.

She could hear the note of warning in his voice and thought about choosing her words carefully, but there was no way of sugar-coating them—and wasn't it dishonest to even try? He seemed to think he could get away with saying all these cold and horrible things without having to justify them to anyone—and wasn't it time he did?

'I'm curious about *why* you distrust women so much,' she said slowly. 'Why you're so dead set against marriage and having children to carry on your line. I don't understand why you neglect this beautiful castle, but can't seem to let it go. Why, Romano?' She sucked in a deep breath, her gaze taking in the suddenly rapid rising and falling of his powerful chest. 'Won't you tell me?' she finished quietly.

CHAPTER NINE

KELLY'S QUESTION HUNG in the air like a guillotine and for a second Romano was tempted to move away from the blade's sharp reach. To shove aside the rumpled bedding and peel himself away from her naked body and put as much physical distance between them as possible. Because that was his default reaction whenever this kind of interrogation occurred. He always preferred to walk away rather than confront emotional demons, or answer intrusive questions.

But for once he didn't want to leave the cushioned satin of her delectable body. He liked the way he was lying, with those abundant curls splayed across his chest and her soft breasts pressing against him. He wasn't just feeling sexually replete, he was also feeling unusually... comfortable. And not only was the concept of comfort unfamiliar to him, it was never a trait he associated with any of his lovers.

But that was the thing about Kelly, wasn't it? She broke the mould, defying his best attempts to categorise her. Forbidden to him for many years—firstly, because of her age, and then because of his perception about the kind of person she really was. And when at last he had been unable to resist her, all his preconceived ideas had been blown out of the water when he'd discovered her innocence...

Which she had kept from him.

Yet his anger at having been tacitly deceived by her had faded, especially since she'd told him about her mother's bitterness towards men-which went some way towards explaining Kelly's own behaviour. And wasn't he fast discovering a primitive and previously unknown side of himself, which was positively *revelling* in the fact that he was her first and only lover?

But that posed its own particular danger, for he had zero experience of virgins. Wasn't there a chance she might fixate on him or grow to idealise him? To see him as the answer to her dreams, despite his stern warnings to the contrary? He knew who he was and was cynical enough to comprehend that his hard body, keen intellect and colossal fortune more than made up for the fact that he had a heart of stone, which was why women fell for him in droves.

He didn't want to hurt her. Even he wasn't cruel enough to do that. She had told him plainly that she knew the score. That she accepted him for who he was. Yet hadn't he looked into her bright eyes a couple of minutes ago, past the shimmer of the tears she had indignantly denied, and seen something else? A flicker of affection, which could easily assume a rampant life of its own if he fanned the flames. Wouldn't the ugly truth cut those burgeoning feelings down to size, like the sweeping scythe which decimated a field of ripe wheat?

'You want to guess why I don't trust women?' he said slowly.

'I'm thinking it's because maybe someone broke your heart.'

His laugh was bitter. She really *was* idealistic. Better tell her the truth. 'Not exactly.' He paused. 'How much do you know about my mother?'

'Not very much.' She shrugged one bare, freckled shoulder. 'Only that she was the first wife of Floriana's father—your father—and she died years ago. And that, well…' She hesitated. 'Nobody really talks about her.'

'Because very few people know anything about her,' he ground out. 'And that was deliberate. The facts were hidden. My father made sure of that. There was no social media to allow for other people's version of events and the twisting of the truth.' His words trailed away, because this was forgotten territory. How long since last he had entered this particular minefield? Not since he had walked out of the office of the therapist assigned to him in his early teenage years, never to return.

'What was she like?' she asked, her soft words punctuating his thoughts.

He tried to be objective. To piece together the fragments of things he had been told and the stuff he'd found out for himself. Far worse, of course, were the things he now allowed himself to remember… He swallowed. His own disturbing reality, which surfaced from time to time no matter how deeply he had tried to bury it. He'd often though it strange that there was a verb 'to dream', but no equivalent for the flipside of dreaming. Nobody talked about 'to nightmare', did they? And yet that was what his early childhood had been. A living nightmare.

'She was very beautiful and very rich,' he began heavily. 'The only child of elderly parents who were entranced by their ravishing butterfly of a daughter and completely spoilt her.' He gave a short laugh. 'Like so many before him, my father fell hopelessly in love with her, and she was pregnant with me when they were married. But very quickly, she began to be disillusioned with her new role.'

'Go on,' she prompted as his voice faded.

'She got in with a wild crowd and grew to hate this *castello* and the life it offered,' he stated, his mouth hardening. 'She began to spend more and more time with her new friends in Rome.'

'With you?' she asked quickly.

'Not initially,' he answered. 'For a while I was left here, with my father and a nanny.'

'And you were…happy?'

'How could I be?' He gave a bitter laugh. 'She might have been the worst mother in the world, but she was still my mother. And aren't children living examples of the concept of hope over experience? They keep on going back for love from their parents, time after time, no matter how often they get pushed back. Don't you know that, Kelly?'

'Yes,' she agreed quietly, remembering the way she used to secretly dream of her father coming to find her, despite all the unflattering things her mother had said about him. 'I do.'

He pulled her closer and now he was back there, frozen in that snapshot of time. How could the image still be so sharp, even after all these years? 'And then, one night, she came here with a boyfriend in the howling rain and they bundled me into a car and sped off into the night.'

'And nobody stopped them?'

'No, Kelly. Nobody stopped them because in those days society was heavily weighted towards the mother's wishes. Some of my male friends in the throes of acrimonious divorces tell me it still is,' he added caustically. 'She was apparently a consummate actress who convinced everyone she couldn't bear to be parted from her only child. When required she was able to play the part of a loving mother while for the rest of the time, she took her pleasure in drugs.'

'Drugs?'

'Why so shocked? Plenty of people get addicted. Her drug of choice happened to be heroin.'

'Romano—'

'No. I'm giving you the facts. Which you asked for, remember?' he bit out. 'But if this is going to deteriorate into a mess of emotion then I'll stop right now. I told you. Crying leaves me cold.'

'I'm not crying,' she said, for the second time, but this time her voice was sombre rather than defiant as she jabbed at her eyes with her fists. 'Tell me what happened.'

He made a harsh imprecation beneath his breath. 'Long story short? She overdosed and nobody knew about it. Even I didn't at first, and I was alone in the house with her. At least not until after a couple of days of being unable to wake her, when I went to the front door of our place in Rome. I remember the door being so heavy and almost impossible to open,' he reflected, as if this were important. Because wasn't that an infinitely preferable memory than the vision of his mother's waxy corpse, and the first fly buzzing in through the window to land on it, and the tears which were stream-ing down his cheeks as he was gathered into the horri-fied embrace of a kindly passer-by? 'Perhaps if I'd raised the alarm sooner they could have taken her to hospital to have her stomach pumped and she might have sur-vived, but we'll never know.'

'How old were you?'

'Five,' he stated abruptly.

'Oh, Romano,' she breathed, and he could hear the horror in her voice.

'No,' he said, steeling his heart to the distress which was clouding her beautiful eyes. 'I told you because you asked and, for some reason, I wanted to tell you, because you know little of the ways of the world. To explain why I have no intention of ever marrying or having children of my own. But that's it. That's all. I don't want your sympathy, however well meaning, and I don't want to discuss it any further. Do you understand?'

Tiptoeing his finger slowly down over her belly, he saw her eyes darken although she had started biting her lip, as if she despaired of her own reaction. 'This is what I want from you, Kelly. The only thing. An uncompli-cated liaison. We take our pleasure until the well has run dry. Which it will.' His voice dipped as he resisted taking the finger further and he waited until he could sense her growing restlessness before he framed his next question. 'So. Is that enough for you?'

Was it?

Kelly's head was still spinning from all the things he'd told her and she was having to work very hard to hide her reaction. But it wasn't easy. Her instinct was to cradle him tightly. To try to absorb some of his obvious hurt—though you could never really take someone else's pain away, could you? But his words had come as a terrible shock. She'd suspected there'd been some dodgy stuff in his past but the horror of his early years surpassed her worst imaginings. Didn't it make his cold and critical attitude a lot more understandable?

She wondered if that was the real reason why he'd been so opposed to her friendship with his half-sister. Not, as she'd initially thought, because he was a snob—but because he'd thought she was leading Floriana astray, as his own mother had presumably been led astray. And she had allowed him to go on thinking of her as that wild person, hadn't she, especially after he had rejected her and she had been nursing her hurt pride? In fact, hadn't she gone out of her way to encourage him to still think she was a party animal? If she'd known about his background, would she have behaved any differently? Of course she would. But the gift of hindsight was a wasted gift.

She stared up into the ebony glitter of his eyes, trying to reduce the facts down to the bare essentials. He still wanted her and she still wanted him. What woman *wouldn't* want him? But he had spelt out in coldly pragmatic terms exactly what he was offering her.

Sex.

Nothing more and nothing less.

Not compassion, or understanding, or sympathy.

It wasn't going to grow, or evolve into something more. He wasn't going to suddenly decide he'd been a fool and fall to one knee with a diamond sparkler in his hand, in front of a technicolour sunset. And if she started wishing for those sorts of things then it would show and he would run a mile. If she wanted him, she had to be practical and not hanker after the unattainable. But that didn't mean she couldn't give him affection, did it? Her heart gave a sudden lurch. Because wouldn't this big, proud man have missed out on a lot of physical warmth in his life?

So she snuggled up closer, her silent acquiescence causing the rigid weight of his erection to nudge insistently against her belly and for a moment she felt shy as well as excited. Did he guess as much? Was that why he put his mouth to her ear, his breath warm against her skin?

'Show me what you want, *la mia piccola*,' he instructed silkily. 'Do not be nervous.'

Boldly, Kelly reached down to encircle the silky pole within her fingers, feeling his involuntary shudder of pleasure. 'In that case... I think this,' she murmured throatily. 'This is what I want.'

'You must come to Turin,' Romano announced, without any kind of lead-in.

From across the other side of the fire-splashed room, he could see Kelly watching as he pulled the cork of a dusty bottle of wine he had just retrieved from the cellar. She was naked beneath his silken dressing gown, which swamped her as she sat curled up on a velvet sofa, nibbling at a grape. On the floor before her lay the debris of a cheeseboard, for they had been picnicking before the fire in one of the castle's reception rooms, silently watched over by the sombre portraits of his ancestors.

Yet this rather domestic scene was liberally doused with feelings of confusion because Romano was aware that his mood was uncharacteristically carefree. For three whole days and three whole nights he and Kelly Butler had paid little attention to the convention of meal-times—or, indeed, to any routine at all. Like teenagers or nomads, they had eaten when they were hungry and drunk when they were thirsty. Bath-time had served an infinitely more satisfying purpose than simply getting clean, morphing into long and sensual encounters involving slippery sessions of sex. He had been utterly absorbed in the pursuit of pleasure and that had inevitably spilled over into other areas of his life.

Unusually, he had instructed his office not to bother him unless it was urgent. He had put Graziana on leave and issued stern instructions for the security detail to retreat to the outskirts of the estate and leave them unobserved to do as they pleased. And they had certainly been doing that. Romano felt his groin harden. They'd been having sex at any and every opportunity and for once the *castello* had shed some of its grimmer associations. For so many years his visits here had been functional, almost grudging—yet now, for the first time, he found himself enjoying the many erotic possibilities offered up by the medieval stronghold with all its hidden nooks and crannies. Hadn't there been something curiously triumphant about ravishing her on the ancient oak dining table, which could seat twenty-four? Or to have her suck him to sweet oblivion at the very top of the house in a forgotten room where a maid must once have slept?

He stared almost resentfully as Kelly's nimble fingers hovered over the mound of fruit before popping another juicy grape between her glistening lips, and he swallowed. He had never given a woman so much constant attention before, nor existed in such a constant state of arousal.

He'd thought...

What?

That his appetite for her would have waned a little by now?

For sure.

Not sexually—for he was a man with remarkable appetite, technique and stamina who could pleasure women for many hours. But after seventy-two hours without a break from her company—effectively incarcerated with her in this hilltop *castello*—he had expected the rapid onset of boredom and ennui. He had anticipated an increasing desire to get away from Kelly Butler and return to his preferred state of solitude.

But that hadn't happened.

Again, he frowned.

He just couldn't seem to get enough of her.

Was that because her innocent eagerness for his sexual tutelage made her utterly irresistible, or because she was endlessly provocative in everything she did and said, without her actions seeming in the least bit contrived?

He felt...

Trapped?

He sighed as he poured two glasses of the rich wine and crossed the room to hand her one.

Not trapped, no. Nobody was keeping him here against his will and there was nothing to prevent him from walking away any time he wanted. Instead, he felt compromised—as if Kelly Butler were taking something from him without asking. Without him having given his permission for her to do so.

Her soft voice broke into his thoughts, reminding him that he'd just asked her a question.

'Sorry. Nice offer, but I'm afraid I can't come to Turin,' she answered firmly, before taking a sip of wine.

He studied her thoughtfully, thinking how ungrateful she could be. Was she unaware of the compliment he was extending, by inviting her into his city home? As always, meeting resistance stirred his interest. 'Why not?'

She shrugged. 'I've got to get back to England to sort out my life. Obviously.'

He made a sound of impatience. 'That can wait.'

'No, Romano. It can't wait. And it's slightly insulting of you to be so dismissive of my needs. We've already delayed my journey home for three days and I can't keep swanning around this Tuscan castle with you and pretending it's all normal, because real life is waiting in the wings. I need to find myself a new waitressing job—and, since the weather is picking up, I need to get back on my market stall, because trade is always very good in the springtime.'

Trade? *Trade?* Romano glared. Did she take some sort of perverse delight in reminding him of the disparity between their two lives? he wondered. He knew perfectly well that he could ease her financial woes in an instant, but something told him that not only would she view such an offer with disdain—it could also backfire on him. Might she not misread his motives and accuse him of trying to pay for sex, before slamming her way out of the castle in a fury? Because she really did have a temper to match that red hair, he conceded hungrily.

'Surely you are allowed to have a couple more days' holiday before you return to the daily grind?' he questioned, in his most reasonable voice.

Kelly took another sip of wine and considered his question. Would a few more days really make that much difference? Probably not. The money she'd earnt from cleaning his castle would be more than enough to tide her over until she found a new waitressing job and she'd heard that Granchester's newest restaurant would soon be recruiting for staff, though annoyingly it happened to be a pizza parlour. She sighed. If she was hoping it was going to be easy to forget all about Italy once she left the *castello*, she could think again.

But for once it wasn't her precarious finances which were her top priority and today it wasn't even the concern that she might be falling for the billionaire. Correction. *Was* falling for him. There was no doubt in her mind about that, despite the fact that he had explicitly warned her not to. But how could she help herself when, for her, he was the real deal? He made her laugh. He challenged her. He made her feel sexy. He brought out the best in her and for a person who'd spent her life racked with self-doubt, that meant a lot. She chewed on her lip, tasting the juice of the grape she'd just eaten.

No. Her current fears weren't about something as straightforward as the inequality of their feelings for one another, but were rooted in a far more practical cause. She'd woken alone in bed that morning, knowing Romano would have gone downstairs to make a pot of the strong coffee he favoured—apparently not trusting anyone who wasn't Italian to concoct a brew which was in any way drinkable. Idly, she had glanced across at her phone and noticed the date and…and…

Her heart had pounded and she had sat up in bed, rubbing furiously at her eyes as if to clear her vision and remedy the obvious error.

It couldn't possibly be the twenty-eighth!

But it was. All day, as they said.

She had rapidly done a raft of reassuring sums in her head and told herself not to be so ridiculous. The first time she'd had sex with Romano had been on the night of the christening, which hadn't even been in the middle of her cycle. And he had used protection every time. Obviously, the reason her period was late was because a lot had been happening. Big stuff. Once-in-a-lifetime stuff. There had been the initial stress of seeing him again when she had arrived at the storm-lashed castle and then the total weirdness of them becoming intimate in spite of all their differences. And yes, he'd lost his rag a bit when he'd discovered that she'd been a virgin. But they were in a totally different place now. They had reached a sort of sensual compromise. With no drama and definitely no future. They were supposed to be enjoying all the incredible pleasures of the present.

But she was late.

She was late and she was *never* late.

'I don't understand why you're looking so concerned,' he observed and Kelly looked over at him with a start, relieved to be plucked out of that nagging arena of worry, even if it was only temporary.

'Is it really such a monstrous suggestion to ask you to come with me to Turin?' he continued coolly.

'Why are you so keen?'

'Your lukewarm attitude is surprisingly enticing,' he conceded drily.

'But that isn't why you want me to come,' she observed.

'Not exactly.'

'Why, then? Tell me, Romano. We agreed to be honest with one another, didn't we?'

He nodded. 'I just don't think we're done yet, do you?' he said softly, his black gaze boring into her.

No, they weren't. Not as far as she was concerned. Sometimes Kelly thought she would never feel they were done. And although he wasn't exactly pleading with her to accompany him, she forced herself to think sensibly. Surely it would be better to be *with* him, rather than going back to England on her own and driving herself mad with worry? Because what if she *was* pregnant?

It was the first time she'd allowed herself to even frame the word in her mind and with it came a series of powerful images. Suddenly, she could see herself standing on a freezing market stall, a slight bump beginning to show. She would be wearing a pair of those fingerless gloves which always left her with icy digits—her mind obsessing about a future she'd always been determined never to have. A future like her own mother's. Bearing the baby of a man who didn't want a baby. A man who would probably reject her, just as her father had rejected her own mother. And yet, if she was...

If she *was*, then she would deal with it—whatever fate threw at her and whether Romano wanted to be involved with his child or not. And she would do it without bitterness or resentment. If she had a daughter, she wouldn't try to poison that child's mind against men in general and one in particular. Not like her own mother…

And what the hell was she thinking of, sipping wine?

'Okay, I'll come to Turin,' she croaked, quickly putting the glass down.

'Don't overdo the enthusiasm,' he observed wryly as he sat down beside her on the velvet sofa, turning her head to cup her chin within the warm cradle of his palm. 'Are you okay?'

'Wh-why?'

His thumb traced the edges of her lips in a gesture which felt misleadingly like tenderness.

'You look very washed out, that's all.'

Oh, God. Wasn't that a tell-tale sign? Should she tell him what was on her mind? No. That would be insane. Maybe if she was two weeks late, rather than two days. Kelly cleared her throat. Surely she wasn't self-sabotaging her first sexual affair by being unnecessarily neurotic? 'I'm not surprised I look washed out,' she joked weakly. 'I'm suffering from a distinct lack of shut-eye.'

'But we have been having regular siestas,' came his purring objection.

'Which are also supposed to involve sleep.'

'How can I sleep when I can't keep my hands off you?' he admitted huskily, tugging at the belt of her silken dressing gown, so that it fell open, her breasts already peaking towards him.

'Good question,' she mumbled as she homed in on his seeking lips and gave herself up to the rapturous touch of his hands. And this bit was easy, she thought. Almost too easy. Everything he did to her she loved. *Liked*, she corrected firmly, reaching for the zip of his jeans. Love had no place in a vocabulary where Romano Castelliari was concerned and if she told herself that often enough, she might finally get around to believing it. But the act of making love was pretty hard to beat. It could make your body feel as if it were soaring and that your heart was melting like marshmallow.

It could even temporarily remove all those nagging worries from your mind.

CHAPTER TEN

'WE'RE GOING TO need to go shopping.'

At the sound of Romano's soft interjection, Kelly turned round, wearing nothing but the silk shirt he'd impatiently discarded within minutes of arriving at his Turin residence. She had been staring out of the window at the leafy garden square beneath his vast apartment, not quite able to believe she was really here.

It was all a bit much to take in. She had suspected he would live somewhere grand, but the reality of his home had surpassed all her wildest imaginings. Romano's apartment was part of a converted eighteenth-century palazzo and she'd never seen anything like it. Domed ceilings were exquisitely decorated with intricate frescoes and the marble floors were strewn with silken rugs. It had several reception rooms. A gym. A kitchen you could get lost in. It even had its own library, with leather-bound spines which looked worryingly old. She kept expecting someone to ask her to produce her ticket to prove she'd paid to get in. She'd really had no idea that people lived like this.

But it wasn't just the splendour of the building or the nearby city surroundings which were so achingly impressive—it was the evidence of Romano's life. His real life. Because this wasn't a castle he'd inherited, which he seemed to be conflicted about for perfectly understandable reasons. This was his *home*. With paintings and cushions and velvet drapes and photos in solid silver frames and one photo in particular, taken at some Premio Mondo race, possibly in Monaco. In a blur of sprayed champagne, he was standing next a driver who was holding aloft a glittering trophy and Romano had his arm round a woman—a blonde, Kelly noted sourly—who was looking up at him, and laughing.

It wasn't simply that the blonde was beautiful—which she was—it was just that captured moment of intimacy, as if she were completely dazzled by the gaze of the Castelliari racing tycoon. And her clothes. Oh, her clothes. She was dressed in the sort of outfit you might see within the pages of a glossy fashion bible, most of which probably wouldn't have survived the celebratory champagne bath, thought Kelly a touch sourly before she realised that Romano was looking at her and was clearly waiting for an answer.

'Why do we need to go shopping?' she questioned, automatically enjoying the golden-olive gleam of his naked body as he lay sprawled against the snowy backdrop of the rumpled sheets. 'I thought you said someone had been in and stocked the fridge.'

'Not for food,' he said impatiently. 'I meant to buy something for you to wear.'

Kelly tried not to react negatively to his emphatic statement but she was already stiffening defensively. 'I thought you said you liked me best when I wasn't wearing anything at all,' she objected.

His mouth gave a close approximation of a smile.

'This much is true. Your body is much too delicious to be covered,' he agreed silkily. 'But you can't stay naked all the time and I thought we might do a few things while we're here in Turin. Go to the opera, perhaps?'

'And my clothes aren't good enough, is that it?' she demanded, remembering the way he'd looked down his nose at her when she'd arrived at the church for the christening in her cheap, flowery dress.

There was a pause. 'I think you know very well they aren't, *cara*. You came to Italy with barely enough stuff for the weekend, and a pair of jeans which you've dried on the radiator, really isn't going to work in this kind of environment. You will stand out for all the wrong reasons.'

His voice was almost gentle and wasn't that in itself *patronising*? Once again, Kelly bristled. 'I don't want your charity.'

'It isn't charity, Kelly,' he answered patiently. 'You can leave them here when you go back to England, for all I care.'

'What, so my replacement can wear them?'

'I've never met anyone with your particular petite and curvy dimensions, but, if you must know, you're the only woman I've ever wanted to dress as well as un-dress,' he offered, his voice now tinged with a mild ir-ritation. 'But that's all I intend to say on the subject and I certainly don't intend to wrestle you into a dress shop on the Via Roma. I thought it might be fun, that's all.'

Their eyes clashed in silent battle until at last she gave a shrug. 'Okay,' she sighed, because he did have a point. She definitely didn't have enough clothes with her and, unless she was intending to hit Turin wearing her Ragno uniform, she couldn't drag out her claret velvet dress *again*. 'If that's what you want.'

'There's only one thing I really want right now. So take off that damned shirt and come over here,' he instructed throatily, making no attempt to hide the hardening at his groin.

Undoing the buttons with trembling fingers and casting aside the costly garment, Kelly went into his waiting arms, wishing she weren't constantly see-sawing between happiness and sadness. It was as if she'd been placed on an emotional roller coaster which was speeding out of control and she didn't know how to get off. She knew why they were here, because he'd told her—supposedly to empty the well of their mutual desire.

But as far as she was concerned, Kelly suspected it would never run dry, especially as with every day that passed, her heart became more and more engaged and not just her body. She found herself wanting to press her face close to his and tell him she'd never believed anyone could make her feel this way. Romano was someone she just couldn't get enough of, and she had convinced herself that as long as she kept that unwanted truth to herself, everything would be okay. In a normal world it might have been.

Except...

She swallowed.

Except that her period still hadn't come, and now she was five days late.

And sooner or later she was going to have to address that.

But not now. Not when his hands were on her breasts and he was pressing her down against the mattress and moving over her. His kiss was deep and drugging as he drove one hard thigh between hers. Her hungry fingertips explored the silk of his skin, kneading luxuriously at all that hard flesh. Every one of her senses was engaged... The evocative scent of sex perfumed the air as he directed her to stroke on the condom and she revelled in his hopeless groan as she demonstrated this newly acquired skill. With a strangled moan he entered her and she came almost immediately and it wasn't long before Romano was choking out his fulfilment in a way which had become achingly familiar, and Kelly felt a great sweep of unwanted emotion as she tightened her arms around his back and tried to hold onto the moment for as long as possible.

Afterwards they moved apart and lay there in silence until the ragged sounds of their breathing had calmed. But instead of staring at the beautiful frescoed ceiling, Kelly shut her eyes until she was sure that the tell-tale shimmer of tears had retreated. And only then was she able to turn to him with a super-bright smile.

'Okay,' she said carelessly. 'Let's hit the shops.'

'No, that one,' affirmed Romano decisively as he watched the stylist dangle two contrasting gowns in front of the diminutive redhead. 'The silver.'

Lounging back on the leather sofa with an untouched goblet of champagne by his side, he waited until Kelly emerged from the changing room in his chosen gown, rather concerned to see that she was biting her lip.

'What's the matter?' he questioned.

'You don't think it's a bit...'

'A bit what?' he prompted, the flicker of a smile beginning to play at the edges of his lips.

She shrugged her silk-clad shoulders. 'Revealing?'

He was tempted to tell her in soft and very graphic English that the dress was relatively modest when judged against the standards he was used to. It wasn't slashed to the thigh, or plunged deep to the navel. Just a shimmer of silvery fabric, which made her look like a fallen star. And though he might wish to feast his own eyes on her body, he was damned if he wanted other men seeing too much of it. But she might easily misinterpret such a possessive statement and there was always the chance that it might be overheard by someone and fed to the salacious press.

'No, I don't,' he said coolly and then, turning to the stylist, who was failing to hide her apparent joy—probably thinking about her commission—he nodded his head. 'We'll take it.'

The silver dress was packed up and dispatched to join yet more shiny carrier bags, which would be delivered to his apartment later. Only one had been held back, on his instructions, and he gave a nod. 'Why don't you put that one on?' he suggested silkily. 'You can wear it out to lunch.'

Ducking back into the changing room, Kelly slithered into the outfit which Romano had selected, wondering if she should object to his bossiness in deciding what she should wear. Yet why waste precious time and energy by making a fuss? It wasn't as if it were going to make any difference in the long run, was it? She was still going to go her way and he his. And didn't part of her revel in the way his black eyes smouldered with undisguised passion when he saw her in something he particularly liked? Didn't it thrill her and still shock her a little bit that she was capable of making him react like that?

The full-length mirror reflected back an image which was quietly expensive, because everything she wore *was* expensive. Eye-wateringly so. Beneath a chiffon dress the colour of ginger tea, she was wearing new lingerie, which was managing to do some gravity-defying things to her breasts, as well as silk stockings and a ridiculously lacy little suspender belt.

Her eyes narrowed. Dressed like this, she would be able to move around without judgment or censure in Romano's high-octane world, that was for sure—though part of her felt like an imposter. The poor girl dressed up to the nines who was only sharing the billionaire's life for the briefest of tenures.

Had she settled for too little? Allowing him to dress her up like a doll, while inside her head was whirling as she tried like mad to reassure herself that her period being almost a week late wasn't a big deal at all. But it was—of course it was—and sooner or later she was going to have to do a test. She chewed on her lip. And since it would be practically impossible to go to a local pharmacy on Romano's territory without incurring a mild interrogation, that meant she was going to have to tell him.

Romano, I think I might be pregnant.

No. That gave it the spurious air of being something they'd planned. Something they might be happy about.

Romano, I'm worried sick that I might be pregnant.

That was certainly more accurate. Her heart clenched. She would have to say something on those lines.

But not today.

Today she was going to pretend that this was for ever…

With a final adjustment of her curls, she walked out of the changing room to where Romano was waiting like a watchful panther, and she wondered if he was expecting her to do a twirl, or to parade before him in her cream high heels so he could watch the delicate silk chiffon brushing against her thighs. But instead, he placed his hand in the small of her back, his thumb making enticing little circles as he propelled her through the prestigious store and outside, where a limousine was waiting.

'Where are we going?' Kelly asked, sliding onto the back seat of the luxury car.

'I'm taking you out for lunch.' He put his hand on her knee. 'Hungry?'

She supposed she should be. It was a long time since breakfast, which he had fed to her while she had been sitting on the breakfast bar of his amazing kitchen, again wearing nothing but one of his shirts. But it was difficult to be enthusiastic about food when his fingers were creeping beneath the hem of her dress like that.

'Sure,' she said, trying to keep her voice from trembling. 'Where are we going?'

Annoyingly, he removed his hand from her thigh. 'Wait and see.'

He took her to a light and airy restaurant, with olives trees dotted around a large terrace which commanded impressive views over the city. Kelly had been expecting ostentation and a lavish display of wealth but to her surprise it was neither of those things. It was a quiet and traditional place, serving Piedmontese food, which was ambrosial, especially the pudding—which initially she tried to refuse.

'Try it,' he said, forking into a slice of *torta* and extending it towards her. 'Go on. Turin is famous for hazelnuts,' he added as she began to nibble on the rich cake. 'Ever since Napoleon banned chocolate imports from England in the nineteenth century and the local chefs had to find something else to use in their desserts.'

'Is that so?' she said, holding back a smile as he delivered another forkful into her waiting mouth.

'Would you like to hear more about the history of Turinese cuisine, Kelly?' he questioned gravely.

'Absolutely. I'm sitting on the edge of my seat waiting,' she said, meeting the playful gleam in his black eyes.

It was the most delicious and frustrating meal she'd ever eaten and it seemed to take a lifetime before they were back in the limousine and he could push her back against the soft leather seat, his mouth on her neck, his hand on her thigh.

'Now then,' he murmured hungrily. 'Where was I?'

'I think you know. But just for the avoidance of doubt.' Instinctively, she wriggled her hips to position herself. 'You're in exactly the right place.'

'Who taught you to be so bold, Kelly Butler?' he growled.

'Why, I think that would have to be you, Romano Castelliari.'

With a low laugh, he raised the darkened sound-proof window between them and the chauffeur as he brought her to an ecstatic climax and then, back in the apartment, he stripped off their clothes with unsteady impatience before tumbling them down on his vast bed.

'*Porca miseria*, what is it that you do to me?' he uttered, his hands moulding themselves over her quivering breasts before tracing down to the moist bud between her spreading thighs.

'Was that a serious question?' she gasped as she felt his erection nudge impatiently against her.

'No,' he husked, his big body positioning itself over her before empaling her with one hard and emphatic thrust.

Rocking in time to his glorious rhythm, she soon felt the ecstatic squeeze of her approaching climax, her back arching helplessly as she pulsed with pleasure beneath him. And afterwards Kelly had to be super-vigilant as he held her tightly in his embrace, her cheek resting against the muscled silk of his shoulder. She wanted to whisper that she had never felt so wanted, nor so cherished, and she wanted to tell him that she was frightened she might be carrying his baby. But the insane thing was that part of her *longed* to carry his baby. Was that the natural projection you made when a man had managed to burrow his way into your heart and you were terrified you were falling in love with him?

They spent most of the afternoon in bed and then a lot of time in the bath before he left her to wash her hair and then laboriously dry it into glossy ringlets. She had just finished putting on the silver dress and a pair of matching strappy shoes when Romano walked into the bedroom, wearing a black tux, which made him look impossibly handsome and yet somehow…remote.

His face was serious as he handed her a slim leather box.

'What's this?'

'Why not have a look inside?' he suggested.

She did as he asked, blinking in surprise as she flipped open the lid to see a pair of dangly diamond earrings dazzling against a backdrop of indigo velvet. Kelly was a silversmith who knew practically nothing about diamonds—apart from the words she'd heard used to describe them, like *Ashoka* and *brilliant* and *marquise*. But anyone could see that these were pretty special. It made her feel quite faint to think how much they must have cost.

'Are these on loan, or something?' she joked.

'No. I bought them. I thought you could wear them to the opera tonight,' he said, the gleam of his ebony gaze sweeping over her. 'They work well with that dress.'

'But…surely some of my own would work better? I mean, mine are silver, like the dress. And you never know…somebody might see them and commission a pair!'

'I would prefer you to wear these,' he insisted, holding one out towards her, the white fire of the precious gems flaming over his olive skin.

She opened her mouth to object before asking herself if this was a battle really worth fighting, before obediently clipping them in to stare at herself in the mirror. But it hurt that he didn't want her to wear the jewellery she'd made herself. As if he was rejecting the person she really was. Did he worry that the silver danglies might look cheap and downmarket in the lavish setting of the city opera house?

She stared at the incandescent rainbow flash of diamonds which could certainly never be accused of falling into that particular category. In any other circumstances she might have quipped that she hoped they were properly insured, because what if one fell off while she was in the loo? Yet there was something about his proprietorial expression which stopped her and, indeed, something about the whole occasion which felt skewed. He'd thrown a lot of money at her to change the way she looked and he'd succeeded. But as she saw the priceless stones flashing at her ears she recognised that the transformation was now complete...she really *wasn't* Kelly Butler any more.

And if she wasn't herself, then who was she?

A rich man's mistress with a terrible secret nagging away inside her.

A secret she dared not share.

'Let's go,' he said softly as he opened the bedroom door for her to exit before him.

Romano frowned as she nodded her head without really looking at him and found himself wondering if he had offended her in some way. Yet how could he have done? There wasn't a woman in the world who didn't like diamonds, and the bigger, the better. He'd had enough hints dropped to him in the past, though he'd never actually bought a lover jewellery before. And they were an investment, weren't they? Kelly would be able to take the earrings with her. Because he didn't want to see her broke, or struggling in the future. He would have no problem with her selling them as soon as she went back to England and gaining a comfortable financial cushion.

He stared out of the window as the bright lights of Turin flashed past in a blur on their way to the opera house, wondering how much longer she would stay.

Would he decide when that moment had arrived?

Or would she?

And why was he viewing the prospect with increasing reluctance?

A pulse began to pound at his temple as the car drew up outside the Teatro Regio, and beside him he felt Kelly stiffen. Reaching up, he turned her face towards him and in the dimness of the car he was aware of her strained expression.

'What's the matter?'

Her nonchalant shrug didn't quite disguise the faint frown lines on her forehead. 'I've never been to the opera before.'

'So what?'

'Oh, come on, Romano. Even you can't be that insensitive.'

'Even me?' he echoed. 'Am I that much of a brute?'

There was a pause. 'Only sometimes,' she said softly.

Her fingers reached up to touch his jaw and something about the tenderness of the gesture made him jerk his head back as if he'd been scalded, but she rested her hand back on her lap as if she hadn't noticed his instinctive recoil.

'I'm scared of feeling out of my depth,' she continued, her voice sounding forced. 'Of everyone else knowing how to behave, but not me.'

'Well, unless you're planning on getting up in the middle for a comfort break or leaping on stage to join in with the main aria, I'm sure you'll be fine.'

'Stop it.' Her lips started to twitch. 'I'm *serious*.'

'And so am I,' he said, relieved to have broken the sudden tension which seemed to have descended on them. 'Just follow everyone else's lead—that's how everyone learns. We're here and it's going to be fine. You might even enjoy it. Come on.' He stepped out of the car to the inevitable flash of cameras and, despite being taller than usual in her sparkly shoes, she looked so small and vulnerable as she slid to her feet beside him. Was it that which made him hold his hand out to catch hers, or the sudden desire to make amends for his occasionally brutish behaviour?

Her fingers laced in his, they entered the iconic building, with its eye-catching scarlet seats curving beneath the bright spill of modern chandeliers.

He glanced up towards one of the boxes to see an instantly recognisable figure, his old face as wrinkled as a walnut, and Romano's lips curved with faint amusement to see Silvano di Saccucci. The last time they'd met the octogenarian had been bad-temperedly refusing to sell him his company because he disapproved of his lifestyle. Yet now the old man was inclining his head politely in his direction and Romano found himself automatically returning the courtesy, before giving Kelly's fingers a quick squeeze.

'Okay?' he questioned.

'So far, so good.'

She looked up into his face, his diamonds glittering like ice in the thick fall of fiery hair, and as he smiled back he could hear someone nearby murmuring his name with a note of surprise. His first thought was that this outing was definitely going to provoke gossip in salons across the city.

And the second, which followed on almost immediately, was that he really didn't care.

CHAPTER ELEVEN

KELLY TOOK A sip of coffee, although it was difficult to focus on the heady brew when her attention was completely dominated by the sight of Romano reading the newspaper on the other side of the breakfast bar. Did he sense that she was watching him and was that why a speculative smile was curving his lips?

She took another sip, trying to calm the clamour of her senses and to quash that annoying little spark of hope which never seemed to go away.

Last night he had been different. He'd held her hand in public and silently handed her a pristine handkerchief when the tears had poured down her cheeks at the end of *Tosca*, reassuring her that, although he loathed tears, crying at the opera was the exception to the rule. She had sniffed and giggled at this and he had kissed her passionately in the back of the limousine on the way home and in that moment she had felt very safe and wanted and protected.

But that was just wishful thinking. That was what she needed to remember. It didn't mean anything, she told herself fiercely. It was simply another illustration of his mercurial nature and she needed to be constantly aware of how dangerous that could be if she started misinterpreting it and mistaking it for growing affection. She started speaking—mostly to steer her thoughts away from their current pointless path. 'I didn't quite catch the name of that man we met at the opera last night.'

'Silvano di Saccucci. He's a very famous car manufacturer,' he supplied in answer to her raised eyebrows, as he lowered his newspaper. 'Who seemed to like you,' he added thoughtfully. 'A lot.'

'Well, I liked him, too. He was really sweet.' Initially, Kelly had been nervous when they had been invited into the old man's box, but the octogenarian had quickly put her at her ease, although she had refused the flute of chilled champagne which someone had tried to press into her hand.

'And what were the two of you talking about so intently?' Romano enquired curiously.

'Oh, he was asking me lots of questions. How long I'd known you. How we'd met. Stuff like that.' She put her cup down. 'But then he said something a bit odd.'

He raised his eyebrows. 'Really?'

'Mmm. He told me I wasn't like your usual girlfriends.' She pulled a face. 'Which obviously, I knew. But it was a little bit personal, considering we'd only just met.'

'Maybe it was your sunny disposition which invited his confidence,' he suggested carelessly. 'What did you say in response?'

'I told him that I could hardly believe my luck to be dating a man like you and that every night I said a quiet prayer of gratitude.'

He frowned. 'You *are* joking?'

'Of course I'm joking!' She slanted him a smile. 'I

said you could be a real pussycat at times, even when you were trying very hard not to be.'

There was a pause. 'Are you trying to ruin my reputation, Kelly?' he taunted softly.

'Or improve it?' She tilted her head. 'Your phone's vibrating, by the way.'

He glanced down at the screen, raising his dark eyebrows in surprise. 'Speak of the devil,' he murmured, clicking to connect the call. *'Pronto, Silvano,'* he said. *'Come va?'*

Kelly watched as the billionaire rose to his feet and began to pace around the vast kitchen, speaking to the old man in fluent Italian, so she didn't have a clue what he was saying. But at least the conversation gave her a moment's breathing space. Time to reflect on what was happening. Or rather, what wasn't happening. She needed to focus on the difference between fantasy and reality.

On the table lay the yummy remains of the fresh bread, which had been delivered barely an hour ago. Beside them stood a jug of coffee as dark as treacle and a dish of iced pineapple, which Romano had deftly sliced himself—and all this against a backdrop of Turin, which looked as pretty as a picture postcard. The situation felt intimate and yet weirdly normal and at times it almost felt real. Like a real relationship. But it wasn't, and she wasn't sure how much longer she could carry on pretending everything was okay, when everything most definitely wasn't okay.

She almost wished he would start being mean to her again, the way he'd done in the past, because that way she could manufacture a row—allowing her to blurt out the awful truth and then deal with his reaction. But he wasn't being mean. On the contrary. This morning, he was being unbearably thoughtful and his exemplary behaviour was adding a big dollop of guilt to the already uncomfortable mix of her emotions.

Romano was ending the call and she could see an expression of unexpected delight lightening his carved features as he put the phone down. 'Well, well, well,' he said slowly.

'Good news?'

'You could say that,' he agreed, shaking his dark head in disbelief. 'Silvano is willing to go through with the sale after all.' He must have seen her look of confusion, because he started to explain. 'It's a deal I was trying to broker with him before the christening. An iconic car factory I've been chasing since for ever, but he refused to sell it to me, even though I offered him a price which I doubt anybody else could match.'

'So what do you think swung it?' She blinked. 'The money?'

'No, not the money.'

'What, then?'

He hesitated for a moment and then walked towards her, pulling her off the bar stool and into his arms, and instantly she was enclosed in the warm power of his embrace. 'You did,' he said softly, nuzzling her lips with his own. 'You swung it.'

She pulled back a little and blinked. *'Me?'*

'Mmm.' He was busy exploring her neck with his mouth and Kelly was having to concentrate very hard not to let her eyes flutter to a close and give into his lovemaking, but she mustn't. She really mustn't.

'Why should it have anything to do with me?' she questioned weakly.

At this, he drew away from her, his black eyes as watchful as she'd ever seen them, his ebony stare underpinned with an element of calculation. 'If I answer that question, will you answer one of mine in return, Kelly?' There was a pause. 'And answer it honestly?'

Kelly's heart started thudding and she couldn't decide whether it was through fear or excitement. Was he implying that sometimes she was dishonest? And didn't he have a point—even though at the moment he was unaware of it? 'Sure.'

He nodded. 'Silvano didn't want to sell to me because he didn't approve of me, or my supposed playboy lifestyle. He's a very old-fashioned man whose wife and only son were tragically killed in a car crash, so he had nobody to leave his company to. Maybe it was that which made him determined to sell to a family man— one with traditional values, much like his own. And I definitely didn't fit that category.'

Kelly licked her dry lips. 'So what has all this got to do with me?'

'He thinks I'm a changed man.' There was a pause. 'And that my relationship with you is different.'

'Different?' she questioned weakly.

'Mmm. He seems to imagine that I have radically altered my playboy philosophy.' His black eyes were glinting out a mocking challenge. 'And that I should make you my wife.'

'Did he? Well, obviously *that's* not going to happen.' Did that sound convincing enough? she wondered. She pulled away from him and took a step towards the breakfast bar, needing to put some distance between them. Because she still hadn't heard what he wanted to ask and that was making her feel scared. She cleared her throat. 'Now it's your turn. You wanted to ask me something, didn't you?'

He frowned, as if taken aback by her words. He probably couldn't believe she'd steered the conversation away from the subject of marriage, which presumably would have had most women gagging to hear what he'd said in response to the elderly tycoon. In any other circumstances Kelly might have been among their number. But not now. Because the giant elephant in the room was threatening to trample over everything and yet Romano didn't even know it existed.

'It's just that sometimes you look as if all the cares of the world are weighing down on your shoulders,' he said softly. 'Why is that?'

Kelly swallowed. 'Is that what I do?' she prevaricated, her voice cracking a little.

'*Sì*. Especially when you think nobody is watching.'

His voice was gentle as she'd ever heard it but that was misleading. Thank God she had stepped away from him and could grip the kitchen counter with fingers which suddenly felt boneless. Because now she felt like the biggest fool in the world. Worse than a fool. What had she *thought* he was going to ask her?

To spend longer here with him?

Or had she thought he was going to take the elderly Italian's advice and ask her to *marry* him?

Afterwards she would regret the way she said it—her unfounded disappointment colouring her delivery and making her words unnecessarily clumsy. 'My period's late,' she stated baldly.

For a moment she thought he hadn't heard her, because he didn't say a word. But then she saw she'd made another major miscalculation because his powerful body had stilled, like a wild predator disturbed by an unexpected crash in the jungle. And when he spoke it was in a tone she'd never heard him use before, not even when he'd been at his most disapproving—clipping each syllable out as though they had been fashioned from unyielding chips of marble. 'How long have you known?'

'I don't actually know anything yet. I haven't done a test and—'

'How long?' he cut in.

'When we were at the *castello*—'

'You mean you've known all this time?' he demanded. 'All the time you've been here? You must have thought about it at least a hundred times a day.' He shook his head incredulously. 'And yet still you said nothing?'

There was genuine appeal in her voice. 'How could I?'

'It's quite simple, Kelly,' he answered cuttingly. 'You just open your lips and the words come out—the same ones you've just used. I'm not asking for a definitive answer but at least you could have done me the courtesy of sharing your fears.' He gave a bitter laugh. 'Though why should I imagine you would behave in a manner which could in any way be considered honourable? You're a woman, aren't you, who learnt to lie and deceive from the moment you first opened those big green eyes?'

The world tilted. His contempt was tangible and Kelly's throat felt as if someone were pressing all the air from it. 'How could I have forgotten what a cynic you are?' she breathed.

'Not a cynic, *cara*. Let's just call it dealing in facts, shall we? But I'm curious,' he added, his voice growing steadier now and somehow this new and icy calm was as intimidating as anything which had come before.

'What did you think would happen, by not telling me?' he mused. 'That I would grow to find you indispensable? That all this time alone with me would allow you to showcase your many charms and enable you to seduce me—'

'I thought we'd already done that bit!'

'I'm not talking about sex!' he bit out. 'I'm talking about trying to worm your way into my life by showing me that domesticity isn't necessarily a thing to be avoided.'

'Wow. I've never been compared to a worm before—but I've certainly thought it about a few men in my time and I'm looking at one right now!' she countered furiously. 'And this isn't *real* domesticity, Romano—not with unseen servants drifting in and out, catering to your every need. It's all make-believe. In fact, nothing about your life is real. You don't have real relationships—not with your family, nor with your lovers. Everyone you deal with forms part of some sort of *transaction*, don't they?'

They stared at one another, both dragging in furious breaths. Suddenly he grabbed his phone and stormed out of the kitchen, and she could hear him getting his coat from the hallway before slamming his way out of the apartment.

She waited until she was certain he'd gone, until the vast apartment was completely silent, and then Kelly stumbled into the sitting room, her knees giving way as she flopped onto one of the giant grey leather sofas. She wanted to rage and howl and hurl some of the fancy velvet cushions against the walls, but she didn't dare risk damaging any of the priceless artwork and, besides, what was the point? Who was she most angry with—him, or herself?

Why hadn't she told him before?

She knew why.

Deep down wasn't she just as guilty of playing make-believe as Romano? She'd wanted to hold onto what they had, without reality intruding. To carry on pretending this was a real relationship, instead of something calculated and temporary. But that was always going to be a doomed venture—like trying to preserve a bubble and prevent it from bursting.

So now what?

She looked around, knowing she couldn't stay here, wondering whether she should just pack her bag and get a bus to the airport. She didn't want to be seen to be running away, but what was the alternative? Meekly waiting for the angry tycoon to return home and hoping he would offer her a lift in his fancy limousine? Why, she'd rather walk barefoot to the airport than have to throw herself on his mercy.

Slowly, she made her way to the bedroom, the un-made bed testament to the passionate night they'd spent together, and Kelly despaired at the futile clench of her heart and the fact that her anger had been re-placed by a sudden terrible sadness. Because, in the end, sex counted for very little, didn't it? It might be a very enjoyable exercise, but unless there was some sort of shared emotion it meant about as much as going for a run in the park. *She* had been the one to read too much into it, who had silently nurtured her own hopes along the way. Had she thought she could help heal Romano's wounded heart through intimacy? Did she think she was any different from all those other women who must have tried before? Her! Market trader Kelly Butler without a penny to her name.

Didn't matter now anyway.

Retrieving her small suitcase from the giant wardrobe, she began to pull out the few clothes she'd brought with her. Into her suitcase went the plain underwear and the handmade silver jewellery he hadn't wanted her to wear to his fancy function. Next, the functional jeans and 'best' dress. As for the rest of them—the silks and satins, the cashmere and the wretched diamond earrings—they could all stay here, for they had no place in her life back in England.

Lastly, she peeled off Romano's oversized shirt—replacing it with the clothes she'd originally travelled in. But it was only when she was bending over to zip up her case that she felt the first low tug deep in her belly and crammed her fist in her mouth to silence her involuntary gasp of pain.

It was quiet in the apartment when Romano let himself in and for a moment he wondered if Kelly had gone.

His brow furrowed.

Had she?

But his intended search halted at only the second room because there she was, standing in the smallest reception room and staring out of the window, her shoulders hunched. She turned as he entered and something about her expression set his senses on edge, because this was a version of Kelly Butler he didn't recognise. Not just because her features were so pinched, but because her eyes were shuttered and wary. She looked...lost...

A sudden flicker of conscience began licking at his heart but he blocked it ruthlessly, for he never allowed himself to feel regret. Or pain. Been there. Done that.

Unbuttoning his cashmere coat, he withdrew a paper package from the inside pocket. 'Here,' he said gruffly and placed it on the black marble coffee table.

She stared at it uncomprehendingly. 'What is it?'

He supposed he could have made a clipped suggestion that she open it to find out but her appearance was so *fragile* that he couldn't contemplate such an offhand response. 'A pregnancy test,' he said, the words sounding thick against his tongue.

He hadn't been expecting her to laugh until he registered that no humour was involved in the sound she made. 'I don't need one,' she said dully.

'What do you mean?'

Another laugh, only this time even more hollow. 'Oh, come on, Romano—I appreciate that you're operating out of your comfort zone here, but surely you did enough biology at school to realise that I don't need one because my period has come.' She swallowed. 'I'm not pregnant. Okay? You're safe.'

His mind was swirling with so many thoughts that it took a while before her words made any sense, but there was no answering rush of relief. He felt... He shook his head and glared at her as, unexpectedly, his heart clenched.

He didn't know what he felt.

'Obviously I would like to go back to England as soon as possible,' she continued woodenly. 'I've had a look at flights and I should easily be able to make the four o'clock. And no—before you offer—I don't want to go home on your private jet. Though I would appreciate a lift to the airport because I don't really know my way around Turin's public transport system. And I would like to go alone.' She forced a smile. 'I think that would be better for both of us—well, certainly for me—if we went our separate ways as soon as possible.'

He shrugged, his gaze briefly flickering to the green cross on the front of the pharmacy bag before lifting his eyes to hers. 'If that's what you want,' he said.

'That's what I want.'

She was staring at him and it seemed strange to have her so close and yet not have her close to him. And she was chewing on her lip, like somebody in an examination hall. As if she were deciding whether or not to speak and then she nodded, bright curls rippling down her back as she obviously came to a decision.

'Would you answer me one question before I go, Romano? As honestly as I answered yours?'

Only one? he wondered as he looked at her enquiringly. 'If I can.' And in an odd kind of way this request reassured him, because now he was on familiar territory.

Did you ever love me, Romano? Will you miss me— even a bit?

But, as usual, Kelly Butler defied his predictions.

'Did you deliberately take me to the opera,' she said slowly, 'knowing Silvano di Saccucci would be there?'

'Scusi?' He frowned. 'Why on earth would I do that?'

She shrugged. 'To play the part of a man completely captivated by his new girlfriend. Because you gave a wonderful performance, I must say. You weren't behaving like a playboy at all.' She was biting the words out as if she had rehearsed them. 'Even I was a little taken aback by all the hand-holding and the way you gave my tears your unexpected seal of approval. In fact, it was a display so convincing that Silvano actually suggested you marry me. Which meant you'd hit the jackpot, didn't it? He had tacitly approved you as a potential family man and actually rang up the very next morning and offered to sell you his business. Bingo! Result!'

The accusation took his breath away. It hung between them like a spider's web—almost invisible to the naked eye but strong enough to capture every toxic fear and suspicion and leave them dangling there. 'You really think that of me, Kelly?' he breathed. 'That I am capable of such deceit and manipulation?'

'Well, why wouldn't I?' she countered quietly. 'Because isn't that exactly what you think about me?'

For a while there was silence, broken only by the sounds of their breathing as they surveyed each other from opposite sides of the room, like two prize-fighters in a cage.

'What an exquisite irony it is to share such a compatibility as this,' he said at last. 'To be so equally balanced in our mutual mistrust of one another. And yet what unites us ultimately destroys us, doesn't it, Kelly?' He gave a bitter laugh as he turned away. 'I'll phone for my driver.'

CHAPTER TWELVE

THE MARKET WAS depressingly quiet. Or, at least, Kelly's section was. In fact, she'd had a total of two customers all day and only one of those had bought something. Most people were congregated on the nearby stalls, filling their bags with vegetables which had just been reduced in price, because they were closing soon. Or buying the few remaining burgers, which made the air smell thick with fried onions.

And it was cold.

Unseasonably cold. The pale sun glinted on the metal jewellery as she carefully packed it away in her ruck-sack and totted up the day's miserable takings. As she unlocked her bicycle, Kelly shivered, wondering how much longer she could keep going with the belief that one day this was going to become a business capable of supporting her. Because markets like these were a place where people built dreams and, more often than not, those dreams didn't survive. Would she become like all those other hopefuls who'd had them crushed— her features growing sharp and disillusioned and her eyes bitter? How long before she accepted life on life's terms and became a full-time waitress, or retrained to work in an office?

And hadn't her general disillusionment been compounded by the fact that her heart was aching so badly, even if she did manage to hide it behind her bright market smile? No matter how many times she tried to convince herself that a brief sexual fling shouldn't hurt like this, it didn't actually change anything. The pain of missing Romano was physical. She kept expecting to wake up one morning without that awful sinking feeling and the bitter realisation that he was no longer in her life. But so far it hadn't happened. Was that because he had affected her on so many levels? She had thought she was having his baby and, even in the midst of all that worry, hadn't her heart *wanted* that, even though her head told her it would have been a disaster?

The only bright light on the horizon was having paid off her debts with the money she'd earned from cleaning his castle. She'd been slightly taken aback by the amount which had been transferred into her bank account from Castelliari Industries and pride had made her want to question whether he'd paid her too much. But then she imagined how that particular conversation might have gone. No doubt the arrogant billionaire would have accused her of using the call as an excuse to speak to him again. As if she wanted to!

Liar, liar.

Of course she wanted to. She wanted him every minute of every day. And night.

But she needed to stop playing back the tape of their brief relationship because it was over and she was just going to have to get used to it. It had been six long weeks since she'd left Tuscany and she hadn't heard a thing from him, and although deep down she knew there was no reason to hear from him, that didn't stop it from hurting. How easily he had forgotten her.

Removing her heavy apron, she stuffed it in her rucksack and was about to get on her bike when she heard someone saying her name and her throat dried at the sound of a horribly familiar voice.

Horrible?

Who was she kidding?

It was a voice of velvet and steel, which was doing dangerous things to her blood pressure. But it couldn't be his voice. Not Romano's. Not here and definitely not now, on a cold April day in England. Had she been thinking about him so much that she'd made herself believe she'd magicked him up, like a schoolgirl with a crush on a popstar? Heart crashing, she lifted her head.

No, not magic at all.

Or maybe it was. How could it be anything else when he seemed to look more alive than anyone else around him? Somehow he managed to stamp his presence indelibly on whichever landscape he was inhabiting with his powerful body, jet-dark hair and the glittering ebony of his eyes. And here, against a faded and cold English backdrop, he appeared even more vibrant than usual.

'Romano,' she said faintly, trying to get her head around the fact that he was standing at her market stall, attracting a lot of attention from everyone in the vicinity, especially the women. 'What on earth are you doing here?'

'Why do you think I am here?' He raised his dark brows. 'You think I wish to buy some earrings?'

'Why would you do that, when we both know you turn your nose up at silver in favour of your precious diamonds?' she sniped. 'Anyway, you're too late. I've packed away for the day.'

'So I see.' He held her gaze with a steady stare which seemed to burn right through her skin. 'I wish to talk to you.'

She tried to stay calm but it was difficult not to react to his shimmering sex appeal, which was making her want to burrow her hands underneath that soft navy jacket and massage the hard flesh beneath. But she was vulnerable around him and she needed to protect herself. The time for make-believe was over. This was reality.

'What about?' she demanded baldly. 'I thought we'd said everything there was to say.'

'Not here,' he said with a formidable clench of his jaw. 'In private.'

Kelly opened her mouth to tell him not anywhere, but then she shut it again. Because of *course* she was curious to know why he'd turned up like this. Perhaps he was so impressed with her work that he was going to offer her a permanent cleaning position at his Tuscan retreat! Keeping her expression neutral, she nodded, determined to make it clear which of them was in charge.

And it wasn't him.

'If you insist,' she said coolly.

He narrowed his eyes, but not before she had seen the glint of surprise sparking in their ebony depths, as if her response had surprised him. 'So, where?'

This was her opportunity. She could suggest the new Italian restaurant where she'd managed to find herself a job, because she would pay good money to see his appalled reaction when he spotted pineapple pizza on the menu. Or she could show him some of the nicer bits of

Granchester, to illustrate that you didn't have to live in a castle or a multimillion-pound apartment to enjoy beautiful surroundings. The park, say…where the spring flowers currently bursting into bright bloom made it resemble the set of a Hollywood musical.

And suddenly Kelly realised she was in danger. Real, emotional danger. *Flowers? Musicals?* What was she *thinking?* That he would start whirling her round the bandstand and crooning in her ear? Why not let him see her as she was? As she really was, without all the Cinderella trappings he'd insisted on lavishing on her. Because surely if she reinforced the differences between them it would kill off this thing between them once and for all. And she needed that. For her own peace of mind, she needed that.

'You can come to my flat,' she said. 'Do you want to write down the address?'

'I know the address.'

Of course he did. Yet another demonstration of the true reach of his influence. A man with all the facts at his fingertips and all he had to do was to snap them and someone would come running. Well, not me, she thought fiercely. Not me.

'I can give you a lift,' he added, with a glance at the nearby side road, and for the first time Kelly noticed the pale blue racing car with the scarlet trim, which was attracting the attention of a cluster of teenage boys. As a symbol of his wealth and power, it was quite something, but all she could think about was that hideous uniform she'd been forced to wear.

She gave him a tight smile and pointed to her sturdy old bike. 'I'll make my own way, thank you.'

* * *

Her home was much smaller than he had imagined and that was saying something. Romano's body tensed. He was a man who considered himself worldly but he couldn't deny being unfamiliar with material poverty. The exterior of the apartment block was tired, with peeling paint in the communal areas, and it was situated in a decidedly insalubrious part of the city. Jamming his thumb on the bell, he waited, and didn't part of him wonder whether she would refuse to answer?

And then what?

Suddenly the door opened and there stood Kelly and the air felt as if it had been punched from his lungs. He had thought she might change—that she would have replaced her working clothes for something more feminine and flattering. But no. The thin overcoat and fingerless gloves had been removed, but the sturdy jeans and sweater remained. Her green eyes were narrowed at him with undisguised suspicion and there was a mulish tilt to her chin as she studied him.

'Well?'

'You wish to leave me standing on the doorstep, Kelly?'

'I don't think you'd really like to hear what I wish,' she answered ominously, before pulling open the door and stepping back. 'I suppose you'd better come in.'

He bent his head as he stepped inside, for the walls of the tiny apartment seemed to shrink and envelop him. But on closer inspection, the interior was surprisingly clean and bright, and strategically placed mirrors seemed to double the space and available light. There were sprigs of greenery in a rustic pottery vase and vivid paintings on the walls, the landscape of one which he vaguely recognised. And the room felt like something he *didn't* recognise.

It felt like home.

He waited for her to speak. To demand to know why he was there, her voice possibly trembling with hope and expectation, but she said nothing. Just looked at him calmly, through the half shuttering of long lashes, which didn't quite conceal the flicker of disquiet in her eyes. He thought of all the things he could say. The diplomatic words he could weave which would have the required effect of bringing her from across the room and into his arms.

But suddenly Romano realised such half-heartedness would get him precisely nowhere. That, more than anything, he owed her the truth. Because Kelly Butler *was* different from other women. She always had been. She would not be short-changed. She was proud and strong and fearless. Wasn't that one of the reasons which made him…?

'I miss you,' he said simply.

'Miss me?' she questioned sharply. 'Or mistrust me?'

'That feeling has faded,' he admitted huskily. 'And I understand why you kept your pregnancy fears hidden.' He expelled a heavy breath. 'Why would you confide in me when I could be so damned unforgiving?'

Still she didn't say anything, though her lashes opened a fraction further.

'I miss you like hell,' he growled. 'I didn't think I would. I kept telling myself you were nothing to me. That you'd been a thorn in my side for longer than I could remember. But nothing I did or said or thought could kill my desire for you, Kelly. It didn't matter how much I tried to convince myself otherwise, it changed nothing. I wanted you more than any other woman. I still do. I can't stop wanting you, in every way,' he declared huskily, and this definitely *should* have provoked a reaction—preferably the kind which would have her smothering him with grateful kisses, which would mean he didn't have to say anything more.

But she didn't move or utter a single word and, eventually, Romano gave a ragged sigh of capitulation.

'When we had sex,' he said, 'I thought that would be the beginning of the end—'

'Wow.' Her eyes dazzled him with their emerald light. 'Is that how you regard all your liaisons, Romano?'

'Yes,' he answered frankly. 'Because that is what happens. I want something until I don't. I get bored. Restless. Just not with you. I have wanted you since the moment I first saw you, even when you were forbidden to me. But in you I saw danger.'

'Danger?'

'Sì.' He paused. 'Because you bring out a side of me I never knew existed.'

'Which side is that?' she questioned, her voice low.

How much did she want from him? he wondered impatiently. Wouldn't she be satisfied until she had wrung every last emotion from his body? More importantly, was he going to let her get away with that?

But he had no choice. If he wanted her, it had to be on her terms. No. Their terms. It had to be honest, right from the get-go. *He* had to be honest. He could see that now.

'It was safer not to feel. Not to attach to anyone.

Never to…love anyone, because I didn't know how. Nobody had ever shown me the way,' he admitted heavily, acknowledging the bitter truth for the first time in his life. 'Even my father found it hard to love me because I looked so much like my mother. That's why I hung onto the *castello*, even though I didn't want to live there. Because *he* had left it to me in his will and to pass it on to someone else felt like a betrayal of that gift.' His stupid voice was breaking and suddenly her self-imposed exile seemed to be at an end for she was crossing the room and putting her arms around his neck and reaching up on tiptoes so she could stare into his face.

'Deep down, I knew that,' she whispered, her breath warm against his lips. 'How could you ever trust your feelings—or anyone else's—after the kind of beginning you had? You saw things no child should ever have to see, Romano, and you learned that the only way you could survive was by protecting yourself. By building walls around yourself and keeping everything which made you vulnerable locked away inside. Once you let me get to know you a little better, I could see that so clearly. Occasionally, I saw a glimpse of the man I knew existed behind all those high walls. Who was thoughtful and funny and clever. And I…'

Romano waited as she hesitated in that way she had, of seeming to think carefully about her words before she said them—only this time they came bursting from her lips like a torrent of sweet petals.

'I admired that man,' she breathed. 'I applauded the way you came through all that tumult to survive. But I couldn't tell you, or show you—because you'd told me not to. In fact, keeping my emotions out of it was one of your stipulations for continuing our liaison. I thought you were being cruel and controlling. It was only as I got to know you better that I realised you were simply being careful.'

'But not any more!' he declared urgently. 'I behaved badly. I shouldn't have insisted you wear those damned diamonds, I should have let you wear what the hell you pleased, because you are you, and it is you that I love. I love you, Kelly Butler. That's…that's all.'

'No, that's not all, because I have some things you need to hear, too,' she whispered, her fingertip tracing the curve of his lips. 'You need to know that mistrusting *you* was a way of protecting myself, because I was terrified of falling in love with you and getting my heart broken—fulfilling all my mother's dire predictions about men. But she was wrong, and I'm not frightened any more. I'm free to tell you that I love you, Romano. I always have and I always will.' She gave a helpless shrug. 'I just can't seem to help myself.'

Romano made a choking sound as, tangling his trembling hands in the thick mane of her hair, he drove his mouth on hers—in a kiss of passion and possession he would remember for the rest of his life. He thought about asking her where the bedroom was, though the place was so small he could probably work it out for himself.

And he didn't want to wait, or delay.

He couldn't.

He was pulling off her clothes with an exhilaration and urgency which made him feel about nineteen and she was tugging at his shirt with equal zeal. His jeans only made it as far as his ankles and so did hers, their flesh warm and giving where they touched, and he gave a groan of feral bliss as he pushed inside her tight, wet heat.

'*Porca miseria!*' he choked out helplessly.

It was over very quickly.

'Too fast,' he murmured.

'Maybe we could do it more slowly next time.' Snuggling up to him, Kelly yawned, thinking that she'd never been lying half naked on her sitting room carpet with a man before and she was rather enjoying this very different perspective of her apartment.

For a while she stayed there, holding him close and savouring the moment while thinking that life had never felt quite so perfect as it did now. She stroked a stray strand of thick ebony hair away from his forehead.

'So what kept you?' she murmured.

'Hmm?' He turned a little.

'Have you only just decided you couldn't live without me? It's been six weeks, you know.'

'Have you been counting?' he teased.

'Trying not to,' she admitted.

He sighed. 'I had things I needed to do before I came to you.'

'Things like?'

'I've been to France to stay with my nephew and niece. To get to know them a bit better, as you suggested to me so very vehemently, *la mia cara.*'

She wrinkled her nose. 'Flo didn't say anything to me.'

'I asked her not to.'

'Right.' For some reason this pleased her, that for once *Romano* was enjoying his sister's confidence instead of her. Because that was the way it should be. She stroked his chest with the tip of her finger. 'What else have you been doing?'

'Signing the castle over to Floriana and her family.'

'Gosh. And won't you mind...letting go?'

He shrugged. 'Not really. The proprietorial side of my character felt a fleeting sorrow, *naturalmente*. But you were right. I don't want to live there permanently and I assume you don't really want to either?'

Kelly held her breath at the potential significance of this question, but she certainly wasn't going to be *pushy*. 'I don't care where we live,' she told him truthfully.

But he didn't appear to be listening. He was looking at the wall. At the painting she'd done just before she'd gone to art school when he'd cruelly rejected her suggestion of going on a date. Now it seemed that her romantism and disappointment had been apparent—showing in every fine brushstroke of the picture, making the flowers seem especially bright and the sky so darkly sombre. It was a painting of hope and despair, she realised—only now all that despair had melted away.

'That's a painting of the school,' he said slowly.

'It is. A view of the summer house near the tennis courts,' she said, meeting the question in his eyes. 'During the school holidays we always stayed put. We couldn't afford to go on holiday and my mum got paid extra for being on the premises, which sometimes made me feel like I never got away from the place. But I was allowed full use of the art department and that was brilliant.' She shrugged. 'I don't know why I'm telling you all this.'

'Because I want to know. I want to know everything about you, *la mia cara*, and I intend to spend the rest of my life finding out.' He picked up her hand and kissed each finger in turn, his gaze not leaving her face. 'So will you marry me, Kelly? As soon as possible?'

'Will I marry you?' She laughed with sheer and exultant joy. 'Hell, yes.'

Had she thought that life couldn't get any more perfect?

It was just about to.

EPILOGUE

'*CARA?*'

Romano's voice was silky as Kelly turned to look at him, basking in the coal-dark brilliance of his eyes. She'd thought he was asleep after that particularly passionate bout of lovemaking but, there again, he never failed to surprise her with his powers of recovery. 'Mmm?'

'You're okay?' he purred.

Lazily, she trickled her hand down over his chest, biting back a smile as she felt his wriggle of faint impatience when her fingers came to a teasing halt. 'Why, Romano Castelliari, I think you want me again.'

'Always,' he affirmed hungrily. 'But you haven't answered my question.'

She let her gaze drift over him, thinking he looked like a marble statue as he lay in the silver-coated moonlight with only a sheet covering his magnificent body. 'I've never been more okay,' she assured him. 'It was an absolutely gorgeous day.'

'So everyone said.'

She gave a sigh of contentment. Today had been the christening of Floriana and Max's third child and this time Riccardo and Angie had flown in from America with their family to the Tuscan *castello*. The ceremony had been held in the Castelliari church but this time Kelly had been delighted to observe that Romano's rugged features had shown no trace of anguish or bitterness, for his demons had been vanquished. By her, he said. His beautiful wife. He said a lot of nice things like that.

It had been great to get all the cousins together— Angie and Riccardo's two, Floriana and Max's three and Kelly and Romano's sturdy little toddler son, Vito. Kelly smiled.

'Why are you smiling like the cat that got the cream?' he probed.

'Because I'm happy. And I'm also curious.'

'Oh, you're always curious,' he murmured, his hand cupping her breast. 'Go on, then. Satisfy your curiosity. Ask away.'

'Does it feel weird for you?' she probed. 'Knowing it's not your castle any more? That we're staying here as guests for the first time?'

He considered the question, then shook his head. 'Not at all. Max is a good estate manager and the family is happy. And, to be perfectly honest, I'm much happier about their children being brought up in Italy.'

'You're so traditional,' she teased.

'And you love it.'

'Mmm. That's probably because I love you.' She told him that as often as possible, feeling he had a lot of love to catch up on, and every day she somehow loved him a little bit more. It was slightly scary to realise that nearly three years had passed since that afternoon in Granchester when he'd asked her to marry him. The following morning she had left her tiny flat and never gone back, moving permanently to Italy—a country she now considered home.

They had wed very quickly, in secret, in a small venue overlooking the green sweep of the Piedmont hills. Neither of them had wanted a fuss, or press, or any intrusive questions about why they weren't marrying at the family castle. Kelly had barely paid any attention to her dress or her flowers. The day had been about them, and their love. And she had cried. Of course she had. But Romano was a dab hand at dealing with tears these days, drying them tenderly with his pristine handkerchief, just as he had done on that night at the opera.

Her life had changed in so many ways when she'd left England. Exactly nine months after their wedding, their son Vito had been born and was the light of his adoring parents' lives. What a wonderful father Romano was, she thought lovingly. So tender and so strong.

She was still making jewellery—very part-time—but had come to an executive decision on what would be more likely to sell in the more affluent circles in which she now moved. She certainly hadn't started using diamonds but was now crafting her distinctive dangly earrings in gold and was doing better than she could have ever dreamed. Sometimes she had to stop and ask herself if this was real life, it was so good.

'You're pregnant, aren't you?' Romano said suddenly.

She nodded, continuing to trace the outline of his lips with the tip of her finger. 'I think so. I mean, I'm only a bit late and I haven't done a test yet but I just feel *different* somehow. Does that sound mad to you?'

For a moment Romano couldn't speak, the lump in

his throat was so damned big. And then he looked at her shining eyes and the thick fall of hair and the way she was smiling at him and he pulled her closer so that she could hear the loud thunder of his heart.

'No, not mad,' he purred.

It sounded perfect.

She was perfect. In every way.

And when he had finished kissing her, he would tell her so.

* * * * *

Were you swept up in the drama of
His Enemy's Italian Surrender?
Then why not try these other steamy
Sharon Kendrick stories?

Her Christmas Baby Confession
Innocent Maid for the Greek
Italian Nights to Claim the Virgin
The Housekeeper's One-Night Baby
The King's Hidden Heir

ROYAL FIANCÉE REQUIRED

KALI ANTHONY

MILLS & BOON

To Ally, Fiona and Louisa.

I can never thank you enough
for helping me to wrangle my recalcitrant hero
over coffee, cake and a day of writing.

And to my daughter, Miss 15.
Who told me my texting style was weird
and that now she'd fixed it for my story
she deserved some credit (and commission—
but that's an argument for another day!).

Here's to you, my darling girl.

PROLOGUE

STRING LIGHTS DRIPPED from myriad small trees filling the palace ballroom. Halrovia's Spring Ball was famed for its opulence, and this year the organisers had excelled with their theme: a Midsummer Night's Masquerade. Anastacia turned, gazing up at the canopy above her which glittered as if the room were filled with fireflies. The lighting was lower than normal, making the space look somehow mysterious, like a wonderland. Huge urns dotted the room, spilling with flowers and fruits. The assembled crowd drifted through the room masked, costumed in jewel colours, twittering like tropical birds.

The sense of the whole evening was...expectant. As the Halrovian royal family's middle child, she'd been taught many lessons about how to comport herself with restraint befitting her position as the country's 'perfect princess', which the press and therefore her people had dubbed her. She was sure, if her mother saw her now, another rule would be added to the *long* list: *don't twirl about looking awestruck*.

But her mother was in another corner of the room entertaining official guests, among them the Crown Prince of Isolobello who rumour had it, was going to offer for her hand in marriage tonight. Rumour had it wrong. Ana had eyes; she could see what others refused to—that Prince

Caspar had no interest in her. Her parents would doubtless be disappointed, but she wasn't. Caspar was handsome and kind, the type of man she could make a friend. They had similar charity interests, such as in child literacy. She'd be prepared to do her duty, if it came to that, but it never would. A friend was all Caspar would ever want to be.

Now her sister, Priscilla… Ana was sure Caspar didn't have *friendly* thoughts in her direction, given the way he stared at Cilla when she walked into a room as if he'd been clubbed over the head.

To have someone look at her like *that*—not with simple appreciation, or even lust, but with a yearning, a consuming…*need*. Ana didn't want just a *good friend* for a husband, though for someone in her position, whose parents expected the eldest daughter to marry a prince, she should have counted friendship as a bonus. Was it wrong to seek more? Ana scanned the crowd, searching for…

No. Wanting more was a dangerous thing for a woman in her position with expectations placed on her since birth. Yet for her whole, young life of twenty-four years she'd craved it. She'd rapped up her desires deep inside, locking them away. She knew she was lucky, always with a roof over her head, and not any old roof but a *palace*. She had sumptuous food on her plate and staff to look after her.

With those privileges came great responsibility. She had a duty to uphold, obligations to her family name and to Halrovia's people. She carried out those duties because it was the right thing to do—such as marrying someone her parents selected because that would be good for Halrovia. It was another way she could serve.

Yet why did she always feel so *starved*? No one would ever know. All people took note of was how she appeared, as if that was somehow her measure as a person. There were endless reports of her 'flawless blonde hair', following every change in its style with breathless anticipation, people waiting to copy it. Commentary about her famed pale-blue eyes, a feature of the Halrovian royal family, and her skin, over which the beauty magazines waxed lyrical, imagining her onerous routines to keep the march of time at bay. The paparazzi constantly tried to take photographs of her body. Ana's private secretary had reported that a shot of her wearing a bikini—as if she'd ever be allowed to wear one—would earn a photographer thousands of dollars, and never mind one who could photograph her doing something less than perfect...

She was trapped by her genetics which no one could look past. Everyone saw who they wanted to see with her. Nothing out of place, restrained, smiling on cue, the perfect princess. Yet there was a question she asked herself every morning as she looked in the mirror, staring at her imperfect self. Who was Anastacia Montroy, Princess of Halrovia? She had no answer to that question.

Ana breathed in deeply, shutting her eyes for a moment, allowing the intoxicating scent of exotic flowers to overwhelm her senses. Tonight, she didn't want to comport herself with restraint. She craved chaos and magic, a little something for herself. To shed the expectations of others like a skin that she'd felt she'd outgrown. Wasn't that what the spring was all about—renewal?

She'd dressed for it. In ordinary circumstances, her mother would never have permitted her gown. Tonight, she was supposed to catch a prince, so allowances had been made. No neat and tidy hair; hers tumbled in unruly waves wound with flowers. She'd been explicit about her dress. Ana had wanted a cross between Botticelli's two famous paintings: *The Birth of Venus* and *Primavera*.

Her dress maker had delivered. The fabric was a sheer net covered in silk flowers. The nude lining clung to her body. Cleverly hand-painted with shading, it looked as though she wore nothing other than strategically placed blooms which appeared to wind lovingly around her. Her mask was made of feather butterflies. It was breath-taking. Caused her mother to scowl. Made Ana feel bold. And tonight it wasn't a prince's attention she sought to catch.

Ana took a deep breath. She shouldn't be trying to catch anyone's attention. She had people to meet, alliances to shore up, a prince to dance with so appearances might be maintained, whilst both of their imaginings lay elsewhere—Caspar's with her sister, who was oblivious to his attraction, and hers with someone she could only ever view from afar.

'Your Highness.'

Her belly fluttered as it filled with the feather-winged butterflies of her mask come to life. That male voice… Deep. Decadent, like a fondue of dark chocolate. She wanted to dip herself into it and drown. Its accent was a heady mix of French, the country of his birth, and Australian, the land of his father.

Ana turned, slowly to savour the moment of seeing this man up close for the first time tonight. Would that sensation of breathless anticipation ever change around him?

She tried to repeat the mantra as he came into view: *princesses don't marry commoners*. Perhaps in some royal families, not in hers. Yet the reasons for that were hazy, and tonight all a voice shouted in her ear was, *why not?*

She knew the answer with an unshakeable certainty, for this man at least. A man like him could never be pinned down. He filled her view. Aston Lane. Tall, broad, knock-out handsome. Heir to the Girard family champagne fortune. Billionaire businessmen in his own right, his daring was renowned in yachting, mountaineering…a thrill seeker. Her heart hammered in her chest. Aston Lane looked like her every midnight fantasy come to life.

'Mr Lane.'

She held out her hand, for no reason other than so he could touch her—the only touch that would ever be allowed between them. His own engulfed hers as he took it. No soft, smooth palms for this man; his were roughened, as if he knew hard work. The heat of him was like electricity rico-cheting up her arm as if it were a lightning rod, the shock exquisite and yet almost painful. Aston bowed over her, his lips never touching but his breath a warm gust against her flesh that left her quaking with pleasure, goose bumps pep-pering her skin, even on this mild evening.

'You look incomparable, as always.'

He towered above her. She wasn't a short woman, yet he was a man who could make her feel small and precious. His inky dinner suit wrapped a powerful body. A waistcoat, not of white or black, but of a deep-green threaded with gold and patterned with leaves. His vivid blue eyes seemed to be smiling behind a mask of a burnished pewter, golden horns curling from it. The expression moulded into the mask it-self, one of wry amusement, almost mischievous, yet with a bite. He looked like an embodiment of the chaos she craved.

'Thank you,' she said, wondering how she managed to speak at all.

Here was the man she'd been looking for. The one that stole her breath and almost all her reason every time she saw him. A man she'd first met when he'd come to talk about trade of his family's wine, then he'd conquered one of Hal-rovia's highest peaks. He'd conquered her with a mere smile.

'I'd hoped to see you tonight,' he murmured.

The breath hitched in her throat and she almost blushed.

She wanted to say, *And I, you.* But she wouldn't. It would give too much away, and her breeding taught her *never* to do that. Anyhow, Ana wasn't fool enough to believe anything could come of this. The man was notorious, linked with many beautiful women, though none had lasted longer than six months. Instead, she could dream. Dreams were all she really had.

'Who are you supposed to be?' she asked.

'Who do you think I am?'

With his horns and wicked gleam in his vivid blue eyes that would tempt the hardiest of mortals, he could be Lucifer himself. She wouldn't give him or his undoubtedly healthy ego the satisfaction, no matter how much she wanted to. Even though it was an ego rightly held, one that deserved praising.

'A satyr.'

His full and tempting lips curled, and his wickedness intensified. 'And will you be my nymph to frolic with?'

His voice was deep, softly spoken, words for them alone. Her body heated. Was spontaneous combustion a thing? If so, she was ready to burst into flames. What she wouldn't give to *frolic* with him, even if it was impossible. The flirting would always have to be enough.

'You have me mistaken. I'm the goddess Flora.'

'Ah.' That one word contained so much as his gaze drifted over her in appreciation. Everywhere it slid, she sensed it like the stroke of his fingers. 'You also have me mistaken. I'm a god.'

She didn't doubt it. 'Who?'

That curl of his lips again, then he let out a pained kind of sigh.

'You disappoint me, Your Highness. I thought you might have guessed, given my family's history.' He held his arms out to the side and took a bow. 'Bacchus.'

Now it was her turn to give him an appraisal and take him in with no shame. The height and breadth of him. His pristine dinner suit, stitched so finely it seemed as if it had been sewn directly onto his powerful body. The way it gripped his shoulders and thighs led her to wonder what he would look like without any clothing at all. Her breaths came shallow and fast, not helped by the intricate corsetry of her dress that pulled her in and pushed her out in all the right places, giving her the perfect silhouette—or that was what her dress maker had told her. If she didn't watch out, she'd become quite dizzy. It was as if she'd been tossed into a kind of fever dream she didn't want to wake from.

'The lack of toga tripped me up.'

A waiter walked past. Aston snatched a glass of champagne for each of them. The Girard family's Grand Cru, their Soleil label. It was one of the reasons Aston had been invited here. Ana took a sip and the perfect bubbles sparkled across her tongue.

Another waiter came with canapés. Aston selected one delectable looking bite for himself. She'd eaten a light meal before she'd come. Her mother would never have approved of her having more, no matter how sublime the palace kitchen's creations. Her Majesty believed it was unseemly to consume finger food, and heaven help it spilling on a gown. Ana shook her head, regretting it the moment the waiter left.

Aston finished his canapé and took another healthy sip of his champagne, reported to have been named after him by his parents. He was a man who seemed to relish life and the pleasure it could provide him, like the god he claimed to be tonight.

'I do believe Bacchus is most often portrayed...' he leaned forward, and she leaned in towards him '...naked.'

The delicious sensation of heat scorched over her again,

no doubt colouring her cheeks. Her parents would be outraged. She was...*enthralled*.

Unbidden imaginings began to drift into her consciousness: how he might look when the refinement of his perfect evening dress was stripped away to bare skin. She'd never much thought of such things before but, the moment she'd first been introduced to him, those kinds of erotic visions had clung to the darkest recesses of her consciousness like a limpet.

Where was the perfect princess tonight? It was as if she'd disappeared. But what was the Spring Ball if not something where, for a little while, she could allow herself the fantasy that she might flirt with a man like Aston Lane and ignore the expectation that she was to marry a prince? Especially when said prince wanted her sister rather than her.

'I don't know whether I should be relieved or disappointed, Mr Lane.'

He chuckled, the deep, throaty sound rolling over her with all the thrill and expectation of thunder heralding a storm. Even under his imposing mask she could see the corners of his eyes crinkling. 'It didn't seem the kind of party where either mode of dress, or lack thereof, seemed appropriate.'

She shouldn't ask, but she couldn't help herself. The world in which she moved was a rarefied one. 'And how often do you attend those sorts of parties?'

He winked. 'Whenever I'm invited.'

Though she wasn't entirely sure he was being serious, from the pictures taken by the dreaded paparazzi she could well believe it. Not that she had often taken to the Internet to look at him—not at all. Yet his existence seemed intoxicating, like the champagne for which his family was renowned, full of sparkle and...life.

'You clearly move in different circles to me.'

'I believe the goddess of spring and fertility and the god of wine and ecstasy would move together extremely well if they found themselves in the same circle.'

He leaned into her again. She leaned into him. It was as if they *needed* to be close to one another. She couldn't help it, absorbing the warmth which seemed to radiate from him, catching his scent—green and fresh, with a bite. 'Think of the things we might do.'

The things she imagined… She'd watched one video of him free-climbing, the way he'd tackled the rock face, the sheer power of him lifting himself. His strength astonished her, the focus… She'd spent days wondering what all of that power and focus would be like when fixed on her. Yet, no matter how she might have dreamed, here they were.

'Sadly, we're mere mortals, not gods.'

'You'd make a man feel like one.'

His voice was like a murmur, as if he were imparting some deep secret. Her breath caught. Everything seemed to still. She could take compliments, but Aston Lane scrambled her brain, and all sensible thought fled. For a moment, she *yearned*. Instead, Ana took a gulp of the chilled bubbles as the warmth of a blush rose to her cheeks again. Everything about this, them here together in this magical forest, seemed to speak of possibilities.

'And I hear congratulations might be in order, if you believe what you read.'

Reality came back in a rush. It was like being doused in a bucket of iced water.

'What have you been reading?'

'You and Prince Caspar. A joining of the houses of Montroy and Santori. *Marriage*.'

He said the last word as if it was something poisonous.

It was a salutary reminder of who they both were, of what her parents would and wouldn't allow for Halrovia's perfect princess. She took a slow breath, not wanting the moment to end. What did it matter if she clutched onto the fantasy for a little while longer? Reality could wait, although it was time for a little truth. She took another sip of the perfect champagne to fortify herself.

'Are you a betting man, Mr Lane?'

Whilst many people might believe he had no limits, there were things Aston did not do. He wasn't cruel. He didn't toy with women's hearts and he most certainly did not corrupt virgins. Not that there were any in the circles in which he mixed. Yet here he was, in a secluded corner of a ballroom wishing for a blistering moment that he didn't have his principles.

Tonight, Princess Anastacia was a goddess embodied in human form. Regularly feted as the most beautiful woman in Europe, her style was coveted and copied by women around the world. It was no surprise. He'd first met her on a trade mission, poised and every bit the 'perfect princess' the press had dubbed her. As cool as the snow-capped peaks for which Halrovia was renowned. The 'Ice Princess', as some of the less kind commentators called her.

There was nothing icy about her tonight. She looked like the most exquisite hothouse bloom. Almost…fecund, with her slender waist and the gentle flare of her hips, her breasts swelling above a neckline that scooped low. Her blonde hair wasn't in a tight chignon, as was her usual style, but spilling over her shoulders in gleaming waves. She wore a dress that, when he'd first seen it, had made his breath stutter, because from a distance his fertile imagination had almost convinced him she was naked underneath, covered only by twisting vines and flowers.

Are you a betting man, Mr Lane?

Those luscious lips of hers were parted, as if in anticipation. He could read the signs from her throaty voice, the way her pupils darkened behind her mask. He knew them well. In other circumstances, he'd bet he could have her in his bed within an hour. What an enticing thought, albeit an impossible one in *any* circumstances.

'I've been known to take a risk or two.'

More than one or two. His parents constantly tried to get him to settle down, especially now he'd announced his next conquest: a plan to climb Everest. His father's ice-axe was in his office, ready to join him as he summited. That news had not gone down well over a dinner of cassoulet at the family's château. He'd two years of gruelling training ahead of him, something that his mother and father could never understand.

Live for me.

They were last words his brother Michel had spoken to him, said years ago when his brother's time had run out. The pain might now cut more like a blunt blade than a sharpened one, but it was ever-present. Still, from that day, Aston had vowed to live life enough for both of them.

But tonight wasn't about loss. It was about living, the promises he'd made: a soft launch of Girard Champagne's Grand Cru, Soleil. Aston was all about the champagne which had made his family famous. What was the saying? *Wine, women and song...* Give him wine and women any day. His family's incomparable champagne and the magnificent woman before him with her eyes sparkling the pale blue of aquamarines and her plump lips a soft and pouty rose. Except, she was the marrying kind. The kind he would never touch. The kind that might cause him to lose focus...

He knew well what a loss of focus could do to a man, the fatal consequences. Michel had paid that awful price. Anyhow, why settle down when life was a feast to be gorged upon and not a Spartan meal for two? Though he wondered whether Anastacia Montroy wasn't the type of woman he'd always hunger for, one for whom his appetite would never be sated...

The princess's lips curled into an enigmatic smile. 'Then tonight you should lay all your money down on my never being engaged to Prince Caspar.'

Excellent.

Though why that word should hook his imagination like a fish on the end of a line he couldn't say. Her observation was only interesting because, politically, she and Santori would make the perfect couple, even though that thought made his fists involuntarily clench. At least she didn't seem aggrieved. However, his observation didn't change the reality—she was off-limits to anything other than some flirting, with the desire to make her flawless golden skin flush once more, never anything further and *never* anything over which her family would call for pistols at dawn.

Princess Anastacia raised her glass and drained it; no elegant sips for her any more. She looked as if she wanted to celebrate, not seek commiseration.

'You don't seem unhappy about that revelation,' he said.

She lifted one slender shoulder in a nonchalant shrug. Everything about her was so measured and perfect. How he'd love to be the one to mess her up, if only a little, to see the princess wild and unrestrained. Since his brother's death, it had been his mission to take every adventure and keep the promise he'd made on the day Michel had died. Princess Anastacia looked as if she needed a few adventures of her own, not an arranged marriage to some stranger, prince though he may be.

The princess looked out over the crowd to couples on the dance floor, almost in yearning. He followed her gaze. Santori was there, dancing with a woman in a glittering frost-blue ball gown. Was Anastacia wishing she were there in his arms, rather than here, perhaps rueing the loss of the prince to another? If she regularly hit the 'world's most beautiful' lists, being passed over must sting. All he knew was that Santori was a fool if he couldn't see the worth of the woman before him.

'Since you're not about to be swept away into some fairy tale, would you care to dance?' he asked.

If a prince was happy enough to pass up his chance to get this woman into his arms, Aston would take it instead, for the next few moments at least. He held out his elbow. She took it, her touch light and delicate, her fingers tipped in shell-pink polish.

The princess looked up at him and smiled. 'Who's to say the fairy tale isn't what we make of it, Mr Lane?'

It was as if he'd been flung into the lava flow of the last volcano he'd trekked up. He *burned*. He couldn't wait for their bodies to be aligned, moving in synchronicity, even if it was only on a dance floor. Aston led her through the crowd as people turned, watching them—the bad boy of champagne and the perfect princess.

On the dance floor, couples drifted to the rhythm of a string quartet playing something slow and sultry. He took her into his arms, his hand spanning her narrow waist. The warmth of her seeped into his palm. Her scent was sweet and fresh, like a flower garden.

Sweet. He must not forget.

Virginal. Shouldn't forget that either.

As he looked down at her then, into her azure eyes framed by the mask of tiny butterflies, the reasons for that seemed hazy.

'You should call me Aston.'

'Should I?'

Her lips parted and he drew her closer as they moved in perfect step to the music. She didn't hesitate, instead melting into him. Who'd have guessed that Princess Anastacia would be the perfect fit? The crowd seemed to fade, as if it were only the two of them, and the music with its seductive lilt.

'What should I call you?'

He craved to hear her say his own name, breathily, gasping in his ear as he made love to her for hours. Her lips parted. Could she tell what he was thinking?

'"Your Highness" would be proper.'

'What if you didn't want to be proper?'

Even in the low light her cheeks darkened. The beautiful flush of colour made her glow. 'I always am.'

The words sounded bitter in her mouth. Poor princess. Did she feel trapped in her cage, gilded and beautiful though it was? He swung her out. She executed a perfect turn and came back into his arms in a rush, even closer now, if that were possible.

'Lucky for you, I'm not. For tonight, I'll call you *ma déesse*…'

Her mask shifted, the little butterfly wings fluttering as she raised her eyebrows. '"My goddess"?'

'Oui. Bien sûr.' He pitched his voice lower, softer, as if the words he was about to impart were a secret between them. 'Of earthy delights.'

'Don't you mean "earthly"?'

'No. I know exactly what I said.'

He might have imagined it, but he was sure she let out a sigh. Even part-hidden behind her mask her gaze pinned him as they simply moved together, lost to everything bar the music, in the same rhythm as his heartbeat. Then the music began to slow, a coda to his time with her, even though he didn't want the dance to end. The string quartet stopped playing and, whilst he loosened his hold, she didn't move from his arms. Another song started. Keep moving? Let her go? Take her to a darkened corner, press her against the wall and kiss her?

So many choices…only one of them a good one.

'May I cut in?'

Aston wheeled round and almost shouted, *No!* Yet the voice was from the man to whom Princess Anastacia was supposed to become betrothed tonight. Perhaps Santori had seen the light and wanted an engagement after all? It was more than he could ever give this woman.

'Of course,' he responded, almost through gritted teeth, but he still handed her off, watching as she was swung away from him into the crowd of dancers. Though, as the couple came into view once more, Anastacia wasn't looking at her prince.

She was looking at him.

Aston turned away from her. Tonight was about business, not pleasure, and business was something he did well. Yet, as he stalked back into the throng of people, he couldn't shake the intense sensation he had misplaced something vital.

Something that one day he'd crave to recover.

CHAPTER ONE

Six months later

ANA SAT AT her dressing table, hardly able to look in the mirror. Today was supposed to be an important day, one she could barely draw up enough emotion to dread. Her mother had said she must make an effort. When had there been a time in her life when she hadn't; hadn't done everything that was demanded of her? She gritted her teeth, adjusting her fringe and the rest of her hair to hide the angry pink scar that marred her temple, threading into her hairline.

Her doctors promised that there was revision surgery for it, and the other scars that were more easily hidden by her clothes. They said that they'd fade in time. If only the memories would, and that all her scars could be so easily dismissed. She shut her eyes against the jolting vision of crushing steel and shattering glass, then the ominous silence, hands pulling her from a crushed vehicle, the pain, a voice in her ear...

Ana sucked in a sharp breath, supressing the memory. Her heart pounded a panicked rhythm, a sick acid sensation climbing to her throat. She swallowed it down, opened her eyes and truly *looked* at herself, staring at the woman who looked back at her. Still Anastacia Montroy, but in all other ways changed. It felt as if she'd aged a hundred years in the space of a mere six months.

The door of her room cracked open, and her mother swept inside in a perfumed glide. If Ana had once been called 'perfect' she'd only been a pretender to the title, because her mother was in *all* ways a picture of perfection. Never once had Ana seen her with a hair out of place, her clothing anything other than immaculate. Today, the Queen was dressed in a pale-blue suit that accentuated her eyes of a similar hue and made her blonde hair gleam like spun gold. Pearls clasped at her throat, she looked as cold and forbidding as the snow-topped mountains for which Halrovia was famed.

'Incomparable', her father had once said of her mother; he hadn't necessarily meant it as praise. Her mother wielded that perfection like a blade. Her sister, Priscilla, had once been the recipient of most of her mother's cutting comments. No longer. Prince Caspar had proposed to Cilla soon after the Spring Ball and she'd moved to Isolobello, becoming assistant to Halrovia's ambassador there till she and Caspar eventually married—a clever request of the Crown Prince to get his beloved closer to him, one that her parents hadn't been able to refuse.

Now the Queen's laser focus was turned on her. The once 'perfect princess' who had been dubbed…imperfect, a disappointment, when she'd spent her *whole* life trying to live up to the impossible standards set for her by her family, the public, the press. She'd never failed.

Till that dreadful night six months ago. In the aftermath of the Spring Ball, the press had constantly questioned how Prince Caspar could have passed up a famed beauty like her, wondering why he'd chosen Cilla, unfairly dubbed the 'plain princess', instead of the supposedly perfect one. The shock of *that* announcement had caused a stir, ripples in the press that lasted to this day, where she was concerned at least. What everyone had failed to realise was that Ana couldn't capture a man whose heart had already been taken from the moment he'd set eyes her sister.

She'd been angry for Cilla, who few people had ever seen the true worth of because she didn't fit the Montroy family mould. And for herself, because no one could look past her appearance to the very heart of her. That fateful night, everything had reached breaking point. She'd been so tired of being good all the time, the press asking what was wrong with the perfect princess. Why hadn't she been able to snag a prince? All she'd wanted was to live a little. To go out, like any young woman in her circle might, to take to the casinos and clubs of Monaco. To flirt and have fun. To wear a scandalously short red dress. To pretend for a moment she wasn't perfect, that she simply…*was*.

But it had ended in a terrible car accident that had changed her life. She considered herself lucky—at least her body hadn't been completely shattered, unlike that of the friend she'd been in the vehicle with. Carla was still in hospital undergoing rehabilitation. She might have been able to walk today, had she not been in the company of a princess.

You'll scar, and no one but me will love you now…

That voice…a man's voice…whispered as she'd lain bleeding, trapped in the wreckage of the car. No one had believed that the accident had been something more sinister, that it had had something to do with who she was rather than a series of random events culminating in one, catastrophic moment… Some days, even she'd convinced herself it was a product of her shocked brain. Yet she'd *heard* it.

No one but me will love you now…

Ana almost laughed. How true that portent had become in the voice of the man she'd been trying to escape on the night of the accident. The man no one believed had been sending her anonymous letters ever since he'd glimpsed her on the night of the Spring Ball.

She'd always received fan mail—but then some had begun to come in via her private secretary that made her senses scream on high alert. It was the way they'd been phrased. They'd sounded just like the man she was sure wrote them, somehow…oily. She hadn't been able to put her finger on it, other than the sentiments had made her deeply uncomfortable, made her skin crawl. Still, everyone had dismissed her concerns. Her parents had said she was just being dramatic.

That night had changed the way her country and her family saw her. Had left its terrible scars, physical and emotional. Yet no one seemed to care.

Ana greeted the woman who was more monarch than mother.

'Mama.' She gave a small curtsey.

Her mother's eyes narrowed, looking her up and down, no doubt searching for flaws in the conservative navy dress she wore with its high neck, long sleeves, skimming just below the knee. Impeccably tailored, it hid a multitude of sins…or the evidence of her failings.

The Queen's lips thinned. 'You're wearing that? You look more like a nun than a woman about to become engaged.'

The problem was, she didn't feel like a woman about to become engaged, particularly since she didn't yet know who her mythical fiancé was supposed to be. A fire of anger lit in her belly. At least with Caspar they'd been given a choice—thrust together on an expectation, yet never forced.

This? It had been presented to her as a *fait accompli*. Ana felt as if all her choices had been stolen from her. She suspected it was because her parents believed she'd made such a hash of capturing Caspar's attentions that they wouldn't give her a chance to ruin an arrangement with another person they'd chosen for her. She took a slow breath, through the hurt and the ache.

'The dress has pockets,' she said, hating that her voice somehow sounded small.

Her mother sniffed, looking down her nose at Ana from her towering heels.

'Why does a princess require pockets?'

To hold her phone, which gave her constant updates and alerts about the man she believed had followed her to Monaco that terrible night. He was from one of Halrovia's oldest families. Rich, titled...*entitled.* Count Hakkinen, the son of one of her father's former advisors. A man who had caused the skin on the back of her neck to prickle unpleasantly the moment she'd been introduced to him.

Yet what confessions could she make when no one believed her? They'd whisper that she was attention seeking, not telling the truth, trying to avoid the consequences of her actions for her friend and the crown.

'Why do I need to marry?'

She'd been prepared to marry for duty six months ago, but the near-death experience had brought her life into sharp focus. Why should she settle down, be stuffed back into a box everyone had created for her, rather than one she'd designed herself? Especially to someone whose name she didn't know. She'd planned for Caspar, after having been pushed in his direction—she had at least *liked* him—but now she found herself wanting more. Why wasn't she allowed to find love?

Her mother stalked up to her and Ana almost took a step back. Queen Beatrice reached out and tugged at Ana's fringe over her temple, adjusting it some more, eyes narrowing.

Had she been able to frown, Ana was sure one would have bisected her mother's brow. Yet her mother would allow nothing to crease her flawless skin, no lines at all—smiling, laughing, nothing.

'You well know the answer to that question.'

The fire in Ana's belly guttered and died. It was true; she did know the answer.

When she'd seen Hakkinen in the casino that night, she'd been sure he was following her. She'd caught glimpses of him in every club they'd visited, lurking in the shadows, as if waiting to strike. She'd been terrified. She'd needed to get away before he did something terrible to her, to Carla.

They'd hurried into a cab. The driver was unlicensed, had drunk too much and taken prescription medication. Ana hadn't known, or she would *never* have entered the vehicle. Her family had had to spend a fortune to buy the horrible, grainy pictures of her being extracted after the accident so they would never hit the news services. Scrubbing the internet. Photos of her dress as red as the blood marring her skin, Hakkinen by her side...

During her recovery, the news stories about her had become even worse. There'd been talk of her being a 'precious princess', shirking her duty when all she'd wanted to do was hide from the looks of pity from the doctors, nurses and palace staff, because of her scars. As if all the charity work she'd done was meaningless in the face of her imperfections, even the new charity she'd started to little fanfare: the Cygnet Centre. It paid for children in medical need around the world to have life-changing reconstructive plastic surgery. Despite everything, she hadn't been allowed time to recover from the wounds to her body and her soul. Not to mention wanting to hide away from her fear that the man who'd been pursuing her might be lying in wait...

Then the focus of the press had turned onto Gabriel, Halrovia's Crown Prince—her somewhat uptight brother, yet a person who cared deeply about his country. They'd searched for flaws in him, ones he and his family kept hidden. Palace courtiers had fears for her family's very existence.

Those were cracks she'd brought to the family's foundations. And now? The atonement was hers to make. She needed to become perfect again to save the royal family's reputation.

She wrapped her arms around herself till her mother gave her *the look*, one that froze like the winter wind. So she adjusted how she stood, as she had been taught, arms relaxed by her side, though everything about her was wound tight.

'Who is this man I'm supposed to become betrothed to?'

It seemed important—*should* be important. Like every princess who was required by their family to marry a suitable prince if humanly possible, she knew who the available ones were. The ones you hoped might be chosen, the ones you didn't...

'*Will* become betrothed to, Anastacia. I'm sure you'll be satisfied with him. He's acceptable in almost every way.'

'*Almost* every way?'

The Queen's lips pursed, as if she'd tasted something unpleasant. 'He's a commoner. However, his mother and I knew each other at school.'

Her mother still hadn't given her a name, but it was pointless asking again. When the Queen didn't want to do something, she didn't, end of story.

'You and Father said I'd be expected to marry a prince, or at the very least nobility...' Ana's voice sounded somehow distant, as her mind worked through the possibilities and came up with nothing.

Her mother tilted her head to the side and gave a tight half-smile. Ana hated that look. It screamed of pity, that her daughter wasn't the vaunted beauty any longer, as if her scars had somehow tarnished her worth. Because in the end what Ana had learned was that all anyone had truly cared about was how flawless she'd appeared—her mother most of all. What that look of the Queen's told Ana was that no available prince must want her.

Who she was inside didn't matter at all. Yet she was more than how a dress might hang on her body, or her good skin, shiny hair or anything that had to do with how she looked.

Her mother's private secretary entered the room without knocking, giving a discreet cough. 'Ma'am…'

Her mother checked her elegant platinum watch, then pinned Ana with her glacial gaze. 'It's time.'

With those words she began walking to the door and Ana followed. The Queen's heels clicked like daggers striking the marble floor of the hall, tap, tap, tap. Ana felt as if the sound was counting down the time to her doom.

'Halrovia's royal family has been the country's bastion for over four hundred years, upholding everything that is right and good. Each of us must do our duty for the family, Anastacia. Your turn comes now. Your *second* chance to do your duty.'

A terrible sense of unfairness overwhelmed her. Before the accident, she'd accepted that her life was in many ways her country's. Had worked tirelessly with charities, even the one she'd recently established on her own. She'd done everything that had been expected of her. When had it ever been enough? She'd toed the line, had never stepped out of bounds. She'd come to realise that the love and acceptance of her parents was entirely conditional.

Bile began to rise to her throat.

'Caspar wanting Cilla was not my fault.'

The sharpness of her mother's responding gaze would have eviscerated anyone else. Once, Cilla had borne the brunt of her mother's disapprobation; now it was turned on Ana.

'Yet why did he choose her over you? What did you do?' The accusation stung because it was the question everyone else was asking too, and the question that was unasked: *what is wrong with you?*

'I didn't do anything. I was myself. *That* was the problem. I was the wrong daughter of the House of Montroy. Caspar and Cilla fell in love.'

To her, it seemed romantic. Her sister always sounded so happy when they spoke on the phone, inviting her to visit Isolobello any time she wanted, especially if she needed an escape from the expectations that bound her.

'*Love.* What use is that when it makes you forget where your duty lies? It had always been the hope of our family that you and Caspar would be together. No matter. When you're finally married, it will silence the critics. Your father and I are resolved. This is a sensible choice.'

What sort of man did her parents believe was sensible? It brought to mind someone bland, grey-suited, grey-haired, maybe older. Perhaps bland and sensible were good? She could melt away from publicity and everyone would forget her. There'd be no more pity, there'd be nothing. She'd simply disappear. She could live her life any way she chose without the public or her parents caring about her. Yet why did those thoughts make her feel that she'd be missing out on something real?

They approached her father's study. The huge, oak doors loomed ominously in the otherwise bright hall, the windows to her left giving her views of the capital of the country she'd spent her whole short life representing. Her footsteps slowed. She didn't want this, not right now. Maybe if she had more time... Her breaths came short and sharp. Where was all the air?

Her mother stopped, her private secretary at her side. 'Anastacia, compose yourself. This man clearly found you attractive at the Spring Ball...'

Her heart stuttered for a moment as conflicting emotions coursed through her. Relief. Excitement. Dread.

'He danced with you three times.'

Aston Lane? It couldn't be. Yet he was the only man she'd danced with three times that night. Once, she might have been thrilled about this. But everything was different now. She wasn't the perfect princess any more. She was someone else entirely. Someone she didn't recognise. The woman Aston had danced with at the Spring Ball had ceased to exist and another person had replaced her. That woman wanted to hide away and lick her wounds. Her now seemingly childish fantasies about a man she might have dreamed of were one thing, but reality?

You'll scar, and no one but me will love you now...

She was flawed in every way. For a few blissful moments that night, she'd been thought of as a goddess. She'd held tight onto that, a precious memory when everyone was now so focussed on her flaws. She wasn't a goddess any longer.

Her mother's private secretary gave the door a sharp knock and Ana flinched as it opened. Her heart beating a sickening rhythm, her breath heaving in her chest. Ana followed her mother into the room, wishing time could simply rewind. She fixed her gaze on her father, who stood as they entered. He looked satisfied, perhaps relieved. Her mother broke into as warm a smile as Ana had ever seen, for a man she could not look at as the breath crushed in her chest like the weight of the world sat upon her.

'Mr Lane,' her mother said in greeting. 'How pleasant to see you again.'

Aston was a man who'd always tried to live in the moment. Since Michel had died, he'd fought not to dwell on the past, or fear for the future. In recent months, he'd been suffocating in both, a state forced upon him by his parents. Now the future had been thrust in his face in the shape of a woman— a seeming lifeline, a breath of oxygen. A woman he'd only admit in his quieter moments he'd thought far too much about in the months since the last Spring Ball.

You must marry...

It was something he'd not contemplated for himself, yet an edict from his parents he couldn't ignore—to settle down when settling for anything was not where he saw his future lying.

When he did consider the future, it was tied up in the direction of his business interests or the next adventure to take, the next mountain to climb—keeping his promises to Michel, carrying out his dream of standing on the top of the whole world with his father's ice-axe in his hands. What man *wouldn't* want that, instead of being tied to another? A wife would only distract him from his dreams. Yet his parents had been clear—the Girard Champagne company was to be left to his cousin unless Aston managed to find a wife.

When his training for the Everest climb had first commenced months before, the hints had come. First from his father then more explicitly from his mother, until their last argument. "Find a suitable wife," they'd demanded. What the hell did that even mean? Why force this upon him?

Though he suspected what their reasons might be. Finding a wife to gain his inheritance of the company whose history ran rich in his veins would consume all of his time. Time he'd planned to spend training for the promise he'd made to his brother, to climb Everest. But if he married? He suspected his mother and father believed that the prospect of a wife would be enough to entice him to abandon the climb altogether and focus his attentions on the business alone. That he'd lose his urge to conquer mountains if he could find contentment closer to home. They presumed, since they were happy in their own marriage, that marriage was a state he wanted for himself.

Why do you always need a bigger mountain to climb Aston? Isn't living life well challenge enough for you?

His mother's words. She'd never understand. Aston took a deep breath through the anger still burning like acid through his veins at the hurt over what his parents had demanded of him. Blackmail was never something he'd expected in his life, especially from them.

He'd almost told them to go to hell. His fortune was his own. Whilst some might have accused him of being one, he was no 'nepo-baby'. Give him a hundred dollars, he'd turn it into a hundred thousand without blinking. He had investments that were all his. He didn't need Girard. Yet he hadn't been able to walk away. The wine was his life. Some laughed and said that, if you cut him, he'd bleed champagne. He wouldn't lose the company to a man like his cousin— someone who did the books but didn't understand the company's *soul*.

In any case, they were wrong. Nothing, nobody, would prevent him from fulfilling his vow. Marrying for love? All love did was hold you back, destroyed your resolve, distracted you. Distractions on a mountain could have fatal consequences—a fall, shattered bones...

I want to stand on top of the whole world.

Words he'd often heard his brother say. And now Aston was determined to fulfil a promise. To carry out Michel's dream of standing on the summit of Everest with their father's ice-axe in his hands.

He clenched his fists, then relaxed them. Memories of Michel had no place here. For now, they needed to stay locked in a vault of the past.

'Your Majesty. Your Highness.' He gave a short, polite bow, focussing on the princess, even though this was a done deal. He might not be happy about it, but he wasn't ill-mannered enough to show it to the woman who was to become his wife. 'The pleasure is all mine.'

That was no lie, so far as Anastacia was concerned. He'd forgotten the effect she had on him, relishing and rejecting it at the same time. The sight of her was a physical thing, like a blow to the head knocking the sense right out of him. Though, as he looked at her, he realised that she seemed little happier than he was at the prospect of an engagement. He didn't question why that thought irritated him, like a burr in his shoe.

In fact, she looked almost unrecognisable from the woman whose visage had crept through the cracks in his consciousness more times than he'd cared to admit. At the Spring Ball she'd been like a tropical ginger flower, vibrant with the hint of spice. Now it was as if she were an arctic white peony—pale, impossibly beautiful yet would bruise at the merest touch.

Today, instead of a rosy flush of health her skin held no colour, as if the life had been sucked from her. Her eyes were a little too wide, her features pinched. Her hair had changed; no cascading golden waves or sophisticated chignon, which had once been her signature. Now it fell shorter around her shoulders, with a heavy fringe framing her face.

In a plain, albeit impeccably fitted, conservative dress, she looked as if she were heading for a day in court rather than celebrating her betrothal.

Where was the earthy goddess he'd danced with at the ball six months ago? Where, even, was the 'perfect princess'? He'd not paid much attention to the goings on in Halrovia in the past months. He'd been too immersed in the launch of Girard's latest signature Grand Cru and the early stages of training for his climb on Everest.

Then his parents' edict had come, and his focus had turned to finding a suitable wife. He'd even engaged a professional matchmaker, until he'd realised only thoughts of one woman entered his head when contemplating marriage: Anastacia Montroy. Once that idea had struck, it wouldn't let go. No one else would do. How could a princess be anything other than suitable?

The King motioned to a lounge area in the cavernous study. 'Please, let's take a seat.'

As they moved towards the seating area, the Queen gave her daughter a quelling look. The atmosphere in the room was an uncomfortable one. Aston accepted it was likely that monarchs rarely had commoners entirely relaxed in their presence, however there was an undercurrent here he couldn't place.

It was at odds with the King's reaction when Aston had seeded the idea of his interest in their daughter, with his expectations low as a commoner but his hopes high because of their family connection. From first mention to final agreement, it had fallen into place with laughable ease. When they'd said yes, it had been a personal triumph, the first step in reclaiming his family's legacy and fulfilling the promise to his brother. He'd been told Ana was satisfied with the arrangement, and he hadn't much thought about it till now, because this was a business deal like any other.

What had changed? If only he could get the princess alone to ask her. Aston was sure any reluctance she might have could be easily overcome. He wouldn't allow anything to impede the marriage he'd negotiated.

They all took their places, the Queen in one grand brocade chair, the King in another. He took the sofa, supposing it was natural for her parents to seat the soon-to-be betrothed couple together. With another meaningful glance from her father, Anastacia took a seat with him, but not close as one might expect if this was to be a happy or desired union. She lowered herself elegantly onto the cushions, pressing herself into a corner, crossing her legs at the ankles, folding her hands in her lap.

'We should discuss dates for a wedding,' the King said.

'It's modern times, so we don't propose a long engagement,' the Queen added.

That got Anastacia's attention. Her head jerked up and she stared at her parents as though she didn't recognise them. When he'd been forced to consider marriage, he hadn't thought of a long engagement either. Whilst his parents weren't old, his mother's insouciant attitude to her high cholesterol and her love of good food, wine and the occasional sneaked cigarette with friends, much to her doctor's dismay, made an earlier wedding of greater import than ever before.

Yet, even though this was a state he didn't want, he found his thoughts speeding straight to the wedding. Anastacia in her bridal whites, a veil over her face, walking down the aisle towards him. Given his views on love and marriage, he wasn't sure why the vision running through his head was so enticing, rather than leaving him cold. Pictures of a wedding night burst vivid in his head: Anastacia spread out on the bed, skin naked and exposed to him alone. Would he be the first man who'd ever seen her, who'd ever made love to her?

A burn lit inside him, something hot and demanding. His consciousness was assailed by a night and three dances when they'd moved seamlessly in each other's arms.

I believe the goddess of spring and fertility and the god of wine and ecstasy would move together extremely well...

If nothing else, they could have that together.

His fantasies from the night of the Spring Ball had been one thing. Now reality overcame him in a rush. He had to shut the thoughts down because there was no way he could politely adjust himself in his seat. The fact that he was sitting in this study, with his soon to be parents-in-law who were a king and queen, should have been enough to quell any errant desire. Yet he felt like a teenager again, with inconvenient erections springing up any time he'd thought about a girl, rather than a seasoned businessman of thirty-two. If the situation weren't so laughable, he might find it embarrassing.

He glanced over at Anastacia to ground himself in the reality of what he was being compelled to do, but she wasn't looking at him. She seemed intent on staring at her hands clasped in her lap, not relaxed in the chair, her back straight and stiff. As if she'd noticed him watching her, she unclasped her hands and reached one up to adjust her fringe.

'I thought...' Finally, Anastacia spoke. Not to him, but to her parents. They didn't seem to listen.

'As you would know, Mr Lane, our youngest daughter Priscilla is marrying the Crown Prince of Isolobello in eight months.'

Aston didn't know. He had no interest in the personal machinations of the royal family. His thoughts were on business, keeping his name in the will and climbing Everest. Anything else was peripheral. 'It wouldn't do for the weddings to clash, so we thought earlier rather than later.'

He glanced at Anastacia again. Any meagre colour in her cheeks drained away.

'Moth—Your Majesty—you know how long it takes to make a wedding dress.'

This was not going as he'd expected. What had happened between the night of the ball, when Anastacia been all flirtation, to now? He'd been passenger enough in this scenario, allowing their exalted majesties to direct the negotiations because he hadn't wanted the deal to sour. Now it was time to make a stand for the woman he didn't love, but would defend as his future wife.

'You'd look beautiful in whatever you chose to wear. Designers will fight to dress you for your wedding. No matter how soon the date, they'll achieve miracles for you.'

The faintest hint of colour bled back into her cheeks. The corners of her pouting pink mouth flicked into an almost-smile, before returning to a neutral line.

'Halrovia's designers are dressing royalty for our youngest daughter's wedding, Mr Lane. They have no time to spare, even for miracles.'

At her mother's words, Anastacia seemed to shrink further into herself. This was a woman who had swept across a ballroom, leaving people falling over themselves in her wake. A goddess. *Ma déesse*…his goddess. Becoming less didn't suit her. A pilot light of anger flicked to life in his gut.

'Then Her Highness can name a French designer and I'll ensure they have time for miracles.'

A silence fell over the room before the King clapped his hands. 'Excellent, then a dress will be no impediment. What date suits you for the wedding, Mr Lane? We can coordinate our diaries.'

With a quick wedding and honeymoon, he could ensure his inheritance was secure and make the climbing season for

Everest in eighteen months' time. His dream to conquer the highest summit and the training it required would be back on the agenda and hopefully soon to be on track. His parents would be unable to object, since he'd done what they'd asked. Even better, he'd be marrying a princess, one who'd been trained for a political type of marriage. There'd be no uncomfortable expectations such as love to complicate everything. He could live his life and she could live hers, because that's how she'd been raised. No complicated emotions to mess up everything. His focus would be uninterrupted.

Perfect. What his parents didn't understand was that he wasn't only living life for himself, but for Michel. For a promise between brothers that he wouldn't break.

'I'm in your hands, Your Majesties. Though perhaps Her Highness and I could have a discussion in private regarding the arrangements, since I've always considered a wedding is more about the bride than the groom.'

Her parents gave each other a quick glance, and to Anastacia a sharp one. Were they thinking to refuse him? How…quaint to believe they had any control over this where he was concerned.

He turned his attention to Anastacia. 'I suspect the garden would be pleasant enough at this time of the year, Your Highness.'

She smoothed her hands down her dress then stood with only a moment's hesitation. She looked down at him, her gazing morphing into something flinty, sharp, slicing right into him. He relished it, the flare of fire in her that burned, hinting at the woman beneath. The one who didn't want to hide. She raised an eyebrow and the corner of his mouth kicked up in response.

'Are you coming, Mr Lane?'

CHAPTER TWO

ANA WALKED THROUGH the vast palace halls with Aston beside her. He didn't try to make conversation. There was no flirtation. They moved in silence other than the echo of their footsteps on the polished marble floors. That didn't stop her body reacting to him. Her mind had blanked the moment she'd set eyes on Aston Lane, the first time since the Spring Ball, in his impeccable dark suit, crisp white shirt and vibrant blue tie, the colour of his eyes. Dressed for business, the only problem being the business was *her*.

Ana's thoughts churned as violently as her belly, which seemed as if it contained a nest of vipers, twisting and knotting. Only a short time ago, it might have been her dream for her parents to suggest marrying this man. It was a secret fantasy that had begun the moment she'd met him. Once, all the girls at her school had talked about crushes and practised signatures in the name of whichever boy had snagged their imagination. Back then, she hadn't understood, marvelling at the choices the other girls seemed to have had. All she knew was that she'd be marrying a prince and he'd be chosen for her.

On meeting Aston, she'd understood the strength of a crush. Thoughts of him had filled her waking moments, her dreams. Love. Marriage. Impossibilities. But what had they hurt? When immersed in those dreams, she'd been the

Anastacia before her accident, his goddess. He was the man who'd seen her, craved her. Her fertile imaginings had taken root when she'd been another person altogether.

Now she'd been thrust into a kind of nightmare.

She'd known there was an expectation she'd marry someone her parents had chosen for her, yet seeing Cilla and Caspar fall in love, rapidly, deeply and irrevocably, had planted a seed that perhaps it was something she could have too. That, whilst she might have to marry a prince, there was *hope* for more than a sterile relationship borne of duty. Something to aspire to.

Hope was such a cruel thing when so viciously cut down. She wasn't a goddess any more. She was unmistakably mortal, not the woman he'd met at the ball—the woman she'd wanted him to see, to take notice of. That woman was now a ghost. She clenched her fists, nails cutting into her palm. Her parents, she might excuse on a more charitable day. Aston...? She'd always thought of him like the elusive lynx that stalked the alpine forests here—wild and free, impossible to pin down. Somehow those thoughts had given her a futile kind of hope that maybe there was something more for her.

'Where are we going?' he asked.

She realised that she was walking faster now, though his long strides kept up with ease. Yet no speed was fast enough. She wanted to break into a run to escape this. The feelings. The humiliation that she was being sold for a quick wedding like the damaged goods she was.

'To the maze.'

It was a place she often went to contemplate. Deliberately taking wrong turns, sitting in the garden chairs placed at the dead ends, surrounded by the high hedges. Her parents never understood why she didn't simply take the shortcut straight to the centre, with its grand fountain and shaded pergola. She believed they missed the point. It was about the journey, not the destination.

'Trying to lose me so quickly?' he asked.

'What if I said yes?'

She arrived at the palace doors and opened them wide. The air was cool, the sunlight sudden and bright. Ana squinted.

Aston cocked his head. 'That would be disappointing. Since it seems like I've only found you again.'

She looked up at him and his intense gaze fixed on her, almost as bright and blazing as the sunshine outside. It was as if he was trying to peer right into the heart of her. She didn't want to be exposed, for him to witness her cracks, her flaws. He'd only known her as the perfect princess. She feared what he'd think of this changed version of herself.

'I wasn't lost. I was right here.'

Except she had been lost. In many ways, she was *still* lost. It was as if she had no tether at all.

'I was told you were happy with the arrangement. That suited me. There'd been plans for you to marry Santori without a fuss, so it seemed logical to me at the time.'

Logical. She didn't know why the use of that word in this situation stung. In her fantasies, she'd expected more—for him to want her, to love her. They'd been a safe kind of thing, and she'd known deep in her heart that they were unattainable. Now she only felt disappointment so heavy and oppressive it might crush her. That he was…settling.

Aston Lane was a man she'd always believed wouldn't sell out or sell himself, and yet he'd done that and bought her in the process, not for love but for some other reason. She'd thought he was a man who struck his own path. Yet he'd chosen a predictable one, in her world at least.

'How gratifying romance isn't dead.'

His expression changed to something fleeting, softer. 'I recognise the error. A goddess like Flora should be nurtured—worshipped.'

They hadn't even stepped into the sunshine and it was as if she'd gone up in flames, self-combusted at the thought of what his brand of worship might be. Oh, the tempting, tempting words slipping from his tongue... Was it the truth? Or was he like the snake in the garden of Eden, filling her head with pretty lies to get what he wanted?

She stepped through the doorway and down a short flight of sandstone steps to a gravel path. The tall yew hedges loomed large in front of them. The voice in the back of her head wouldn't stay quiet. What could he possibly want with her? He was a man with the world at his feet. Yet she drove those feet forward to the entrance of the maze, where she hesitated. Aston stopped beside her, his presence palpable, like a living thing it loomed so large.

'I think you'll find I'm not a goddess and that I have feet of clay.'

He made a show of looking down at her shoes and back to her face. His lips curled at the edges into the hint of a smile. 'Let me be the judge of that. I'm sure you have very pretty feet, even if of clay.'

She snorted, an un-princess-like sound, and caught herself. Aston grinned, so devastatingly handsome he could have taken her heart and torn it in two and she'd hardly have noticed, caught in the heat of his gaze, the glorious flash of his smile. But that was all a trap.

'Before an official announcement of any engagement, I'll be visiting my sister. She's invited me. I've said yes.'

It was truth and a lie. Her sister had invited her to stay but Ana hadn't accepted. She hadn't wanted to involve Cilla in her problems. Her sister had her own wedding to organise and deserved this time, the joy. But perhaps staying in Isolobello would give her some clarity to come to terms with what had happened. How this was the price she was expected to pay for that night in Monaco and what had followed. To accept the crushing of her dreams. Moreover, it could be an escape from everything, most of all herself.

Aston frowned for the briefest of moments.

'I see we have a lot to discuss.' The lack of an immediate refusal surprised her. Instead, he motioned to the maze's entrance. 'Let's begin. Which way, Princess?'

His voice was soft and deep, better suited to midnight than mid-morning. How would it sound, whispered into her ear in the darkness? She rubbed the centre of her chest, her heart fluttering against her ribs.

'I'll go straight ahead and you can take the left path.'

Whilst it wasn't sporting, the path ahead was a shortcut which took her directly into the centre of the maze. There she could sit and try to untangle her knot of feelings, whilst Aston tried to find her. She dared a look at him. The corner of his mouth had quirked again into a knowing smile. Was she so transparent?

'No chance. You know the way and I don't. I'd be lost without you.'

There was that fluttering in her chest again, joined by warm sensation flooding over her. Now they were outside, it was probably just the sun.

'Don't be so sure I'll show you the right direction,' she said. If she went straight ahead, he'd know she'd been planning to cheat, so she turned left. He laughed and a sparkle of goose bumps shimmied down her spine at the sound.

Aston adjusted his long stride to fit hers, walking at her side. 'I'm happy to follow.'

'I thought you'd be more of a leader.'

They strolled along the gravel path with the hedges above their heads. Something seemed to bloom in the moment, become almost pregnant with expectation, even though she wanted to run from it.

'I'm happy to see where you take me…for now.'

There was something slightly ominous in those last two words. 'Fine. How about you pick the way next?'

'You're prepared to take your chances with me? That's gratifying.'

'I'm curious to see whether you'll succeed or fail.'

They reached a crossroads in the maze. She knew the way, of course: right. Which would he choose?

'I'm not one for losing, Princess—at *anything*.'

More words of warning, she was sure. Aston stopped for a moment, as if deciding, then took a left. They walked a little way and reached a dead end.

'You're not going to make it easy for me, are you?' he asked, making his way to an alcove cut into the hedge. There sat a beautiful, creamy marble sculpture of a woman in classical style. A stopping point for contemplation. Aston studied the sculpture for a moment.

'Venus, I believe—the goddess of love,' he murmured with a grin. 'A sign, perhaps?'

'Of the universe mocking us.'

There was no love here; he knew it, she knew it. Once she might have had fantasises that this man could fall in love with her when no other woman had seemed able to tame him. But even she'd been sensible enough to know that they weren't rooted in reality.

Aston's expression was unreadable. Of course, being a renowned businessman, he'd have to know how to keep a poker face.

'The universe wouldn't dare mock a goddess.'

'And yet here we are, Mr Lane.' She nodded to the statue, one of her favourites in the whole maze. 'What do you think of love?'

He shrugged in a dismissive way. 'It's a strategic campaign of sorts.'

'You make is sound like a kind of…battle. Have you ever been in love?'

The answer to that question seemed important. Never having been in love herself, she could only guess what it was like. And she'd never know, because she'd never be given the chance. Once, it hadn't been something she'd dwelled on too much. Now a wash of sadness flooded over her.

'No.'

Short, sharp and to the point. No embellishments or sweet words. A hint of where he stood on the matter for future reference.

'Then how are you qualified to say anything about it?'

She looked up at him. His jaw now a hard line, his eyes flinty. 'I've lived long enough to bear witness.'

Ana was left to wonder, what had Aston seen that had left him so cynical? He'd never been in love. Was that by choice, or by cruel accident? What experience had framed his views? His parents? They were a reported love-match. His father was an Australian wine maker who'd fallen for Aston's mother. From what she'd read about Girard and the family story, it sounded romantic. Though who knew? People wrote about her family all the time and hardly any of it was the truth. She knew from bitter experience that the Internet was full of lies.

But, from Aston, she wanted to find out more. Curiosity gripped her. She'd seen enough to know women fluttered about him like hummingbirds to a feeder of sugar water.

He'd obviously had plenty of opportunity, so why *not* love? It seemed like a normal, human thing to desire. Hadn't the Trojan War been fought over it? For sure, wars had been fought over less…

Aston turned from Venus and began walking back the way they'd come as she hurried to catch up.

'Let's get on the correct path,' he said.

She wasn't sure he was talking about the maze.

They took no detours now, heading the right way, him striding forward with purpose. She reached her hand into her pocket and touched her phone, but its notifications had been blissfully silent. Her thoughts whirred as they walked, Aston's gleaming leather shoes crunching a relentless rhythm on the gravel. To the end, when she knew what Aston sought was a beginning.

Her questions remained. What was the point to this? It wasn't love. He wouldn't need to marry for…for…sex. She'd seen enough on the Internet of any number of beautiful women gracing his arm, looking very…satisfied, like cats having stolen a few laps of cream.

As they made the final turn, she couldn't hold in the question any longer.

'Why marry, if not for love?'

The words blurted out of her. His pace faltered briefly before picking up even faster. It was almost as if he was trying to outrun the question. A strange observation. She'd always believed a man like him to be fearless. He'd have to be, from what she knew of his mountaineering. Why should a question like that worry him?

'I'm told it's a good time to settle down,' Aston said, as they walked through the last break in the maze.

A beautiful fountain lay in the middle of an open space, with the water trickling with a gentle sound. To the left sat a small pergola covered in vines. Under it was a garden lounge, where she'd spent as many moments as she'd been allowed, contemplating. Too many moments contemplating him, if she was being honest with herself. Till the accident had stolen everything away from her.

He led her under the shade.

'Time?' she asked, curiosity getting the better of her. 'You're what—in your early thirties? Such an old man.'

He stood so tall and imposing beside her. His dark hair was slightly unruly, as if he'd raked his fingers through it rather than used a comb. A slight stubble shaded his jaw. He looked somehow…wild. Whilst staring out at the fountain was something Ana found calming, it appeared Aston didn't feel the same. His jaw was clenched hard.

'You'd be surprised.'

'I would. Who thinks it's a good time? Not you, by the sounds of it?'

Aston cocked his eyebrow. Those eyes of his were like shards of blue glass, gleaming and sharp.

'My parents.'

It sounded as if it cut him to say the words. His voice was rougher, in a way that spoke of pain, not pleasure.

'Do you do everything your parents tell you to do?' she asked. He struck her as a man who listened to no one.

Aston gave another seemingly nonchalant shrug, but she could see the tension marking every part of him. 'Do you?'

'Some of us have greater choices than others. You seem to have more than most. I was simply curious.'

'That's not all you're curious about. I can see you have so many questions begging to be asked.'

'How do you know?'

Most people didn't glean anything from her. Some unkind people had called her 'the ice princess'. That had been a carefully cultivated persona. Emotion hadn't been valued in her family. Ana had learned years before that to get any attention from her parents she needed to be quiet, dutiful. She was their mirror. They wanted only to see themselves when they looked at her. Viewing themselves as perfect, they'd expected the same from their children.

'A world of thought shows in your eyes. You seem… worried.'

He saw too much. It was as if a hand gripped her throat. Marrying meant there'd be no hiding from him. He'd lay all her wounds bare, wounds she wanted no one to see— particularly him. Because if she showed him her deepest hurts and fears and he didn't believe her, was disappointed? It would crush her.

'If I ask questions, will you answer them?'

He raised his eyebrows, as if surprised at the question. 'Of course. I'm not interested in secrets.'

A tension that had been ratcheting tighter and harder seemed to ease a little, like a garrotte loosened at the last moment, allowing her to take a breath. She didn't know this man, not really. Yet he seemed willing for her to know him. And there was one question her ego had been pressing to get an answer to.

'Why marry *me*?' He climbed mountains into the clouds whilst she was so…earthbound.

Aston quirked one dark, strong eyebrow. 'Why *not* marry you?'

Ana crossed her arms. 'That's no kind of answer. You promised.'

He blew out a slow breath. 'You're a princess. Our mothers knew each other. There's a family connection. You understand marriage for practical reasons, not love. Ergo, you're perfect.'

It all sounded so sensible, as her parents had claimed: *this is a sensible choice.* Yet her body carried the evidence of her imperfections which her mother couldn't let her forget. And she'd rather stopped wanting to be sensible...

'What if I don't want to be the perfect princess any more?'

'Who do you want to be instead?'

Wasn't that the question? 'I—I don't know.'

It hurt to make that admission, the uncertainty of it. She wanted so desperately to discover herself, but didn't know how. So much of her life had simply been dictated to her.

'No matter what you say, you'll always be perfect to me.' He looked down at her with his brilliant blue eyes, the colour of alpine gentians that dotted the mountains in spring. Something about him in that moment seemed so serious and solemn. Had she been a romantic any longer, she might have believed him.

Ana shook her head. 'You don't know me at all.'

He didn't deny it. 'There are other considerations.'

'Which are?'

'Do you remember the Spring Ball? How we danced?'

She'd been thrilled each moment in his arms at the strength of him. How safe she felt. How desired and desirable. Telling him as much might leave her exposed. When so many people had tried to strip her down to her essentials, she still wanted to keep some things close.

'I danced with many people that night,' she said, as if the time spent with him was of no consequence—another lie she told to protect herself.

Whilst she'd danced with many, she only remembered one. As long as she lived, she'd never forget how it had felt to be in his arms, which made this situation even more dangerous. He wanted the woman she'd been. That woman had been a fantasy created by others, like her own fantasises about him.

'Perhaps I should remind you.' Everything was hushed here at the centre of the maze, protected from the real world by the high hedges. The only sound aside from their voices was the twitter of birds in the shrubbery and the tinkle of the water from the fountain.

Aston stood back and gave her some space. 'Care to dance?'

CHAPTER THREE

'*Care to dance?*'

Memories came rushing back of a magical night when, for a few breathless moments, Ana had allowed herself to believe anything was possible. Aston held out his hand, palm up. She looked at it, recalling the way it had felt against her skin—not soft and weak, but the hands of a man who knew hard, physical work. Hands that, in the midnight hours, she'd dreamed of having on her body. It was so tempting to touch him again.

But, if he discovered her scars, what would he think of her? He was seeking perfection. In that, he'd be like everyone else. Pity from her family was one thing. She didn't think she could survive his pity too.

You'll scar, and no one but me will love you now...

She shut that voice down. It would *not* control her.

'There's no music,' she said, her voice sounding somehow faint and far away.

Aston cocked his head, as if listening. 'There's bird song. Some might say it's more beautiful than any string quartet you could provide.'

'This isn't a fairy tale where animals become musicians.' She looked down on her prim, navy dress. Her heart beat hard and fast, her breath catching in her throat. 'Or Fairy Godmothers wave a wand to create a ball gown.'

'Who's to say the fairy tale isn't what we make of it, Your Highness?'

Those words of hers were thrown back as a reminder. Was he mocking her? Yet the look on his face wasn't mocking. It was open. His lips curved in the slightest of smiles, as if he knew: she was *afraid*.

'A simple waltz, perhaps?'

If he'd known history, he'd have understood nothing about the waltz was simple. It had once had the power to shock society, couples close in each other's arms. Though she supposed times had moved on, and she didn't want to show him that she cared.

'Whatever you like,' she said with all the dismissiveness her princess breeding could muster, although recognised she probably sounded more petulant than haughty.

Reaching out, Ana placed her hand in his, trying to ignore the electric shock of sensation as their skin touched. Aston didn't move for a while, simply holding her gaze as firmly as he held her hand. The blue of his eyes, which should have been such a cool colour, seemed to smoulder as a spark lit in her belly, a pilot light of desire. She wanted to look away, to break the contact that seemed far too intimate, but she couldn't. It was as if he had her in his thrall.

Then he began to reel her in to him, slowly, like a fish on a hook, and she was helpless to resist. Whilst she might have tried to be dismissive of the man, there was no way she could dismiss this, dismiss the way their bodies fit. She was shorter than the last time they'd danced, wearing lower heels today. Something about being in his arms again gave her that same sense of feeling cherished and protected as last time. The tingling warmth flooded her, the *need* to press closer than was polite or even necessary.

It was cool under the vine-covered pergola yet being so

near to him was almost like being slowly roasted alive. She took a deep breath, which made it worse, because she sucked in the smell of him—something rich and earthy, like sun-warmed stone and the hint of mountain evergreens, a wild kind of scent that whispered of untamed peaks and daring. It was the essence of this man.

He began to move then in the one-two-three, one-two-three of the waltz, leading her. Her body melded seamlessly with his. He looked down at her. His hold was gentle, as if he were cradling a precious Ming vase. Although, hadn't life taught her that she was all too breakable? Yet something about this seemed so simple—their closeness, the desire for Aston to absorb her into him. The bright sunshine, the vibrant birdsong in the maze's privacy. Though the truth of it was impossibly complex—she'd wanted him, yet when presented with the reality she wanted to run away as far and as fast as she could.

To be with him would be her destruction. To run might save her. Because his desire for her was not for the woman, Ana Montroy, but for Princess Anastacia.

'I'm convenient.'

She needed to remind herself of the truth of it. He wanted *what* she was, the external; not *who*, the woman inside.

He leaned closer into her, if that were possible when they were dancing together. The rhythm of the dance lost now in a slow sway. His breath caressed her ear.

'Convenient doesn't have to mean cold.' His words were low and deep against her ear, the merest brush. A shiver of pleasure tripped through her. 'Without the complication of love, this can mean so much more. Passion without constraints. *Imagine* it.'

No constraints, when her whole life had been full of them. It was as if he reached into her heart and dragged out her deepest desires. Yet they were for the woman she'd been before. Letting go of constraints, restraint, never ended well.

One night in Monaco had proved that.

Ana pulled back and put some distance between them, even though they were still in each other's arms. She looked up at him. A gentle breeze picked up, flicking her fringe. His eyes narrowed a fraction and appeared to focus fleetingly on her temple. She wriggled out of his arms and turned away, adjusting her hair. Her heart began to beat thready in her chest. Had he seen her scar? Did he even know what had happened to her those months ago? She didn't know why it was so important that he not, only that she wasn't ready to flaunt her wounds, especially not to him.

It all seemed so futile. The spell cast over the past moments disappeared. The pressure simply to run began to weigh down on her.

He'd not pressed his claim to her hand in marriage, yet he clearly believed it was a done deal. So why was she hesitating? She had to fix the damage she'd caused to her family's name, the negative press.

Convenient doesn't have to mean cold.

He'd see *all* of her. The breath snagged in her throat. She wasn't prepared; she wasn't ready. She'd begun to realise that her whole life was one lived in a gilded cage. She'd always been a captive, no matter how pretty the bars that held her. Ana began to pace. A new tempo entered her head: duty, freedom, duty, freedom…

She almost walked into a solid, hard body.

'Goddess?' Aston had placed himself squarely in front of her.

Marriage to him was her duty. Duty be damned. She wanted to run. To freedom.

Going to see Cilla would give her space to think… That was all she needed right now.

'I'll give you my decision in two weeks,' she said. The words were hard to get out, her voice barely loud enough to hear, too breathy, like she couldn't get enough air. 'I'm visiting my sister—'

'You don't want to visit your sister.'

'I—I *do*.'

'It's a ruse. A delaying tactic. The question is why? What are your fears? Because no matter, if you tell me, I'll try to ease them for you.'

Was she so transparent now? That alone was terrifying. How could she possibly explain her fears to him? What could she say to him that she hadn't said to courtiers, her mother, father and brother? No one believed her apart from Cilla. She couldn't take that chance with him.

'Who's to say I fear anything?'

Lies. They could choke her.

The phone in her pocket buzzed once. She flinched. The only alerts she'd ever set were for Cilla and…she almost hyperventilated even thinking about him: Count Hakkinen. The man everyone believed was her rescuer. All they'd seen was him trying to pull her from the wreckage of the car, not how he'd been following her that night, the chase that had caused the accident in the first place. She should take the phone out and check, though she and Cilla had only spoken that morning…

Aston cocked his head. But the look on his face of patient acceptance told her she was transparent as glass.

'Do you want adventure? I'm an expert. Do you want to bargain with me? I'm a reasonable man, especially where you're concerned.'

Adventure? A bargain? He was offering her…choices.

Ana hesitated. She looked at him, *really* looked, and saw what she hadn't noticed before because she'd been tangled in her own head. The way his nostrils flared. The sheer intensity of his gaze, how it didn't shift from her. The desire burning from him. It was like he needed her in some way. A jolt ran through her, a spike of sensation totally unfamiliar.

A sense of her own power.

'What will it take?' he said. His voice was low, decadent, tempting as her favourite dessert. He was offering her the world right now, if she simply knew how to reach out and take it.

'What will it take for you to postpone the visit to your sister and come with me instead?'

Aston didn't chase women. He'd promised himself after Michel's accident and death that any pursuit was pointless. Sure, flirtation and the inevitable delicious consequences were all part of the game. But he'd never been about the long term, a fact he'd made clear to every woman he considered a liaison with. He'd never led anyone on with sweet words and false promises. He wished Michel had done the same all those years ago. He'd witnessed his brother's obsession and heartache over a woman, his loss of focus on a climb, with tragic consequences.

Nothing would distract from Aston's quest to climb Everest. His survival and success depended on it. He'd stand on top of the world with that ice-axe for Michel—for himself.

Yet here he was, pursuing as he'd sworn never to do. Instead of seeming like some tiring, futile kind of game, there was something about it that thrilled him. The planning. The chase. The prospect of bargaining. His heart pumping as if he were about to tackle a sheer rock-face—the seeming impossibility of it till he found that narrow handhold, a crack, a way in.

Anastacia Montroy had a unique allure. She was the *perfect* candidate to restore his inheritance. Now all he needed to do was to convince her to come away with him, because it was clear she wanted an escape of some kind. If he allowed her to run to her sister, he was certain that he'd never get her back, which was untenable. And he had the perfect weapon: her desire for him. Hence, the chase.

'What will it take, *ma déesse*?' he said again. 'I need to know.'

Ana frowned, the cutest crinkle of her brow. Her confusion was plain.

'You mean…leave?'

'It's clear you don't want to stay. Your parents are intent on a quick wedding with no interest in your desires. Whereas with me…'

He let the sentence hang, allowing her to fill in whatever possibilities her imagination could conjure, because he saw the want. Saw the dark flare of her pupils, the rosy blush that brought life back to her pale cheeks.

'W-when?'

'Today, if you wish… My yacht's in the harbour. She's ready to go at short notice.'

'It would be scandalous,' she whispered.

He pulled his phone from his pocket and made a show of looking at it.

'*Pardon*, I had to check the year. It seems we've left the 1800s. There wouldn't be a scandal and, if there's a story to tell, we write our own. People love to believe in love and whirlwind romances.'

A story like that wouldn't be a hard sell. His business in Halrovia, and now this trip with his well-known yacht in the harbour, would lead people to form their own conclusions. When the engagement was inevitably announced, an astute reporter would put together the trail, leading everyone to conclude this had been a grand and secret love affair rather than some clinical arrangement.

Such a story would likely be a balm to the princess's ego. Why wouldn't she want people to think he'd whisked her away as a romantic gesture, rather than the truth? It would also suit his purposes for his parents to imagine this relationship as a love match rather than what it truly was. There'd be no explanations required. They understood love at first sight, claiming it had afflicted them from the moment they'd first met.

'You don't understand,' Ana said.

'Then help me.'

'My parents would never agree to me going away with you unless we're officially engaged.'

It was the first hint she might capitulate. His heart pounded at the thrill of whatever deal might come.

'Don't fear, Princess. They will.'

Convincing the King and Queen would be easy, especially when he told them it was the choice between the trip or Anastacia refusing him outright. They wanted their daughter married quickly, and this was the perfect way to ensure it happened without a fuss.

Anastacia's lips parted. There was such hope on her face at the tiniest prospect of escape. He'd never stopped to think what her life might be like, trapped in a gilded cage. The mere thought made his skin prickle and itch. There was no doubt she was a woman he needed to set free, to open that cage door and let her fly. Although, sometimes birds didn't want to leave their cages when it was all they knew, even with the door thrown open.

'Have you ever heard the phrase "ask and you shall receive"?' he asked, realising she might never have been given a choice. 'You're allowed to ask for what you want.'

She nibbled at her plush lower lip, her white teeth sinking into the pink flesh. 'Then I—'

Aston perceived the faintest of sounds: a buzz, like a phone alert. It wasn't the first one he'd heard in the maze. Anastacia turned away, reaching her hand into a well-hidden pocket of the demure yet tantalising dress, and pulled out her phone. Her mouth opened slightly and she paled, gripping the post of the pergola. Her fingers blanched white, as if she was going to faint on the spot. He moved closer, in case she did.

She looked at him, eyes wide, then back at her phone screen.

'Bad news?' he asked. Or was it a lover? Was that why she and Santori hadn't married, because she wanted someone unsuitable instead? It could explain her family's easy acceptance of him, the desire for a quick marriage.

Something tore through him, hot and potent. Everything inside roared in rejection of the prospect. She didn't look like a woman in love now. She certainly hadn't been the night of the Spring Ball, given the way she flirted with him. Though she could have been trying to make someone jealous. He knew all about manipulation, having witnessed it happen to Michel and being unable to stop it…

No.

He'd been sure that any attraction had all been reserved for him. That night, she'd been a woman…*wanting.* Instead, if he wasn't mistaken, the look on her face now was one of real fear. He'd seen the same in Michel's eyes on the last day of his life. Aston was struck by the overwhelming urge to reach for her, hold her; ask what made her afraid. Instead, he held his ground. He wasn't a man who gave women false expectations.

'Would you keep me safe?' she asked.

Her voice was almost a whisper. Her arms wrapped round her waist. Her body was taught, as if getting ready to flee. Everything inside him stilled. The atmosphere changed. Even the bird song had dropped. A chill settled over him, as if he had been caught in a sudden fog. All of him was on high alert.

'Are you in danger?'

'People tell me I'm not.'

'What do you tell yourself?'

She said nothing, just looked at her phone again, then to the exit of the maze. There was a story here, but first he needed to secure a deal between them. Then he could take some time to discover what had caused this reaction. The pinched look on her face… None of it made sense. Why would she need protection? She had a family to look after her—a *royal* family. Yet she asked whether *he* could keep her safe. For a fleeting moment, it made him want to be that man for her.

'You're a princess. Of course you should have personal security, that's a given. You'd only ever have the best. I care for what's mine.'

At those words, Anastacia seemed to recover from whatever her phone had shown her. Her spine stiffened, as if she'd found her resolve, and he saw the glimpses of her strength. A woman who looked as if she knew what she wanted and would take it. His blood ran thick and hot at the thought that what she wanted was *him*.

There you are. The goddess of the Spring Ball.

'I'm not yours…yet.'

She would be. He'd said those words with no thought, but

he recognised the truth of them, even though he'd never expected to consider any woman as his own. Aston wanted to say that if she was a betting woman she should bet on having his ring on her finger and being in his bed in under a fortnight, yet he didn't. Whilst he was no romantic, he understood how the game was played. Perhaps he could give a little to get the reward he sought.

Her.

No, not her: Girard. *Always* Girard.

'You haven't answered my question. What will it take for you to come with me today?'

'We don't know each other,' she said. 'A marriage would be a disaster if we couldn't stand the sight of each other after a few weeks.'

He had no doubt their chemistry would carry them through and, in the end, what did it matter? His inheritance would be secure and he'd be gone half the year, climbing. They wouldn't have to see each other if they didn't want to. He didn't stop to question why those thoughts didn't sit comfortably with him. Why they somehow lacked...

He shook himself from his introspection. 'Let's make a deal,' he said, his voice somehow strange, urgent and rough to his own ears. 'Come away with me today. I'll keep you safe from whatever it is you're afraid of. Get to know me. Then, if you agree that an engagement would be an advantage to both of us, we'll marry. You don't like what you see? I'll take you to Isolobello, to your sister.'

'You sound certain of yourself.'

If only she knew; losing her was not an option. A flash of need roared through him—a desire to conquer, not a mountain but a *person*. What he wouldn't give to take her now. To kiss her, *show* her what they could...no, *would*...

be together. He breathed through it. Where was his own steely resolve now?

'The choice is simple—yes or no. What'll it be, goddess?'

Aston knew the chance he was taking with that final question, the risk. Yet the certainty remained. She desired him, and he desired her. That was a simple truth he could work with.

She cocked her head. Her winter-blue gaze locked with his. It was as if she was trying to chisel into the soul of him with a pick forged of ice. Was she making him wait? *Oh, Princess…* The punishment would be so sweet when he could turn the tables.

'Okay,' she said.

Not a 'yes', but an agreement nonetheless. An unexpected lightness washed over him. Aston flashed her a smile. He began to walk towards her. She didn't back away, standing her ground, unafraid, of him at least.

'I'm honoured. Now there's one thing I'm certain of,' he said, slipping his arm round her waist, leaning down and murmuring into her ear, 'It's time for you to live a little.'

CHAPTER FOUR

ANA STOOD AT the bow of the yacht as they left the marina, gripping the railings till her fingers blanched white. The water was an impossible kind of blue ahead of her as they left the harbour towards the open sea.

People might have thought that as a princess she had a life replete with choices. Carriages, crowns, a world in which she could do anything she wished. That was so far from the truth, it was almost laughable. She was chained. The restraints might have been gold and jewel-encrusted, but she'd never really had freedom.

Today, yet again, she was left with no real choices. The alerts on her phone in the maze hadn't been from Cilla. They'd been notifications about Count Hakkinen. A news report announcing he was to receive an award for bravery for saving her, or so the story went. Dragging her from a crashed car after her accident when she was certain he'd been the one doing the chasing. Her parents knew how she felt and what she feared, and yet they proposed this. How *could* they?

As part of her role as princess she'd been asked to hand out medals for various sorts of awards. Ana bet anything that her parents would ask her to give the medal to this man to prove to her that her fears were imagined. Groundless.

She couldn't do it. *She wouldn't*. How could she face him? They'd have to shake hands. He'd look at her, search for her old wounds, knowing that she was scarred and all the while believing that no one could love her but him.

That had left her with only one option. To join Aston on his yacht for this farcical trial to see how they'd get on together. It had been presented to her as a choice, but what choice did she really have? She'd needed an escape, and Aston had given her one, but could she afford to say no? If she did, he'd deliver her to her sister, but she'd be back to the beginning and without options. No real assets or means of her own, her parents' determination that she must marry for duty, Count Hakkinen... In the end, this time away seemed more about putting off the inevitable than learning about whether she and Aston could get on.

At least leaving had been easy enough, as he'd promised. He'd spoken to her parents as she'd packed her bags. She didn't need to take any sentimental gifts because her parents weren't into sentimentality. The family photos were all formal portraits. Nothing was candid or unscripted, for fear that it might find its way into the press. No selfies for her. Her clothes were all chosen for her by a stylist. There were colours she liked but nothing she owned ever felt like it had been her own choice. It was as if she was a blank canvas.

For how long had she simply been a passenger in her own life?

She'd packed everything into two suitcases. Aston had told her if she needed anything else he could source it for her. It was a generous offer, but she wasn't fool enough to forget that everything came with a price. People always wanted something from her; he was no different.

The final goodbyes from her family weren't about best wishes, but a reminder about appearances. To be discreet. Not to create a scandal. Her parents clearly thought this was the quickest way to ensure the marriage, given her obvious reluctance. She wondered what Aston had said to them, though it hardly mattered. Getting away was the main aim. She'd worry about the rest later.

Scandal, she was happy to avoid. Discretion didn't trouble her, especially when she wanted to fade into the background. No way was she going to flaunt herself and draw Count Hakkinen's attention. The end game of marriage was a problem but, as Aston had said, what her parents didn't know about their private agreement wouldn't hurt them...

A shiver of sensation ran up her spine. Not unpleasant, rather signifying a presence.

'You make the most beautiful figurehead,' Aston said, voice a mere murmur on the breeze. They might only be words, but she wasn't immune to them. Ana closed her eyes for a moment, relishing the compliment. The sun on her skin. The salty tang of the air.

'Thank you.' She faced him, the breeze ruffling her hair over her face. Ana reached up and checked her fringe, brushing it to cover her forehead.

'Before we spend too much more time together, am I breaching propriety by calling you Anastacia now? Or are you going to require me to call you "Your Highness"?'

'No, of course not. Anastacia is fine. Or Ana.'

'Ana.'

The way he said it, softly. Gently. Almost on a breath, like a whisper imbued with a kind of tenderness entirely unfamiliar to her. A tone that made her believe for a fleeting second that she was someone special.

It had been a mistake, telling him her name's diminutive. The name that not even her parents or brother used. Only Cilla and a few close friends. It implied a greater intimacy between them than there truly was, yet she couldn't take the words back now. She was stuck with it, that creeping level of familiarity that seemed to erode all of her well-preserved boundaries. She wanted to keep calling him Mr Lane. But that would never do, not now. The barrier had been breached for ever.

'Aston,' she said, trying his name out. It was so new and unfamiliar, it felt unexpectedly intimate. She needed to keep reminding herself that this thing between them was convenient and nothing more. Using his name was nothing special. 'Where are we heading?'

'Why don't you let this be a surprise, see where life takes you?' he said. 'Of course, if it gives you a greater sense of security, I'm happy to let you know.'

How well he read her. Her life had held no real surprises. Every part of her day in the palace was diarised. Simply 'seeing where things took her' wasn't in her repertoire. But she supposed this journey could be about discovering new things. Discovering herself…

'I suppose I could leave myself in your capable hands.'

'I'm sure you'll find them more than capable, when the time comes.'

Her lips parted, as the breath hitched in her chest, heat rising to her cheeks. 'Your confidence no doubt gets you into trouble.'

'Plenty of time to reap the rewards of that trouble later.'

He smiled. This man was a danger when he did; he was so handsome, it was blinding. She almost needed sunglasses for the glare. Since coming on board the yacht, he'd taken off his jacket. Removed his tie. Her gaze fixed on the base of his throat, the brown skin there. The way a dusting of hair sprinkled on the slice of chest she could see. She wanted to bury her nose at the base of his throat and breathe him in. His scent, of old granite and spice, catching on the breeze.

'You've heard what I have to say on the subject.'

'I promise to take your lead.'

She tried to rein in her emotions, the way her heartbeat became thready and out of control around him. How there never seemed to be enough air to fill her lungs when he was close. Ana turned, putting him behind her again to peer into the water below them. The bow of the boat cut through the deep blue. She caught a grey flash in the wave below them, then another, breaking the surface.

'Dolphins riding the bow wave.' Aston leaned forward, forearms on the rail next to her.

'Oh. That's…magical.'

Four of them surfed ahead of the yacht, occasionally leaping out of the water, so joyous and free.

'I've never seen them leaving Halrovia's harbour before. It's lucky for you.'

She wasn't one for signs, but somehow this felt like a good omen, something positive in an otherwise difficult day. Ana kept watching till the dolphins peeled off either side of the yacht and disappeared into the depths. The magic of the moment broke and reality intruded about what she was doing, because she wasn't free like the dolphins. A lack of some tether made her anxious, not relaxed, like everyone might assume.

Aston straightened. 'Do you want to see your room? I'm sure you'd like to settle in.'

Anastacia nodded and he led her below decks, through a long passageway ending in a suite. The carpet on the floor was thick and plush. The whole room an opulent display of glass, sleek lines and neutral, modern styling. Her two suitcases sat on the floor ahead of her. What must Aston think? Surely it was a sad indictment of her life that this was all she had to bring with her? But as she looked at him, he wasn't focussed on her meagre belongings, but at the expansive bed overlooking the ocean, then her.

'This is the master stateroom,' he said. 'I hope it meets your expectations. You should find everything you want here. If you don't, a phone on the bedside table will connect you to my staff. I've asked my Chief Stewardess, Ricci, to give you anything you need to make your journey a comfortable one.'

Being Aston's yacht, Ana was certain the master stateroom would normally have been inhabited by him. 'Isn't this your room? I don't want to usurp you.'

She wasn't sure she wanted to sleep in his bed either. There was something entirely too intimate about the thought of lying where his own body had been. Thoughts came to her mind unbidden. Did he sleep naked or clothed? She shut them down.

Aston shrugged. 'You're not. It's only mine when there's no one more important on the yacht.'

'Who measures a person's relative importance here?'

The corner of his lips curled up into a sly kind of grin. 'Me, of course.'

Heat rushed to her cheeks again and Ana was sure her they were now a rosy red. What was she, a woman of twenty-four or some teenager with a full-blown crush? Right now, it was hard to tell.

'I'm grateful.'

'It's no sacrifice. Hold your gratitude for later, Princess, when your thanks are deserved.'

'How many staff do you have working here?'

'Twenty. If Ricci is unavailable, you'll be able to find someone else quite easily.'

So it wasn't as if she'd be completely alone with Aston on the yacht. A sensation, something suspiciously like relief, washed over her.

'You're welcome to explore anywhere on board. There's nowhere off-limits to you.' He motioned to a large wardrobe. 'Clothes are in there. You can select whatever you want to top up what you've brought till we can reach landfall. There'll be something to fit. If you like it, it's yours.'

She walked to a door and opened it to find hangers draped in myriad soft fabrics of bright colours.

'Who do you keep these here for?'

They were all women's clothes of impeccable quality. Were they kept for lovers? She didn't know why it was so important to know the answer to that question.

'I use my yacht for business. I find that people appreciate the extras I provide them whilst they stay here.'

'How…calculating of you.'

'I prefer the word *shrewd*. Anyone who stays on *Reine de Marées* will remember their time on her.'

'*Queen of the Tides*. Are you expecting me to remember mine?'

'*Oui. Bien sûr*. I'll ensure it.'

She glanced at the clothes in the wardrobe again, all women's, looking like all kinds of sizes. 'And when not you're conducting business here?'

A look passed over his face, something stark that, if she'd been asked, looked a lot like isolation.

'I always sleep alone.'

The last rays of sun sank below the horizon as Aston waited on the yacht's deck. The lights of the Italian coastline twinkled in the distance as he breathed in the salty air of a cool autumn evening. It had been months since he'd felt such peace. A calm washed over him, a settled sensation. Nothing at all to do with Ana, of course. It was the same feeling he had when he climbed the mountains. The silence. Presence in the moment. No past, no future. It was the same on the ocean, the vastness of it all. Whilst he had a firm view of his own importance, he enjoyed the sensation of being insignificant for a few moments in his life. It was freeing.

Whilst his parents' edict had impacted his equilibrium, he hadn't realised how easy the idea of having a wife would be. He didn't really think too hard about whether it was the woman rather than the state of being itself. That was introspection he wasn't required to make. It was enough to have Ana here. The rest would come, he was certain.

He walked to the table for two, set out of the breeze, because Ricci had told him Ana had worried about it earlier—something about her hair. Strange, but then he'd do what it took to make her life comfortable, show her how easily they could work together, to be so much more. The table was set as he'd asked, for an intimate dinner for two: tea lights, flowers, gleaming crystal glasses and sparkling silverware. He'd requested something romantic so the external lights had been dimmed and string lights hung in their place, imbuing the space with a magical kind of ambience. It was an odd sensation, seeing the setting. He'd never asked for anything like it ever before.

A time for firsts, for him.

For Ana, too.

He wanted her as any man would want a woman he was attracted to. But thoughts of 'firsts' led inevitably to the thought that he would be hers. Be the only man to witness a look of pleasure slide over her face as he touched her, entering the tight, wet heat of her for the first time. Teasing her nipples till she gasped as she came. It was all he could do not to stalk down to her room, kiss her and take things to their glorious, inevitable conclusion.

His *need* for this woman, the hunger for her, had many

reasons. Call him old-fashioned, but as his wife Ana would be his to protect. That naturally had evoked all kinds of complex and perfectly natural feelings. He'd had no one gracing his bed for some time so that was the clear reason for this drumbeat of desire which pounded through him, that was all. That was all it could *ever* be.

He made his way towards the railings of the yacht once more, into the dimness of dusk, adjusting himself in his trousers. It wouldn't do to have his future fiancée walk out onto the deck seeing him flagrantly aroused. She wanted to be kept safe, and he'd ensure she always felt that way around him. It was a promise, and he knew how important they were to the living and to the dead.

'This looks beautiful.'

Ana's voice sounded surprised, in a good way. Something deep inside him curled with primal pleasure that she might have liked what he'd done for her. She'd changed from this afternoon, and it was with slight disappointment that he saw her wearing something she'd brought herself: a black dress with three-quarter sleeves. It was attractive the way it fell softly round her calves, and hugged her curves, but it didn't satisfy him in the same way wearing something he'd provided might have.

Time.

That was what she'd asked for and no doubt she was still asserting some control over the choices she made, and excluding him from the equation. No matter. He was a patient man, with big plans. He could wait, a little while at least.

'You look beautiful,' he said. Her hair hung loose, the fringe covering her forehead. She reached up and adjusted it, looking self-conscious as she did. At what he'd said or something else, he couldn't be sure.

'Thank you.'

Ana smiled, but it was what he might have called her business smile. Something that seemed easily practised but didn't touch her eyes. He wanted her real smile, the one reserved just for lovers who knew each other's secrets. Once again, he was sure that would come. It was more important to get an engagement ring on her finger. His plans for that would be executed once they'd arrived in Paris.

He approached her and Ana stood a little straighter. She seemed to stiffen. Aston didn't want that but appreciated it might take a while for her to relax around him. She'd probably never been alone with a man who wasn't her family or otherwise a long-term employee. 'Please, come to the table. Dinner will be served soon.'

He placed his hand on her lower back and she didn't object. Her body was warm under his palm. Her hips swayed as she walked. When they arrived at the small table, he pulled out the chair for her.

'That's really not necessary,' she said. Yet she moved to take it anyway.

'I was taught to be a gentleman,' he murmured into her ear and relishing the scent of her, sweet and floral. 'It's absolutely necessary.'

She sank into the chair as he pushed it in. Was it his imagination or did she sit a little fast, as if her knees wouldn't hold her up? Not so unaffected as she pretended, then. He grabbed a bottle of champagne from the ice-bucket and deftly opened it with a quiet hiss, pouring a glass for each of them. He'd asked Ricci to leave them alone as much as possible tonight. Seduction couldn't start with too much interruption.

'When will we reach land?'

In such a hurry to leave…or perhaps she'd forgotten some things that she needed. They'd left in a little bit of a rush in the end.

He smiled, trying not to take it too personally. 'Tomorrow, in Nice. Would you like to do some shopping there? Or perhaps in Paris when we arrive? This afternoon I asked my banker to extend you a line of credit, and that'll be available to you by the time we reach shore.'

Her eye's widened, gleaming like tropical pools in the soft light. 'I…thank you. I have my own things. Enough, I think. Though you haven't told me what might be expected of me.'

Expected? He wondered again about her life, supposing that it would be full of expectations, closely diarised. Whilst that was largely his life too, he still enjoyed moments of freedom with no plans, just going where the mood took him—something else to offer to her.

One of his staff arrived and served them with an entrée of scallops in their shells. Aston was confident she'd enjoy it. He'd asked Ricci to discover her likes and dislikes, her favourite foods.

Ana cut into the tender flesh and took a small mouthful. Her eyes briefly fluttered shut with pleasure. The look on her face…was that how she'd look when underneath him? That same kind of bliss? He hoped so. In fact, he'd ensure it.

'There's not a great deal planned,' he said. Plans would come in time. A new wife for him—a confirmed bachelor known only for short-term relationships—would create a stir. The publicity would be good for Girard. Even his parents would be keen to exploit it. 'I expect we'll want to eat out, so a few casual dinners. Meeting my parents. My mother will want to impress, so it's likely any dinner will be formal.'

He sampled his own entrée, which was as superb, as he'd expected.

'Your parents?'

Perhaps, with his comment, Ana might think things were

moving a little faster than she'd expected. 'If they "catch wind" of you, so to speak. Should my mother find out I'm living with a woman, she'll be curious, since I never have before. I've no immediate intention of telling her about you, though. You wanted time. I'm giving it to you.'

Ana seemed to relax at that, not sitting so stiffly any longer, and relishing the remains of her scallops. 'Your father's from Australia?'

Aston didn't think too hard about why her knowledge of his family made him pleased. He liked that he interested her too.

'*Oui*. He travelled to France to learn old-world wine-making techniques, which is how he met my mother.'

'That sounds romantic.'

More talk of romance. He was now pleased he'd asked for the table to be dressed this way, and for lights to be strung.

'They've been married over thirty years.'

His grandparents had been sceptical at the time, but his mother was a force of nature, and she wouldn't listen to their pleas for caution when she told them she'd fallen in love with the Australian boy.

'Have you been to Australia?'

Aston nodded. 'My mother's parents demanded their grandchildren be born in France, so my parents obliged. But my father wanted me to know his country, so I did a lot of my schooling there, spending summer holidays at the beach. Working in my father's family's vineyard.'

'It sounds wonderful.'

They'd been some of the happiest times of his life with his Australian relatives. There was something relaxed about them. He'd gone to school during the week, and at the weekend had worked among the vines. He'd surfed and fished, living an idyllic life in the sunshine.

'It was. I try to visit as often as I can.'

'I've always wanted to travel there but I haven't had a chance. There's been no cause for someone from my family to visit in an official capacity.'

Aston finished his entrée. 'What about holidays?'

'My family always take their holidays locally, to support the economy.'

When there was a whole world out there to explore? He couldn't imagine it. Poor princess.

'Perhaps I could show you one day?'

A honeymoon on one of the tropical islands, perhaps? They could bask in the sunshine there. Swim in pristine water. Make love in the moonlight on a secluded beach. Though where these romantic notions came from, he had no idea.

'I'd like to see a wombat, or swim with dolphins—maybe even a whale shark.'

Ana seemed more…alive when she talked about those things. She might have led a sheltered life, but he'd known underneath there was a woman who wanted to burst out and see the world.

The things he could show her. Yet he had plans. For the next eighteen months he would be all about training to make what would be one of the climbs of his life. Though right now he didn't understand why the thought of all that planning and preparation exhausted him, when he usually found it invigorating. It had to be the pervasive stress of securing a wife, that was all. Once he was married, everything would change.

'I've seen a wombat in the wild,' he said.

Her eyes widened. 'Really? Where?'

'One night as a teenager. Near my family's vineyard. It was grazing.'

'Like a cow?'

With the look on her face, her eyes sparkling in the candlelight, she made such a beautiful picture. He would tell her stories about all of Australia's wildlife if it kept her looking at him with such fascination.

'*Oui*. They eat grass.'

'Who knew? They seem so sweet and round and cuddly.'

He chuckled. 'Round they might be, but sweet and cuddly, *non*. I'm sorry to disappoint. They're grumpy.'

'Never. I don't believe you.'

'My cousins dared me to approach it. I'm sure they knew. Trust me, when that wombat hissed and charged, I ran.'

Ana's mouth broke into a beaming smile, lighting her up from the inside, more beautiful than any sunset nature could provide. When she laughed, a joyous sound, it was like something lit inside him too. He couldn't help it, he began laughing with her in a way he hadn't for months.

'I'm trying to imagine it. You, being chased by a grumpy wombat,' she said, wiping at her eyes.

'It wasn't an edifying display. I learned wombats are best viewed up close, in zoos.'

She pouted, but the corners of her mouth still quivered with mirth. 'Now I'm disappointed.'

'Dolphins and whale sharks are a far easier ask. Trust me.'

Ana cocked her head. That look on her face was almost as if she was trying to decide whether she'd take him up on the offer. Everything in him stilled, but she didn't make any more of it. Still, it felt like a kind of breakthrough, that trust would come if only he was patient.

He took his glass of champagne, chill under his fingertips, and raised it.

'A toast,' he said.

'To what?'

'To us.'

'There is no us...'

Yet. It was only a matter of time. He had no doubts. Aston knew attraction when he saw it. Every time she looked at him, it was obvious she wanted him.

'There will be.'

'Don't you find the idea of an arranged marriage anachronistic? How do you even go about something like that?'

One step forward, two steps back. She wasn't going to make this easy, but he did like a challenge.

'Remember I said you interested me?' Her lips parted in a gratifying way. Her pupils were wide and dark in the low light. 'When doing business, I asked after you to your father. And the rest, as they say, is history.'

It had been natural to ask after the princess those times he'd seen the King. His mother had known the Queen, and that connection made it easier. Conversations had been surprisingly cordial as he'd mentioned his parents' desire for him to marry. Soon, the conversations had been less about the business of champagne and more about the business of negotiating his engagement to marry a princess who, when he looked back now, had been conspicuously absent in the whole deal.

In the end, finalising the arrangement had been surprisingly easy. Likely Ana wouldn't want to hear that story about how quick her family had been to give her away.

He took a bracing sip of his champagne, one of Girard's finest vintages.

'It still doesn't answer why a modern man would choose this method.'

Because it hadn't been a choice but a necessity. A suppressed anger in him sparked. He tried to tamp it down.

'You could ask yourself why a modern woman would agree if she found the idea so objectionable.'

Anastacia had been prepared to marry Santori. Was the problem here that he wasn't a prince? That she felt he was somehow beneath her as a commoner? He gritted his teeth and breathed slowly through the annoyance of the thought. She could have told her parents to go to hell, but she hadn't—so she must be at least somewhat interested.

'And yet here you are, wanting to marry me because your parents think it's time.'

Touché, *Princess*. It wasn't the whole story, but there was no need for her to know it all.

'That's different. You have siblings. Your brother's the Crown Prince. There's a certain freedom for the one who isn't going to carry the family mantle. The heir doesn't have as many choices. I have obligations.'

Ana put down her glass. 'So you have no "spare", as royalty like to call it?'

He didn't like thinking of Michel that way. They'd been brothers, best friends, then the universe had cruelly snuffed out Michel's life. To this day Aston had trouble fathoming how a person so full of a desire for living could simply cease to exist.

'No,' he said. It still made him want to rage at the unfairness of it all. 'I'm all there is.'

Aston's staff had served the main course. As Ana sat across from him, eating a delectable dish of duck, she couldn't help but think once again how stark he looked. As if he carried the weight of the world. She wanted to reach out, to comfort him.

He'd made two telling comments.

I always sleep alone.

I'm all there is.

She'd had trouble accepting the first, but now she wasn't so sure. He seemed to hold himself apart. In a world of people rushing about, she could see him standing solitary, as distant and as solid as one of the mountains he climbed.

'I've always wondered, was it difficult being an only child?'

She had siblings, and in many ways at least she and Cilla were united against a common enemy: their parents. Gabe was distant, but Ana had little doubt, if the crunch came, he'd be there for her as much as his role and his own emotional intelligence allowed.

Aston stopped eating, carefully placing down his knife and fork. He took a sip of his champagne. His Adam's apple bobbed distractedly as he swallowed. He looked so handsome in a blue-and-white-striped shirt, sleeves rolled up showing his strong, tanned forearms.

'I had a younger brother—Michel. He died.'

Ana's heart missed a beat, her stomach clenching uncomfortably. She had no words. She felt awful for raising a sibling in such an unthinking way. She reached out her hand, placing it over his, and squeezed. His skin was warm to the touch.

'I'm so sorry.'

'It was a long time ago,' he said, but he didn't move his hand from under hers. He simply looked at it. She didn't know what to do now, and didn't want things to become awkward, so she slowly pulled her hand away, immediately missing the connection her touch gave them.

'Is that why your parents want you to marry?'

He shrugged. *'Peut-être.'*

Perhaps.

It seemed there was more to the story, though she appreciated she might be touching his tender points. Ana couldn't imagine what it would be like to lose either of her siblings. She also had a little more understanding for what might be driving his decisions.

'I understand dynasty—royalty, remember?'

'The need for heirs. Someone to ensure the family legacy.'

Ana stilled. *Children*. She hadn't really thought about wanting them before. They were simply expected for someone who was going to marry a prince. Now the idea of children was tangled up with the need to bare herself. The thought of that…

The air cut off in her throat. What was this proposed marriage, the need for a legacy, if not for children as well? Still, he wasn't pressuring her. He said if she didn't like what she saw he'd take her to Isolobello and there'd be no need for an engagement. She just needed to remind him.

'I can't make promises.'

His gaze was like a pilot light, blue and bright, shining directly onto her. His attention made her question everything about herself.

'You did. I'll ask nothing of you you're not willing to give.'

Was this how she wanted her life to be—a negotiation, a series of bargains? It reminded her that Aston wasn't the man of her fantasies. A sense of powerful disappointment hit her once more. The main of duck, which at first she'd thought was delicious, now seemed dry and tasteless. This— running away together on a magnificent yacht with a man so handsome it could break her heart—should have been everything she'd dreamed of. She hated that the reality was all so artificial, so hollow.

'How romantic.'

'What about this—' he motioned to the table '—isn't romantic?'

'Because it's contrived.'

She couldn't escape the stabbing sense of unfairness that this would never be more. Even if she wanted it to be, he'd talked about a convenient relationship without love being freeing. What if she *wanted* the love?

'Romance is one of the most contrived things on the planet,' he said. 'You think otherwise? Why? You were prepared to marry Caspar Santori, and don't tell me that had anything to do with romance.'

When would people ever stop reminding her of it, as if her inability to marry the man was a kind of personal failing? 'That's different.'

'How? Explain it to me.'

Her problem was, she hadn't been attracted to Caspar. Aston, on the other hand... Tonight he was dressed in casual chinos which hugged his narrow hips, his shirt gripping the hard planes of his body and his broad shoulders. Maybe everyone was shallow and all that mattered was how they looked, the objectification.

Yet Caspar hadn't done to her what Aston did whenever he was near—didn't cause the frisson of pleasure and expectation that seemed to ripple through her at his attention. His mere presence causing goose bumps to sparkle across her skin. And when he looked at her, truly looked, the heat threatened to scorch her.

Being near Aston Lane was like sitting too close to a bonfire. She was bound to get burned.

'Princess, you could destroy a man's ego if he didn't have a healthy one. You devour me with your eyes, yet spit me out with your words.'

Was that what she wanted? She wasn't sure of anything any more apart from the need to get away. She'd been trapped this morning and going with Aston had seemed like the best worst choice.

She couldn't sit here any longer, not with the flowers on the table, candles and string lights. The place was dressed up for romance, the pretence making a mockery of the word. Ana stood, making her way to the stern of the yacht. They were clearly a fair way offshore, but the lights on the land hugged the horizon. She wished she could be there, feeling grounded, rather than this sensation of being cut adrift.

'When people try to escape it usually fails, because what they're running from is most often themselves,' Aston said. His voice was close behind her, so he must have followed from the table. She gripped the yacht's railings to tether herself. It was as if he saw her better than she saw herself.

What if she agreed to marry him, what then? She'd have to expose herself and if Aston was revolted by her scars, rejected her, where would she be? She wasn't sure she'd survive it.

'Have you ever been in a situation where your choices have been taken away?' she asked.

'We're all constrained in some way, whether in reality or of our own making.'

'I have trouble accepting that where you're concerned.'

Yet his words had sounded so heavy, like a dead weight dragging him down under the waves.

'Everyone has their shackles, Princess, yet most people are blissfully unaware of what holds them back.'

She turned. He stood there, so tall, so imposing, seemingly strong and solid. To look at him she wouldn't sense there was a single crack in him, yet every word suggested chinks in his armour.

'What are yours?'

His expression changed fleetingly. It was almost as if he winced, as though recalling something painful. He didn't seem present. There was a distance to him, as if he was far away somehow, all the while standing in front of her.

The silence stretched. She was about to say his name, to bring him back from where his memories seemed to have taken him, when a gust of breeze blew. Aston's eyes flicked to her temple. She reflexively moved her hand to check her fringe. He was too quick, gently grasping her wrist in one hand, the other reaching out to brush her fringe out of the way, exposing the ugly scar. She turned her head, her heart beating a sickening rhythm, the bile rising to her throat. His question would come. How much to give away in answering it?

Aston let her wrist go, as if her touch burned him.

'What happened to you?'

She couldn't look at him. She wouldn't allow herself to see the pity on his face. She'd seen enough of it to make her sick to the stomach. Still, Ana had to give him some answer. He didn't need the whole story, just a simple truth.

'It was a car accident.'

'When?'

'A little over six months ago.' Just after the Spring Ball.

'I didn't see anything in the press.'

She kept her eyes downcast, focussing on his shoes instead—deck shoes, she mused.

'It was there, for a while. It wasn't big news.'

All lies. Her parents had paid a small fortune to kill the story, and had bought the most egregious pictures. Though if someone knew what they were doing and looked hard enough she suspected it would be easy to find. The Internet was for ever, after all, so the royal press secretary continually reminded her. Still, not all the stories could be suppressed, like the lies about her being a party girl, avoiding her responsibilities. They continued to follow her...

'Do you have other injuries?'

'I had some. They're better now.' Carla hadn't been so lucky…

Aston slipped his hand under her chin and tilted up her head. She didn't want to meet his gaze but didn't want him to think she was afraid either. The conflicting sensations warred within her. She wanted to break away, to flee, but there was nowhere to go.

'Is this why you asked whether I could keep you safe?'

His voice was filled with empathy, yet with a core of steel. The look on his face wasn't one of pity, but of resolve. He might have told her about his brother, yet she sensed there was so much about him that he held back. Why should she be the one to have to share everything when it was clear there were things he didn't want to disclose?

She jerked her head from his grip. If she told him about Count Hakkinen and he didn't believe her, she wasn't sure what she'd do. It would be another wound she'd have to re-cover from.

'I think I'm done eating now, and I'm very tired. I'd like to return to my room.'

Aston frowned. 'Ana, you…'

She held up her hand, invoking an attitude even her mother would have been proud of.

'"No" is a complete sentence, Mr Lane.'

He had the good grace not to follow her as she walked away.

CHAPTER FIVE

THE MAIN SUITE was a beautiful room, with views of the ocean beyond complementing the earthy colours inside. The water gleamed a glorious, vibrant blue. Almost the same blue as Aston's eyes. Ana didn't want to think of that, of them and how they pierced her, looking for a way in. She didn't want her secrets laid bare—not yet. Perhaps never, even though it seemed unavoidable now, all because he'd seen her scars.

Ana knew she was hiding. She hadn't gone to breakfast on deck this morning, asking for it to be brought to her room. Unable to face Aston and the inevitable questions that would lead to the accident and talk of her stalker. She felt a clawing fear that Aston wouldn't believe her about that, and where would she be left?

But thinking about it…*really* thinking and not driven by the panic of the evening before… Ana realised he'd seen her scars and still the world kept turning. It hadn't ended. Even more, Aston hadn't appeared disgusted by them. There hadn't been a look of pity on his face. Some shock, yes. Then had come the concern and his question of whether this was the reason she'd asked if he could keep her safe. It was as if he'd cared. Had thought about her first, before himself. Sure, he'd pushed her a little, but he hadn't demanded anything as she'd walked away. He'd taken no for an answer.

Ana knew she couldn't hide there all day. It was coming to lunch and Ricci had let her know there'd be food on the deck soon. She checked her phone. A reflex, even though right now she had nothing to fear. There was a message from Cilla with one word: *Okay?* She responded with a thumbs-up. She checked in on her friend, Carla, who was fine. Ana felt a stab of guilt that she didn't know how long it would be before she could visit her friend again, but Carla said that her physical therapists were pleased with her progress and that she understood why Ana had wanted to leave.

It all meant that Ana had no excuse to stay in her room any longer. She didn't want to be a coward. She'd been afraid for so long, it'd be nice to find her courage again, to face Aston, because he'd been right: she was running away from herself.

Ana fished through the clothes in her wardrobe, outfits she'd brought with her that she thought might be good for a yacht. Nothing held much interest—practical neutrals, mix and match, easy to grab and throw in a suitcase before she'd left. Instead, her gaze was drawn to the array of resort wear in jewelled colours and silky fabrics. Some were barely there, which she looked at with a kind of yearning. She wanted to show courage, but she wasn't ready for Aston to see everything. Not yet.

Instead, she chose a silk dress in a caftan style that gathered slightly at the waist to give her shape, and otherwise floated about her body. She ran her hands over the exquisite fabric, so soft and beautiful in pinks and blues, crystals stitched around the deep vee of the neck. Something about it made her feel pretty, probably the first time since the accident.

She could do this instead of hiding away like a little mouse. There were also apologies to make of sorts. Lying in bed reflecting obsessively over their conversation the night before, she'd realised some things. Some of the conversation had been fun. Aston had been trying to make her comfortable. He'd shared things about himself. And, if she truly wanted to try at marriage, she couldn't flee at the first sign that things were getting difficult.

Ana selected a pair of flat gold sandals from an array in the wardrobe that seemed the best match for her dress, then set off through a carpeted passageway towards the bow of the yacht.

Outside on the deck the sunshine was bright, so she slipped on a pair of sunglasses against the glare. Ahead of her a small table was set with some drinks on ice and other refreshments. Her stomach growled. When had she last experienced real hunger? Most of the time over the last six months she'd eaten for fuel, forcing herself because her appetite had disappeared. It was a strange sensation, that gnawing feeling in her stomach. She selected smoked salmon blini and ate it. She had another, then grabbed a small bottle of sparkling water from a bowl of ice and cracked the seal. She took a sip of the chilling fizz before walking further out onto the deck.

A large, aqua-blue pool lay ahead of her. In it swam Aston, slicing through the water with powerful strokes as he reached the end, executed a perfect turn and came towards her. Another turn and he swam away. She was transfixed as he continued, lap after lap, by how his body cut through the water like his yacht had done, slicing through the ocean as it had left Halrovia's harbour. The rhythmic splashes were somehow soothing as she watched the power of his body, the water coursing over his back as he maintained his solid strokes.

Then, as he reached the end of the pool furthest from

her, he stopped. Grabbed the edge for a few moments as if catching his breath. Placed both arms on the side of the pool and launched himself out of it. The water sluiced over his bronzed skin as he hauled himself from the water, wearing only black swimming trunks that gripped his muscular backside.

She'd seen men in states of undress before when Halrovia had hosted international swimming competitions and she'd handed out medals to the winners. Those men had all been powerful athletes with smooth skin and the typical swimmer's shape, with strong physiques and peak fitness.

None of them had affected her like this. She was pinned to the spot. She couldn't take her eyes from Aston, couldn't stop her gaze roving over him. The solidity of his shoulders looked as if they could carry the weight of the world. She watched the bunch of his biceps, the taper of him, his narrow waist, lower…

Then he noticed her. His mouth curled into a slow smile as he stalked past a sun lounger and grabbed a towel, lashing it round his waist. The bottle of sparkling water almost slipped through her nerveless fingers as he approached. His towel hadn't helped. It simply drew her attention to the smattering of hair on his muscular chest, the trail of it that bisected the muscles of his abdomen, disappearing below the knot at his waist. The way the droplets of water on his body sparkled like diamonds in the light. He raked his hand through his hair, rivulets of water dribbling down the sides of his neck, his pectorals.

She didn't know where to look or what to say. He stood near her, grabbed a bottle of still water, opened it and put the neck to his mouth, tilting his head back and gulping it down, Adam's apple bobbing. When he finished, he placed the bottle carefully on the table.

'Good afternoon. I see you found something to wear. I hope the selection was a reasonable one?'

He seemed so formal today. Perhaps it was unsurprising that after last night the conversation might be a little stilted. It was then that she noticed that he appeared breathless. A man like him looked in peak fitness. Surely he wouldn't have been puffed out by a mere swim? Although, he'd been pushing himself, like those champion swimmers, almost as if he'd swum a race.

'It was, thank you. How long have you been in the pool?'

He checked the time on the watch, still on his wrist. 'Around an hour.'

An hour? 'You looked to be swimming hard.'

He shrugged, the muscles of his shoulders bunching distractingly as he did. 'I like to train.'

'What for? Your climbing?'

He smiled, as if she'd somehow made a confession by revealing she knew of his exploits. It was an incendiary curl of his lips, slow, deliberate, setting her on fire. What she wouldn't give simply to dive into the pool herself to get away from the sensation, to cool down. There was a selection of swimwear in the clothes in her wardrobe. Once she might have worn it. There were no paparazzi here to take photographs and sell them to the press. But her scars were things she hid, not flaunted. Maybe one day she'd be brave enough. Today was not that day.

'I need the stamina, the endurance. It's useful, not only for my climbing.'

She swallowed, her mouth dry even though she had a drink in her hand. A trickle of perspiration slid down the back of her neck. 'I'll have to take your word for it.'

'I'm happy at your easy acceptance of what I say, Princess.' His intense blue gaze fixed on her. 'But please,' he said, motioning to a casual seating area with soft-looking couches. 'We should sit.'

She led the way, not wanting him to get too close, really not wanting him perhaps to put his hand on the small of her back and guide her, as he'd done as they'd been walking up the gangplank onto the yacht, and when he'd helped her to her seat over dinner. She knew what his touch was like, how heated, branding her. She liked the burn of it a little too much.

Ana sank into the soft cushions of the outdoor lounge, placing her bottle of water on the table in front of her, crossing her legs at the ankle as she was taught to do, her hands positioned primly in her lap. He on the other hand seem to sprawl, still with a towel wrapped around his waist. His bare chest was an impossible and distracting display. He didn't make any effort to find a shirt. Did he know how he affected her? Most likely. If she was asked to describe the expression on his face, she'd say he was amused.

He looked at her shoes. 'You lied.'

Her heart pounded at the shock of his comment. What did he know? Had he found something on the Internet?

'When?'

'Your feet aren't made of clay, and I was right—they're pretty.'

She couldn't help herself. The shock of it—she burst out laughing. The earlier tension faded away. 'No one's ever sung the praises of my feet before.'

He grinned. 'That's a terrible oversight, but I didn't really want to talk about your feet, alluring as they are.'

Her nerves began to kick up again. 'Okay.'

'You have charity interests—child literacy, correct?' he asked.

Ana sat up a little straighter. That was the charity she

supported in Halrovia because of Gabriel… Still, Aston's knowledge of it was unexpected. When she'd first met him at a trade delegation, they'd talked, but she didn't recall having mentioned it.

'How did you know?'

Then there was her new charity too, one close to her heart after her accident. Realising that, whilst she'd had the opportunity for reconstructive surgery, so many children didn't. Ana wanted that to be her new focus, something tangible she could do to help.

'I'd have thought it obvious,' Aston said, in a tone that suggested her question came as a surprise. 'You interest me. When people talked about you, I listened.'

The words seemed almost dispassionate, yet his gaze, the clear-crystal blue of his eyes, his focus, was all on her. She had no doubt that the interest meant something more. Something *far* more.

'We should also discuss your needs ahead of our engagement,' he said, catching her off-guard. He'd given her what she really needed, an escape. She wasn't sure what else he was talking about.

'*Potential* engagement,' she corrected him. 'And my needs are simple—safety, as I've said before. Freedom to carry on my charity work. Doing some good for the world…'

'Your desires, then.'

No way would she prise open that hornets' nest, especially when some days she hardly knew herself. People tended to give her what they thought she wanted, especially if they wanted something in return.

She clasped her hands on her lap. 'This might all be temporary.'

'I understand. I'd also prefer to set us up for success, rather than presume failure in the beginning.'

'I don't want to feel obligated when I can't repay you.' Or to feel any more bought than she already did.

One of his staff approached, asking if they would like anything. She declined. Aston asked for a coffee.

'Let's presume you had a wish list,' he said. 'Things you wanted to set up a new life. What would you ask for?'

A new life… Was that what she was doing? It was so tempting to think so. Maybe she could try to move forward rather than staying constrained by her recent past.

There were some things that concerned her. When Cilla had left for Isolobello, the employment of her staff had been terminated. Her lady-in-waiting—the palace 'fairy god-mother', as everyone called her—had followed Cilla. The rest had been let go. Ana feared for the people who'd worked in her small office if she were to leave. They relied on her for their incomes. She'd taken a personal approach in employing them—they were those in need, who might not or-dinarily have been offered jobs by the palace. She loved the team she'd worked with. Ana didn't want to see them suffer because of what had happened in recent days.

'I have staff—my lady-in-waiting, my secretary… I'm not sure they'd have roles in the palace without me. I want to ensure they're taken care of.'

The staff member returned and gave Aston his coffee. He took a long draw from the cup. 'Give some thought to any others. If you live outside of the palace, you'll need to set up your own office. It's sensible to keep staff you're famil-iar with. Who work well with you. You had other interests, organisations you supported. If supporting any in Halrovia isn't open to you, perhaps you can find the others.'

He clearly didn't recognise the Cygnet Centre as her new endeavour, but that was no surprise, since the charity was still a fledgling one. Ana's head spun at the pace this was taking, how matter of fact he was about her having an office of her own, even with all the uncertainties between them. Her own parents had never really concerned themselves with what interested her. So long as it didn't disgrace the family's name, that was all they cared about. Yet Aston sat there as if keen for her to establish her own life with his help.

'I'll give it some thought,' she said.

A problem remained, a large and insurmountable one. She had no real money of her own. It was customary for her family to make a settlement to their daughters on marriage, but that wouldn't come till the day she had a wedding ring on her finger. She had a small inheritance from her grandmother, but nothing that would support the number of staff she needed. Her heart sank. People often expected that, because she was royal, she had riches, when her allowance had all come from her parents. She had nothing to call her own.

'Put together a list of those you'd like to work with. I'll hand it to my team and they can make the first approach, unless you'd like to do that personally?'

'I… I…'

'Something wrong?' he asked.

'To pay for staff I need money and I have…none.'

The intensity of him seemed to soften.

'Chère.' He shook his head. 'I have companies who can employ them on your behalf. I've told you—ask and it will be done.'

'There's always a catch. What do you want?'

'Eventually?' His gaze dropped to her hands. 'My ring on your finger.'

Yet the look in his eyes spoke of so much more—heat, desire. His nostrils flared, his pupils dark in the ocean blue of his gaze. She couldn't help her reaction; her nipples tightened in her bra. The whole of her sparked with a delicious heat of her own, an ache deep inside that she craved him to fill. This man was a danger to her equilibrium.

'You also wanted to know if I could keep you safe. I want to ensure that you feel you are, always.'

She paused at that, at their conversation last night. She had things to say, things she'd so far avoided. Ana smoothed the fabric of her dress. 'You haven't asked any more about my scars.'

Aston picked up his coffee and drained the cup. He set it carefully down on the saucer.

'You said no. I stopped asking. You'll tell me when you're ready. Everyone's entitled to their secrets, Ana.'

She shivered at the way he said her name, softly, deliberately, as if she was special. 'As easy as that?'

How could it be, when everything in her life lately had been so hard? She didn't trust anything sold to her as simple.

'Why wouldn't it be?'

She had no response. It was as though he really cared, when no one bar Cilla had before. She didn't know what to say. 'Thank you' didn't seem enough.

'*Pardon*, Monsieur Lane.'

'Excuse me,' he said to Ana, before turning his attention to over her shoulder. '*Oui*, Ricci?'

'I have your head vintner on the phone.'

Aston's expression became pained. 'I'm sorry. I need to take this. He usually only contacts me when my mother's been unreasonable.'

'Of course.'

'We'll take this conversation up later if you like. In the meantime, have you eaten anything?'

'I…' She hadn't wanted much before but, now he'd mentioned food, her stomach grumbled noisily again. 'No. I wasn't hungry earlier.'

'Ricci, please ask Chef to prepare something for Her Highness to eat.' He pinned Ana with his intense gaze once more. She felt like a butterfly skewered by some ardent collector. 'I want to ensure her stay on *Reine de Marées* gives her everything she desires.'

CHAPTER SIX

Aston sat with Ana at his favourite Paris café, drinking coffee after eating a late lunch. They'd taken a spot on the pavement under some umbrellas, allowing Ana to people-watch, which she appeared to enjoy. Usually he didn't have time to simply sit, but today he hoped it would be another beginning of sorts.

'No' is a complete sentence, Mr Lane.

He'd taken care in the few days since leaving the yacht not to press Ana, accepting the firm boundary she'd put between them. The 'Mr Lane' had stung in surprising ways, as it hadn't been said with flirtation, but he knew what she'd been doing—protecting herself—so he'd kept any conversations between them neutral. Talk about where she might like an office, were she to set one up—in his apartment or Girard's Paris headquarters. Nothing difficult to answer because there was more to the story behind the scar on her temple, her fear.

He could work on her fears once she trusted him a little.

Building that had started when they'd made landfall. She'd blushed as he'd handed her a credit card in her name, but it gave her freedom. He wanted to show her a possible future, not dwell too much on the past.

'I hope I look suitable for whatever outing this is. You've been very mysterious,' she said, smoothing her hands over the skirt of a demure, pale-grey suit. It had three-quarter sleeves that he had little doubt hid more scars. He ached inside at the way the accident seemed to have changed her from the confident, sensual young woman he'd first met, to someone filled with uncertainty.

'Business wear' was all he'd told her, and he was wearing a suit himself. He'd wanted this to be a surprise, one he hoped would be a breakthrough between them.

He smiled. 'You look perfect.'

Yesterday he'd sent Ana with his secretary and security to do some shopping, whilst he'd worked and trained in his home gym. She'd come home with a few packages, fewer than he might have liked, but she looked pleased. Had she bought the suit then? He liked to think that she might have. She'd been a little mysterious about what she'd purchased but he'd been telling the truth when he'd said everyone was entitled to their secrets. He hoped she'd tell him hers in time.

Something about her was still wary, hesitant. He knew what she needed—an unmistakeable commitment. He'd realised now why her hair had changed, why she covered herself. Why she might want to hide the scar on her temple she refused to talk about, and others that he suspected her body bore. To him, it hadn't changed her desirability. He simply had to show her.

'I'm still curious about whether you've had any other Australian fauna mishaps.'

He chuckled. 'Nothing, other than walking into a large spider's web at night. That wasn't pleasant.'

She shuddered. 'No, I'm guessing not. I'm a bit disappointed you don't have other stories.'

'I have *plenty* of stories.'

He'd like to make more with her. He had his diving certification. They could swim with dolphins or whale sharks any time she wanted.

'Stories… What mountains have you climbed?'

Some days he thought too many, both physically and emotionally. He had many more to go. He wasn't sure why that thought exhausted him, when once standing on top of a mountain had only filled him with exhilaration.

'Those you may know? The Matterhorn, Mont Blanc, Kilimanjaro…' There'd been others, difficult climbs, all leading to his quest for Everest.

'Is there a next mountain?'

'There's always another,' he said, deliberately vaguely. She didn't need to know, not now. He wasn't sure what he'd do if she expressed any concern about his intentions.

'I just thought, with all the training… I wondered what you had planned.'

Ana's phone buzzed an alert. She bit her lower lip, grabbed it and checked the notification, seeming satisfied. She put it back down. He hadn't missed that a notification in the maze seemed to have been the catalyst for her leaving with him…

Time—that was all she needed.

'All I have plans for is today.'

Aston checked the time, his heartbeat kicking up in his chest in anticipation. His car would be coming round the corner soon. Today would be their first public outing together, and by the end of it he felt assured things between them would have changed for the better. He needed them to, if he was to take Ana to meet his parents. He couldn't have her looking like a terrified rabbit in a snare. What would that say to his mother and father about him? He wanted a woman, if not in love, then in lust. Though why he should care, he wasn't sure. It wasn't as if he'd sought out a relationship based on love at first sight, like his parents.

A kind of dull ache settled in his chest, almost like regret. He ignored it.

'Time to go?' she asked.

'*Oui.*' He stood and helped her from her chair, and she gifted him one of her rare and precious smiles. Had she been freer with them before her accident? He wasn't sure. He hoped by the end of today he'd be granted more of them. When he'd gone through the catalogue after it had been delivered to his office, he'd known this was an event he wouldn't miss. He'd registered immediately.

Aston held out his arm, as Ana wore heels and the footpath was a little uneven. She took it, walking down a side street as their car eased into place. His driver opened the door for them, and Ana got in.

Aston took a long, slow breath. He had his own journey to take, mapped out years before, but he could give Ana beginnings—a life of her own, a fresh start. Reasons for her to agree to this marriage, her future. It all began with success this afternoon, and he was not a man to fail.

When he succeeded, everything would fall into place.

Their car pulled up at gleaming white building with blue awnings. A uniformed man opened the door and Aston exited the vehicle, holding out his hand. Without thinking, Ana placed hers in his. Aston's warmth engulfed her. His fingers gripped hers gently, yet she could feel the strength in him, his solidity. She looked up at him, his eyes the same glorious blue as the sky on this bright autumn day. The faintest of smiles hovered on his too-tempting lips. She could sit and simply gaze at him, like her favourite piece of artwork.

He raised an eyebrow and his smile deepened. His masculine features seeming to soften. Ana came to her senses. She couldn't sit here in the car all day. She got out and stood. His height and breadth and all that banked strength somehow made her feel safe.

The man was temptation personified. *Why not simply give in?*

Her stomach twisted in uncomfortable knots. He wasn't horrified by the red, still angry-looking scar on her temple. After the initial questions, he'd been happy to give her space, to divulge what she wanted to in her own time. It had been considerate. He'd placed no pressure on her at all, letting her set the pace. Yet, she held herself so tightly, she wasn't sure she knew how to undo herself and let go.

Convenient doesn't have to mean cold...

The man would have warmth enough for both of them.

Aston led her into the building through a magnificent foyer. A floor of black-and-cream marble polished to a mirror shine. Huge vases of opulent blooms dotted through the space.

'What are we doing here?' Ana asked. Aston seemed to know where he was going as he led her down a corridor.

'We're going to an auction.'

'Why?'

'You'll see.' He gave her another blinding grin, one that seemed full of self-satisfaction and...mischief. A smile that set her heart thumping. Being around this man was an adventure in itself.

Everyone seemed to know him here; he was acknowledged with knowing nods by staff. They were directed to a room at the top of a winding marble staircase, and Aston led her through the assembled crowd of people, his hand gently resting on her lower back. The atmosphere was a rarefied one yet bristling with energy and excitement. Just the place that Aston would enjoy... She didn't know why she thought that, whilst *knowing* it with certainty.

He guided her to the side of the room with another group of people. 'I'll be back in a moment,' Aston said. 'Save me a seat.'

He walked away, and she couldn't help but admire his broad shoulders, hugged lovingly by a dark suit jacket. The length of his legs and how he always seemed to stride with such confidence and authority. Yet he'd left her to herself and her thoughts. Not really a pleasant place to reside.

Ana glanced at the people round her and took a deep breath, trying to settle her growing nerves that twisted higher and tighter. When she'd been shopping, Aston had sent her with his private secretary and a discreet personal protection officer. Today, they'd come here alone. Still, there was no reason to think anyone would know where she was. In Halrovia, all her moves were diarised in a court circular, her royal engagements publicised. With Aston, no one knew what they were doing. None of their time was advertised or documented. She couldn't help feeling thankful at the anonymity of it all, keeping her safe.

Aston returned after a few short minutes and took a seat beside her. The smile on his face was warm and genuine, self-satisfied. It made her heart flutter in anticipation, his mood so infectious. In his hand he held a paddle with a number on it.

Ana frowned. 'What's that for?'

He sat next to her. 'I'm bidding.'

'What are you buying?'

'An engagement ring for you.'

Her heart stopped for a second, then bounded to restart, as if it had been shocked.

'But…but…why?'

'Don't you believe you deserve it?'

Ana had no words. She leaned back in her comfortable seat, looking at the people around them all with paddles of their own, oblivious, flipping through catalogues, talking. Whereas she sat silently, unable to say a word. She hated that this was even a question for her. Once, her first thought would always have been, *of course I deserve it*. Now? She didn't feel worthy.

'But nothing's agreed.'

'I'm a man who likes to be well prepared, but you're under no obligation to accept me. Still, there's no harm in having the perfect ring in case you do. I saw the auction advertised and thought of you immediately.'

Had he?

Aston leaned over to her, so close, she could sense him. That smell…was cool, like the granite of the mountains surrounding Halrovia's capital. The slight salt of an ocean breeze, the wild and enticing scent of spice… She could breathe him in for days and never get tired of it.

'Sit back and enjoy. Auctions are fun—the thrill of the chase.'

'Where's your catalogue?'

'I don't need one. I know exactly what I want.' She didn't think he was talking about the jewellery. His eyes darkened. Goose bumps peppered her skin at the intensity of his attention.

'What if we don't win?'

'I won't fail because what I have in mind is perfect for you. Nothing else will be good enough. You'll soon discover when I want something, I do everything in my power to get it.'

Aston's intensity thrilled her. Even more so, the realisation that he'd thought about this, planned it for her benefit. When had anyone ever done anything like that? Never, that was when. Most of the time people only expected things of her. They didn't much think of what she wanted at all.

The auction began with a fanfare. Exquisite jewels were projected onto a large screen, diamonds bigger than quail's eggs. The jewellery twinkled like constellations as the auctioneer coaxed the best price for the purchases. She couldn't help being caught up in the bidding. All the while, Aston quietly narrated the purchases—who had bought a diamond brooch for his mistress, what collector had won an emerald-and-diamond rivière to lock away in some vault.

He was expressive as he spoke, and at first she was terrified that with an errant flick of his hand he might purchase something he didn't mean to. Aston had laughed, deeply and throatily, reassuring her that that only happened in the movies. After that, she'd allowed herself to get carried away by the excitement as jewel after jewel sold to a hammer strike.

Then the auctioneer began to speak. Aston stiffened, alert, like a predator waiting to pounce.

'Now for lot twenty-one. This is a six-carat, internally flawless, cushion cut, fancy vivid-blue diamond set in platinum...'

A picture flashed up on the screen of a ring being modelled by a woman. Ana couldn't help herself; she gave a little gasp and stopped focussing on what the auctioneer was saying. She turned all her attention to the magnificent stone of deep-blue with an extraordinary internal fire. Had she been asked to choose her own engagement ring, she couldn't have imagined anything more perfect.

Ana knew without any doubt this was the ring Aston would bid on for her. He looked over at her with an intensity that burned. She realised then that the vivid blue of the diamond was the same colour as his eyes. It would be a reminder of him on her finger for ever.

'We'll start the bidding at two million.'

Two *million*? Suddenly it was hard to breathe. Aston did nothing, lounging back and watching the bids progress higher and higher, although the tension remained. He was coiled like a spring. The bids reached five million and he still hadn't made a move. It was too much money, that was why. She didn't know why her heart sank a little. Perhaps it was the thought of having something so beautiful on her finger before realising it wasn't going to happen. She might have worn all manner of precious gems, but none of them had been her own.

The bidding slowed when Aston raised his paddle.

'Six million.'

There was a collective gasp in the room, excited chatter at a new bidder entering the fray. Aston's bid seemed to reignite interest. The ring hit almost eight million euros.

'What are you doing?' she whispered.

'Bidding on your ring,' he replied with a grin, although his focus was all on the auctioneer. 'Eight-seven-five.'

'Eight million seven hundred and fifty thousand.'

His jaw was hard, his concentration intense as he watched the other bidders around him. That sort of money, all for a ring to grace her finger? She thought of what that sum could do for a charity instead of her. This was a convenient relationship, all fake. A wall of guilt crashed over her like a tidal wave. Carla was in hospital and here she was in an auction, with a man bidding on such an extravagance...

'You need to stop,' she snapped.

'Nine-point-two,' he said, and turned to her, eyebrow cocked. 'Why?'

'It's over nine million euros to put a ring on my finger. Think of what that could do for a charity.'

'I'll donate an equivalent amount to a charity of your choice. Just name it. Because I see this as an investment.'

'In what?'

'In you. This is your ring, *ma chèrie*. If you don't want it, let me know. Ten-point-one.'

The atmosphere changed again. She could sense the thrill rippling through the room. She wanted the ring, wanted him to keep bidding to see how much he was willing to pay. But at the same time a voice began to whisper nastily… *No one will love you now…* And, once she thought it, she couldn't shut the voice down. It repeated over and over, making a farce of everything, especially since it was the truth—Aston *didn't* love her.

He held up his paddle again. Another number, another increment. It was a fight between a phone bidder and him as to who would win the prize, when all Aston would win was her.

'Stop,' she said.

'I'll stop if you kiss me.'

She was aware of the hum of the room but, at his words, all her focus fell to Aston's lips—how perfectly etched they were, how full. Would they be soft or hard against her own?

A bid was raised by another party. Aston's pupils dilated. 'Twelve million.'

He didn't take his eyes from her, as if daring her to stop him. Ana didn't know what to do. All she knew was that she needed this riot of sensations to stop because they threatened to overwhelm her. Part of her wanted simply to fade away but Aston was pushing her into the blazing spotlight.

She was dimly aware of the auctioneer calling for more bids. The corner of Aston's lips curled and she knew she had to end this. She grabbed the front of Aston's shirt and tugged. His nostrils flared for a brief moment as he descended on her. There was no finesse in what she did as their lips crashed together.

It was only then she realised her fundamental mistake, her belief that she had *any* control here. The kiss had been designed to stop things, yet she was flung into a maelstrom. She hadn't known what to expect from a man whose body looked as hard as Aston's, a man who she was coming to learn worked out for a few hours every day in the early morning, but it hadn't been tenderness.

His free hand cupped her cheek, holding her close. His lips were feather-light on hers, so gentle, so soft. Such a contrast to the strength of him under her palm. There was so much banked power in him. She could sense a quiver of his muscles, as if he was holding back when her brain kept crying *more*.

She began to tremble against him as the heat roared through her, burning any hurt and fear away to nothingness. How she craved the abyss. Her lips parted and their tongues touched. She wanted so much more, becoming lost in it, all slick and hot. The world was simply white noise around her. She wanted him like nothing she'd ever wanted before. It consumed her, a craving so sharp and intense it hurt. This was a need that reached inside and tried to tear out her soul.

Then things slowed once more and became syrupy. Aston eased away and all she wanted to do was chase the kiss. She noticed then how heavy his breaths were, panting gusts matching hers. She stared into his eyes, into those deep pools of blue. She wanted to drown in them. A smattering of laughter sounded through the assembled crowd. The room slowly eased back into focus.

'No more bids?' The sharp fall of a hammer cracked through the room. 'Sold to Aston Lane for twelve million euros.'

CHAPTER SEVEN

THEY WALKED OUTSIDE into the bright light of the afternoon. The feel of Ana's kiss still on Aston's lips; her hand in his, as natural as breathing. Her ring glittered in the sunlight. His bank had transferred the funds immediately after he'd notified them at the hammer fall. There had been no delay. Then he'd taken the gem from its blue velvet box and slid it onto Ana's finger, to the smiles of the auction house staff. The ring had been the perfect fit.

Something primal erupted deep inside him, the sense that this was his claim over her. In the space of a short afternoon, any remaining distance between them had been breached. It was so deeply satisfying. There was no more wanting, as if he'd had his fill, was replete. For much of his life it had been as if he'd been looking for something. Now he was overwhelmed by the sense that today, he'd found it.

He tried not to think too hard about that, living only in the now. Ana's palm was warm against his. The sense of rightness on a back street in Paris, when his whole life had been spent chasing the next big adventure. He'd never seen a person as an adventure before but something about the simplicity of this moment had adrenalin coursing through his veins. There was a feeling deep in his gut that his life could irrevocably change if he allowed it.

A large black car slid into place on the street ahead of

them. The driver stepped out to let them in, but Aston didn't wait. 'To the apartment, please,' he said, opening the door himself.

His hand was on the small of Ana's back, guiding her in. She sat slowly and elegantly, swinging her legs into the vehicle and sliding across the seat as he followed. She tried to move over to the other side of the car, but that was too far, like a world away. He grabbed Ana's hand, hauled her to him and cupped her face, her skin soft and smooth under his fingers.

His lips descended on hers as her hands roved over his chest, clutching the fabric of his shirt. Everything about them together was hot and hungry. Time lost meaning. The car could have been moving, or it might not have gone anywhere at all as Ana's lips opened underneath him. Their tongues touched, sliding over each other. The connection was deep and immense, unfathomable.

The need for her hit him thick and sweet, like a syrupy dessert wine, the most addictive intoxicant. He could drink her in and still never get enough of her. Aston craved more, everything. To drag her onto his lap, strip her clothes and make love to her here in the back seat, with the world passing by them.

His hand reached to her breast, his thumb tracing over her nipple, a hard peak under the fabric of her impeccable suit. She arched into his hand and moaned, deep and low. Ana deserved more than this. She needed a bed with luxurious linens, not some fumble in the back seat of a car. Especially not for what he knew would be her first time. He tore his mouth away. His breath was heavy, her lips a deep plum, her eyes glassy.

'Name a charity,' Aston said, his voice unrecognisable to his own ears as the words ground out of him.

'The Cygnet Centre.' Her own voice was low, sensual, unlike how he'd heard her before. The sound of it shot like an arrow straight to the heart of him, then much, much lower.

Aston fired off a quick text to his assistant to arrange an immediate donation of twelve million euros to the charity in Ana's name.

A sense of urgency gripped him then, as if he had no time to lose. They'd marry in the Hôtel de Ville near the Girard château and celebrate the reception in one of the vineyards. If a religious ceremony was important to her, there was a chapel on the grounds.

The plans shaped in his mind. Her walking down the aisle in a dress of white… Yet he hadn't actually asked her to marry him, not officially. He'd slipped the ring on her finger in front of the staff of the auction house because it had been expected, yet the words hadn't been there. Everything had been assumed.

The car pulled to a stop and the driver opened the door. Aston got out, held out his hand and Ana placed hers into it. He didn't know how he managed to get to his apartment without stripping her bare. As it was, he pressed her into the back of the lift and kissed her mercilessly again. They tumbled out at his floor. He fumbled the lock on his apartment door as if he was some teenager on a drunken night out, and not a man of thirty-two in control of his faculties.

As they entered his apartment's entrance hall, he swung Ana into his arms, kicking the door closed behind them. He strode through to his bedroom, his lips hungry on hers, their panting breaths mingling. When they reached the room, he placed her reverently on the bed, where she sat, so prim and perfect. He tore off his jacket and dropped it to the floor, yet as he looked down on her something in her expression changed. Her teeth worried her lower lip.

Uncertainty... *No!*

His brain shouted the word. Aston didn't want to stop. He was harder than he'd ever been in his life. Every part of him felt as if it would crack, he was wired so tight. Yet, for him, desire had always been a two-way thing. It was vital for both people to want, enthusiastically and equally with no hesitation. He took a long, slow breath.

'I want you,' he said.

She looked at his groin, her pupils darkening, her lips parting. It was all he could do not to groan.

'I guessed.'

He'd never considered English as his second language. He'd always thought of himself as having two. His first memories were speaking both French and English fluently. Now he could barely get out the words in any language.

'Problem?'

Ana sat up, chewing on her lower lip. She wrapped her hands round her waist. Perhaps she wanted an official engagement before intimacy? He could ask the question, one that would seal their fate together, yet it didn't seem the right time. There was a ring on her finger, and for now that was enough. He didn't believe the absence of the words 'will you marry me?' was the impediment here. Aston still sensed the heat between them, raging like a wildfire. He was surprised the paint hadn't blistered on the apartment's walls.

She dropped her head and her heavy fringe fell over it.

Scars. It was daylight. Ana was afraid of what he might see. He walked to the bank of windows and gently drew each heavy curtain closed against the bright afternoon light. Everything seemed softer, muted.

'Better?' he asked.

'Thank you.'

He didn't think of himself as a tender man, but she needed

some tenderness. Aston walked towards her and took her hands in his.

'Will you let me see you now?'

She bit into her lower lip again. It must sting, the way her teeth cut into her pink flesh. He wanted to kiss all her pain away. She nodded.

'Let's start with what I already know.'

She tilted her head up to look at him. Aston reached out and gently brushed her hair out of the way. She closed her eyes as he looked at the scar threading into her hairline. He bent forward and kissed it, feather light, relishing her exhale as he did.

'It doesn't change the way I see you, *ma belle.*'

'It changes the way everyone else does. It changed me.'

'What's outside isn't important. You're kind. You care about your staff, charity—they're the things of value. *Who* you are inside.'

He reached down to the top button of her jacket and raised an eyebrow, preparing her for the question to come. 'Allow me?'

The corners of her mouth lifted in a trembling smile. He would kiss every scar on her body, every imperfection as she perceived it, to bring a true smile to her face. His fingers weren't as steady as they could be on the buttons because of the anticipation and part concern about needing to manage her fears in a way that would heal and not hurt. What if he got it wrong? He tried not to think of it and concentrated only on her.

Ana's jacket fell open to an elegant, embroidered camisole underneath. He held his breath in anticipation. She flinched a little and he was unsure whether it was pain or fear of what he might see, so he took it slowly, sliding the fabric from her shoulders. The scar revealed itself, marring the top of her left arm. Parts were thicker than normal skin, raised and red.

'Does it hurt? Does *anything* still hurt?' He wanted to give her pleasure, not cause her pain.

'Not really. Not any more.'

He knew, though, how emotional wounds could cause more pain than the physical. He had years of experience. Aston leaned down and kissed the still angry-looking skin.

'Anywhere else?' he asked. 'I'll kiss each one.'

She shook her head. 'I needed you when I was covered in bruises.'

An ache bloomed in his chest. Had anyone looked after her at all when she'd been hurting?

'I can go one better. I'll strip you bare now and kiss every part of your body till the concept of pain leaves your consciousness for ever and all that's left is pleasure. You, crying out my name to the room.'

Her lips opened, almost as if in shock at his promise. *'Oh.'*

It could have been the low light, but her pupils were huge and dark, drowning out the pale blue of her eyes. He bent down and slid a hand behind the swell of one of her calves. Aston eased off one nude stiletto and did the same to the other. Held out his hand and she placed hers in it without hesitation. He helped her up and undid the zip of her skirt. It slipped to the floor, leaving her in the exquisite camisole and panties of fine French lace. She was every fantasy brought to life. He wrapped his arms round her, kissed her. Let Ana feel just how much he wanted her. The kiss deepened and she began to grind herself against him. Needy, wanton. Clearly craving more than he was giving her.

Good.

He wanted her desperate, out of control, to stop her mind thinking and allow her body to take control, to take over.

'Lie back on the bed,' he murmured in her ear, kissing down her neck till she moaned. His hands stroked her back, goose bumps blooming on her skin. Aston backed her to the side of the bed and she sank into the soft covers, head on the plush pillows, lips apart as if there wasn't enough air in the room to catch a breath.

He held her gaze as he kicked off his own shoes. Slowly undid his shirt, tugged it from his trousers. Dropped it to the floor. Her breaths became audible. The shuddering inhale, the soft exhale. He undid his trousers and pushed them down his legs. He left his underwear on for now, so Ana could take time to get used to the idea of him, how they would fit together. His body objected, wanting to be free of the constraints of the tight fabric.

Patience.

Her eyes widened as he allowed her to take her fill. Aston sucked in his own steadying breath as she stared at him, his torso, his arousal. Once he thought she'd seen enough, he took off his socks and moved beside her. He breathed the scent of her in, like the sweetest of spring roses.

'The kissing all over starts now,' he said, in part-anticipation, part-warning. He gently lifted the camisole over her head and dropped it beside them. Her bra matched her panties, sheer, delicate lace, her nipples straining against it.

'Someone looks to be needing attention,' he said, dropping his mouth to one nipple, then the next, tonguing their tight peaks in turn till Ana writhed underneath him. Driving his own need higher and harder. He unclipped her bra and tossed it away. Cupped her breasts and rubbed his thumbs over her nipples as she arched back, panting. He dropped his head to her throat, trailing his lips down her body. Then he heard it, the breathless chanting of, 'Please, please...'

'I know what you need, Princess. Let me give it to you.'

His lips seemed to burn against her skin as he kissed down her body. He hooked his fingers into her panties, inching them down her legs as she struggled to get free of them. Once off her body, he rid himself of his own underwear, gritting himself against the feel of the coverlet on his overheated flesh.

She'd come first. He'd ensure it. Aston lowered his head to between her legs, splayed open as if inviting him. He kissed there, breathing in the heady scent of her own arousal, which made his head spin. *Mon Dieu*, the *need* for her... It clawed at him, demanded he rush to be inside her like some wild and rabid beast. He'd not experienced anything like it. He wanted to let it off the leash, to simply *take*.

But this was her first time, not the last time. He could be gentle, reverent, take his time and make her wait. It was what she deserved, the glorious mindlessness of pleasure. He used his tongue and his mouth to drive her higher and higher till she began to moan. He toyed at her entrance with his fingers, marvelling at how slick and wet she was, all for him. She began to beg once more, so he slid one finger inside, joined by another, in and out. Her breaths were mere pants. Ana was reduced to a creature of desire and feeling, and nothing more. It was a marvel to see her unbound, like some miracle. Then he curled his fingers inside and found a spot that made her stiffen. He concentrated on her clitoris and sucked. Her breathing stopped, then she threw her head back and wailed his name...

Just as he'd promised she would.

Everything exploded in a shower of light and sensation. Ana had never experienced anything like it. Time held no meaning bar this one, perfect moment. She floated as wave after wave of pleasure swamped her body. Drifting, untethered, but in a way that *freed* her. Then slowly she seemed to come back into herself. Her nerves still shimmering, over-sensitive.

She was aware of Aston sitting up briefly, opening the drawer of his bedside table. Protection. Then he returned, his kisses gentle, coaxing, setting her on fire again when she'd thought the pleasure of the moments before had extinguished it. She ran her hands over his muscular body, relishing how warm he was, how strong and sure. Relishing the contrast between her and him, the stiff hairs on his chest, arms and legs, rough against her skin. And even though her world had exploded around her, she still felt empty and wanting.

Aston rose over her. She parted her legs and he settled between them, forearms either side of his head, his thumbs stroking her temples.

'I like my ring on your finger,' he said.

'I like it too.' It was too extravagant, too much, yet no one had ever done anything like this for her before.

'You know, I'd marry you tomorrow if the laws in France allowed it, but you deserve more than a rushed day, which isn't exactly how you want it.'

The sentiment seemed so tender. Aston was thinking of her again. He'd seen her worth not in how she looked but who she was inside. That meant more to her than the ring, or promises of a wedding. Something inside her seemed to crack and break, as if allowing space for him. She knew there was no going back, not now.

He kissed her again. The tenderness had gone. This one, hot and feverish. His fingers at her nipple, his weight against her. Their bodies moved, creating a sweet ache inside. A need began building again, tighter and tighter, as they rocked together. His hardness slid against her. She wanted to be filled by him, to experience that blissful sense of release and floating once more. She lifted her hips as Aston eased himself inside her. She gloried in the feeling. The pressure, the fullness. He stopped, toying with her nipples again, sensation spearing between her legs as he slid forward and seated himself deep in her body.

'Good?' he asked.

'Yes.' The word was almost only a breath. How close she felt to him in this moment. How much care he'd taken. There'd been no pain, only pleasure. He began to rock again, as if allowing her to get used to his size, then he really moved, thrusting in and out. She ran her hands down his body to his buttocks, feeling the way his hips flexed. The muscles as he drove into her in a hypnotic kind of rhythm. Becoming one. She was lost in the wonder of it, the dizzying sensations. The clawing need as it built again, deeper, a relentless ache. And then it came over with a roar of heat and ecstasy, as Aston groaned his own release.

Ruining them both.

CHAPTER EIGHT

ANA WOKE AND STRETCHED. Her body ached in the most delicious of ways. She and Aston had made love for most of the afternoon before, exploring each other's bodies, learning what it took to make each other sigh and moan. It gave her such a sense of power, to have seen him come apart because of her. Then they'd eaten a quick dinner, tumbled back into bed again and made love through the night.

Now Aston lay beside her, blissfully asleep. She knew that he usually woke early and trained. For what, she still wasn't sure, as he avoided the question, but for now it didn't matter. There was something satisfying about seeing him simply rest when usually he appeared to be a person who truly burned the candle at both ends.

She rolled over to check the time on her phone, but it wasn't beside her bed where she usually kept it. It must have been in the lounge area. That was the thing about leaving with Aston—she hadn't needed to obsessively check her daily alerts. It had stopped being a reflex because no one except her family knew where she was.

Her stomach grumbled, telling her it had to be well past breakfast. She got out of bed carefully so as not to wake him. Crept out of the room to her own *en suite* bathroom and looked in the mirror. Grazes from Aston's stubble had marked her skin. She touched the areas, loving that he'd left them on her. They were marks she didn't mind. They didn't mar her. They were a reminder of the earth-shattering pleasure he'd given her.

She tidied her hair a little and threw on a silk gown, not yet wanting fully to clothe herself. She relished the sensation of the smooth fabric on her overheated skin, imagining it was his hands stroking her.

Perhaps she could get them both some breakfast? They could eat together, then spend the day in bed. She didn't have anything on, nowhere to go. Ana grabbed her phone and made her way to the kitchen where she found some fruit and yoghurt. She loved Aston's apartment. The honey-coloured herringbone parquetry. Ornate plaster ceilings. Tasteful furniture, a mix of antique with some modern touches. This place had a soul.

She opened the French doors to her favourite feature, a little balcony overlooking the Eiffel Tower, where she put down her bowl and sat. She couldn't help holding up her hand in the warm morning light, turning it so the magnificent diamond she hadn't taken from her finger flashed as it caught the sunshine.

She guessed it meant that she and Aston were now engaged. He hadn't asked, but she'd sensed the finality of it all in the kiss at the auction, the moment he'd slid the ring onto her finger. Then they'd made love for most of the afternoon and night. What was that if not confirmation that the deal between them had been sealed? She didn't need Aston to make a performance out of it and officially ask her to marry him in some romantic gesture.

Although, Aston *could* be romantic—the dinner on his yacht with the beautiful candles, flowers and string lights were proof... Her heart tightened at the memory, something like disappointment, but she had no right to that emotion when what they'd agreed was clear. Their relationship wasn't about love or romance. It was a convenience, and that was enough. There was no point dwelling on any of it.

She took a spoonful of her yoghurt and checked her phone. As she did, she noticed the messages from her parents' number, although she was sure it was their private secretary who'd sent it.

We requested discreet. However, we offer you congratulations on your presumed engagement. Please advise when the announcement is formalised.

How did they know? Her heart began to thump a sickening rhythm. There were no court circulars to talk about her comings and goings or engagements as a member of the royal family.

Then she saw a text from Cilla.

OMG Ana, is this true!?!?!

The text linked to an article and she opened it. Immediately wishing she hadn't. It was a piece about the auction, mentioning the record price per carat for a fancy blue diamond. Who purchased it. Talk of a mystery woman. She shut the piece down and looked for more. The Internet was awash with it. Rumours about the mystery woman turned into rumours that it was her, before some entertainment sites formally named her as the recipient. An anonymous attendee at the auction had apparently confirmed it, and their kiss. The press wrote how they were waiting for an announcement from the palace. The tabloids had delved into the romance, fictional though it might have been. There was talk of Aston's business in Halrovia, perhaps signalling the commencement of a love affair for the man who had once been a confirmed bachelor.

It was like a juggernaut bearing down on her. She'd lived the past days in relative anonymity, no one knowing where she was going or what she was doing. That had been a kind of bliss. Now there was speculation as to where they might be staying, identifying his apartment in the seventh arrondissement as the most likely place. Showing pictures of the previous real estate listings. Its last sale price before Aston bought it and was reported to have done an extensive renovation.

She dropped the spoon and it fell into her breakfast with a clatter, spattering yoghurt on the table and on her. She couldn't breathe. She didn't know what to do. Could anyone see her out here? The street was lined with trees. She tried looking through them at the properties opposite. Were they homes available for rental? Was anyone watching? Waiting, for her? Ana peered over the balcony to the road below. There was a man across the street, standing looking at the building. He wore a hat pulled low but something about the shape of the body, the way he held himself, seemed familiar.

She pulled back, gasping for air. It wasn't possible, was it? Could Count Hakkinen have found her here? With the news reports, everybody would know where she now lived. It was only a few hours' flight from Halrovia to Paris. She didn't know what to do, where to go. Panic gripped her as she struggled for each breath. Ana stood, trembling, her legs barely holding her as she ran into the apartment...

Hitting a strong, solid wall of male flesh as she did.

'Whoa!' Aston said, chuckling as he caught Ana just inside the door to the terrace. 'I'm happy to see you too.'

He could say that with honesty. The afternoon and night

had been more than he could have dreamed—though he'd known how their passion would burn together from the first night they'd met, so it shouldn't have come as any surprise. This morning he'd slept in, and had been a little disappointed not to find Ana in bed with him, because he'd woken with the inevitable erection and, even though he had planned a few hours of training, thought they might spend the most of another day in bed together. However, this greeting would do nicely…

Except as he held her he noticed her trembling, as if she was freezing. He placed his hands on her shoulders and looked down at her. Her face was deathly pale, her eyes wide. It was a look familiar to him from those final, terrible moments with Michel when he'd paled, gripped Aston's hand and said, 'I think I'm going to die… Live for me…' and then crashed.

The look on Ana's face was fear.

Would you keep me safe?

Are you in danger?

All of him stiffened, on high alert. He'd asked that on his yacht, but Ana hadn't really answered. He'd told her he cared for what was his. What had he missed?

'*Ma chèrie*, what's wrong?'

'I can't…'

Her breaths came in heaving gulps. He led her inside to the sofa, sat down and took her with him. He simply wrapped her in his arms and held her.

'Tell me. Take your time. Nothing can harm you here.'

He stroked his hand over the fine silk of her robe and cradled her till the tremors that racked her body eased and she was ready to speak. To let him know what was wrong.

'It's everywhere.' Her voice was the barest whisper. 'We're *everywhere*—the ring…us…where you live.'

Ah.

He wasn't sure why that stung, the thought she was upset that their engagement, such as it was, had been picked up by the press. He checked his phone. The stories weren't unexpected. Where he lived was no secret. There was a text from the private secretary to her parents, admonishing him for not keeping things discreet. Asking for their official announcement, which he was happy to ask his own team to draft.

'It was to be expected. Nothing remains secret for too long. They were going to find out soon enough.'

'I thought I had time.'

Her voice sounded shrill, panicked. He released her and took her chin, tilting up her face so he could see her. Ana's eyes were full of tears. He didn't have much time for sentiment or feeling, but his heart cracked, seeing her like this. He'd skirted around the situation for too long. Usually Aston knew when to keep his cards close and when to play them. Right now, they needed to be in play.

'Why are you afraid?'

'No one believes me.'

'I will.'

He waited, and a story simply came tumbling out of her about a man she believed had been sending her fan mail that made her skin crawl. How she thought he'd begun to follow her. Then about a night in Monaco…

'I was with friends. I'd been sure I'd caught glimpses of him earlier in the night. Then I *saw* him, in the casino. He smiled at me. It was *knowing*. I had to go. I asked a driver to take me away and my friend followed to make sure I was okay. All I'd wanted was to have fun, to live a little…'

She told him about an unfamiliar driver, a potent combination of alcohol, prescription medication and speed. An accident which had hurt her friend Carla badly, and had hurt Ana too. She talked about her crushing guilt, the way she'd been treated by the press, her family.

The anger ignited and began to burn in his gut like acid at how afraid she sounded, at how her parents didn't believe her. How the man she blamed for it all was going to be granted a medal for bravery for pulling her out of the car when, in truth, the accident had been due to the terror he'd caused her and *no one* but her sister had supported her.

'And I heard his voice as he was trying to pull me from the car: "you'll scar, and no one but me will love you now."'

Aston had never considered himself a violent man but, right now, it was all he could do not to break something, anything within reach. Though that wouldn't help Ana. She needed his calm, his control.

'Now he knows where I am. I—I think he was downstairs, watching. Or maybe I imagined it.'

Aston gently placed Ana on the sofa next to him. Stood, and strode to the terrace. Her breakfast sat spoiling in the sun, yoghurt splattered on the table-top. He looked out over the street but couldn't see anyone. That didn't mean someone wasn't there...

'There's no one...' he said as he came back inside. Ana's face began to crumple, tears welling in her eyes. She needed to know that he wasn't someone who'd ignore her very real fears. 'Goddess, I believe you.'

He had influence and power, so the fix was easy enough. Aston called his security firm in her presence so she could hear what he was doing. He told them the situation, and then called the building's owners to updated them on his arrangements. The place was secure, but more would never go amiss. Within the half hour, there would be residential security in the building, and if he and Ana left the premises, close personal security would guard them. It had been laughably simple. How her family, a *royal* family, hadn't done the same was inconceivable.

Finally, he contacted the building's concierge to give him some warning and to ensure that nothing which hadn't been vetted by his security was to come to their apartment.

'Monsieur Lane, there's a delivery of flowers here for Her Highness—red roses.' Aston stiffened, turned and gave a reassuring smile to Ana before leaving the room so she couldn't hear him.

'Is there a message?'

'Oui.'

'Read it, please.'

'It says…"it isn't over until the wedding ring's on the finger".'

A volcanic heat began simmering in his gut. Aston gripped his mobile so hard, he feared he would crack it.

'Who are they from?'

'The card doesn't say, *monsieur.*'

Aston asked for the flowers to be left for his security detail to deal with. Perhaps they'd provide some evidence as to who'd sent them, perhaps not. For now, he needed to take care of Ana. He went back into the lounge area, where she huddled on the sofa, looking small and pale, her arms wrapped round her middle.

She looked up at him, eyes brimming with unshed tears. 'Your address…'

He knew what she feared, and her fears were clearly justified. Aston sat back down on the sofa and took her into his arms again. 'I have more than one place to stay around the world, and many friends. The man doesn't have the resources I do. He'll never touch you.'

She seemed to relax a little at that, softening in his arms. He appreciated her trust, and would honour it.

'With the news today, there's no doubt my parents will want to meet you. The timing couldn't be better. I've recently purchased a property in Épernay that's known only to my lawyer. We can travel there by helicopter and no one will have any idea where we're going. We'll have some time before the inevitable invitation from my parents. Their château is only a short drive from my farmhouse, so we won't be in a car for long. Security will always be with us.'

'Thank you. I don't know what to say.'

He tightened his arms round her. '*Ma chèrie*, you don't need to say anything.'

Aston was confident nothing could touch her, or him. It was her fear he needed to assuage, to soothe. No wonder she'd seemed so worn down, a different woman from the one he'd met at the Spring Ball, because her life had in all ways changed.

'For now, we have plans for the day.' She tensed a fraction in his arms. By the end of this, she wouldn't. She'd be confident in him, his abilities. 'You need food. You need coffee. Then I'll take you back to bed and hold you till you believe that I'll do what I promised you in the maze. I *will* keep you safe. Because I care for what's mine.'

Aston stood with Ana in his arms. As he carried her to the bedroom once more, he ignored the training he should be doing to prepare for the mountain he'd promised to climb.

Aston picked up the dossier of material gathered by the security firm he employed. They'd been thorough, and they'd not taken long to get the information he'd paid them handsomely for. Whilst the Halrovian royal family had tried to prevent reporting about Ana's accident and its aftermath, pictures still existed for those who knew and had the determination to find them. The bile rose to his throat at the voyeurism, at how people had seen fit to take photographs rather than help. Only one person had approached the crumpled car, trying to remove Ana from it, but this man was no rescuer. Aston clenched his fists, his jaw: Count Hakkinen, Ana's tormentor. The thought of his hands on her lit him up with near-incandescent fury.

He breathed through the anger, not stopping to question why he was being affected this way. She'd kept photographs of some of the anonymous letters sent to her. Whilst he could understand why they might have been dismissed, there was a sense of malevolence about them that he would never have ignored. From her report and timelines, his security team believed that the man's behaviour had been escalating. Sadly, the flowers sent to their apartment hadn't yielded any clues. There were no fingerprints and the message was typewritten. But he had enough. He'd put a stop to Hakkinen's harassment of Ana and, if it didn't stop, he would crush the man like a cockroach.

Ana suspected her parents had fancied him as a suitor for her sister, Priscilla. Aston knew men like Count Hakkinen and could identify them a mile off: rich, with an inflated sense of entitlement. Believing he was owed a princess, so taking the one who remained unattached. The one who would likely have scars. Such arrogance, audacity…

Aston hadn't forgotten the words Ana had heard in her ear the night she'd been injured. No wonder she'd seemed changed, with no one believing her, with the guilt. She'd have been plagued by self-doubt, wondering what was real and what was imagined. *He* believed her, and Hakkinen would pay. The count was down on his luck, a well-hushed-up financial scandal having significantly reduced his social capital, meaning he'd been cut loose by most of his contacts. Did he seek to recover his position through a princess? *Never.*

Yet something in the back of Aston's brain prickled, almost like guilt. Wasn't he using Ana in his own way, to ensure his inheritance? Perhaps, but unlike this man, who only saw fit to torment her, Aston would look after her, encourage her interests, worship her body.

He was *nothing* like Count Hakkinen. That man might be an aristocrat, but he was craven and dishonest. Aston's security had easily discovered how far the rot went. His house of cards would take laughably little to bring down should he not do *exactly* what Aston demanded. The man might think himself better than anyone else, with his title and tenuous links to the royal family through his father. It was *nothing* compared to Aston's reach and influence.

He checked his watch. Ana was now safely ensconced in his Épernay farmhouse, well-guarded by personal protection officers. Today she was occupied in back-to-back meetings with her staff, and also with his accountants, to discuss her charity interests. She'd been excited about those things, and this had given him the perfect opportunity to take a helicopter flight to Paris, under the guise of conducting business, to meet with the Count.

Aston never again wanted to witness the fear he'd seen in Ana's eyes. He hadn't wanted to tell her of this meeting, either, in case that fear returned. Only when he was sure Hakkinen had been dealt with would he provide her with the reassurance she needed. Aston had promised to keep her safe, and he would. He always kept his promises.

The journey to the hotel where the count was staying didn't take long from Aston's office in La Défense. The man had no idea that Aston would be calling today but, from reports he'd had from the security operative watching him,

Count Hakkinen was a man of routine, and at this time of the day he'd sit in the hotel's café and eat breakfast. This morning, Aston hoped he would make that meal curdle in Hakkinen's stomach.

On arrival, Aston was happy to see the hotel had a faded elegance—the type of place an aristocrat down on their luck might stay. His security operative nodded to him on the street as he entered the tired-looking café with its pretensions to grandeur. He spied the man he was looking for immediately, having seen enough photographs in the dossier still sitting on the desk in his office. Hakkinen's gaze rose to Aston over his coffee cup, eyes widening as he put down the cup and stood. To challenge? To run? Aston had no idea, but he was prepared for anything. This man was a nobody, as Aston would soon show him.

Hakkinen held his ground but the tells were there. The way he fidgeted with the cuff of his cheap looking ready-made shirt. The convulse of a swallow. Still, he attempted a business-like smile. Aston saw right through him, and could almost smell the fear lingering in the air.

'Monsieur Lane. To what do I owe the pleasure?'

'There's no pleasure to be found here, Hakkinen. *Sit.*'

The man's face reddened. His jaw hardened. Aston stood there, unmoving. Waiting. Hoping that the man would try something, because his loss in any challenge would be swift and assured. But, in the end, Count Hakkinen sat. He was a coward and Aston knew he would always prevail.

Aston waited a few moments, staring the count down, then unbuttoned his jacket and took a seat, lounging in the chair as if he didn't give a damn. In many ways, he didn't— not about the man sitting opposite him at least.

'Leave my fiancée alone. Your pretensions that you could have any chance with Her Highness end today.'

Hakkinen's face reddened. 'I'm not doing anything to your fiancée.'

Liar.

'You might have fooled some, but you'll never fool me,' Aston snarled through gritted teeth. '"It isn't over till the wedding ring's on the finger"? You're right, it hasn't even *begun* where you're concerned if you don't leave France immediately.'

If Aston wasn't mistaken, he saw an avaricious gleam in the count's eyes.

'There are things you don't know about Her Exalted Highness,' Hakkinen said with a sneer. 'She's not as perfect as she pretends. How would you like all of the information the palace tried to hush up about that night released to the press? The driver of the car—'

'Was someone she had no control over. Her Highness doesn't have to pretend to be anything around me. There's nothing you could say that will make me think less about her.' That was a certainty. Aston gave a cold, hard laugh. 'But *everything* I know about you, on the other hand...'

'You have nothing on me.' Yet the count seemed to pale, fidgeting with his coffee cup.

'Want to bet the meagre remains of your fortune and failing reputation on that?'

A harried-looking waiter came to the table and asked Aston if he would like anything.

'*Un café,*' Aston said, pinning Hakkinen with a cold glare. 'On Count Hakkinen's bill. Now, where were we? Yes. I was asking whether you were a betting man. But I'm short on time, so let me lay my own cards on the table.'

Aston's coffee arrived. He pushed it away. He'd never had any intention of drinking it but took perverse pleasure in the knowledge Hakkinen was paying for the beverage, even if it was only a few euros.

'The only story the press will be interested in is the one I'll provide them should you not do everything I say—a full investigation of certain irregular charity transactions. You talk about a hush-up? I have evidence about the repayments you made to cover up the discrepancies. Then there are your debts. I know where the cracks are in your business, all your weaknesses. If you don't leave my fiancée alone, there will be a takeover and I will ensure it's hostile. You'll be left with nothing. Completely ruined, financially and socially.'

Aston had never believed a person's face could turn truly white, but he witnessed Hakkinen's do so in that moment. It gave him a brutal satisfaction—not only the pallor of the count's skin but the way his hands trembled, the sweat beading on his upper lip.

'You think you can do that to me?' the man asked, voice a bare whisper.

'I don't think, I *know*. I have an informative dossier all about you. A few words in the right ears and your fall from grace will be so complete there will be no rising from it. You're no Lazarus.'

Aston stood, and loomed over the table, lowering his voice to inject cold menace. Hakkinen shrank back in his chair.

'I'm a fair man and will give you *one* chance. But, if I hear even a rumour that you're in the same *country* as my fiancée ever again, I will end you.'

Aston took the time to button his jacket, turned and stalked from the café, sending a quick text to his driver as he did. Positive Hakkinen had heard the message he'd delivered, loud and clear. He checked his watch as his car pulled up at the hotel, sliding into the rear seat. His pulse beat hard and fast. In less than an hour, he'd be back at the farmhouse. He could go for a training run to burn off the sickening remains of his fury, then arrange another meeting with his fellow expedition members to plan for the Everest climb. No, not *could*—he *would* do all of those things and more, even though right now the weight of them exhausted him.

Yet all he craved, more than any promise he had ever made to the living or dead, was to make love to Ana.

CHAPTER NINE

THEY'D TRAVELLED IN secret to Aston's Épernay property a week ago. It was a magnificent, sprawling stone farmhouse on fifty acres of land. Aston had arranged for on-site security, who lived in a converted barn a discreet distance from the main house. She welcomed their presence, even though for the main they stayed out of sight.

It was as if she could finally relax. Aston had taken some time away from work to spend with her, apart from a brief trip back to Paris when she'd been sorting out staff and her new charity. Aside from the early hours, when Aston took to his gym or put on a heavy pack and trekked across the land in training, they'd explored the countryside. He'd taken her to Reims, where they'd visited a cathedral, a museum and had a quiet dinner. He'd promised her a balloon flight over the vineyards.

Then their nights…when it was as if she came alive. The hunger, the need, consumed her. The depth of her emotion she had trouble fathoming some days might have scared her a little, had Aston not always been a grounding presence. When one night she'd cried because the orgasm, what he made her feel, had been too much, he'd simply held her. Kissed away her tears and made love to her again, slow and aching.

Then the very next morning he'd gone out to train once

more. She admired his dedication, and loved what it did to his body, all the hard, tempting muscles, but she worried about him. Worried about how tired he sometimes seemed, as if what he was doing was an obligation. She'd tried to raise it with him, asking what mountain he was planning to climb, but his response was always the same. He'd dismiss her concerns and then kiss her till she forgot any questions and simply immersed herself in the passion that exploded between them.

He worshipped her, like the goddess he'd proclaimed her to be at the Spring Ball. Her scars were ignored. They'd become part of her. Even she was coming to accept them, feeling…beautiful once more. He'd given her that—a sense things were possible again. That there was an exciting life and a future ahead not only for her, but for *them*.

As if she'd conjured him, the man walked into the room, showered and wearing a dark suit and blood-red tie, whilst she stood in the middle of their bedroom in only a robe. He was so handsome, so solid. He was kind to her in ways entirely unfamiliar. Everything Aston did made her feel safe and wanted. Not for what she looked like but who she was. She felt it when they discussed her charities, his own interests, how they might work together. He treated her like a true partner.

It was as if he'd finally woken her from a life where she'd been sleepwalking. She hadn't known how exhausting the constant tension had been, always being on edge. What Aston had done for her fuelled an anger that her parents could have done something too, had they wanted to. But she didn't have time to think about a family who hadn't thought much about her.

Although thinking of family… It hadn't taken long for Aston's parents to extend an invitation to the château and tonight she'd be meeting them for the first time.

'Not quite ready yet, I see.'

He gave her a wry and knowing grin. Her heart fluttered. Aston might be handsome all of the time, but when he smiled it was as if a supernova had exploded in the room. She looked at the bed, the clothing on it. This was an important night, and she had no idea what to wear.

'It's easy for you. A suit's like a uniform.'

'It should be easy for you too. You'll be magnificent in whatever you choose.'

'How about you choose for me?'

His smile softened. 'It would be my pleasure.'

He moved to the bed to sift through the clothes, where only last night they'd made love and she'd come so many times she'd begged him to stop. Yet even though they'd plunged into an exhausted and replete slumber, he'd still risen at four and worked out for two hours.

'This.'

He held up a dress in fabric of gleaming duchess satin with a boat neck that his secretary and the woman in the boutique had begged her to try on and buy, so she had. It had three-quarter sleeves. Sleek and impeccably fitted. Its styling was reminiscent of fifties elegance yet carried a flirty edge, with a little bow belt.

It was blood-red, the same colour as Aston's tie. The only other time she'd worn a little red dress... Her breath caught, her heart rate kicking up. She couldn't, wouldn't, remember. Instead, she focussed on Aston, and her heart-rate settled.

'You'll look magnificent in red, *ma déesse.*'

My goddess.

The emotion welled inside her, a sensation that she could do anything. Around Aston, her fears seemed to fade. It was as if he saw *her*, the woman, not the 'perfect princess' on her shaky pedestal. It was a position she'd never wanted but had been given regardless by the press, the public and her own family. Ana had come to realise the night of the accident wasn't her fault. She'd done nothing wrong. She and her friend had been victims of circumstance; she wasn't being punished by the universe. She'd wanted to wear a red dress once. Why couldn't she wear one tonight, on this important night, meeting her future parents-in-law?

'Would you help me do up the zip?'

'I'll help you dress…and undress later.'

A glorious wave of desire washed over her, her nipples beading in her bra, a warmth blooming at her core as Aston carefully removed the dress from the hanger and undid the zip. He handed it to her. She stepped into it and turned her back to him. He lifted her hair and goose bumps sparkled over her skin. As Aston began slowly doing up the zip, his lips dropped to the base of her neck, drifting over her skin in feather-light kisses. Her eyes fluttered shut.

'Are you trying to convince both of us to stay home?'

'It's just a taste of what's to come,' he murmured against her overheating flesh.

'Promises, promises.'

'They're something I always keep. Rest assured, I will deliver.'

She smiled as he inched the zip slowly upwards, tooth by tooth.

'Is that a promise or a threat, Mr Lane?'

Aston chuckled, the sound dark and throaty as he finished with the zip, hooking the dress at the top. 'It can be anything you want, Princess.'

In that moment, she couldn't answer. It was hard to breathe, with the effect he had on her. Instead, she turned round and smoothed her hands down the perfect, heavy silk, doing up the belt. 'What do you think of your choice?'

'*Parfaite,*' he said.

If a look could set her on fire, Aston's could burn down the house. He stalked to the dresser, as if he somehow needed to get away from her, picking up her ring which she'd placed in a small bowl whilst she looked for something to wear. He made his way back to her and gently took her left hand, sliding the magnificent gemstone onto her finger. It twinkled in the soft light.

'However, I'm coming realise a terrible omission. I never *asked* you to marry me.'

He was right; those words had never been said. Now they felt important. So much had changed. When she'd first left the palace all she'd wanted was to flee. He'd taken her away, given her space and time, and since then everything had been assumed. She couldn't imagine her life without Aston in it.

'Your ring on my finger and an official announcement is kind of a giveaway.'

He'd been right: convenient *didn't* mean cold. It was as though she was already bound to him in ways she could never have anticipated. A formal proposal seemed unnecessary, yet why did she feel too big for her own skin right now? Her hands trembling, heart pounding in excitement.

'Your acceptance is important to me. To hear the words, not to assume.' He cupped her cheek. 'Will you marry me, Ana? My princess, my *goddess.*'

Tears burned her eyes, the back of her nose. This moment was so perfect and precious in its simplicity, brimming with emotion. She was so thankful that he'd helped her overcome her fears. The words from that night of her accident—*no one but me will love you now*—held no power any more.

Though in reality none of this was love…was it?

'Of course there was never a doubt,' she said. 'You've given me everything.'

Though a tiny thought niggled the back of her consciousness. Had he truly given her himself? There was so much she didn't know…

Aston dropped his head and kissed her gently, reverently, on the lips.

'How I'm going to worship you later,' he said. And there it was again, in the rumble of his voice, part-promise, part-threat. 'Now, *on y va*, before you convince *me* never to leave.

Ana knew she'd be counting down every second till they returned home again.

Aston steered the car down the narrow roads from his farmhouse to his parents' château. He should be tense about it. This meeting was a critical one, cementing his and Ana's relationship in the eyes of his family—securing Girard in the process. In many ways he understood it would be difficult. He hadn't really seen or spoken to his parents since their argument in anything other than a superficial way or when necessary for the business. Yet, despite the importance of this evening, a calm settled over him.

He glanced in the rear-view mirror at the vehicle following with his personal security, then to Ana, who sat in silence next to him. Once he might have schooled her on what to say to his parents about their relationship. Now he didn't feel the need. The proposal tonight had cemented something, an honest and meaningful moment between them. Whilst he might not have wanted his parents to know their relationship was a convenient one, it didn't feel so convenient now. Their attraction was a truth and everything between them felt real with her in his life, his bed, his future… Still…her silence now troubled him. What was she thinking? Was she having second thoughts?

Impossible. She'd all but suggested they might like to forgo dinner and spend the night in bed together instead. That didn't speak of regret, but passion. Of course, it could be the simple fact of the car journey. Now he knew about her accident, her injuries, he took extra care on the drive.

'You're quiet,' he said.

'We're visiting your parents. I'm finding the thought quite daunting. Usually when I'm meeting someone new a staff member would give me a dossier I could read about them. I feel under-prepared.'

He turned into the long, gravel drive of the place that he still thought of as home, even though he had houses all over the world.

'There's nothing more to know than I've already told you,' he said. 'You'll be perfect.'

Even in the darkness he could tell she stiffened. 'I'm glad you have faith in me.'

'Don't underestimate yourself.'

'Everybody else seems to, of late.'

They pulled up at the front of the château. The grand building and the trees that flanked it were lit up with accent lighting in the darkness.

'"Everybody" is not me. Remember who you are, *ma déesse*. Charming, kind…my parents will love you.'

Ana turned to him, the warm light from the house and garden painting her in gold. She smiled and his breath caught. Each one was such a rare and precious gift. Something seemed to snag in his chest—an unfamiliar sensation, hinting at possibilities which might be his if he simply reached out and took them.

'Thank you for reminding me.'

'Toujours,' he said as he leapt out of the car and went to her side, helping her over the gravel drive to a broad stone staircase leading to the house. He took her hand, threading her fingers through his as they walked up the stairs. She was wearing heels, after all. He didn't want her to twist her ankle on the stone surface.

'This is magnificent,' she whispered, the sound of wonder in her voice.

He chuckled. 'You live in a castle.'

'Whilst I lived there, most of it is a workplace rather than a home.'

As they reached the front door, Aston pulled a key out of his pocket. If he were formally disinherited, would his parents ask him to return it? It gave him a moment's pause, hesitation. He reached out to put it in the lock when the door opened like a miracle. His parents must have been waiting for them on the other side. Knowing his mother, probably keeping an eye on the security camera in anticipation of their arrival.

He stiffened as his parents stood there. Since their argument, their demand he find a wife, he'd only spoken to them over the phone. His grip on Ana's hand tightened involuntarily. She squeezed back, then glanced up at him with an eyebrow raised, a question on her face. He relaxed his fingers so as not to crush her.

His father was the first to smile. His mother soon followed. Ana wouldn't know, but Aston could see the slight strain on both of their faces. Their expressions were not as open as he would otherwise have expected.

'Hello, I'm Simon. This is Camille. Come in! Welcome to our home.'

They followed his parents into the house, to a sitting room where Aston knew pre-dinner drinks would be served. Aston introduced Ana with her official title. She blushed, her cheeks reddening, her flush heightened by the glorious colour of her dress.

'Please, call me Ana.'

His mother walked up to Ana and kissed both her cheeks. 'I cannot believe I had to find out my son was engaged this way, through the *media*.' She glanced over at him, the words almost a rebuke, but also an acknowledgement of the distance between them.

'We wanted to tell you, but we were outed before we could,' he said.

'It was all very sudden,' Ana added.

'And the ring. Excuse me for being gauche, but I must see the treasure which led me to discovering my son was engaged.'

Ana held up her hand, the perfect gem glittering in the light as she and his mother talked about the auction, the excitement.

With his mother and Ana engrossed in conversation, his father put a hand on Aston's shoulder, an affectionate gesture. 'You did well, son. I thought we could open this.'

He handed Aston a bottle. Aston whistled.

'The 1972 vintage.' It was a collector's item, their most sought-after vintage of all.

'Of course. It's not every day our son gets engaged to a princess. You deserve the best.'

Aston might have imagined it, but his father's eyes looked a little glassy in the lights. Simon turned away and began to pour, then handed out the glasses.

'I'd like to propose a toast,' he said. 'To Aston and Ana. Congratulations. May you be as happy as Camille and I are.'

Aston took a sip of the magnificent wine. Its appearance represented a clear thawing of the *froideur* that had been between his parents and him. Any issues in their family tended to be settled at the table with food and wine. Hopefully tonight was no different.

Ana came to his side, smiling as she raised her glass and drank. She looked happy and more relaxed than he had ever seen her before. He watched on as she and his mother talked about her family, her school days. Ana laughed, listening to his mother recount stories of the antics the girls had got up to when they'd boarded. Ana's mother had seemed to stay well out of most of the trouble, but still, anything that made Ana happy pleased him.

'How did you both meet?' his mother asked. A loaded question for sure, but an easy one to answer.

'We met at a trade mission.' Aston stilled. Ana answering first came as a surprise.

'The moment I saw him, he caught my eye.'

Her admission surprised him even more. He'd had no idea she'd remembered him. That day she'd been the perfect ice princess—cool, polite, the consummate royal. Ana looked up at him with a gentle smile on her face. Her eyes were full of emotion, something soft and warm. Warming him to his frozen core.

'She caught my eye too,' he said, the truth. He'd wanted to crack through her hard shell that day and find the woman beneath. The woman he saw now. 'Then the Spring Ball. She was a goddess.'

'You were a god.'

They were having a moment, something profound, he just couldn't name what it was. Simon clapped Aston on the shoulder. 'This story sounds familiar, doesn't it, Camille?'

'*Tout à fait*. Although, I hope my son's proposal was more romantic than his father's.'

'Why, what did Simon do?' Ana asked.

His mother put her hand to her chest. 'He made me climb a *mountain* with him.'

'Goodness, which one?'

This was an old story, one of his parents' favourites and one they often told. His father chuckled. 'Camille makes it sound like a trial. It wasn't so much of a climb, more like a walk—easy.'

'It took *five* hours uphill. And Kosciuszko is a mountain. You told me it was the tallest in Australia. I thought it would never end.'

'You survived.' His father sounded wounded, but it was all an act. He still had a huge smile on his face.

'I suffered, but then he went down on his knees and proposed, so I forgave him and said yes.'

'Well, Aston didn't ask me to climb any mountains,' Ana said.

They all laughed, and he wondered, what if he'd asked? Would she have agreed? It seemed vital somehow to have the answer, although he didn't know how to get it from her.

She gazed up at him, her eyes gleaming in the soft light of the room. 'But it was a romantic proposal nonetheless.'

'As we would have expected,' Aston's mother said, her own eyes glittering too, as if with tears.

A knot seemed to tighten in Aston's throat. He took another sip of wine and swallowed it down.

A woman came through the doorway, one of the kitchen staff, who usually worked in the château's restaurant.

'Ah, dinner is served,' his mother said. 'To celebrate this momentous evening, we have our chef cooking for us. Please, come through to the dining room.'

Aston slid his arm round Ana's waist, the exquisite red fabric of her dress smooth under his palm as they followed his parents through. As he pulled out her chair at the table, his parents gave Ana an indulgent smile.

A satisfaction settled over him that he hadn't felt in years, perhaps not since Michel's death. Everything was falling into place. For once, things were going to plan. The moment was so perfect and real, he might have scripted it.

As Aston sat at table, Ana placed her hand on his thigh and squeezed. They'd marry, he'd climb Everest, then look to the next mountain as Michel would have wanted. But, for now, there was nowhere he wanted to be in the world more than sitting next to her.

The dinner was exquisite, made by the chef from the château's starred restaurant. Salad with vinaigrette, fish, boeuf Bourguignon, cheeses and an apple tart. Now Ana was delightfully full, replete with impeccable wine, food and conversation. Camille and Simon were gracious hosts. From Simon, Aston had inherited his blue eyes. From his mother, the dark hair and her effortless style. Such a handsome couple, she could see the love shining between them. The way they spoke, looked at each other. The glances. Their shared history and intimacies.

'Love at first sight', Aston's father had said. She believed it. Why hadn't Aston wanted something like that for himself?

She caught my eye too... She was a goddess...

Her breath hitched, the memory of that Spring Ball now fresh in her mind. The story they'd told. The attraction instant, like a thunderclap, for her at least. Had it been the same for him?

So many questions to which there were no answers, yet it all felt so real. She looked over at his parents and him, deep in conversation in the room they'd retired to for coffee after the meal had finished. There was a still strange undercurrent she couldn't place, something that made her senses prick up, although it had eased as the night progressed. She could be overreacting, yet if the past six months had taught her anything it was that she should take notice when anything didn't feel quite right.

It was clear his parents loved him deeply. Yet for some reason he held himself a little apart, somehow separate. She had trouble understanding it, but knew she needed to ask the question. Later, when they reached the farmhouse.

She sipped her coffee and looked into the fireplace, the flames crackling low, likely lit for ambience, more than the temperature. It added a beautiful glow to the elegantly furnished room that was full of French antiques like the rest of the house.

'I'm so pleased he found you.'

Ana looked up. Camille stood next to her, a picture of sophistication in a fitted black dress with a beaded neckline.

'So am I.' It wasn't hard to be honest now, about this at least. Ana couldn't imagine being anywhere else than with Aston.

'As a mother, I was gifted two wild sons. They took after their father.'

Simon didn't look wild now, but not exactly tamed either. Though Ana had seen a gleam of mischief in his eyes earlier in the evening when he'd talked about his proposal.

'I'm so sorry for your loss.'

'Thank you.' Camille gave her a wistful smile. 'I wondered what Aston might say to you about Michel. The loss is hard enough to bear for a parent but for a brother… They were inseparable. "The sun and the moon", I called them.'

'You named your last Grand Cru after Aston.'

She'd known that much. It had been well advertised.

Aston was the face of Girard, and such a handsome face too. It was no wonder they wanted to capitalise on it.

'*Oui*. Michel was darker, more intense. Always another mountain to climb for him… Those two boys, forever planning their next adventure.'

Ana thought about the early mornings, the relentless training, how Aston pushed himself.

'I don't think Aston's changed very much.'

His mother frowned, the movement so fleeting Ana wasn't sure she'd truly noticed it. 'You'll be good for him. He's always been searching…'

Ana suspected that he still was, and that she had no control over it. He continued to hold something back from her and tonight, she'd witnessed him holding back from his parents. What was it that drove him? She began to wonder whether he was truly happy with his life. Something painful and insecure knifed deep. Was he happy with her?

'You know, when they were younger, he and his brother had plans. Michel wanted to climb Everest, all the highest mountains in the world. He wanted Aston to follow…'

'That must have made you worry.'

'I still do. Aston was determined to try Everest himself. Even after his father failed and his brother's climbing accident…'

Ana stilled. It was as if her heart skipped a beat. Was *that* what Aston was training for? Why would he hide it from her? Something must have shown in her expression.

'Did you not know?' Camille asked.

Ana recovered herself and gave Camille her princess smile. Warm, practiced. Granted so many times it was imprinted on her muscle memory.

'Of course,' she lied, hating herself for it, but she was

also practised in self-protection, especially after the last six months. 'But I didn't know about Simon trying, that's all.'

'When we married, had children, he stopped climbing the highest and most dangerous peaks. That's what we hope for Aston. That with love and children he learns it's the simple things that can be the true adventure.'

Ana wasn't so sure. She didn't know what to say. She grappled to keep the conversation going, remembering her breeding: *if all else fails, talk about the person you're speaking to. Smile, nod and engage, even if you're dying inside.*

'You seem to have found that with Simon.'

They appeared to have a love that books could be written about. That movies could be made of. The dashing wine-maker from Australia and the chic French champagne heiress. Proof that love at first sight could happen, and could last.

'I knew, from the moment we met, that I would always run into Simon's arms if he held them open, and he would always catch me. I only hope the same for you.'

It was the kind of love Ana had dreamed of, but never expected. A love she'd always wanted for herself. A dream she now realised had never really died, and had been reignited by Aston over the past few weeks.

A dream she feared might now be slipping through her grasping fingers.

His parents' driver picked them up to take them back to the farmhouse. Camille had offered a room at the château, but Aston had refused. Ana was happy about that. Tonight she'd learned so many things she wanted to talk to him about. Too many questions swirled in her head. Would he answer her if she asked? Her heart leaped to her throat, beating a sickening rhythm.

Aston held out his hand as they sat in the back seat, and Ana placed hers in his, their fingers twining together, grounding her. Part of being married was working through problems. They'd work things out. Love would come...

Love? Where had that thought come from? She needed to remind herself that Aston had sought convenient, even if he hadn't meant cold. Goose bumps shivered over her skin as she'd remembered his return from Paris. The passion. How he'd bent her over the kitchen table, lifted her dress and made her cry out his name.

'That went well,' Aston said. 'What did I tell you?'

'I liked your parents a great deal.'

She meant it. They were a wonderful couple, warm and genuine—so unlike her own. Aston had been lucky with them. How would her life have been if she'd had the same? It didn't bear thinking about.

'They liked you.'

'I hope so.'

'How could they not? How couldn't anyone?' Aston raised her hand to his mouth and kissed it. His lips were warm against her skin. Even in the back of the car, in the relative darkness, she could feel the heat of his gaze on her, the need, as if he couldn't wait to get home. Her heart rate picked up. She couldn't wait either.

There'd be no talking tonight, and that was okay. There was always tomorrow.

The car pulled up at their front door.

'Would you like a nightcap?' Aston asked as they got out of the vehicle and went to the front door. They'd had a magnificent cognac before leaving the château. That final drink had made her feel quite giddy.

'No, I think I'd like to go to bed.'

The minute she said it, he eased her up against the stone

wall of the entrance and pressed his lips to hers. The kiss was soft, slow, passionate.

'What was that for?' she asked with a laugh after he broke away, leaving her breathless.

'For being perfect. I know you don't like the word, but you are. Own it.'

He had some lipstick on his mouth from their kiss. She swiped her thumb gently over his perfect lips to wipe it away. He caught the digit between his teeth, his tongue smooth and slick over the pad of the pad her thumb. She had extensive experience of how that tongue of his could work magic on her body, make her mindless. As it was, all of her seemed to turn liquid. She wanted to melt into a puddle on the doorstep. She wondered how he managed to get the key into the lock and let them in.

She sauntered ahead of him as he followed, giving an exaggerated sway of her hips because he did that to her— made her feel beautiful. He'd shown her the power of her own sexuality. He groaned behind her as she began to walk up the stairs.

'That dress will be the death of me. I've been wanting my hands on you all night.'

She made to turn as she entered the bedroom, but he placed his hand on her shoulder, stilling her. 'Let's get you out of your clothes.'

'What about yours?'

'Ladies always come first.'

Heat and need roared through her. She well knew how much pleasure this man could give her. She grew slick and wet between her thighs. Would there ever be a time she wasn't ready for him? She couldn't contemplate one.

He reached round her waist as she leaned back into his

muscular body, her backside nestling against his hardness. She wiggled a little, for effect.

Aston chuckled into her ear. 'Witch.'

'I thought I was a goddess,' she said through a smile.

'If you don't behave, I'll revise my opinion.'

'I don't think you want me to behave, not really.'

Aston hesitated for a moment, his breaths heavy, before unclipping her belt and letting it fall to the floor. Then he pulled back and took her zip as he'd done earlier this evening, but this time in reverse, inching it down slowly, revealing her skin to the cool late-night air. As he did, Aston gently traced a finger down her spine. She shivered.

'Cold? I'll keep you warm, *ma déesse.*'

So, she was still a goddess. Ana smiled. Tonight, she felt like one. Aston eased the dress off her shoulders. It fell to the floor. Then he swept her hair forward, his breath drifting over her skin at the back of her neck. She closed her eyes at the pleasure of it, arching back as his lips touched the top of her spine.

'You'll be the death of me,' he murmured. His hands stoked her gently, stroking the pale pink lace of her panties, her bra. Her nipples peaked where his fingers touched, as Aston plucked at them as if he were playing the finest of instruments. He certainly knew how to play her body.

'Not too soon, I hope,' she said, although he could be the death of her too, through unadulterated pleasure.

'Greedy.'

'For you, always.'

'Then let me oblige.'

He unhooked her bra. It fell to the floor with the rest of her clothes, then Aston walked round to her front. Everything about him was taut—how he moved, the skin over his face betraying tension at having to maintain control. She loved how she affected him. Loved how he affected her too. He cupped her breasts, stroking his thumbs over her nipples, teasing them till they budded to tight peaks. The sensation arrowed between her legs, which trembled, almost unable to hold her upright.

'Oh, God,' she said.

'You called?'

He knew the effect he had on her and clearly enjoyed it. His grin was a wicked one. Aston shrugged off his jacket and tossed it onto a chair. His belt and tie were gone in a rush too. Then he dropped to his knees in front of her, slipped her panties down her legs to the floor and she stepped out of them, and out of her shoes too, because she was now unsteady in her heels. Her toes sank into the plush carpet.

He slid his hand round to her buttocks, looking up at her, that sly, knowing grin still on his face. Then he brought his mouth to her centre. His tongue toyed with her body, the merest of touches. Not enough to take her over the edge, but enough to have her going up in flames. Ana speared her hand into his hair and gripped tight. He chuckled and kept licking and sucking until she was mindless, grinding into him. Yet he never gave her *enough*.

When he finally pulled away, she moaned, though it was almost a whine. Needy and desperate after being held on the brink of release.

Aston stood.

'Bed,' he growled. His voice was on edge, almost feral. She crawled under the covers, pulling them back for him too as he rid himself of the rest of his clothes. He was magnificent in the lamp light. The shadows his muscles etched. The strength of his biceps, the washboard ridges of his abdomen. Standing there, thrillingly aroused. He found protection and sheathed himself, then crawled over to her like a huge, hungry predator.

Her pounded at her chest, she was so aroused. Wet, ripe. Needing him in a way that was mindless, borne of pure instinct. She arched up into him as his weight came down on her. His body rocked against hers, a blissful promise of release. Her eyes fluttered shut as he positioned himself, notching himself at her centre. Her hands slid round his waist, feeling the power of his muscles under her fingers.

'Open your eyes,' he whispered, and she did. The look in his own eyes somehow melting yet hard at the same time. 'You're so beautiful when taking your pleasure. I want to watch you come. Want you to watch me.'

He began to ease into her and she moaned, not closing her eyes as he'd asked, watching him. The intensity of his gaze, his focus, was all on her. He thrust in gentle strokes, her body moving in perfect time with his. Something about this moment, their love-making, was so aching, so slow. His rhythm was deliberate and constant, building a burn between her thighs, deep inside. It was like a vice, the relentless twisting, tighter and tighter.

A small frown formed on Aston's brow, but they didn't take their eyes from each other. It was as if they had opened a door and were looking into each other's souls.

'A-Aston... Aston...' His name came out as a chant as she teetered on a terrifying edge, afraid to fall because she feared something about tonight would change everything. All the while tears formed in her eyes, blurring him because the pleasure was so sharp and sweet she could hardly bear it.

'I'm here. I understand,' he said, his voice tight, as if barely holding on himself. 'Come for me, *mon amour.*'

My love.

With that, she threw herself over the edge into oblivion.

CHAPTER TEN

ANA SAT AT a large table in the rustic farmhouse kitchen, draining her second coffee of the morning. Once again, she'd woken alone. She checked the clock on the wall. Aston had been gone for three hours this time, and they'd fallen asleep in each other's arms, exhausted, past midnight. He must have had no more than four hours' sleep.

Waking alone didn't bother her so much; it was more than that. After the dinner at his parents', she'd begun doing some research into what it took to climb the tallest mountain in the world, the risks. She'd seen the photos and videos—they were awe-inspiring, terrifying. She'd seen the bodies of those who'd failed. It had taken her down a rabbit hole of trying to understand him, what it took to climb the 'eight thousanders', as they were called—the tallest and deadliest mountains in the world.

As she'd thought before, she loved what the exercise did for his body, but now hated what it appeared to be doing to him. Hated how tired he seemed, although he tried to hide it well. If he'd appeared happy with it all, if he'd confided in her or was excited in any way, then maybe she could get excited too. But all she was left with was creeping fear and dread. On some of those mountains, a third of people who tried to climb them died. Luckily, Everest wasn't as bad as that, but still…

She'd tried to talk to him again about when he might be planning his next climb and where that might be. She knew from her research when the best season was to climb, so she guessed it wouldn't be for a while, but she didn't know how he could keep going like this. Burning the candle not only at both ends but seemingly in the middle too. No matter how subtly she tried to bring up his mountaineering, he fobbed it off when she hinted at wanting to talk. Kissing her until all she craved was him and everything else was forgotten.

He worked and trained and they made love, but he didn't seem *happy* to be doing it. She wanted him to be happy so badly, it had begun to make her desperate. She suspected all the research hadn't helped. She'd watched videos of mountaineers, trying to understand why they climbed the tallest peaks. Trying to understand *him*, because he was opaque as a thick fog. But it scared her even more to realise some of the videos she'd watched were from people now dead, lost to the mountains they'd climbed. If only he'd confide in her, just a little, she might understand. That was all she was asking for—him to reassure her this was what he wanted. That he was doing it for himself…and not someone else.

Movement at the door roused her from the dregs in her coffee cup. Aston walked into the room, smiling when he saw her. As always, it made her belly flutter.

'Good morning,' he said.

'Good morning to you.'

The fresh smell of soap and what she could only define as the scent unique to Aston, earthy and wild, threatened to scramble her senses. His hair was still damp. He hadn't shaved, a stubble grazing his jaw. He looked as handsome as ever, in jeans and a polo shirt, yet she saw things that he might not when he looked in the mirror. The dusty colour under his eyes. The lines deepening at their corners, bracketing his mouth. It spoke to her of stress, of tiredness. She loved his drive, his commitment, but it seemed that it was driving him into the ground.

Ana tilted up her head and he captured her lips. Her heart pounded at the conversation to come, part-excitement, part-trepidation. They broke apart and Ana twisted the engagement ring that sparkled on her finger in the morning light.

He poured himself a cup of coffee, grabbed a croissant delivered by the local bakery and sat across from her.

'So, where did you go this morning?' she asked. She'd guessed, but wanted him to tell her. She wanted to lead into this conversation slowly because she wasn't sure how it would go.

He shrugged. 'I went for a run.'

If it was anything like the other days, he would have taken a weighted backpack with him, to increase his effort.

'Why?'

Aston tore off a piece of the buttery croissant and washed it down with a mouthful of coffee. 'As I've told you, climbing requires me to maintain a level of fitness that sitting in a boardroom doesn't give me.'

'To climb Mount Everest?'

'If you knew the answer to the question, why did you ask it, *ma chère*?'

From the cool tone of his voice, she was aware she was prodding a sensitive place, but she didn't know why. She wanted him to explain so she could understand him better. There was something that kept him apart from her, when she craved to get even closer. She'd seen that closeness in his parents, and between Caspar and Cilla. Couldn't she have it for herself?

'Why do you want to climb Everest?'

Aston became deadly still as he regarded her, eyebrow

raised. 'Why would I not? I'd be standing on the top of the world.'

Except, they'd been his brother's words, going by what his mother had told her. And here she was walking into dangerous territory. It required her to challenge him when it was something she was unfamiliar with, that she wasn't certain of.

'Are you sure it's *your* dream?'

He put down his cup, placing his napkin in his lap.

'What is this about?' The sound of his voice—not just cool, but icy, like a frigid winter wind—should have sounded a warning. She carried on regardless because there was a need inside her to understand, to reduce the panic that seemed to build each day, the more she thought about things. In this case, what she didn't know might hurt her, especially if it hurt Aston.

'After you've climbed Everest, what then?'

He shrugged in a dismissive kind of way, and she was certain that he wouldn't stop, that he'd keep exhausting himself, keep going, till one day he climbed the last of the eight thousanders or died. But, if he finished climbing the tallest peaks, what then? Would he be happy?

She wasn't so sure. Ana knew she put a smile on his face but there was something more, something missing. They might lose themselves in each other's bodies, might make love for hours, but he remained as remote as the mountain peaks he climbed. He'd been right. Convenient didn't mean cold. Until Aston, she'd never truly understood how close to the flame she could fly. Then something else welled inside her, a sensation so big and all-encompassing, she refused to name it.

'Climbing Everest is dangerous,' she said, trying to tempt him into answering.

Ana realised her error immediately. He pinned her with his flinty-blue gaze. 'Life's dangerous. You can cross the road and be struck by a car. You can fall down a flight of stairs and break your neck. Nothing's guaranteed.'

'But that's not placing yourself in harm's way. How many people died on the mountain last year?'

She knew the answer. Seventeen. She knew the answer for every year for the past ten, the grim toll, the statistics.

'Stop speaking in circles, Ana. You have something to say? Say it.'

'I don't think this will make you happy. I think the thought is making you miserable.'

Nothing about it seemed to give him any joy. It was as if this was a kind of obligation, not a challenge he truly wanted to make his own.

'What would you know about my happiness?'

She reared back a little. What would she know? It was all Ana thought about. She wanted to wake up to him each day and go to sleep with him at night. She wanted him to be happy with *her*. Happy with his choices in life. She just wasn't sure he was. She had to make him see what he'd come to mean to her, because surely that meant something to him too?

'I'm getting no sense of excitement from you about this. All I feel from you is obligation, that you're doing something you don't really want. I'm terrified that's not going to be enough to get you to the top of that mountain and to keep you safe. And the thought of you not being safe is untenable to me.'

Aston stood, raked his hand through his hair and began to pace. He could see where this was going, as it had before with Michel. An old and familiar story. He'd been fooled into believing that this woman wouldn't hold him back, yet here they were.

Live for me.

He tried every damned day, living life enough for two men.

'Are you trying to change me? Because it seems, when I put a ring on your finger, you were happy enough with me then.'

Except that wasn't true. Their whole relationship had been based on a crumbling foundation. She'd agreed to marry him because she'd been afraid. He'd only proposed to ensure his inheritance. That was the deal. Nothing more, nothing less.

'Aston, we didn't know each other. And, now I do, I'm trying to make you see.'

He wheeled round. She still sat at the table, gripping onto her empty coffee cup. 'What? That you're yet another person trying to tell me what to do?'

'Your mother told me—'

'Ah.' He could imagine any number of things she might have said to Ana, filling her head with stories over dinner. 'I see where this is going. What did she say?'

Ana stood now, slowly, carefully, approaching him as if he was some kind of wild animal fighting to break free of restraints. He felt it, the past six months compressing upon him, crushing the life out of him.

'That your brother had always wanted to climb Everest. A-and I think that's the thing. You don't really want to want to do it for yourself, but you don't know how to let it go.'

The *audacity*. She had no idea how long he'd planned, what it required, what he would sacrifice. How gruelling it would be to make the climb and then to keep going.

'You could never understand—a woman who's been caged her whole life, with no sense of adventure.'

As he said those things, she jerked, as if having taken a blow.

'You're blaming me for something that's out of my control. I was limited by my family and my role. It *doesn't* mean I don't have a sense of adventure or want to do things. But I'm not going to irrationally risk my life for a dream that isn't mine.'

It was as if an awful history was repeating itself. He remembered those days, talking to Michel about a woman he'd met. Remembered how desperate he'd been to keep her, but at the same time how torn he was, being asked to give up what he loved. Aston had thought then that he was witnessing the limits of pain. How naïve he'd been; it had only been the beginning.

'You want to hear about my brother? Let me tell you a little story. Michel had one love in his life—climbing the mountains. Until he met Greta.'

How desperately in love Michel had seemed, how obsessed. Because his brother had always had a dark side to him. It was as his mother had said. Michel had been the moon, Aston the sun.

'She was meant to be a holiday romance. Michel had plans for life, plans we were working on together.'

To reach the top of the world had always been Michel's dream, taking the ice-axe from their father's own failed expedition. He'd wanted Aston to join him—two brothers climbing Everest together. He'd sold it with a kind of religious zeal that was impossible to ignore.

'But with Greta, their relationship, there was always some drama, some crisis. She wanted his only focus to be her. Everything else came second.'

Ana stood there, arms round her waist, her teeth worrying her lower lip. 'How old was he?'

'Nineteen.'

'So young.'

Too young to be in a coffin in a graveyard. Aston had raged at the universe for a year, for taking him.

'He didn't want to stop climbing. But she told him it was her or the mountains, one or the other. He wanted both.'

Aston turned his back. He couldn't look at Ana's pity. She'd never understand. She was just another woman trying to change a man, to fit him into her own image.

She'd taken enough from him already. Even now, it was near impossible to get out of bed in the early mornings. He had to drag himself away from her. If he wanted to climb to the top of that damned mountain and keep climbing, she could not win this battle, never. The promises he made, his life, depended on it.

'My brother had some of the most single-minded focus I've ever seen in another human being, yet on his last climb he wasn't thinking about what he should be doing, but of a choice—Greta or the mountains. On a climb where there should have been no distractions, no loss of focus, he was thinking of her. He fell and he died.'

Aston gripped the counter-top till his fingertips blanched white. The pain of that day was never ending. 'Because of a woman, he died for love.'

The pain in Aston's voice threatened to break Ana. What a burden he carried, one that no one saw. She understood now what drove him. Why he was lashing out. What he held back. She wanted to go to him, hold him, but she re-alised that he was a man with an ego showing his wounds. It had been difficult enough for her, being honest about her own. She was sure he wouldn't react well to pity. For now, all she had was words.

'I'm sorry. So sorry that happened to Michel, to you and your family.'

He gave a bitter laugh. 'And yet here you are, trying to do the same.'

She shook her head, even though he couldn't see her, holding onto the bench-top as if it was the only thing keeping him upright. 'I won't. I want you to do it for the right reasons. Tell me you want this. Tell me it's your dream and I won't say anything else.'

'Lies. You need to be reminded, Ana—this was meant to be a convenient marriage, nothing more. You know why I married you? The real reason?'

It was as if she'd swallowed something bad, now congealing in the pit of her stomach. Here was the real story. Did she want to hear it?

'You said it was time to settle down.'

'My parents demanded I marry or they'd write me out of their will. Girard would no longer be mine. But I knew the real reason. They knew I'd do anything to keep Girard and they hoped that once I was happily married, I'd forget all about this climb. But they were wrong. You see, like my brother, I have two loves—the mountains and the wine.'

Not her.

No one but me will love you now...

She tried to shut that voice down but it kept whispering, taunting her with what she'd never have. Aston's love.

'My father and mother erred. No person will ever prevent me from making that climb. I asked you to marry me because it was the way to keep Girard and the mountains. Why should you have cared? I believed you understood the meaning of a convenient marriage. Now this.'

He saw her as standing in his way when that wasn't what she was trying to do at all. She wanted to free him. And yet she now began to see this for what it was...

'You're afraid.'

'I fear nothing.'

'You're afraid to let love into your heart, because you fear it might be more like Michel's relationship than your parents', but even more—there's a risk it'll open another door. One that doesn't keep you locked in the past. That moves you forward to something different, to something better.'

'Don't fool yourself. This relationship gives us both something we need. You, safety. Me, my inheritance. But don't ever think to change me.'

'I'm not thinking to change you. I—I…' She couldn't finish the sentence with the words she wanted to say because they were too big and too terrifying when everything was unravelling horribly. 'I want you to do it because it's something you want. Not because it was a dream of your brother's which he can't fulfil.'

'Enough,' he said, his hand slashing through the air like an exclamation mark. 'You know nothing about me, you know nothing about life. You want to stay in your little cage? I will not join you there. If you're asking me to choose you or the mountain, you'll be disappointed in my answer. So, let's keep this to what it is. A convenient relationship and nothing more.'

Ana realised in that moment there was no moving him. The pain of it tore her heart in two because she knew what this sensation was now. One that filled her with wonder and dread. One that terrified her and thrilled her. She was in love with him and Aston could never love her back. He'd never give her all of himself. He'd always look at that ring on her finger and know how much she'd cost him. He might be faithful, they might make love, but he could never *love* her. She couldn't live with that because if she tried, she'd die a little every day till all that was left was a shell of herself.

'You've made yourself very clear. But I deserve more,

not someone who sees me as something they bought for a record price per carat. I deserve to be loved.'

Ana took off her ring and placed it on the table. She felt the loss of its presence, its weight, immediately. It was as if she'd been cut adrift again. But what did it matter? Self-preservation meant she had to leave, not stay. She drew herself up with all the comportment she could raise, from what she'd been taught. For a while, she'd loved pretending with him—just being Anastacia Montroy the woman. Not the perfect princess, not a princess at all. But it was time to call upon all her royal breeding to get through the rest of her life without him.

'You say I'm trapped, but I'm not.' Ana turned to leave the room, leave the house. Leave the man she now knew she loved. Unable to stay a minute longer. She blinked her eyes at the burn. They were tears she wouldn't shed, not in front of a man who didn't care. 'It's you. Aston. You're the one who'll always be in a cage.'

Aston sat in his gleaming, modern Paris office in uncomfortable silence. His staff were keeping their distance. His temper was short. He'd lost all motivation. Every morning, waking late. Not training. With no desire for anything let alone climbing to the top of the world. On his desk lay his father's ice-axe, a reminder of the climb Aston had promised to make.

Why did the thought of climbing a mountain now, hold as much excitement as walking up the closest hill? Nothing interested him—not the food on his plate, not the taste of the wines that had made his family famous. It could all have been ash and vinegar. Yet small things still caught his attention: a flash of golden hair. The scent of roses as he walked past the local florist. The bed in his apartment that carried the memories of entering Ana's body for the first time and knowing things had changed for ever. So much so, he'd begun staying at a hotel near his office to avoid thinking of her.

He might try to ignore it, but he knew this feeling. It was like a death, the same finality with which he'd lost Michel…however in this case the person still lived. And in some ways it was worse, to know they were out there but didn't want you.

Aston stood and stared out of the windows onto the city below. Everyone was going about their lives, yet he somehow seemed frozen. He'd never lied to himself before, but he knew he was lying now. Anastacia hadn't walked away, he'd pushed her. Ruthlessly, mercilessly. He had no one to blame but himself.

On his desk, his office phone rang. Strange, since Aston had given instructions to his staff that he wasn't to be disturbed. He'd set his mobile to silent. He still had security keeping tabs on Ana and Hakkinen, just to make sure, since her family hadn't cared enough to listen to her. There'd been nothing to report for over a month. The count had crawled back into the hole from where he'd come in Halrovia, and there he'd stayed. Ana was out in the world too except, rather than hiding, she was living her life. He rubbed at an ache in his chest, one that seemed ever-present.

The phone on his desk stopped then started ringing again. Aston snatched it up to put an end to the shrill sound.

'Allo? Oui?'

'Monsieur Lane, it's your father.'

Aston didn't want to speak to the man, not now. His wounds were still raw. He was in this position because of his parents' actions, forcing him into this situation. Now he'd failed in his engagement, had failed to marry Ana. Would they still require a marriage for him to remain in the will? He had no appetite for it. He didn't care any longer. If his parents saw fit to punish him, to leave Girard to his cousin, then so be it. It was all pointless now, anyway.

'Father, this isn't a good time.'

There was silence on the end of the phone. All Aston could hear was some heavy breathing.

'Aston…' Something was wrong. He could hear it in his father's voice, the way it carried such weight, and cracked. 'It's your mother.'

Bile burned his throat, sour and sickening, as Aston stalked through the hospital's sterile halls. The scent of antiseptic overwhelmed him. He hadn't been into a hospital since the day Michel had died, when they'd been retrieved from that mountain, and Aston had been brought in at the insistence of his family to be checked for any injuries. There hadn't been any that were physical, but that didn't mean he hadn't been mortally wounded that day. The memories were so fresh and acute it could have been yesterday. No matter that there was art on the walls, soothing scenes, this was still a place where death stalked the living.

Aston stopped at a nurses' station and asked for directions. Luckily, his parents had been in Paris to see the opera, so it hadn't taken him long to get here even through traffic. Staff led him to a waiting room where his father sat, leaning forward, forearms on his legs and hands clasped, staring at the floor as if in prayer.

'Dad.'

His father lifted his head. The lines on his face were etched deeply. He'd always been such a robust, healthy man, yet in this moment it was as if he'd aged ten years. He was somehow…diminished. He stood from the chair, as if every move was an effort. Aston strode towards him, everything else forgotten, grabbing his father in a tight embrace. They simply held each other for a few moments as if the past, the present and the future weren't suddenly colliding.

His father pulled back, wiping his eyes.

'Son, you look as much in hell as I feel.'

There was time to discuss that, if it ever needed to be raised at all. That time wasn't now.

'What happened?'

'Your mother's been feeling unwell for a few weeks—nausea, tiredness. We thought it was a virus until she started getting jaw pain. Now they say it's a blocked artery. A "widow-maker", they call it.'

Aston's blood ran cold. 'What do you mean?'

'The main artery to the heart. It's as bad as it sounds.'

His father collapsed into his chair, but Aston couldn't sit still. He began to pace. He couldn't imagine his mother and father not together. They'd had a once-in-a-lifetime kind of love, something Aston had always believed was incapable of being duplicated. Whilst their relationship was sometimes fiery, they hadn't spent a day apart in their thirty-four years of marriage.

'But if there's anything that will keep your mother alive it's the thought of a wedding and having grandchildren. How's Anastacia?'

Her name brought Aston to a stop. There'd been no press about the end of their relationship. He'd remained quiet about it, for her safety. She hadn't said anything either. His parents wouldn't know until he told them and accepted the consequences of his failure. His father looked up at him, his face somehow hopeful in the midst of everything. Aston should lie, so as not to add to his father's concerns, yet the words choked at the back of his throat. His eyes stung. He shut them and pinched his nose, willing yet more grief away before it consumed him.

'Son? What's wrong?'

'You have enough to worry about.'

'Now you're worrying me even more. No matter your age, you are always my child, and you can *always* talk to me.'

So the words tumbled out of him about how they were over. Ana had left France and gone to stay with her sister...

'I won't marry simply to inherit Girard. If that's what you want, the company's all yours.'

He'd never wanted a wife yet, with Ana in his life, Aston realised he wanted nothing else. She was strong, caring, kind. Most people only saw her external beauty but, for him, it was the inner beauty she radiated. Losing her was like losing everything.

His father rubbed his hand over his face. 'We were wrong, your mother and I. That ultimatum... If we could turn back time... But Everest, the rest of the mountains, the risks... It was more than not wanting to lose another child, we simply *couldn't*. There's nothing more unnatural. We'd do anything to protect you, even if it was misplaced. As a parent, all you want is for your child to be happy, and yet you always seemed to be looking for something. We thought if you could find what we had...*have*... Then you arrived with Anastacia and we hoped...'

Aston stilled. He wasn't sure what his father's confession meant for him and the company. But to know that all of this had been futile... What if he could turn back time to a moment when Anastacia had never been his fiancée? What would he have done?

The answer was simple: no matter the pain, he would have done it all over again. He would always catch her if she ran to him. The ache of the realisation almost cut him in two. He acknowledged what he'd done and what he'd lost because he was a selfish fool and a coward.

'There were things said in the heat of the moment.'

He wasn't only talking about that fateful conversation with his parents.

'Is there a way to fix it, with you and Ana?'

'I broke something precious. I don't know how to rebuild from that.'

His father stood and placed a hand on Aston's shoulder. The weight, the warmth, was somehow comforting when Aston knew he deserved none of it after the things he'd said to Ana.

'Saying sorry is a start, which is what I need to say to you.' Simon looked at Aston and held his gaze. The look on his face was earnest. 'I'm sorry, son. All we wanted was for you to focus on possibilities, not the life you'd been leading, where it seemed you were pushing yourself harder and harder without really enjoying what you were doing.'

They were the same sentiments Ana had expressed, and both she and his parents were right. He'd been living the life Michel wanted, not his own. He was exhausted. He loved mountaineering, but he didn't need to conquer them all, and had no desire to stand on top of the world. He enjoyed adventure but hadn't realised he could find it in a person too—in one shining light who cut through the darkness like the beam from a lighthouse.

Ana.

'I hope the pressure we placed on you to marry didn't cause this.'

Aston shook his head and gave a short, sharp laugh. 'No, I did that all by myself.'

By not realising what was important. By trying to avoid love. All this time he'd fought the perceived constraints.

Yet with Ana he'd found his greatest freedom. In trying to avoid pain and a loss of focus, both had found him anyway, enough to tear him clear in two. He hadn't saved himself from anything. Right now, he was suffocating with it.

He'd been too ignorant of his own feelings to realise what was happening. Many climbers fell into serious trouble because of subjective hazards, those of their own making. Failure to analyse conditions, or their poor conclusions and judgement. Despite all his knowledge and planning, with Ana he'd fallen into that trap himself. Now he was reaping the rewards of his own failures. Aston realised that some hurts were too much to heal. He hoped that Ana might see her way to forgiving him—but only if he laid himself bare.

'Do you love her?' his father asked.

'Yes.'

The answer was easy. There was no question about his feelings. He loved Ana and he'd work with everything he had, the persistence and dedication he used in his business and his mountaineering, to get her back. It didn't matter how long it took, because he was sure now that she'd loved him too. He only hoped that the love and concern she'd shown him hadn't died because of the things he'd said to her.

His father gave the smallest of smiles. 'There's no greater feeling, and sometimes bigger curse. And yet I wouldn't pass up a single day of any of it with your mother. I regret nothing.'

Aston tried to imagine a life without Ana. All he saw was long, interminable years of loneliness. A sense of absence that no perilous climb or mountain peak would fill.

Now he knew. He'd never felt more alive than when he was with her. Aston wanted the adventure of the world seen through her eyes. He craved to show it all to her, if she'd allow him.

He looked at his father. The man's gaze was fixed on a point over Aston's shoulder. His eyes widened, then his face drained, pale. Aston whipped round, and there stood a surgeon in her scrubs, face neutral—not grim, but not happy either.

'How is she?' his father asked. His voice was quiet, weak, in a way Aston had never heard before.

'Your wife is a very lucky woman. The surgery went well. A successful procedure.'

The relief was so intense, Aston could barely even thank the woman who had saved his mother's life. His father's shoulders sagged. He put his head in his hands. Aston walked to him and placed his hand on his shoulder. It shuddered under his touch.

Aston didn't much believe in signs but something about today gave him hope. His father had his second chance. Now Aston had to find one for himself.

CHAPTER ELEVEN

'YOU DON'T HAVE to go home just because mother and father say so.'

Ana lounged on an outdoor chaise on a secluded terrace of Isolobello's famed palace, with Cilla on a lounger next to her. Ahead of them a view of the vibrant sea glittered to the horizon with a colour which carried painful reminders...

She caught her thoughts, stopping them from leading to their inevitable conclusion. Instead, she sipped a fruity cocktail as she and her sister watched the world sail by. Ocean liners, super-yachts of the rich and famous and fishing boats. If she didn't think too hard about it, Ana could almost pretend that she was on some holiday, rather than trying to escape what a wreck her life had become.

A cool breeze drifted over them, still fairly warm here on the Mediterranean, rather than with the crisp bite of early winter at her home in Halrovia. Or a rustic farmhouse in rural France... She shut her eyes, but she couldn't escape the last ugly argument with Aston. His rejection of her. His seeming disdain.

How broken her heart was. All she could do was ignore it, because surely hearts mended, given time? Though it had been two months. She thought the pain would have blunted by now. It hadn't. It still caught her unawares, slicing like a paper cut, as fresh as the moment she'd walked out of the door of Aston's farmhouse and asked one of his security team to take her far, far away.

Cilla had offered her a soft place to land when Aston had simply let her go.

'And you don't need your sister here, getting in the way of wedding preparations.'

'Since you're part of the wedding party, and my maid of honour, it's your duty.'

'Since I failed so spectacularly at my own engagement, I wonder why you'd want me.' Ana rubbed her ring finger, where her beautiful ring had once sat, still gripped by the constant sense that something was missing, something she doubted she'd ever find again.

Cilla sat up.

'Don't. *You* didn't fail at anything. If I know you, you tried to do what was good and right and that...' her sister flapped her hands about as if lost for words '...that man, if I can even call him that, didn't deserve you.'

Her support meant everything to Ana. Once, her sister had been all uncertainty—the 'plain princess', as the press had unfairly dubbed her because she didn't look like the rest of the family. Dark hair to their blonde. Petite to their height. Now she'd come into her own.

Ana peered over the rim of her glass filled with the fruity elixir and decorated with a jaunty pink paper umbrella, to glimpse her sister frowning. Priscilla pushed her glasses up her nose. Even through that look of disapproval, Cilla bloomed with a beauty that radiated from within. Love had transformed her, made her believe in herself. A kernel of warmth lit in Ana's heart. Cilla had always been a gentle, studious soul, hard-working, underestimated. It had only taken the right man finally to *see* her...

All that warmth was snuffed out. Ana had thought she'd

found that man for herself, one who saw her, someone she could love and who would love her in return, but it had all been cold and calculated. All to protect an inheritance. Well, she deserved more, so much more, which was why she'd walked away. She hadn't wanted to lose him, but if he didn't appreciate her and couldn't love her, what point was there?

In the end, she knew if she stayed she'd have become a shell, as she'd been before the accident, trying to be perfect. She would always have tried to be the woman he wanted, rather than woman she truly was. In the end, staying with him hadn't been safe. Walking away had been.

'Then why does it hurt so much?' Ana's voice cracked.

Cilla left her own sun lounger and came and sat next to her. 'Because unrequited love is the worst. You do love him, don't you?'

Ana feared she still did, irrevocably. Because she suspected that, no matter how cruel he'd been, he'd given Ana her life back, and for that she needed to be thankful. Whilst leaving him might have meant the end of her security, one of his personal protection officers still went wherever she did. Cilla had tried to shoo him away, but the man was resolute, so they let him follow her about, looming whenever anyone looked at Ana sideways.

Then there had been a letter from Count Hakkinen. She'd refused to read it but Cilla had. Apparently it was an apology and a promise that he'd never be even in the same country as her.

In her weaker moments she knew she had Aston to thank for this, for her safety, though she shouldn't give a damn what he did ever again. He didn't love her back, so there was no point.

'You know I do.'

'Because I know you. Anyway, let's give him something to think about.'

'I don't think he thinks about me at all.'

Cilla grabbed her phone and held it out. She hesitated then plucked Ana's cocktail umbrella from her drink and put it behind Ana's ear.

'Rubbish. He might not be worthy of you, but he'll be looking. How could he *not*? Being awesome is always the best revenge. Now, get that drink in frame and smile like you gleefully burned your last bridge.'

Ana burst out laughing as Cilla took the shot and then showed it to her. It appeared to be a moment of joy, and maybe one that proved she was going to be okay, broken heart and all.

'What are you going to do with it?'

'I'm sending a copy to you, then posting this to my social media, because you look hot in that bikini, and that's what sisters are for. Messages need to be delivered.'

Cilla had become a bit of a darling of social media since her arrival in Isolobello, now granted administrator privileges over the Santori royal accounts. An adoring public constantly tried to guess which posts were written by Cilla, and which ones were courtesy of the family's official social media manager. This shot would likely cause another flurry of interest.

Ana thought she looked like a woman who'd just lost the love of her life, but Cilla had told her earlier, 'Put on some sunglasses and lip-gloss and suck it up, Princess.' So at least she had a little colour to her, though the bikini did make her feel bold. It was the first thing she'd bought for herself on coming to Isolobello, almost a shout to the universe: *just you watch me now.* Before she'd collapsed in floods of tears, weeping on her sister's shoulder.

Cilla held up the final photo for her to see. 'Okay?'

The shot had been cropped so the scars on her arm didn't show, though that hardly mattered any more. Ana knew now they weren't a measure of her worth—just another thing to thank Aston for...

'Go for it,' Ana said, finishing her drink and putting the glass on a side table.

'Done!' Cilla looked so blissfully happy, full of joy. Ana hoped one day that she could find the same for herself. It had been so hard, thinking she had and then having it fall apart and crush her like an avalanche. If only she could see the world through rose-tinted glasses again. That view had been so beautiful, so full of hope.

But loving Aston Lane had been a fool's errand. Like trying to tame the winter winds, or hold back spring meltwater with nothing more than one's hands as it rushed down the mountains. That love would eternally have slipped through her fingers as she'd tried to hold on tighter.

Anyhow, he didn't want to fall in love. He was truly like the god Bacchus at the Spring Ball, which seemed so long ago now. Whilst he might intoxicate her, he'd always remain free.

'Excellent!' Ana said, trying to sound enthusiastic. 'Now let's talk about these wedding preparations.'

'Are you sure?'

'One hundred percent.'

It was a masochistic kind of distraction, Cilla chatting about her dress, about Ana's. About the pomp and ceremony that would overtake Isolobello on the day. About the joy it would bring this island country—the Santori family's beloved heir marrying Halrovia's youngest princess. Ana tried to let Cilla's happiness fill her empty heart with talk of flowers, carriages and the fairy tale, when all Ana felt was somehow small and broken.

There was a gentle knock on the door leading into the palace and courtier walked onto the terrace.

'Your Highnesses.'

He bowed, walked to Cilla and murmured in her ear, then stood back, as if waiting for instructions. Cilla frowned.

'Problem?' Ana asked.

Cilla's eyebrows raised. 'It seems Mr Lane is at the palace and has asked to see you.'

Ana's stomach churned with the ferocity of the waves hitting the rocky cliffs below them.

'I can send him away,' Cilla added in a rush. 'Just say the word and he'll be gone. You don't need to do anything you don't want to.'

Yet that would be putting off the inevitable, the coward's way, and she didn't want to fear anything ever again. Ana took a deep breath. Her whole problem was that being here with Cilla was safe and familiar. In many ways, she'd reformed and burst out in a new skin, yet she still didn't really know who Princess Anastacia was. And she wasn't sure she'd ever discover her, hiding away.

That thought had her rising from the chair. She had desires. She had needs. She had *choices*. She just needed to move forward, and confronting Aston was the first step towards closure.

'I'll see him.' Ana looked down at what she wore, at the bikini top, matching sarong wrap-tied low on her waist. She wasn't dressed to receive visitors, particularly not Aston Lane. 'But I should probably...'

'Put on your armour?'

Her armour...the façade she'd hid behind. Hair, make-up, clothes. First to project perfection, then to hide her scars. In that way, she realised now, Cilla had been always so much freer than her. She'd lived her life eschewing the expectations her mother had tried to force upon her. In the end, her sister had been more true to herself than any of their family.

'What else do I have?'

Cilla stood and placed her hands on Ana's shoulders. She was inches shorter and eighteen months younger, yet Ana felt like a child.

'Yourself,' Cilla said with a patient, knowing smile. 'And she is enough.'

Aston didn't hear a door open—and there was no announcement that anyone had arrived—yet he could feel something. A strange sensation, an awareness of another person with him. There was a change in the atmosphere. Aston turned slowly, his gut churning, filled with anticipation and dread. Knowing with certainty who it was, afraid of who he would see, because of how much he had to atone for. It didn't even seem enough to beg forgiveness after the things he'd said that last, terrible morning. If Ana sent him away without a backward glance, then it would be wholly deserved. Aston could only hope she'd listen.

Ana came into view, standing there in a bikini top and sarong. Her appearance affected him as always like a punch to the solar plexus, forcing the breath right out of him. Today, the scars on her arm were unhidden. After how she'd been with him the first time they'd made love, her reluctance to show them to him, he was filled with pride at how far she'd come. She stood so unashamed, shoulders back, gaze cool and regal. The ego in him, one he tried hard to quash, wanted to believe that he'd played a part in her fearlessness today, but he knew that wasn't the truth. It was all her. Her strength and her resilience was *despite* him, not because of him.

Aston might have smiled had he thought she'd welcome it, because she also had a jaunty little paper umbrella behind her ear. It made him realise that this was yet another sign she'd likely moved on. He wouldn't blame her if she had. Yet he could see the grey shadows under her eyes, how her normally plush mouth was a thin, tight line.

He wanted to go to her. Wrap her in his arms and tell her he was sorry for all the pain he'd caused, but this was no warm welcome. Not that he'd expected it. He considered himself lucky that he'd been allowed in at all, after turning up unannounced. Only some fast talking about how he was Princess Anastacia's fiancé had garnered him any kind of attention.

'Aston. How are your parents?'

So cool, so polite—the consummate princess, the woman from *before*. Before she'd allowed him a glimpse of how deep her passions ran, and that was fathomless. He tried to be heartened by the fact she'd used his first name but knew that, after everything they'd been through, she wouldn't have been petty enough to call him Mr Lane. Should he tell her about his mother? He didn't want her to think he was using it as a way into her good graces, but if he wanted only truth they had to start somewhere, and here was the right time.

'My father's well. My mother's been in hospital.'

Ana started forward, forehead creased in worry. She checked herself, as if some invisible tether had pulled her back. 'I'm so sorry. Is she well?'

His mother's doctor had called Camille 'her miracle'. 'Yes…now.'

'I'm pleased. When you go, please send them my regards.'

Her words stung like the slap of an icy wind. She was the perfect princess, the ice princess. There was not an ounce of warmth in her. Yet he knew how she simmered, what she hid underneath. How he craved to experience it again.

'You could tell them yourself.'

Her eyes widened a fraction, her throat convulsing in a swallow.

'What are you doing here, Aston? I thought you'd said all you needed to. Your message was quite clear.'

The things he should have said instead... How she'd been right. How he loved her. So many opportunities had been missed to build something towering and eternal when all he'd done was to try and tear things down—self-sabotage at its finest. Time to attempt a repair of what he'd so callously broken.

'You were right.'

Ana's teeth began to worry her lower lip. She wrapped her hands reflexively round her waist, then loosened them to drop them by her side.

'In what way? There were so many.'

She'd been right in *every* way.

'I'm a coward, hurting you to protect myself.' He shook his head. 'I love to climb, but I don't want to climb Everest. I don't want to climb any of those mountains. The thought exhausts me.'

'Then why...?'

Now was when he had to lay the card showing one of the most painful days of his life on the table. To give her a glimpse of what had in some ways made him but, in more, had broken him. He'd never really faced Michel's death, even though he'd thought he had over the years since. He'd fooled himself into believing he'd moved on, all the while being stuck in the past as that desperate, guilt-ridden twenty-year-old who'd carried those scars into his future. Though he'd not fooled Ana. She'd seen right through him.

He motioned to an uncomfortable-looking antique couch. 'Would you like to sit?'

She shook her head. 'I'd prefer to stand.'

'Do you mind if I do?' He wasn't sure that his legs would hold him through the retelling of this story.

She shook her head and he lowered himself onto the sofa, wanting to hide his face so she wouldn't witness the pain. But he'd been a coward with her before. He refused to be one now.

'The day Michel died, I was with him. We'd been climbing. Preparing one day for the trip of our lifetime to Everest. To climb the mountain my father had failed to.'

Though that was something only he and Michel had thought. In all the time he'd spent with his father, Aston realised now, Simon had never seen his inability to reach Everest's summit as a failure. Instead, he'd seen his survival in that terrible climbing season as a success, a second chance.

'You know I said Michel lost focus?'

Ana winced. He had no doubt she remembered that conversation, and he hated to bring her more pain, but the past had informed every day of his present and it was time to put it behind him, if she'd allow it.

'It was an error both of judgement and equipment. He fell, was injured—mortally. I… I couldn't save him. He died in front of me as we waited for rescue.'

He couldn't look at her any more. Didn't want to read what she saw on his face. His eyes flooded. He blinked the tears away. Beside him, the seat dipped. Through a blur he saw Ana seated next to him. He felt the warmth of her hand on his thigh. There was comfort in her touch. She was so generous, he didn't deserve it.

'I don't know what to say.'

'Nothing. You don't have to say anything.'

All the words that needed to be spoken were his.

'He knew he was dying. Just before he passed, he said, "I'm dying…live for me".'

The ache inside his chest was a yawning one, a chasm that would never be filled. He chanced a look at Ana and tears brimmed in her eyes then overflowed. One tracked down her cheek. He wanted to wipe it away, but he had no right to touch her, especially not to comfort. It wasn't his place, not yet. If she saw fit to afford him some grace, to forgive him, only *then* would he have earned the privilege.

'Don't cry for me. I don't deserve it.'

'I think you might.'

'It had always been Michel's dream to climb Everest, and the rest. To conquer the world's tallest, hardest peaks. I carried it from the moment he spoke those words to me. But I didn't stop to think.'

His brother had said, 'Live for me'. Not, 'Climb Everest', or Annapurna or K2 or Nanga Parbat. Simply, 'Live.'

'Instead of living my own life, I tried to live Michel's— fulfil what I believed were his dreams, rather than my own. I didn't even know what mine were any more. Working towards Michel's is what kept me moving forwards.'

If he'd been truthful to himself, he would have recognised it years ago. He realised it was what his parents had been trying to tell him, in their own way. To look into the heart of himself to what *he* wanted, not live his life for others. He could now thank them for the push that had allowed Ana to burst into his life. Calling on him to reflect on everything he thought he'd wanted.

'You were young. His death wasn't your fault.'

'I was broken, and I was a fool. I felt guilty. My parents

saw it. They hoped marriage would make me settle down, accept life as it was. And then I met you.'

His chance to make the life for himself he'd been told to live. With a woman whom he admired, whom he loved. Because of fear, he'd thrown it back in her face. He'd hurt her, when he'd promised to keep her safe.

He took a chance and took her hands in his. They were cold. He wanted to show her love, to keep her warm. To keep her with him, if she'd allow it.

'You challenged everything I thought I was meant to do. I'd mistaken Michel's dreams for mine for so long that letting them go would have been like losing him all over again, a second death. In the process, I accused you of things, broke something—us. Something real and right. Something perfect, although I know you hate the word. And for that I'm truly sorry.'

Ana shook her head. 'I never wanted to hold you back, or force you to *settle*.'

He squeezed her fingers. She squeezed back. That one, tiny moment gave him hope.

'With you, I could only ever look forwards. The person holding me back was myself. But no more. I loved you. I *love* you—*jusqu'à la fin de mes jours*. I don't care about an inheritance. I don't care about Girard. All I care about is you.'

I love you—until the end of my days...

Ana looked at where their hands were joined. Somehow, their fingers had twined together as if of their own accord. It felt so right. It was everything she'd wanted, as if they should never separate again. And yet the thought still rang through her head that he *couldn't* love her. Why couldn't she simply believe instead?

'What are you saying?' she asked.

Aston rubbed his thumb gently over the back of her hand. The touch caused a shiver of pleasure to run through her.

'I want you as my wife, if you'll have me. I've never wanted anything more. I was living a half-life, and you brought me back, like a shock to the chest. Made me look at myself, to realise what was important. You—loving you—is what I wanted more than anything, yet pushing you away seemed like the only option to protect myself.'

'And now?'

'It's all down to you. The decision's yours. I'll spend my whole life proving that I'm worthy of you, if you'll let me.'

She looked at him. He was so earnest, open. Nothing was hidden, not any more. The shutters on his heart and soul had been lifted. She saw the love in the softness of his reverent gaze. Did she want him? Could she forgive him?

If he held open his arms... Ana knew she would always run into them.

'Would you catch me?'

The corners of his mouth curled into a slow smile that kindled a flame deep inside her. One she'd never thought she'd feel again.

'*Mon amour*. Come running, and you'll see.'

My love...

'I don't need to, because I *know*. I love you, Aston. For the way you believed me—believed *in* me—protected me. You had my heart before I even realised it could be possible.'

He let go of her hands and reached into his trouser pocket. She missed his touch immediately. She needed him to hold her, never to let her go. When he pulled his hand from his pocket he held a ring box.

'Is that...?'

'The ring, if you want it. Or I'll buy another, if you need

a different memory. Only remember, I didn't buy you. I know your heart was never for sale.'

Ana didn't need to think. She held out her left hand, which trembled as Aston removed the ring from the box and slipped it on her finger.

'I like my ring there,' he said. She smiled, turning her hand in the light so that it glittered.

'Me too.'

He reached out and slipped the cocktail umbrella from behind her ear, twirling it between his fingers.

'Been having fun?'

'I hope to.'

He grinned. 'I've asked you once, but I'll ask you again, because it's what you deserve. Will you marry me?'

Ana tapped her chin. She knew the answer, but making him wait wasn't a bad thing… They had the rest of their lives to spend together, after all.

'Are you a betting man, Mr Lane?'

His pupils darkened. 'I've been known to take a risk or two.'

'Then today you should lay all your money down on my becoming your wife.'

Aston cupped her cheek and lowered his mouth to hers. 'And that, my goddess, is a fairy tale I cannot wait for.'

EPILOGUE

ASTON LEANED AGAINST the railing of a terrace in the cool of a clear, spring morning. The early rays of sunlight painted the soaring peaks of the Himalayas in gold. He and Ana had arrived in Nepal a week earlier, taking a helicopter to this place, one of the highest hotels in the world. Here, with the shutters pulled back on the windows, they could see the mountains from their suite. They dominated every view—from the stone terrace where they ate their breakfast, to the infinity pool overlooking the fir-covered valley below, where he and Ana sipped cocktails in the afternoons.

He reached beside him and gripped the handle of an ice-axe: his father's. The one Michel had wanted to take to the summit of Everest. He held it up against the backdrop of the mountains. Whilst Aston wouldn't be carrying it there, it *would* be going, because today was an important day…

A warm hand slid up his back, fingers threading through his hair. He smiled and closed his eyes for a few moments to relish the touch.

'Hello, my beloved wife.'

'Hello, my equally beloved husband… Do you wish you were making your way up there, to the summit?'

Aston stared at Everest, standing imposingly in the distance. He'd imagined it. Most mountaineers probably had. Imagined the rigours, both mental and physical. The risks.

But it didn't call to him. The answer was a simple one. It had been simple ever since Ana had come into his life.

'Not at all.'

'Not even to stand on the top of the world?'

He turned his back to the view, and Ana glanced at the ice-axe in his hand. He placed it down on a small table and wrapped his arms around her waist.

'The hardest of mountains I've ever had to climb were here.' Aston tapped his head with a finger. 'And here.' He tapped over his heart. 'Everest was Michel's dream. Not mine.'

'I'm glad.' Ana turned round in his arms, her back to his front. She leaned into him as he manoeuvred them both so they could stare at the view together. 'I never imagined this could be so beautiful.'

'I know something that's even more beautiful than those mountains.' He buried his nose in her hair, taking in the scent of her. The smell of flowers, of home… 'You.'

She laughed, the sound like the most joyous of bird songs, filling his heart with happiness. 'Has it been worth it?'

He guessed she was talking about their trip to Nepal, but all he could think about was other things. Such as their wedding at Épernay's magnificent town hall, followed by an intimate religious ceremony in the château's chapel. Ana had been in an exquisite dress made for her by a French designer who had fought to create the perfect dress for a perfect princess—*his* princess. Their reception had been a raucous celebration of life and love in the château's gardens, the ancestral home he loved. Because people were right. If you cut him, he'd bleed champagne.

'It's been worth all of it, being here with you.'

He hadn't realised how hollow and meaningless his life had become. He'd just set one foot in front of the other like

an automaton, until Ana had burst into it. Now every day
was a thrill. He still loved to climb, to challenge himself.
But, even more, he loved coming home to Ana. The way
her love wrapped round him, completed him.

'Are you ready for today?' she asked.

In a few short hours, they'd take a helicopter from the
hotel to Everest base camp. There, he'd hand his father's ice-
axe to a member of the expedition he'd once planned to join
in climbing Everest. That team member would carry it on
their own journey to the summit. It would be like closing a
circle, part of Michel's dream finally realised.

But Aston understood the greater depth of Ana's question. What it meant. 'It's the right time,' he said.

He'd come here not to climb a mountain, but to say good-
bye. Each footstep a homage to his brother's memory. To
letting go.

'You know I would have trekked to base camp with you,
rather than taking a flight?'

Ana had come into her own since they'd married twelve
months ago, showing him her confidence, her curious soul.
It was such a precious gift. Aston had taken time away from
his business and had begun to show her the world. During
their honeymoon, they'd snorkelled with whale sharks and
dolphins. On another trip, they'd hiked to see the pristine
blue lakes and glaciers of Patagonia's national parks. In
Australia they'd even glimpsed a wombat in the wild. Aston
suspected it had been one of Ana's favourite parts of all.

There'd been so many adventures, and so many more to
come. He loved seeing the world through her gaze, relishing her perspective. Discovering that had been a thrill all
of its own.

'I don't need to prove anything to myself, and I don't need

you to prove anything to me either. Being with you, making you happy, is the only challenge I need.'

She wriggled from his hold and faced him, a glorious smile on her face, brighter than the rising sunshine. 'I don't know whether I should take that as a good thing or a bad thing.'

Aston smiled back. 'A good thing. Every day with you in my life is good.'

He'd stopped pushing himself so hard and had begun to truly savour all life had to offer—the big moments and the quiet ones. In a few days they'd be flying home to Paris to a function for her charity, the Cygnet Centre. Soon, they hoped Ana's friend Carla, who'd been released from hospital after a long rehabilitation, would join the charity's board. It was an exciting time for Ana, for him. Together, it was as if they could achieve anything.

'You don't know how happy that makes me,' she said. Her eyes glistened, as if with tears. This trip had been an emotional one in so many respects for them both. A closure of sorts, and a new and exciting beginning too.

'*Je t'aime*. That's all you ever need to remember.'

'I love you too.' She relaxed into his embrace, melting into him. A tempting heat lit in his belly. 'And I'm late.'

'No, you're not. We still have a few hours. If you like…' He trailed his lips down the side of her neck and she sighed before pulling back, cupping his cheek, a rosy flush blooming on her face.

'I do like, but that's not what I mean.' She reached down and took his hand, placing it on her belly. 'I'm…*late*.'

Her eyes lit up in a way he'd never seen before, with radiant joy, hope. Myriad emotions were contained in the pale, eternal blue of her gaze. He didn't think. There were no words. It hit him like an avalanche. Emotion so powerful Aston didn't know what to do with it. His lips simply crashed down onto hers. She threaded her hands through his hair and they kissed as if it were the first and last time of their lives. Breathless, endless. Aston poured everything, his undying love for her, into that kiss. Hoping she could truly understand how much this moment meant to him.

After how long he couldn't say, they eased apart. Ana's lips were red and well-kissed. It was a good look on her, one of his favourites.

'All the travel…' she said, her voice a little breathless. 'I must have messed up the days with the pill.'

'It doesn't sound like a mess to me. It sounds perfect.'

Aston had never thought he could be happier than when he'd first woken this morning. How wrong he'd been. Today he'd finally be letting go of his brother's life. In about nine months, he and Ana would be welcoming a new one into the world. The universe had clearly kept some surprises for him up her wily sleeve.

Ana quirked her perfect mouth, giving him sly little smile. 'You're not afraid this will curb our future adventures?'

Aston looked out over the mountains, their towering, snow-capped peaks gleaming in the morning sunshine.

See, Michel? I'm living… Just as I promised you.

The whole day seemed to brighten around him.

'Mon amour…' Aston tightened his arms round Ana, holding her close. Holding her to his heart, the one she'd filled to overflowing with love. His, always and for ever. 'My life with you is the only adventure I'll ever need.'

* * * * *

MILLS & BOON®

Coming next month

BILLION-DOLLAR RING RUSE
Jadesola James

'Am I that obvious?'

'Weren't you trying to be?'

'Don't be so eager to rush a beautiful thing, Miss Montgomery.'

'Val,' she corrected, her heart thumping like a rabbit's. If this was happening, she couldn't let it happen with him calling her *Miss Montgomery* or, worse yet, Valentina. Not with his liquid, rich voice simply dripping with all the dirty things she presumed he could do to her—it was bringing to the surface something she wasn't ready to explore. Not with him.

And yet, her thoughts were going in directions she couldn't control, while she sat in the booth, heart thudding, mentally grasping at them as they floated beyond her fingertips into places that sent back heated, urgent images that took her breath away with their sensuality. His mouth on her neck, his lips on hers, the softness of his breath on her ear. His hands on her breasts, hips, bottom, thighs. Stroking. Exploring.

Gripping.

Her face bloomed with heat, and it left her body in the softest of exhales before he *finally* kissed her.

Continue reading

BILLION-DOLLAR RING RUSE
Jadesola James

Available next month
millsandboon.co.uk

COMING SOON!

We really hope you enjoyed reading this book.
If you're looking for more romance
be sure to head to the shops when
new books are available on

Thursday 27th March

To see which titles are coming soon, please visit
millsandboon.co.uk/nextmonth

MILLS & BOON

LET'S TALK

Romance

For exclusive extracts, competitions and special offers, find us online:

f MillsandBoon

X @MillsandBoon

⬚ @MillsandBoonUK

♪ @MillsandBoonUK

Get in touch on 01413 063 232

Afterglow Books is a trend-led, trope-filled list of books with diverse, authentic and relatable characters, a wide array of voices and representations, plus real world trials and tribulations. Featuring all the tropes you could possibly want (think small-town settings, fake relationships, grumpy vs sunshine, enemies to lovers) and all with a generous dose of spice in every story.

♪ @millsandboonuk

◎ @millsandboonuk

afterglowbooks.co.uk

#AfterglowBooks

For all the latest book news, exclusive content and giveaways scan the QR code below to sign up to the Afterglow newsletter:

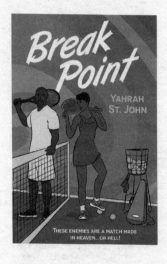

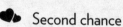
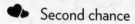
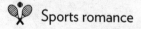
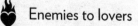

FOUR BRAND NEW BOOKS FROM
MILLS & BOON MODERN

The same great stories you love, a stylish new look!

OUT NOW

Eight Modern stories published every month, find them all at:

millsandboon.co.uk

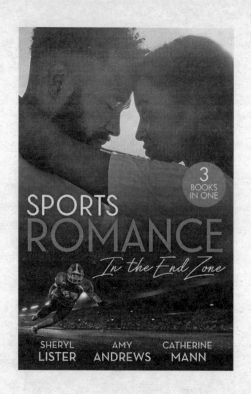